HE GENTLY
HER FING

"What an intriguing woman you are," Paul said, moving closer. "Would you mind very much sacrificing a single kiss to my curiosity? I have to know if you are real."

Sara stood perfectly still, not allowing the warm pressure of his hand on her back to draw her to him. "I don't give kisses as sacrifices," she replied evenly.

"But do you always affect men this way? I've lost a lot of valuable sleep over you lately. And here I am, making a fool of myself one more time with Sara Courtney. Why do you think that is?"

"Maybe you need to learn humility," said Sara blithely, trying to break the rising pull of physical attraction that was growing between them despite their easy banter . . . trying unsuccessfully. . . .

CATHERINE KAY
is also the author
of these titles in
SuperRomance

**DAWN OF PASSION
INTERLUDE**

CRITIC'S CHOICE

Catherine Kay

A SuperRomance from
HARLEQUIN
London · Toronto · New York · Sydney

All the characters in this book have no existence outside the imagination of the Author, and have no relation whatsoever to anyone bearing the same name or names. They are not even distantly inspired by any individual known or unknown to the Author, and all the incidents are pure invention.

The text of this publication or any part thereof may not be reproduced or transmitted in any form or by any means, electronic or mechanical, including photocopying, recording, storage in an information retrieval system, or otherwise, without the written permission of the publisher.

This book is sold subject to the condition that it shall not, by way of trade or otherwise, be lent, resold, hired out or otherwise circulated without the prior consent of the publisher in any form of binding or cover other than that in which it is published and without a similar condition including this condition being imposed on the subsequent purchaser.

First published in Great Britain in 1985 by Harlequin, 15–16 Brook's Mews, London W1A 1DR

© Kay Croissant & Catherine Dees 1984

ISBN 0 373 70127 6

Printed and bound in Great Britain by Cox & Wyman Ltd, Reading

To Stella and her friendly staff—Ron, Hal and Scotty

CHAPTER ONE

SARA PRESSED A FINGER up under the edge of the ill-fitting bouffant-style blond wig she was wearing. The damn thing was hot and itchy. The restaurant was hot too, she thought, despite its glamorous atmosphere.

She was scribbling her observation in a small notebook perched on her lap when she was interrupted by a chuckle from across the table. Bill McCormack's light-blue eyes twinkled at her. "How's the blond bombshell? A bit uncomfortable under all the paint?"

"I'm okay," she said tartly.

He gave a grunt of laughter. "At least no one would recognize you, the svelte Sara Courtney, restaurant critic *extraordinaire*. But what this is doing to my reputation as a man of the world I shudder to think. You look like my maiden aunt."

"Shut up, Bill. You know it's better not to be recognized in these places. Once they spot you as a newspaper critic they roll out the red carpet and you can kiss any objective evaluation goodbye."

"I know, I know," he soothed. "I didn't say it was a bad idea to do it your way. It's innovative, at least. Poor old Everett Costain got the wool and feathers pulled over his critical eyes all the time when it was his column."

"Well, I'm the mystery critic now, and no one will know where I'll strike next." She smiled at him and adjusted the frumpy wig with a decisive tug.

"Sorry, Sara." Bill stifled a chuckle. "It's just that you look so funny—I don't mean to other people, but I *know* you. I must say that Norma did a great makeup job."

"That's right, and she's going to teach me to look like a lot of different people of varying ages.... Now, let's get to the menu, shall we?"

"Ah, yes—business," Bill drawled. "I wonder how many other lucky men in Los Angeles are having a dinner date with a professional restaurant critic—poor devils." He sighed forbearingly.

Le Grand Richard, just off Highland Avenue in the heart of Hollywood, was a new French restaurant. It was small with what Sara would call an elegant peasant decor. It had burst upon the Los Angeles scene with well-orchestrated publicity and a chef who longed to be the darling of the chic set.

Sara acknowledged the hovering waiter, giving him a quick and thorough glance before she started to order. Somehow, the man didn't live up to what he was supposed to be: his suit was some sort of bastardized Breton outfit. It had most definitely not been improved by the addition of a black beret arranged over one eye. He didn't seem comfortable in it, nor with his theatrical Hollywood-French accent. She felt a moment of pity as she looked into his dark eyes; to be a waiter was no soft job. She gave him a reassuring smile and he responded, forgetting his fake French savoir faire for a moment and looking like the tired middle-aged American that he was.

Sara selected sole *au vin blanc* from the menu and vegetable dishes that would challenge the chef's range and authenticity.

"And what am I supposed to have?" Bill said on a querulous note. He ran his eye over the French menu and ordered duck *à l'orange* with a fractured accent. After the waiter's discreet withdrawal Sara gave Bill a whispered tongue-lashing, which only made him arrange his rugged features into a sort of blank mask. He was impossible, Sara thought humorlessly.

"You'd better behave, or I'll find someone else to eat free on my expense account," she warned. His expression changed to hangdog and she had to smile.

"That's better," he said. "A week isn't long enough for you to mellow into a job, but don't be so uptight. And honestly, I didn't know how to pronounce those French words, so I had to make a stab at it. It didn't seem to bother our *garçon*."

Sara wrote more notes: *Not exactly Left Bank*. Unless the food was good she was prepared to be painfully honest with her readers—a first for the *L.A. Chronicle*'s restaurant column.

"Did you ever read one of Everett Costain's columns?" she asked Bill.

"Olive Gadwall, you mean? Sure. I always

assumed the old gal was in the secret pay of the restaurant owners. The writing looked like advertising copy to me...and to everyone else."

Everett Costain's column had carried the by-line of Olive Gadwall for the last twenty years, a name and persona that the old man had invented. It was his little joke, since a gadwall was a tasty European duck. Everyone knew who the coy Miss Gadwall really was, and Everett Costain reveled in the attention he received at his favorite restaurants.

Sara let out a frustrated sigh. "Poor old Everett. I just hope he's happy in his little Irish retirement cottage by the sea."

The wine steward came with clanking chains and keys strung over a red apron. His accent had a genuine flavor as he suggested wines to go with the meal they had ordered. Sara asked about a certain wine in French and he answered in that language. Looking conspiratorial, he admitted that most of the wine on the list was overpriced, but that a certain soft white wine, not too costly, from the Rhone Valley, would be excellent with everything.

Sara questioned him about the restaurant—who had developed it and who owned it. "All of us," he said to her surprise.

"All of you?"

"*Oui*—some of us have been wishing to own a restaurant. Eight old friends. We pooled our savings, and one of us had the power to borrow good sums from the bank. We do everything ourselves." He beamed a proud smile around the room. "I am sure we shall succeed. It is very attractive, *non*?" He bowed slightiy and went about his duties.

The waiter brought a flower-painted dish of the distinctive yellow kind made in Carcassonne on the Spanish border of France, an excellent presentation for the tiny hot bread sticks, thick with sesame seeds and sprinkled with heavy crystals of crunchy salt. Bits of hot, dripping brie cheese, soft and aromatic, were arranged on the tips of toothpicks. Sara nodded in appreciation of this genuine touch of France.

She was just popping a brie appetizer into her mouth when her attention was diverted by a flurry of activity at the doorway. Someone was causing a great commotion. Whoever it was approached their table and passed beyond it to a rustic booth. The excitement centered around a tall, rather imposing man and the willowy brunette on his arm. They were being shepherded by the maître d', assorted waiters, and the wine steward, all looking tense and on their mettle.

The tall man had a mellow, deep voice with a resonance that somehow made attractive his flat New England upper-crust accent. Harvard, if Sara were to guess. He spoke to the hovering help with a sort of overwhelming cordiality, allowed himself and his lady to be seated and accepted a small glass of amber-colored beverage. After he was settled, the restaurant returned to normal, and curious patrons returned their attention to their meals.

"Well..." Bill said, "that's your rival from the *Tribune*."

Sara took a harder look at the man. "That can't be Paul Cabot Edgerton—he's not old enough to be so stuffy."

"Himself. Wine critic without equal. Actually, the last word in taste. His discriminating palate has shaped the opinions of the Los Angeles Who's Who for several years now. He's the uncrowned king of gastronomy."

"Don't bait me, Bill. If that's really Mr. Edgerton, I'm not very impressed with his style."

"He's not a fool, Sara. Sharp of wit, keen of tongue—he delights in reducing his trusting, naive readers to quivering insecurity."

"I've read enough of his columns. He's an ego production all by himself! But I imagined him to be sixty years old, with gray hair and glasses. He's such an awful snob...."

"He's not such a bad guy, despite some of his mean reviews. Even rather nice, I hear. He deigns to help struggling restaurateurs by bringing them patronage. He even publishes the Edgerton list of good waiters and fledgling chefs. He just naturally believes his taste is impeccable and, really, it's not bad."

"You know him?"

"Only by sight. You'd be smart not to jiggle his web by jumping into the critic game too strongly. He might not appreciate a neophyte challenging his opinions."

Sara felt a heated response rising but thought better of it. Bill McCormack got around in society and knew what he was talking about. She had met him about two months ago at a cocktail party and he had helped her get used to her new hometown.

New to California, she was under the wing of her godmother Elizabeth de Lacy, a semi-retired grande dame of music, who still gave the occasional harpsichord concert to select audiences in the music room of her Bel Air hillside mansion. Sara estimated her age to be well over seventy. Aunt Liz had approved of Bill as an escort for Sara, since he qualified on several points: he was a junior partner of a good law firm, never married, came from a fine family, and was a man on his way up. She had waved aside Sara's protests that a twenty-five-year-old woman didn't need such careful scrutiny of her companions. *All unmarried women need a sponsor in society,* her aunt had said.

Sara liked Bill. He was fun to be with and gentlemanly enough not to press for sexual intimacy if she discouraged it. They had developed a kind of camaraderie that was nonstressful. Neither pried into the other's past, but Sara knew that Bill had recently been hurt rather badly in an affair of the heart. She hadn't told him that she, too, had left behind a painful affair six months ago, and that it had been the chief reason for her sudden decision to leave Paris and relocate in Southern California.

For the moment, Bill was just what she needed. His rakish sense of humor made her laugh. After the many years Sara had spent living like a privileged gypsy with her parents in all the finest places in Europe, he had helped to ease her adjustment to life in L.A.

"A penny for them," she heard him say.

"I was just thinking that if anyone had said I'd get this job a year ago I would have laughed hysterically. I guess I miss my friends in the kitchens of my favorite hotels. When I come to a place like this, all sort of unsophisticated and ersatz, I can't help thinking of the real thing." She wasn't able to tell him how her heart could twist at the very sight of certain things that reminded her too painfully of....

Bill was smiling. "What a kid you must have been. I wish I could have seen you pestering the chefs at the Georges V."

"I told you, I didn't pester them." She bristled quickly. "They saw that I liked cooking and they knew I was lonely when my parents were tied up in rehearsals and concerts every night. They were like a family—like a whole bunch of French uncles, and they were wonderful to me. Mine wasn't a regular childhood by American standards. I had my special friends in restaurant kitchens wherever my parents had their concert engagements."

Bill patted her hand. "The story comes out bit by bit. I'd like to hear more about what made you leave the romantic world of Paris and gourmet delights to come here, of all places."

Sara looked at him seriously and took a tentative bite of her filet of sole *au vin blanc*. "I just hope I can handle this job."

"You deserved to get it. The articles you wrote from France for *Epicure International* were great."

"How did you know about those? I didn't use my real name."

"I know. You were the Niece of a Hundred Chefs, or something like that—right?" He sat back and smiled at her disbelief.

"Bill McCormack, how did you know that?"

"Your Aunt Elizabeth, love. A few weeks ago she called me on the carpet—asked me to tea, actually—and looked me over. Very Old World. She told me in no uncertain terms that you were a lady of considerable quality and background and she showed me several of your magazine articles. I think I passed inspection. Elizabeth is a formidable old thing when she's protecting her little lamb, I can tell you."

Sara broke into a broad smile. "Oh, Bill, I'm so sorry! She never told me."

"I assured her I was an honorable gentleman and wouldn't dream of stepping out of line with her goddaughter."

"It was sweet of her to care so much, but annoying just the same. I feel like a five-year-old child."

"Anyway, you'll do just great at the *Chronicle*. Any editor would love to have your talent on his staff. Who else could speak four languages, call the great chefs of the world uncle, whip up a soufflé that can't be surpassed, and write about it so that the reader's mouth is watering to taste it?"

Sara screwed her face into a doubting grimace and inspected the dessert menu. The food so far hadn't been bad. The sauce on the carrots was a bit heavy with cumin and the plates should have been warmer, yet the meal was reasonably well prepared. She had stolen a forkful of Bill's duck *à l'orange*, finding it on the dry side, but quite well seasoned.

After a light and pleasant *sabayon* for dessert she decided to write a modestly positive report. She couldn't fault the service, and the owners seemed to be making a real effort. She wouldn't shoot down a restaurant just because the decor was unauthentic and the waiters' uniforms ridiculous.

After the meal was finished Sara took some time to study her rival from the *Tribune*. Bill sipped his second cup of coffee and didn't make conversation for a few minutes, aware that her mind was elsewhere.

Paul Cabot Edgerton's table was receiving more than the normal share of attention from the staff. She hoped that he was a decent tipper. His face didn't fall into lines of unkindness as she had expected. In fact, as he sat back looking relaxed he was startlingly handsome, capable and somewhat imperturbable looking—a man whose strength might be comforting. She stopped herself in midthought just as she was wondering what it would be like to be seated at his table, the focus of his attention.

She gave herself a mental shake. As far as she knew the man was a stuffed shirt. Anyway, it would be far better not to know him. No—it was positively *essential* that they have nothing to do with one another. She was starting to feel glad of her disguise. If they should meet in some social situation he would have no clue to her real work.

Why did the thought of meeting him give her a small, not unpleasant shiver in her solar plexus? Looking up, she found Bill's eyes on her.

"Are you all right? For a minute you made me think of Auntie Mame having an off moment."

She let her breath out in a quick sigh. "This wig's enough to aggravate a saint! Let's leave." She laid her special credit card on top of the check. It bore the corporate name of a little-known subsidiary of the *Chronicle*'s parent company.

"It's been grand not caring what the total was," Bill said. "I'm happy to escort Olive Gadwall any time."

"The reincarnation of Olive Gadwall, you mean," she corrected. "Dear, sweet, lackluster Olive is going to be singing a new tune." As she reached for her gloves and purse she couldn't resist taking one more look at the man in the preferred booth.

Paul Cabot Edgerton was having what looked like a meaningful conversation with his brunette. His eyes were intent on her face and she was responding with fluttering glances to his undoubted masculine charm. Sara looked away quickly when he glanced in her direction. In that split second their eyes met and Sara felt the impact of his energy. She didn't like responding to him and she stood up immediately, taking Bill's arm to go. Bill proposed going somewhere for a nightcap. But Sara said, "I think we'd better call it a night."

"You do know how to take the romance out of things," Bill said with a wry grin. "How will you ever know what heights we might have reached together if you're always so conscientious?"

At her door he expected a kiss, and she gave it. He had a natural masculine expertise, but when he tried to arouse a response in her she slipped away from his embrace. She wasn't in the mood for something more sensuous and exploratory tonight. She half apologized for not asking him in and shut the door gently but firmly, a little annoyed at herself for not knowing just what she did want from a man anymore.

CHAPTER TWO

THREE DAYS PASSED. Sara had delivered her first story, received a pat on the back from her editor Eric Hartley, and had gone alone to two more restaurants for lunch so far that week. The time in between had been spent at her desk in the *Chronicle* city room reading back issues of Paul Cabot Edgerton's column for the *Tribune*. Curiosity and something more than that motivated her. She had to understand what the Los Angeles readers had been learning about foods from their gastronomic guru. He wrote well. Reluctantly she admired his ironic turns of phrase. He surely knew how to put the finger of acid superiority where it would wither the pompous.

It was Thursday and the first Olive Gadwall byline had come out the day before. Right now the Wednesday food section of the *Chronicle* lay open on her desk top as it had for the last twenty-four hours. She couldn't stop rereading her own words and grinning at the wonderful way her new pseudonym glowed back at her in stunning black and white.

Her Olive wrote rather nicely, Sara thought with satisfaction. Gone was the dry, repetitious syntax of Everett Costain that made every restaurant sound equally nice, if not dull.

There it was, her verdict on Le Grand Richard:

This new restaurant has tried hard to develop a Breton ambiance and I give them an A for effort. There is an underlying tinge of nostalgia and love for the taste, smell and touch of France that arouses my sympathy, since I spent many summers prowling the Britanny coast.

Into this small restaurant has gone a lot of hope and planning. The service is reasonably good and definitely friendly. Often the authentic taste of France moves happily upon the tongue. The *sabayon* was gently flavored, the sole *au vin blanc* napped in a creamy sauce with the delicate aroma of fine white wine and just the right hint of lemon. The accompanying carrots were overpowered by cumin, but the other vegetables were excellent. Only the nests of tender noodles could be faulted—perhaps they need another two minutes on the boil? The duck *à l'orange* was superior, by the way, a fine treatment of a frequently abused dish.

As a counterpoint to her gentle treatment of Le Grand Richard, she blasted the new quarters of a very old society restaurant, calling its sleek decor "stark" and "cold" and the food "not worth the high prices."

The service deserves negative comment. Slow, with a forced courtesy that borders on the supercilious. Or was that only because Olive Gadwall's face is not one of the pampered regulars at the establishment? If that is their policy, then DINERS BEWARE! Being outside the Los Angeles elite shouldn't mean having a table next to the kitchen doors.

Sara felt proud of herself. The column had a new title now—Consuming Passions—a name she dreamed up and urged her editor to adopt. He loved it, and told her so last week.

"It's a different look for our Olive. They'll think the old gal is going through the change of life and getting sexy." He had laughed in his usual booming voice. "Our passionate critic will be mysterious and entirely original. I don't want our subscribers to yawn when they read Olive Gadwall. Those days are over, right?"

So far Sara got along well with her boss. He moved in some of the same music circles that her parents did, and he enjoyed concerts, opera and the theater. Being the daughter of Elena Talbot and Jonathon Courtney may have placed Sara ahead of the other applicants for a job in Eric's department six months ago, but after that she was on her own.

Eric was happily divorced, according to office gossip. His social life was busy—the personable, sought-after eligible male. Hostesses loved him since the worst thing that could happen to a well-planned dinner was to have an extra female, and there were lots of extra women in Los Angeles society. Eric had become a genial and witty escort-on-call. That way he could keep his finger on the city's social pulse, thereby enhancing his work as the food and entertainment editor.

Short and slight, he moved with an athletic bounce that bespoke vitality. His bright, observant green eyes missed very little. He dressed with a sense of relaxed style. His narrow clever face was topped by a well-shaped cap of blow-dried sandy hair.

But he was first and foremost a good editor and knew where to stop his own words. Toughness and decisiveness were his outstanding qualities but so was consideration. The women in the office vied to do things for him and primped hurriedly before entering his glass-enclosed office cubicle.

Sara wanted to live up to his judgment of her capabilities. "This isn't Paris," he had said. "I can't afford the leisurely European approach." He encouraged her to create her own contacts in the food world, and she gave him a series of interviews with society caterers.

She knew when she joined the paper that Eric was grooming her for bigger assignments, even though he didn't tell her his plans. Her name hadn't appeared on a by-line, but he had started assigning her to do some sidebar stories to accompany the Olive Gadwall column. And then one day last month it was rumored that Everett Costain was retiring and Eric had picked Sara Courtney to fill his shoes. Last week he had confirmed the rumor when he handed her a thick pile of old Olive Gadwall columns, ordered her to drop them into the nearest wastebasket and never to emulate Costain's style. "If you do, you're fired," he had said quite seriously. "You have a special flair and I want to see it twice a week without fail. I want you to make Olive Gadwall noteworthy and as long as you avoid lawsuits, I don't care how you do it."

Sara finally stopped gloating over her first article. She spent the day typing notes into the video display terminal she was just learning to use. She had already managed to lose part of an article in the computer memory bank and it had taken an hour to figure out the code needed to retrieve it.

She took a break and looked around from her desk in the corner of the newsroom. Her window overlooked the roof garden of an athletic club and gave her a stark view of congested streets. The late-afternoon sun sparkled against a glass box of a building to her right and the flat plane of the city was dotted with other tall, glass-sided buildings. Sara felt homesick for the uneven skyline of Paris—the curved domes of its churches and the mellow, carved stone of its old buildings. Here everything was so new. Yet, Los Angeles had its peculiar charm, she had to admit, and she felt satisfied with her job. Increasingly, Sara had a sense of settling into a home environment, a sensation that was completely new to her.

It was hard to picture Jacques Renard in the

context of this bright new life. For that, she was grateful. He was still part of the old world.

She drew a deep breath and there was a lessening of the tension that so often accompanied thoughts of her French lover. Now she could almost smile at some of her memories, even the one that had been the first harsh cut into her tender illusions. The incident had occurred shortly before the end of their headlong affair. They were having dinner in an outdoor cafe on the Boulevard Saint-Germain, and Jacques had been talking about his brother Alain, whose wife was expecting their first child after three years of marriage.

"He is delighted," Jacques had laughed. "Of course he will consider Hélène in every way. He has already found for himself a bed friend so that his needs shall not disturb Hélène as her pregnancy grows more confining."

Sara still remembered his exact words. She could see his deep-brown eyes—his most fascinating feature—looking innocently into hers as she asked him, "If we were to have children, would you find a companion also?"

"But of course, *ma petite*, out of honor to you." The abrupt change in her face reflected in his own. "*Zut*—I've waked up your puritan scruples again, haven't I?" He had reached for her hand, but she drew it back swiftly. "You are an infant," he said soothingly. "How have you remained so unknowing in the world of your creative father and mother? They are both worldly people, drinking the pleasures of life, eh?"

"They love each other," she had said sharply.

"Who says they do not?" He sounded patient and a tiny bit bored. "Sex has little to do with love, but much to do with a man's comfort. French wives understand that."

She had stood up suddenly and he had looked surprised. "My father would not. He loves my mother. I don't think that sexual comfort is all that a man should think of when his wife is expecting a child!"

He had smiled, but his dark velvet eyes had narrowed. "So marriage is to turn off all natural instincts toward the other sex. Will you put a sign on a man's chest: This Is Mine?" His expression was a blend of hot and cold. "You are happy to lie in my arms. I am a good lover. Do you think, silly child, that you will always satisfy all of my needs? Unless, of course, you become the femme fatale of an infinite variety of seductions."

His laugh was cutting and ironic and Sara had turned away from him, walking as fast as she could toward the safety of her tiny apartment. She felt so naive...so used! Why had she said anything at all about marriage? It had all bubbled up from inside, from her own most-cherished but terribly traditional female American dream patterns. Love and marriage were supposed to go together like a horse and carriage, weren't they? she thought darkly.

His patronizing laughter haunted her sleepless nights as she wrestled with her pride and the raw hungry passion he knew so well how to draw from her. She saw him once more after that, when he came to her apartment, gentle and loving, intent on soothing her offended scruples. He had proposed living together. "The most practical form of love," he had said.

"And, *chérie*, I remind you I have never said marriage. It is you who have said it. But in the bed you have only purred with delight—no words of marriage were asked of me."

How could she say that she was expecting those words from him—poor, old-fashioned fool that she was?

"We must be mature in our love," he had crooned to her, "learn to live free, not be dependent on words, but only the responsibility of the heart's feelings. These are the best ties between us."

Somehow, she had found the strength to send him away, and she had spent the rest of the day crying into a pillow, trying to decide what it was that she expected love to be. There had to be more to it than she had experienced so far, except for the love her mother and father shared. The only problem was that her parents were such a unit together; even a child could feel a sense of being outside something so splendid and impenetrable.

But now her life was good. The past was the past. At least she had lost her virginity to a virtuoso of a French lover. It could have been worse. She had no miserable trauma to color her future sex life...only a cold place in her heart and a solemn promise to herself: she would never again fall prey to a glib and polished male line—never go limp and grateful when an attractive man paid extravagant compliments to her. And never, *never* believe that a man is thinking about marriage when he takes a woman to bed! There was a deep anger in her about some men's attitudes toward women.

She looked away from the window and stopped the flow of memories. They were best forgotten. It was almost time to go home for the day. She started to straighten up the mess on her desk when Eric Hartley erupted from his office, waving a newspaper over his head.

"Wait until you see this, Sara!" He shoved the paper into her hand, folded to show Paul Cabot Edgerton's column, The Right Table. "You did it!" he chortled. "By damn, Sara, he's turned his cannons on Olive Gadwall. He never even deigned to notice her before." Eric did a delighted two-step beside her desk, causing heads to turn in their corner of the newsroom. "He's insulting as hell about your first column.... He thought the Grand Richard was awful. And you slashed one of his favorite restaurants. This is great, just great! You can both review the same restaurants. He'll be beside himself and he won't know who you are! It's a terrific concept."

Sara had a queer feeling in her stomach. She hadn't expected to take on Paul Cabot Edgerton, at least not so soon. "But my column comes out on Wednesday, a day ahead of his," she said in a tight voice. "He'll always be criticizing *me*, not the other way around."

"That's no problem," Eric grinned. "There's always your Sunday column to start things off and get ahead of him when you want to."

"This isn't going to work, Eric. How will I be able to be at the same place he is, except by coincidence?"

"I'll do a little judicious bribery of parking attendants and doormen. Edgerton has one habit I happen to know about: he likes to eat fashionably late. If you're dressed and ready to go when a call comes, we can have a reserved table at a lot of places under various names. All you have to do is go to the one where he is and let the others go."

Sara shook her head emphatically. "That's ridiculous. Think of the lists of places, the time I'd have to spend, the deception...."

"I'll assign you an assistant to take care of it." He put a heavy hand on her shoulder. "Don't you realize what this means? We've been in a circulation war with the *Tribune* for years. They've got the big bucks, but we're small and clever, and that's why we have the edge. Nothing like a battle of the columnists to increase circulation. The Old Man upstairs looks kindly on editors who can arrange such things."

"I'm not sure I like this..." Sara began.

Eric pointed a long stabbing finger at the folded newspaper in Sara's hand. "Read this before you make up your mind. I'll give you ten minutes." He strode into his office again.

She started to read Paul Edgerton's acid prose and felt herself growing hot with anger. "I have read," he wrote, "the venerable Olive Gadwall's description of Le Grand Richard. Obviously La Gadwall had her bifocals askew and spent the evening meal in some other establishment, since her embarrassingly happy review of the sole *au vin blanc* and the duck *à l'orange* could not possibly apply to the over-cooked travesties of fish and game bird that were presented to me and my companion—especially the appalling duck. Or had Olive sipped too much of the bad wine? As for the three-star restaurant she found so supercilious—are we hearing sour grapes from a critic who is incapable of appreciating a refined setting?"

Sara's temper flared dangerously. It wasn't his opinion of Olive Gadwall's taste that galled her as much as his insulting condescension. She had no respect for a man who used a poisonous pen. She stopped reading, slammed at the On switch of her V.D.T. and started to type:

A word to the man at The Right Table.

A critic should be dedicated to elevating the good, encouraging the not-so-good to be better, and finding decent ways to express displeasure.

I happen to know that Le Grand Richard is a hopeful venture of hard-working people whose combined capital is at stake, as well as their livelihood. This small restaurant is run with imagination and creativity, and the quality of its food, while not that of Tour d'Argent, is nevertheless good and can improve.

She picked up the Edgerton article and read further. His attention had turned to an Italian restaurant in the neighborhood seaside city of Santa Monica. Fortunately, she had eaten there (escorted by a friend of the chef) just before starting her new job. Paul Edgerton claimed in his column that only northern Italy—because of its proximity to France—could boast a fine cuisine, dismissing the southern dishes on the menu.

She typed into the display terminal: "Perhaps Mr. Edgerton is unaware of the development of Italian *novella cocina* in recent years, or of the remarkable subtlety of certain southern Italian dishes served in this fine restaurant. I cannot attribute his crude assessment of Chef Armando's talents to the possibility that the impeccable Mr. Edgerton had imbibed too much bad wine—since there is no wine of that description in Armando's excellent cellar."

As she finished with a last indignant tap of the keys she became aware of Eric reading over her shoulder. She turned to find his clever green eyes on her. He leaned closer to give her flushed cheek a quick kiss and then straightened up, laughing.

"Bravo, Sara—give it to the gourmet princeling." His face twisted in delight. "He'll be livid, just livid. Nobody has challenged his opinion for years. The old Olive Gadwall, if she were real, would be turning in her grave. I'll send Everett

Costain a copy. He may have wanted to say things like this but was too scared." He beamed at her. "You've declared war on the great arbiter of taste. Things couldn't be better! It's a bold move."

Sara sat looking at him blankly. She had only written what she had to relieve her irritation, not for publication. She certainly wouldn't write a column in that tone. *But why not?* she thought. A spark of rebellion, some of the ire that she had buried about Jacques, wanted expression, and this outlet was legitimate. She was sick of so-called sophisticated men and the power they had to manipulate the naive.

"Why not?" she said to Eric with a feisty grin.

"That's my gal!" He laughed so expansively that people around them stopped what they were doing to listen. "I'm going to feature your Consuming Passions on the front page of the section," he said. "It's been buried too long. We'll have the art department do a frame for it. Nobody will be able to miss our new Olive Gadwall." He rubbed his hands gleefully. "We'll update our whole layout, make your column the diamond in a setting of personality bits about up-and-coming chefs, gourmet-cooking societies, wine-tasting parties among the A-list.... The whole first page will be city social. The standard food stuff can start on the second page."

Eric looked so pleased, Sara had to feel good too, in spite of her instinctive hesitation to get involved in an editorial change so fraught with potential problems and tension. As strange as it was, it was a terrific idea.

"Photos," Sara said in the middle of a thought. "What about a color photo on the front page—the specialty dish of a great restaurant adapted to the busy life-style of today's cook? Something like that."

"You bet! Let me call some layout people in for a conference. We'll work it out right now." He dived back into his office and Sara saw him waving his hands descriptively as he talked to the art department on the phone.

A niggling sense of worry made her go cold for a minute, but then a picture of the tired-eyed waiter at Le Grand Richard and the pledged savings of the wine steward came into her mind. She wouldn't turn back. She wouldn't try to be nasty—but after all, she thought with a shrug, Paul Cabot Edgerton had started it....

CHAPTER THREE

IT WAS LATE when Eric finally ended the conference with the art department. Hours had raced past in the stimulating process of creating a new look for the food section. Most of the day shift had long since gone home when Eric leaned back in his antique oak desk chair and grinned at Sara.

"This calls for a celebration, Miss Courtney. I'll take you out for drinks, dinner—the works."

She wasn't sure she wanted to go, but the crackling energy of Eric's enthusiasm was contagious. "I'm not dressed for a night on the town." She attempted to beg off.

"You look beautiful. Come as you are, how's that? I'll find a spot that's not too fancy—just right for two hard-working newspaper types like us. We deserve it."

She smiled agreement to Eric and went off to the powder room to freshen up. It would be fun, she thought, to be just Sara Courtney, no wig, no subterfuge—and on somebody else's expense account. The first week as Olive Gadwall had taken its toll on her nerves.

There was a multicolored silk scarf in her purse and she tied back her rambunctious bright auburn curls with it. The harsh fluorescent lighting showed up a sprinkle of tiny freckles on her fair skin and she rubbed a bit of liquid makeup over them. A touch of mascara on her eyelashes brought out the green-blue of her eyes. After a dab of peach lipstick she was ready, except for a quick spritz from her purse flacon of Chanel No 5, her mother's favorite scent. It always brought into sharp focus a series of memories of premieres and entertainments when, as a little awestruck girl, she had believed her mother to be the most beautiful woman in the world.

Rummaging in her purse for the lipstick, Sara turned up a pair of gold earrings she had taken off a week ago because they had felt uncomfortable with her clumsy wig. They added some dash to her appearance. Her dove-gray soft-knit suit wasn't severe; the pleated skirt moved gracefully as she turned before the mirror of the washroom. She was presentable.

Eric was waiting at his desk, scribbling some last minute notations on tomorrow's work pad. The office staff jumped when one of Eric Hartley's pithy memos was circulated. For all his outward joviality he had the organizational instincts of a military commander. Everyone expected him to move up the ladder with all due speed.

He looked up when she came toward him and gave an appreciative whistle. "You're not a bad looking woman, not bad at all," he teased. His eyes told her that he liked what he saw and she enjoyed his kind of inept flattery. It seemed more face of Paul Edgerton. He held out a large, finely shaped hand and Sara was obliged to put her own into it. His grasp was warm, and a spark of energy surged up the nerve pathways of her arm. "I'm delighted." His rich voice held overtones of sensuality. She felt him raising her hand higher and realized that he was about to kiss it in the best European tradition. Such hand kissing wasn't new to her and she expected him to kiss the air a fraction of an inch above her hand, as was customary. Instead, his eyes drew hers with a steady gaze and his classically defined lips brushed gently against her fingers.

Another and stronger frisson sped up her arm and lodged itself almost painfully in her solar plexus. "Hello," she managed to say. She withdrew her hand from his, feeling his fingers hold onto hers for an extra moment of pressure, as if to assert his male strength. It was a wordless exchange in which his touch said, *I am a man. I know the effect of my energy on a female body.*

She closed her hands around her small purse, still feeling the tingle of his lips and a remnant of arousal. It was too ridiculous, she thought angrily. Her contrary nature was just being titillated by forbidden fruit. She looked back quickly at Eric.

"Sara's only been in Los Angeles a few months," he said in answer to her desperate glance. Good old Eric. He was a master of recouping a tense situation.

But Sara couldn't let it go at that. She had to press at this Mr. Edgerton just a bit—it was a matter of pride. "Yes," she said. "I'm just beginning to know the local celebrities, and I rather guess you're one of them."

Eric's hand tightened convulsively on her arm. "Paul is the well-known restaurant critic for the *Tribune*," he explained quickly. "He keeps me on my toes. All the great chefs tremble at his very presence."

"How nice!" she said too brightly. She saw a puzzled glint sharpen the edges of Paul Edgerton's large, shadowed eyes.

"Eric is too generous with compliments, I fear. I'm only a humble connoisseur of the finer things in life." His gaze was still on Sara, a look of male curiosity she recognized. But it wasn't easy for her to disregard him, nor to banish the slight trembling she was feeling. She tried to appear casual, looking about her at the restaurant while Eric and Paul exchanged pleasantries.

Paul's voice was as resonant tonight as it had been the first time Sara had heard it at Le Grand Richard. "I see you were wise enough to reserve," he was saying to Eric. "The bar is full. I'll join you at your table with the drinks if that's agreeable."

"Fine," Eric said heartily with another unseen prod of Sara's arm.

"Please do." She summoned a gracious smile and avoided looking directly into his hypnotic amber-colored eyes. Like a lion's, she thought. There was an unmistakable animal tension beneath his smooth cultivation. What was this strange contradictory man doing as a food critic?

They were seated at a table beneath the graceful tracery of branches of one of the ficus trees. The Indian hostess fluttered around them like a worried pink butterfly. She called for a waiter who flew to their side. Obviously they were to be well treated.

Paul Edgerton leaned forward in his rattan chair. "Now, my friends, what shall it be? I insist on being your host tonight, since I have intruded so outrageously." He smiled with the self-assurance of a man who expects to be forgiven his charming eccentricities.

Eric opted for a martini and Paul ordered a gin and tonic. He discussed the brands of gin with the waiter and finally was satisfied. Then he asked if the limes were absolutely fresh. "There's nothing so abominable as squeezing a resistant section of hard, juiceless lime," he informed the waiter, who hastened to agree. After requesting an exact ratio of gin to tonic he asked for one teaspoon of honey to be stirred into the gin. He turned his eyes with their odd amused glint to Sara. "And for you, my dear lady?"

"I'll have a *mithi lassi*," she told him, pleased that she knew the name of the traditional Indian drink.

His dark eyebrows rose a little on his broad forehead. "You're sure? *Lassi* is non-alcoholic, did you know?"

"I know." She looked to the waiter. "Do you use buttermilk or yogurt?"

A white toothy smile gleamed on his face. "We

make it of our own yogurt—prepared each day fresh."

"That almost tempts me to have a salt *lassi* instead," Sara said gently, making her expression innocent. "But, no, I do enjoy the rosewater. Give me a *mithi*, please."

She felt Eric's gaze on her. In his eyes was a mixture of disapproval and unholy mirth. He knew what she was doing.

"You're sure you wouldn't like a small sherry to go with your *lassi*?" Paul inquired solicitously. "Perhaps a Moscatel de Setubal. I can recommend it for the feminine taste. It has a tangy nose."

"Just plain sherry," she said. "My taste isn't always so feminine."

Eric made a smothered sound that quickly turned into a cough, and he plunged into a discussion of new restaurants in town. He and Paul threw names back and forth with a sophisticated air, giving one-line opinions. They were both being insufferable. She couldn't decide who sounded more so.

Sara sat sipping at her *lassi* and sherry—the forgotten woman shut out by man-talk. Then her ears pricked up. Eric had just said that he was enjoying the exchange of criticism between Olive Gadwall and Paul Edgerton.

Paul leaned back in his chair. "Really, Eric, everyone knows that Everett Costain has retired and you've hired someone to fill in as Olive Gadwall. The new style of writing is obviously female and amateurish. I would think you'd be better qualified to cover the restaurant scene yourself."

"Come now, old boy," Eric said with a tinge of annoyance. "Olive has more qualifications than I can name, starting with a long acquaintance with the finest kitchens in Europe."

This time it was Sara's turn to send an under-the-table signal to Eric that things were going too far.

"One can't take a female too seriously," Paul smiled lazily. "Present company excepted, of course—and certainly not a woman like your Olive Gadwall, whoever she is. And isn't it time to retire that ridiculous *nom de plume*? I do my work out in the open, honestly and without artifice."

"Olive is quite a lady," Eric answered, invisibly giving Sara's knee a reassuring pat. "A bit of an eccentric, I admit, but with a million-dollar set of taste buds."

"Hogwash!" he snorted. "A *bourgeoise*—a panderer to low tastes, if yesterday's emotional column is any indication. Please, Eric, I beg you, hire a man to do the job. And let him write under his own name. I don't care to spar with a phantom." He was smiling, but his words belied the smile.

"You aren't sparring with a phantom, Paul, and I don't think I'm going to let my Olive go just yet. I'm growing rather fond of the old dear."

Sara wished she could leave. Eric seemed to be reveling in the situation. Worst of all, some very unbecoming emotions were surfacing as she sat close to her rival critic. One part of her response to him was irritatingly instinctual and primitive, while another part of her wanted to hang Paul Edgerton up by his insulting, sharp tongue!

They had been served with a variety of small appetizers, brought unrequested as a friendly gift of the house. Paul Edgerton received them without comment, except for a grunt of pleasure as he munched animatedly. *Probably thinks they're his due,* Sara thought darkly.

She was fond of *bhajia*, the small bits of vegetable deep-fried in chick pea batter. The pungent appetizing taste of coriander, cumin, turmeric and garlic, with a hint of lemon dissolved on her tongue along with the chewiness of the enclosed vegetables.

A variety of fresh chutneys—orange and lemon peels freshly ground together and coconut with tamarind pulp, brown sugar and ginger—were served with tiny hot *chapatis*. Sara made a mental note to explain the concept of *chapatis* to her readers, who were probably already familiar with Mexican tortillas, a distant cousin of this Indian flat dough. These were smaller than the usual *chapatis*, like round crackers, ideal for dipping in the savory chutneys. They were served hot in their basket, wrapped in a saffron colored napkin.

The subject of Olive Gadwall didn't come up again, and Paul and Eric seemed to be enjoying their peculiar situation as representatives of rival newspapers, giving excessive courtesy to one another and showing impeccable manners.

The food was excellent, equal to any Sara had eaten in Europe. She sat silently, savoring the appetizers and thinking what pleasure Jean-Claude would find in them. He had always wanted to adapt some Indian dishes to Western menus. He took the position that some things should be part of a universal cookery to be enjoyed widely, not only in specialized restaurants.

Without being obvious, Sara observed Paul Edgerton. When he wasn't being rude his manners were gracious. He made sure that the dishes of hot snacks were within her reach. He even noticed that she was not a part of the conversation and inquired if she enjoyed Indian food.

"This is very good," she said. Then, impetuously, she added, "There was a small place in Paris that served orange chutney as good as this. But I'm not an expert like you." She had to control her desire to test herself against him.

"You're familiar with Paris?"

"Somewhat."

"I gather that you stayed there for a time," he persisted.

"I lived many places with my parents during my childhood." She sensed Eric impatiently shifting in his chair.

His voice cut in: "Sara's parents are Elena Talbot and Jonathon Courtney."

Paul's face lit up. "My dear Sara, how wonderful! They are truly fine musicians, each a genius. I have admired them for years and I own most of their recordings. It was my pleasure to hear them in Rome three years ago." His eyes were full of a new light and his voice had lost its self-conscious conviviality. "No one can play Debussy as they can. Their piano interpretations are miracles of sensitivity." He smiled with new directness. "How proud you must be."

"I love their music, too," Sara said wistfully. Her new environment held little music except rock and roll from the apartment above hers. And of course Aunt Elizabeth's musicales, those special evenings she arranged for friends and visiting musicians in the grand music salon of her home.

"You're musical also?"

"I was too much of a daydreamer to be a disciplined musician, so I went into other creative areas, like writing, where I'm free to let my imagination go."

Eric trod sharply on her foot under the table. "She's good, too. If she weren't so busy writing the story of her parents' life together, I'd hire her in a minute. It's a marvelous tale covering two continents, and best of all, it's true. A New York agent I know saw her outline and predicts a best-seller."

"Ah," Paul Edgerton said softly. "So you spent your childhood traveling around Europe in the wake of your splendid parents. It must have been rather lonely for you, m'dear."

"I had friends," she protested gently, "and a succession of tutors. My parents never neglected me. We had wonderful times together."

He continued to talk about music, commenting

on the interpretations of various performers, while she nodded in reply.

A waiter appeared at their table. "Do you wish to order dinner?" Sara looked at Eric. Was Paul Edgerton going to be a gentleman and bow out now, or would he continue to be their uninvited guest?

He set down his empty glass. "I think I must leave you two charming people, I do have another appointment at a little Japanese-Mexican bistro." He smiled indulgently. "Heaven help me for trying something completely new, but I've heard about their chef, who sounds imaginative, if nothing else. He has something called Filet Serape, advertised as an 'experience'. And something else he calls the Oriental Cowboy." He rolled his eyes up with resignation. "Probably a steak treated with Japanese *miso*. That's why I came here first, to fortify myself with a gentler cuisine before I meet the improbable Filet Serape. What I must do for my craft!"

He rose before Eric could make a polite protest. "It has been a special pleasure to meet you, Sara Courtney." His hand reached to hold hers in a warm grasp, and she murmured the first cordial words that came to mind.

"If you want a good dessert, order the *kheer*," he said to Eric with an eye on Sara.

Sara couldn't resist a last word. "I hope their *kheer* is custardy and not sticky. It's always a gamble, isn't it? Although I do agree, good *kheer* is a treat." She met his leonine eyes with a smile, but a pulse was beating irregularly in her throat. She so very much wanted to dent his superiority.

He arched an eyebrow toward Eric. "Quite a little epicure you have here. Maybe I should fear for my job." He smiled at his own joke.

"You're safe for now," Eric quipped.

"Please, friends, order with confidence—I wouldn't dream of recommending a sticky *kheer*." He turned away slowly, sending a benevolent command over his shoulder: "Enjoy!"

Sara sat silently while Eric ordered for them: *alu matar*, a vegetable stew; *raitas*, a mix of yogurt and vegetables; saffron rice; and spicy puffed bread called *puris*.

"We'll end with *kheer*," Eric grinned at her wickedly. "My, what kitten claws you have. Not at all the sweet Sara I thought I knew...."

"He forced it out of me."

"Like a gnat buzzing the elephant."

She had to laugh. "I guess so. If he ever finds out who Olive Gadwall is, I'll have to leave town."

Eric chuckled. "He won't find out. What's more, I think he liked you."

"He was just impressed by my parents' names."

"I had a feeling he wanted you to be favorably impressed with his magnificence. Didn't you find him at all interesting?"

"He's impossibly attractive. I've never liked men who were so handsome and sure of themselves. They expect women to fall all over them," she sputtered while Eric continued to laugh.

All through the excellent meal and the perfect,

creamy *kheer* Eric was crowing about the sales potential of the new Olive Gadwall-Paul Edgerton rivalry. He didn't notice that Sara had dropped into an uncomfortable depression. She wanted to blame Eric for creating this tricky subterfuge, but he was just doing what any clever editor might do under the circumstances. She didn't want to fight with Paul Edgerton. She felt silly for having pricked his huge ego in her childish way, tempting as it was. But then she thought about his slashing pen and the harm he could do with it, and she felt better again.

Eric talked shop for a while longer and took her home early to her little apartment, in the center of Hollywood just below Sunset Boulevard. Her building was like dozens of others built in the Fifties replacing the quiet neighborhoods of family bungalows that used to be there.

At the door Eric gave her a light kiss that had no urgency. She could handle Eric without stress. He was too smart a man to start a sticky office romance. But, damn—that Paul Edgerton had gotten under her skin!

CHAPTER FOUR

SO, PAUL CABOT EDGERTON thought she was quite a little epicure—well, he was right. As she closed the apartment door behind her, Sara told herself she shouldn't care what a stranger thought, but his jibes still stung. She had at least as good a culinary background as he did and it grated on her that she had had to sit there and let him patronize her tonight. She even felt protective of dear old Olive, as ridiculous as that sounded.

What did he know of the inner workings of a fast-paced kitchen? He could use his large vocabulary to criticize all he wanted, but she wasn't merely an educated outsider. She had already fought that fight in Paris, where she had had to prove over and over again that she qualified to write about fine foods. Finally *Epicure International* had given her the chance. But even then there were those who felt that a man should have been given the job.

There was something so annoying about food snobs, and Paul Edgerton appeared to be one of the worst, a classic case. There were almost enough irritating things about him to outweigh the disconcerting attractiveness of the man. The odd magnetism, something in his voice—the velvet smoothness of it with its layers of emotional tone...those arresting eyes that sent out an amber charge of voltage when they looked at her. This wasn't the way Paul Edgerton was supposed to be.

She caught herself slipping into the same type of rationalizing that had been the start of her foolhardy affair with Jacques last year. Anyway, this Edgerton person wasn't just any man, he was her enemy—the rival who would cut her heart out and eat it for lunch if he could. Even toying with the thought that he could become more than a distant acquaintance was dangerous, and she had a deep sense of responsibility for her job.

After a long hot shower Sara put on her thick blue terry-cloth robe and fixed herself a cup of aromatic Earl Grey tea. At her small round dining table she began making notes about the Indian restaurant. Later, after studying her Los Angeles street map, she pinpointed certain restaurants to visit within the week. Eric's plan of bribing parking attendants all over town seemed difficult to execute, and she wasn't going to sit around waiting to hear where Mr. Edgerton was having dinner.

Sara hadn't had time to be as thorough in her job as she wanted to be so far, because of the suddenness of her promotion. It wasn't a stroke of luck that had given her this position with one of the two largest newspapers in Los Angeles. She had worked hard to develop her skills. Out of the chaos and pleasant madness of her upbringing she had found a steady point in herself that wouldn't waver no matter what the circumstances. She had proved this steadiness by her quick recovery from the affair with Jacques. Work was the best remedy she knew.

Sara poured another cup of tea and looked through notes for her book about her parents. It was becoming a kind of personal therapy, a way to occupy her mind and find a pattern to her life. So far, she had filled several spiral notebooks with memories of a childhood spent in hotels, concert halls and trains. Her parents were musical geniuses who were completely unprepared for the prosaic job of parenting.

When Sara was fourteen it had occurred to them that their pretty, red-haired, stubborn daughter should probably be in a regular school, rather than catching an hour here and there with tutors and hobnobbing with the kitchen staff of God-knew-what restaurants.

While her parents practiced endlessly for their dual piano performances, Sara would slip out quietly to observe the magical techniques of the *sous*-chefs, the pastry chefs, and the *chef de cuisine* himself, if he was an indulgent sort of man. The unobtrusive child with her bright devouring eyes then experimented with her new knowledge, whether it was in Berne or Bergamo, London or Paris. Life became a moveable feast; the exciting, busy restaurants of Europe felt like home.

Even to such free-spirited people as her parents

Sara's unusual regimen didn't seem proper, and they enrolled her in a Swiss boarding school run by Italian nuns. It was only a matter of weeks before the American child was turning the school's plain Sunday suppers into festive events. When she was eighteen she graduated and promptly enrolled in one of the best Parisian cooking schools.

Sara sat back, put aside her pen and paper and searched her mail for something interesting, maybe a letter from Jean-Claude, her one happy link to Paris now. He was like a brother—sweet, impulsive—and very very good with *nouvelle cuisine*. She knew he was one of the most talented young chefs around, but he feared that he would be an old man before he could work himself up to a high position in a fine restaurant.

She had kept track of his progress through several of the good kitchens in the south of France while she entered college in Paris, intent on refining her skills as a journalistic writer. For all her joy in preparing fine foods Sara knew she wouldn't be spending her life in the tyrannical hierarchies of a European four-star kitchen. How many four-star female executive chefs were there? No. She realized that her future lay in her ability to write discerningly about good food.

The amusing letters she had received from Jean-Claude at the time—so full of French emotion and light-hearted suffering—had kept her spirits up as he shared his victories with her, helping her over lonely times.

But the day had come six months ago when not even he could cheer her up, when all she could think of was running away from Paris as far and as fast as possible. There was only one place she could remotely call home: Los Angeles, where Aunt Elizabeth lived. It was far enough away so she wouldn't constantly be reminded of the places she had been with Jacques, the things they had said to each other...and the utter fool she had been.

Jacques had come along at a time when she was feeling vulnerable and rootless, and practically any man would have satisfied her romantic dreams. She had been a textbook case, a young untried virgin wondering what all the fuss was about. Deep down she had wanted to have the experience everyone else had and, being impetuous, Sara had set out to get it. What a cloud of self-deception she'd ridden on for a while, reveling in the discoveries of her body and the indescribable pleasure of being loved by a man. But she hadn't known the rules of the game then....

But why should she be dredging up all that ancient history? And why did Paul Edgerton's face and voice so unsettle her nervous system? She wasn't about to imagine that he was attractive in a romantic way. She had always abhorred condescending men, and she had every reason in the world to be wary of this one.

What she needed was a jaunty letter from Jean-Claude to clear the air. The phone rang and Sara jumped. It was Norma, her neighbor down the hall, the one who was teaching her to use several styles of makeup as Olive Gadwall. Norma worked at one of the movie studios in Burbank in the wardrobe department.

"Just checking in," her high voice chirped. "In case you had a special assignment tomorrow as 'you-know-who'." She was sworn to secrecy about Olive Gadwall.

"I have a lunch reservation in Pasadena, but the blond wig is fine," Sara replied.

"You should see what I brought home tonight, Sara, flapper costumes from one of the old storerooms. But seriously, do you need me? I can come right over."

"Thanks anyway. If I stay up all night working I should have the perfect middle-aged face, so I won't need makeup help. See you soon."

SARA CHECKED IN at the *Chronicle* early the next morning and worked until eleven at her desk. She had a headache and didn't relish putting on the blond wig for lunch. As she stood next to the water cooler swallowing two extra-strength aspirins, Eric spoke next to her.

"It's all part of the game. Just don't ask me for combat pay."

"I didn't sleep a lot last night," she said lamely.

"Well, I wanted to apologize for having some fun with Edgerton at your expense. It wasn't very gallant of me. But—" he grinned mischievously "—did you see his face when you knew all about his exotic dessert?"

She smiled in spite of her throbbing headache. "He seems to have a hard time with intelligent women."

"Oh, wow—is he going to have a time with Olive!" Eric went back to his office still chuckling.

SARA HAD NEVER BEEN to Pasadena before, a city nestled at the foot of the Dan Gabriel mountains, but she was determined to master the curving old Pasadena Freeway to get to a little tearoom called Stella's Place.

The tearoom was in the Old Town section of renovated turn-of-the-century buildings, and Stella herself greeted Sara with British cheer and warmth. The headache began to ease for the first time that day.

After a potful of English tea and fresh sea bass Giovanni she was feeling positively cured. The apple *tarte tatin* dessert was a delight with its thin crust and well-poached fruit. And best of all was Stella, providing chatty companionship to the plain woman in the blond wig who looked so very much alone. It made Sara feel good that she could say a word of praise about this charming little restaurant and have thousands of people read it.

After driving back home, Sara made notes about Stella's Place and wrote a letter to her friend Jean-Claude who was currently the *sous*-chef of a Michelin-rated restaurant on the southern coast of France.

"You'll have to see me to believe me!" she began. "I'm locked in mortal combat with the lion of Los Angeles food critics, a man named Edgerton. And I *think* I'm having a wonderful time at it. But it's too soon to tell if I'm going to fail miserably in my new job or establish myself as an arbiter of taste. Remember the name Olive Gadwall, because in my next letter I'll explain how important she has become to my life...."

Jean-Claude loved getting cryptic notes from her. They had a playful correspondence that wandered over every subject imaginable. She planned to let him dangle for a week or so and then tell him the tale of poor Olive and the wigs and costumes. Dear Jean-Claude—she missed his impish face.

Her mind was still functioning in French after writing the letter, and when the phone rang she absent-mindedly answered it with, *"Allo, oui?"*

The momentary silence on the other end was followed by a man's voice. "Is this the Courtney residence?"

"Yes, it is," she said.

"Miss Courtney, this is Paul Edgerton."

For a split second she had the wild urge to slam down the phone. What was *he* doing on the other end of her line?

"Oh, hello," she said cautiously.

"Miss Courtney—Sara, if I may—would you allow me to escort you to dinner tonight? Terribly short notice, I know, but—"

"I don't think so, Mr. Edgerton," she interrupted. *Absolutely not!* her mind shouted.

"Might you reconsider if I told you we would dine at Mon Château?"

She had asked Eric about Mon Château. It was that French restaurant with the unlisted number the film colony was raving about. It would be quite a coup to review it over dinner with the enemy—but she couldn't possibly....

"I thought I could show you some of the fine points of food criticism," he continued, "if you'd like to learn."

Something suddenly went *snap* in her self-control. He had said the one thing in the world that would goad her to accept.

"What time will you be by for me?" Sara could hardly believe she was saying the words.

"Say, eight o'clock?" he said smoothly. Sara could feel him smiling, believing that he had offered her an enticing bait. But he couldn't know her real reasons. "The maître d' is expecting me at eight-thirty. It should be a pleasant experience for you."

He hung up, leaving her annoyed. She had jumped too fast. A move like this needed careful consideration. On reflection, she was glad he called. Beneath all his elegant verbiage and Boston Brahmin accent flowed a current of intriguing warmth, as if he wanted to appear cool and flawless for his public, but....

It could be her imagination—the old silly Sara reaching for a dream. This irritating man had been the cause of a restless night for her. She needed to prove to herself that he wasn't worth losing a moment's sleep over.

He wanted to teach her a few of the fine points, did he? No matter what came of this evening, she planned to keep her wits about her. Olive would be there, unseen, but sharp of eye and clear of mind. Olive's point of view should do nicely as she sat across the table from this strange, disquieting man.

A pleasurable sensation shot the length of her spine in betrayal of her warlike thoughts. At least Eric wouldn't have to make reservations all over town wondering where Mr. Edgerton would dine. A short call to Eric's secretary explained the situation briefly. Eric was out, which was fine. Sara didn't have to hear a pep talk about how to play the game tonight.

She looked through her wardrobe considering the psychological impact of one outfit after another. Was it Paul's superior tone that was urging her to look as beautiful as she knew how, or was it defiant one-upmanship? She was every bit as knowledgeable about the finer points of cuisine as he—probably more so, she repeated to herself as she slipped on her emerald-green wool knit sheath. The high neck and long sleeves followed the well-curved lines of her body and bestowed an aura of utter femininity on her.

Her hair wouldn't cooperate in her attempts to make a soft Edwardian rolled style that she hadn't tried since leaving Paris. Tendrils of golden-red hair escaped the bouffant rolls, making becoming shadows near her subtly made-up eyes.

She picked up the heavy gold chain and antique cameo that her godmother had given her on her twenty-fifth birthday. "A lady needs to appear cared for and cherished," Elizabeth had said in her old world way.

Finally she was ready, but ready for what, she didn't exactly know. If there had to be a date with Paul Edgerton she wanted to do it her way. He was the kind of man who had to be met from a position of strength. And he wasn't a fool. She didn't dare reveal too much about herself tonight. It wouldn't take much for him to start putting two and two together and coming up with Olive Gadwall, what with Eric as her date at the Indian place, those impulsive things she said about the *kheer*, and the rash way she had said she was a writer. Discretion was the password for tonight.

The clatter of a diesel engine drew her to the window of her tiny living room. Below, executing a tight parallel parking job was a white Mercedes sedan. Somehow, it fit Paul Edgerton perfectly. The vehicle was just old enough to avoid the label *nouveau riche*.

He stepped from the car, looked up at her building, and set his tall body decisively into motion up the steep steps. Sara looked around her apartment one more time for incriminating evidence of Olive Gadwall. There was nothing in her typewriter except her letter to Jean-Claude, which she slipped into a folder. She would finish it later tonight, when she could add an amusing description of her notorious rival. Her note pads for the book were scattered about her desk and she didn't bother to arrange them. It was better to seem casually creative, with a book actually in progress. Mr. Edgerton could just assume that her doting parents were paying her bills for her. When she opened the door her heart was beating fast.

"I am honored to be your escort," he said approvingly and stepped into the living room. His smile was almost genuine, making deep creases around his fascinating eyes, and Sara had a moment of bemused paralysis before she turned away to pick up her purse and white mohair stole.

She noticed him taking stock of everything in the apartment. "I see you're hard at work on your book." He nodded in the direction of her messy desk. "I admire a writer who sets a schedule and doesn't become seduced by the blandishments of the outside world. I suppose you were going to write this evening, but I came along like a tempter." He gave a little laugh.

"Your invitation *was* tempting, I must admit."

"Then I shan't disappoint you. Mon Château is eager to be reviewed by Paul Cabot Edgerton. Shall we go?" He deftly placed the stole about her shoulders and held the door open for her. The closeness of his body for the brief moment gave her nerves mixed signals.

She caught the subtle scent of a fine cologne and had a stab of response, almost a thrill. It was a memory of something she had known...an uneasy déjà vu.

"You do look lovely," he said, as he opened the car door for her. She was fumbling with the seat belt when he reached across to help her, looking seriously into her eyes. "Thank you, Sara Courtney," he said softly, in a rich compelling tone. "You know, I had to see you tonight, to satisfy myself that you were as...as...remarkably well presented as you seemed last night at that Indian restaurant."

She felt like laughing at his inelegant compliment. "I sound like a fine wine."

"Sometimes a beautiful woman can only be compared with something else equally appealing to the senses," he answered quite seriously.

"I mustn't forget I'm with a gourmet food critic." The smooth compliments made her pull back defensively. His words were too familiar, too much like Jacques' easy flattery.

He started the car and set the stereo to a cassette that played a familiar classical symphony. "I hope you like Mahler," he said.

"I like Beethoven better," she responded quickly, but with a smile. "It's all a matter of taste, isn't it?"

"That's a philosophic question we can discuss over an excellent vintage cognac later tonight. Taste: is it an absolute, an appreciation of the Platonic ideal—or is it something that any Tom, Dick, or Harry possesses...and as such, should it be given equal weight to the opinion of a person of more refined temperament?"

"I think I would enjoy discussing taste with you," Sara said honestly. "You have some rather rigid points of view, and I have some myself."

"You, of all people, who have grown up in the rarified atmosphere of fine music, should understand the prickly problem of defining good taste for the masses."

"The masses?" she shot back. "That's an odd word to use. At least half the people who attend my parents' concerts are rather ordinary, making sacrifices to pay for tickets.... But their love of music transforms them for a brief time. On the other hand, I have also seen the so-called patrons of the arts sitting in their gilded boxes at the Vienna Concert Hall, gossiping through the most exquisite passages of a Debussy reverie. Frankly, I think I prefer the masses."

"A noble sentiment, but you know what I mean, I'm sure. For most people it would be a crime against nature to waste a Monserrat '76 on them when a common house wine would do just as well. That's all I was saying." He sounded defensive. As well he should, Sara thought.

She hoped she could get through the evening without saying anything more barbed than she already had. There was nothing wrong with Mahler's music. In other circumstances she wouldn't have been so quick to take exception to the casual remarks of a date. But this was Paul Cabot Edgerton—and she had an almost desperate need to keep him at arm's length.

He was silent for the rest of the drive to Mon

Château. As they pulled up to the valet-parking entrance he turned to her with a conciliatory smile. "Please accept my apologies. I must have sounded damnably superior."

"Damnably," she said lightly. An electrifying connection of their eyes prevented her from saying more. She smiled back at his serious, almost vulnerable face.

This wasn't going to be as simple as she thought. She wasn't ready for unalloyed charm.

CHAPTER FIVE

THEY HAD ARRIVED at a location on Melrose Avenue known for its antique shops, chic hair salons, and popular little bistros. Mon Château had no sign in front. It appeared to be just one of a line of low, vine-covered brick buildings, its soft Normandy-blue shutters closed to the gaze of passersby.

Inside, the large open room was filled to capacity, with a busy bar along one wall and high-backed upholstered chairs preventing easy identification of the celebrity diners. Paul was greeted with familiarity, the kind reserved for people of importance. He nodded to the maître d', who was an honest-to-goodness Frenchman.

The interior of the restaurant was decorated in the style of a French country house, white rough plaster and heavy, rough-hewn dark beams. A great open fireplace was crackling and fragrant from a genuine oak-wood fire. Sara smiled appreciatively. *This* ambiance was French.

They were seated near the fireplace where they had a good view of the room. A waiter with just the right amount of deference and authority brought the menus to the table and withdrew in favor of the wine steward—the *sommelier*.

Paul and he debated the relative merits of the wines on the handwritten parchment list. A Cos D'Estournel '65, perhaps, or a Bonnes Mares '78?

"We'll start with a Chateau D'Yquem to accompany the foie gras appetizer," Paul said with certainty. When the wine steward raised a questioning eye, Paul added, "You think it a bit sweet for foie gras? The proprietor of Yquem, the Comte de Lur-Saluces, finds it the perfect accompaniment."

The expression on the *sommelier*'s face changed to contrition and the right degree of awe. "But of course," he agreed. He leaned close and said in a stage whisper, "The preview shipment of Beaujolais Nouveau has arrived at dawn today. Would Monsieur Edgerton care to judge the quality?"

Paul smiled knowingly. "If it is as good as last year's it will be a pleasure. Chef Gaston is satisfied with it?"

The *sommelier* nodded. "This time we got the first shipment, three hours before New York. A *grand coup*," he said and departed.

Paul grinned at Sara's peculiar expression. "What are you thinking?"

She bit at the edge of a crusty piece of warm bread. "Do you really know the Comte de Lur-Saluces?"

"But of course," he said in a throaty French accent. "I only wish I had his vineyard."

"Then you really do know a lot about wine?" Ignorance was the best pose for the moment.

"More than most. I dream sometimes of chucking everything and running away to a little hillside château with just the right angle to the sun, and a few choice acres of outstanding vine stock."

"But you choose to stay here, instead? Writing a column can't be all that much fun, week after week. I should think you'd get tired of it."

"Now you're getting too close to my secret self. That isn't done on a first date with Paul Edgerton."

"Sorry," she said. "But you *were* going to tell me how a food critic thinks, weren't you?"

"All a ruse to get you to say yes, m'dear. I don't give away my trade secrets to anyone." His face moved into a captivating smile, showing his fine white teeth and beautiful mobile lips to advantage, while Sara admitted to herself that she was dealing with a very complicated man. Had he already guessed who she was?

The conversation stopped as the waiter brought the tiny plates of paté de foie gras, and the wine steward presented the bottle of Chateau D'Yquem for Paul's scrutiny. Sara watched with quiet cynicism as Paul examined the label, received the cork, sniffed it, set it aside, raised the partly filled glass, gently rotated it against the light, and then very thoughtfully took a small sip between his well-bred lips. "Hmmm," he said. "That will do nicely."

The steward smiled with what appeared to be relief and poured the wine into the two glasses.

"If a restaurant has a list that is first cabin, then I can forgive the minor indiscretions of the kitchen," Paul said.

Oh, yes, Sara said to herself, *quite.*

The pâté melted in her mouth and the wine was really wonderful, fruity but delicate. "A curious union of intensity and elegance," Paul said, sounding like a caricature of a wine connoisseur.

"And it's tasty, too," Sara couldn't help adding once she had sampled it herself.

The warm vegetable salad with truffle dressing tasted not quite right, Sara thought. She would have left out the garlic. "How would you describe this in your column?" she asked.

He looked up briskly, pushing the plate a little away. "Inferior. The garlic competes with the subtle earthy garb of the truffle. A heavy-handed effort at exotica. Everyone's doing truffles lately without the least understanding. You see, the whole business of using truffles is a fine art."

"Are you a truffle expert, too?"

"Among other things," he said easily.

"And what was the wine steward whispering about earlier?" she asked. "It sounded like secret agents and derring-do. Are you also in the wine-smuggling business?"

Paul threw back his head with a laugh. "Did it sound like that? Pardon me for not explaining it to you. Of course you wouldn't know about the great Beaujolais race."

Sara didn't like his assumption that she knew nothing at all about his rarified world. In this case, though, she was ignorant.

"Every year it becomes more of an international race to see which city will have the first taste of the new French harvest of Beaujolais. A few cases of the new wine are spirited aboard a supersonic Concorde plane in Paris and taken to New York, where agents claim it and take it to their secret tasting locations."

"Why all the fuss?" she couldn't help asking.

"Mankind's passion for drama," he said with a shrug. "Lately the event has overshadowed the wine. Beaujolais is a simple wine. The new bottles come from grapes less than four weeks old. Last year's tasting was held here at the California Club one hour after it was served at New York's Knickerbocker Club. And this year we were first. Frankly, I don't become excited by things like who was first or second to taste a new wine. I only care if it's good."

The *sommelier*, as if on cue, brought the precious bottle to the table, pouring some in a glass for Paul's scrutiny. He stood back waiting for the verdict. This was a very serious moment, apparently.

Paul went through the gestures of scrupulous analysis. "Stronger, deeper...much more body than last year's. But don't you think it suffers a bit from jet lag?" His smile failed to alter the sober expression of the wine steward.

"You are a master, Monsieur Edgerton," he intoned. "Chef Gaston feels just as you do. I shall tell him and he will be pleased!"

In spite of her forebodings Sara was having a good time. Paul could be amusing, even educational. She caught herself more than once slipping into the rhythm of his thoughts, reaching to see beneath his pomposity, almost forgiving him for everything. In short, she was doing something she had done once before: falling under the spell of strong male energy. But intellectually she knew what was happening, and she was trying hard to retain control.

The waiter presented Paul his breast of duck with fresh noodles in garlic sauce and brought Sara a veal Cordon Bleu, which she had let Paul order for her. He had specified carrots glacé to go with it.

"Why did you order duck?" she asked. "There were more elegant French dishes on the menu."

"Very perceptive, mademoiselle. I had a good reason, having to do with a desire to clear my palate of the aftertaste from a wretched duck dish I had recently."

Sara knew which duck dish he was referring to.

"I reviewed an inferior little French place last week, to the despair of my stomach," he explained, with a smile of sympathy for himself.

"I know," Sara admitted too quickly. "Le Grand Richard—I read your article about it."

"You did? I'm flattered. Then you *did* know who I was before we met last night...."

"I didn't notice the name of the critic, just the restaurant. You made it sound like a dreadful place. I'm sure people will be staying away in droves."

"As well they might!" he said through a mouthful of duck. "It annoys me to distraction when an ill-trained restaurant critic whose taste is all in her mouth goes limp and hyperbolic about a place just because the chef and staff tried hard. Imagine—they tried hard! Such a place has no right to exist as far as I'm concerned."

"The ill-trained critic as well?" she prompted.

"If you mean that Gadwall creature—exactly! She's a wart on the hide of responsible journalism."

Sara was stunned to hear how much Olive had pricked his sensitive ego. "You can't be as heartless as you sound," she said, retracting any gentler emotions she may have felt earlier.

His dark, expressive eyebrows shot upward. "Not at all, m'dear! I think of myself as a teacher. If anything, my great weakness is my sympathetic nature. Le Grand Richard, for example: I could have rhapsodized over the mediocre food and service, and the terrible wine list. The efforts they made were truly touching. But instead I did the more difficult thing and pointed out for them where they could do better," he said innocently. He sipped at his Beaujolais as if to seal his point.

She pretended to be involved with her veal dish, giving her irritation a chance to settle down. She regretted her volatile temperament at moments like these, when her anger flared too easily. She still couldn't believe he was serious. He was waiting for her to respond to his outrageous statements and she took a chance. "What would you say if I pronounced you a dreadful snob?" She forced a little smile.

An answering smile grew slowly across his face and he reached to take Sara's hand in his. "You must think me absurd, Sara Courtney.... Ever since I picked you up tonight I find myself sounding like the most perfect ass. I'm hearing myself talk and watching your lovely face and those eyes of liquid turquoise, and I'm thinking, *Shut up, Edgerton, you fool! You'll drive her away.* And then my tongue says something else that you must find offensive. Sara, I'm basically a decent man, I promise you!"

She looked at his disarming expression and her heart turned over in her breast. Strangely, she wanted to believe him.

"What kind of spell are you weaving around my senses?" he whispered across the table and gave her hand a gentle squeeze. "I feel like a schoolboy who can't seem to say the right thing. Maybe you should name our next subject for conversation. I've made a hash of it so far."

Sara wasn't ready for the enemy—the man from The Right Table—to smile at her so compellingly. It had been easier to dismiss him as insufferable. She didn't want this explosive chemistry to exist between them.

"Well," she began carefully, "I know we shouldn't talk about music or wine. Politics is a thorny subject, and we'd best avoid matters of taste. There must be something...."

"I have it!" he said in a triumphant whisper. "A burning question from the gentleman: How distant a suitor is Eric Hartley, and what claim does he have on you?"

"Very distant—that was our first date. And my life is my own."

"Aha!" Paul's eyes glinted rakishly. "Then he has made a strategic mistake by introducing us. The race goes to the swift."

"Stop right there," she said. "You're sounding like a social dinosaur again. If there's a race, there has to be a prize, and I'm a bit too liberated to be a prize won at combat between rutting males."

He laughed easily. "Everything I say—absolutely everything—is wrong!" He picked up his newly filled glass and looked at her through the gleaming liquid. "Most females would be delighted to be fought over."

"If you presented yourself to me after a bloody brawl with some rival I would tell you to go and clean yourself up!"

"You would, would you?" he smiled with a wary look in his eyes.

"Yes, I would." Sara stabbed at her carrots glacé for emphasis. She could feel his eyes on her and she didn't want to look at them.

He didn't speak for a long moment. When she looked up again he had a look of intense concentration. "What would you say if I told you I want to see you again—every night if I have to—until I can understand what this amazing feeling is between us?"

"Is that an order?" She cocked a disapproving

eye at him, fearful that he could see right through her.

"Yes, I do believe it is It surely will take more than this one evening for you to straighten me out, don't you think?"

This was much too dangerous a territory to treat lightly. "Pleasant as this is, I'm afraid I won't be free again to see you."

"And I have presumed too much," he said in clipped tones. A mask of politeness was quickly drawn over his face. "As you said, you are a woman who knows her own mind and will decide which suitor to accept."

"Don't put it that way, Paul. There are complications I can't explain now."

"The lady has a past," he said, looking seriously at her flushed face.

"I just need time to be alone," she said lamely.

"Point taken, m'dear. I was never one to intrude. Now, I'll ask again—what shall we speak of? I pride myself on my ability to entertain a companion and avoid controversy, believe it or not!"

OVER THEIR TALL GLASS GOBLETS of fresh raspberries in heavy cream the conversation rambled in every direction. Paul spoke of his childhood, his family's estate near Boston, the horses he adored, and the fact that his family always wintered on the Côte d'Azur.

"Do you know Le Moulin de Mougins near there?" she asked. "A dear friend of mine is the *sous*-chef."

"Of course I know it. A three-star establishment. But I haven't been there for a while."

"My friend is one of the most gifted chefs I've ever known," she said rashly.

"Oh? And how many great chefs have you known?" His tone was lofty again, but Sara couldn't fall into the trap of telling him too much about that side of her life, even if she did want to wipe that superior little smirk from his lips.

"A few. I did call myself a European for some years, you know. Fine food isn't completely unknown to me."

"A miscalculation on my part, and I withdraw my rude question. There are so few females of my acquaintance who know more than where to have their hair done and which health spas are the most punishing."

An honest remark, Sara thought, even if it did show the level of his usual taste in women. And she wished he wouldn't look at her with that knowing expression, as if he assumed he'd win whatever contest he chose. He wouldn't—not even if he did have her pulse under his complete control.

"You're different. You know that, I suppose. You don't have that expectant gleam from beneath heavy lashes, ready to snatch at any compliment. Your body language doesn't send me messages saying full speed ahead. In fact, I think I can truly say that I like you as a person."

"Don't you often say that to women?"

"They don't seem to require it. Just the usual banter. Idle flattery is enough."

"I'm sorry to hear that." She was planning to quote some of Paul's outlandish statements in her letter to Jean-Claude.

"Tomorrow night, then? Will you give me a chance to start fresh with you, now that I've discovered how special you are?"

She hesitated too long and he said softly, "I understand. If it isn't Eric, then it's someone else."

"Paul—listen to me. I know the pitfalls of starting a relationship too fast just because the other person is different from what you've known before." She felt the thrust of remembered pain and tried to stop it from showing on her face.

"Words of wisdom," he said, nodding agreement. "And then we grow afraid of repeating the experience."

"Not afraid, just cautious."

"To the cautious Sara," he said, and raised his espresso cup to her.

He had never looked more handsome. His voice still said that he was completely in charge, but Sara knew that there were great chinks in his armor that would be challenging to study—if she dared.

ON THE DRIVE BACK to her apartment Sara could have kicked herself. The very thought of pursuing a normal dating relationship with Paul Cabot Edgerton was insane. Even Eric would think so, as adventurous as he was. But there was a blind spot in her tonight. The new Beaujolais, maybe.

How could she have known beforehand that Paul would awaken that provocative, tingling feeling inside her? It wasn't simply a matter of not mixing business with pleasure—it was going to be one big complicated mess. And if he ever found out who she was...!

She was like the mythical Pandora, who knew she wasn't supposed to look into the box full of furies, but she couldn't stop herself. Curiosity was what made a fine cook, a good journalist, but it could certainly kill her career if Paul should discover he had been manipulated.

Of course that wasn't her intention. She didn't want to think past the surprising and unexpected pleasure of his company.

She wisely refused his suggestion for a drive out to Venice Beach for a walk on the cool April sand.

"Too fast?" he said. "Too much moon for a lady so recently wounded?" Instead of mocking her, he seemed to be probing, seeing if she meant what she had said.

"I wouldn't call my condition 'wounded,' but I really do have to get some sleep tonight," she apologized. "I didn't get my full eight hours last night."

"Nor did I. Women don't usually make me lose sleep. Did you know that Anne Boleyn held Henry VIII at bay for years, but he finally made her his."

"What an awful comparison! Aren't you assuming too much?"

"I was, and I apologize. It isn't my nature to behead difficult women, I pledge that right now—so rest assured."

"I may not be free to see you again, Paul—really," she said, in an effort to stop this delicious tension between them.

"But, there's always the possibility that you may, isn't there?"

At the door to her apartment he lifted her chin into the dim light and looked at her for a long moment. "Do you know what you've done for me tonight, Sara? You have made me forget for several hours that there's a cold, threatening world out there."

His lion's eyes held hers with compelling power as he drew her close and kissed her very gently on her cheek—no more. He pulled back slowly, as if from a deep and intimate embrace, leaving her completely without words to say.

"More than that," he breathed warmly, "you've made me understand why old King Henry was willing to wait years, if necessary, for the joys he knew would be his...." He blew her a final kiss and strode off down the long corridor, leaving behind a stirring hint of his fine cologne.

What have I done! she thought vainly, while her legs went weak.

CHAPTER SIX

SARA BROODED ABOUT PAUL EDGERTON long into the night. Her mind was turning over like a child's kaleidoscope, making picture after picture, too fast for her to stop it.

Her body was restless, with rushes of sensual response flooding through her every time she visualized herself with Paul. What was so special about the feel of his hand around hers? It was just a hand. But he had some maddening affinity with her that put her completely off balance.

It was silly to be quivering at the memory of his intense and challenging eyes. Had she become so perverse and irrational that she could be sexually aroused by the mere idea of pitting her will against that of an accomplished male chauvinist? Couldn't she stand to be bested by a man whose intelligence and wit were at least as good as hers?

Her mind's picture gallery interrupted her inner dialogue by showing her what it would have been like to have Paul's lips move teasingly from her cheeks, down to the corners of her lips and then to be full upon them in a deep, searching kiss. And then... and then....

Sara threw off the covers and sat up, furious

with herself. These were the fantasies of a frustrated, unfulfilled woman. Or, they could be simple indigestion—too much coffee. She fixed herself a cup of hot camomile tea, tried to read an old magazine, and attempted to sleep again. But always in the back of her mind was the question: What is Olive Gadwall going to do with Paul Edgerton? And what is Olive Gadwall going to do with Paul Edgerton??

SHE WAS AT THE CHRONICLE BUILDING early. The day shift was arriving and Eric waved to her from his office, an eager smile on his face. Reluctantly, she entered his cluttered cubicle. His phone rang and he answered it, at the same time shoving the morning edition of the *Chronicle* across the desk at her while he dealt with the caller.

The name Olive Gadwall shone up at her in gothic print. There was her column surrounded by double decorative lines, and across the top was a parade of small duck silhouettes, in honor of the name Gadwall. She had nearly forgotten Everett Costain's little joke about his pen name.

The whole page was eye-catching; Eric had been true to his word. A luscious color photo of food headed the recipe article below hers. But her eyes were riveted to her stinging condemnation of Paul Edgerton's taste. There it was, leaping from the page. It was horrible.

Eric finally hung up the phone and fixed Sara with a look. "Well, what do you think!"

"It looks...very nice."

"You don't sound too excited."

"It's great, really—but I'm in an awful muddle, Eric."

"Sit down. Tell all."

She perched on the arm of a chair. "I went out with Paul Edgerton last night—to Mon Château."

"My secretary told me. Great balls of fire, woman—how did it go? I've been on pins and needles waiting for you to get in today." His alert green eyes were opened widely enough for the whites to show all around.

"He's an interesting man," she hedged.

"Interesting! Don't tell me the fort has fallen! Does he know who you really are?"

"Of course he doesn't! And the fort hasn't fallen, whatever you mean by that."

He pulled several pages of typed material from his drawer. "Here. It's Edgerton's column for tomorrow—don't ask me how I got it. Read. Then tell me about him."

Sara took the pages from his hand. "I've dropped in twice now to The India Experience," the words said.

> I admit the decor is quite charming and imaginative. The staff is willing to please. However, despite the agreeable atmosphere the food is definitely uneven, the cuisine bland. Somehow, one doesn't expect this in Indian food. The *ghiya-ka-shak*, a sautéed Indian squash, was anything but memorable, and the *alu-matar*, a vegetable potato stew, was drab

> to a fault. The *sabat maahn*, black lentils, should have been pungent, but wasn't; the unsubtle flavor of the entire meal would not urge a return visit.
>
> The rices were pleasant and imagination had been used on the cocktail snacks, but the wine selection was dull and limited. The sophisticated diner will feel cheated.
>
> The dessert list? Adequate. For myself, the fudge-like halvas are always too sweet. But the *kheer*—a type of rice pudding—was surprisingly good. For those who abhor a sticky *kheer*, this one I can recommend.

"All in all," he concluded, "if you go to The India Experience, be prepared to be disappointed."

Sara looked up to find Eric's brightly piercing eyes on her. "Well? Interesting?"

"He's good at damning with faint praise." She felt the first twinges of a new headache behind her eyes. After last night she almost believed that Paul had a nice side—at least she was ready to be convinced. But here he was in print again, showing quite clearly what kind of a man he was.

"But you did like Edgerton," Eric stated. "Have you considered that maybe he *has* spotted you? That remark about the sticky *kheer*... maybe I'm reaching a little, but how do we know just how crafty the old fellow can be?"

Sara was feeling worse by the minute. "Be honest with me, Eric. Did you set up our accidental meeting at the restaurant?"

He barked a laugh. "Now who's drawing conclusions?"

"You said you knew the parking attendants who were willing to tip you off about Paul. I don't want to think that I'm a pawn in a game you've cooked up to raise the circulation of the *Chronicle*."

"Is that how you see me?" He stood up and came around to put an avuncular arm about her shoulders. "I'm not that devious, believe me. But if this thing makes you too uncomfortable, just tell me."

"Well, it does, Eric. I'm not tough enough."

He looked at her thoughtfully. "What if we just let nature take its course? If you do go out with him again you'll know exactly what he's going to review, right? Unless he takes you to a show, of course," he smiled. "His columns should start to get pretty repetitious after you've already covered the restaurants before him."

"What about me, Eric? It's still a game you're talking about. If Paul and I go out again—and I'm not saying we will—I don't want to deceive him. I'm not equipped to do it."

"Okay, then think about his toplofty and cold reviews. Are you going to let him pounce on nice places like that Indian restaurant without standing up to him? We both know the food was good."

"I know," she vacillated. "He shouldn't be allowed to do it. But why does he?"

"God knows. Maybe it's an inferiority complex under all that Boston culture. You could dig under his defenses and psychoanalyze him in your column!" Eric laughed gleefully.

Sara glared back. "That's not funny. I can deflate Paul Cabot Edgerton without dating him."

Eric still grinned. "It's up to you. Now go and write a bangup story about The India Experience. And if he asks you out again—and I'm sure he will—he's going to try to see how much you know about Olive. He'll want you to pump me about her. Just be vague and tell him to ask me himself. As far as he knows you don't know a thing about the inner workings of the *Chronicle*." He patted her hand. "Don't look so upset. It's a journalistic coup!"

She went bleakly back to her desk, barely convinced that she was doing the right thing. She halfheartedly switched on her word processor and started to type:

Today I read with surprise the words of my honorable counterpart from The Right Table. The esteemed Paul Cabot Edgerton has struck out again. I too have dined at The India Experience and have a very favorable report to give my readers.

Since Indian food is one of the most appetizing of earthly cooking disciplines, and a favorite of mine, I simply can't let Mr. Edgerton's prejudicial remarks about this charming small restaurant stand. It has been my good fortune to sample foods from India in many places in the world. I can say without reservation that we should be glad that we have this local example of fine Indian cuisine.

Indian chefs must always take care not to overwhelm the delicate Western taste buds. Our palates aren't trained to appreciate the varied flavors of a very hot curry. Perhaps Mr. Edgerton neglected to see a note on the menu explaining how to order the degree of spiciness: mild, medium, or very hot. Nothing stopped the *Tribune*'s gourmet from using the chutneys—some of which smoke deliciously on the tongue—if he wanted a taste of fire. Blandness at the India Experience is simply a matter of personal choice.

More about Mr. Edgerton's apparent lack of taste perceptions: May I take the liberty to say that alcohol, no matter what the vintage, dulls the tongue, and I was sorry to see a bar at The India Experience. I'm sure it is a concession to Western taste. When the palate is prepared by the sharp taste of yogurt and cucumber, for instance, or by the appetizing tang of a salt lassi, the subtleties of flavor in Indian food become apparent.

Since Mr. Edgerton believes alcohol to be a necessary adjunct to any meal, he should reconsider in the case of Indian cuisine. This is not my opinion alone, but that of Indian friends, such as chef Krishna Ram Singh of the Gujarat in London. It was also expressed to me by Lord Medwin Stanley, whose long acquaintance with India is legend.

She finished, feeling like an offended old maid. *Let him wonder who he's dealing with,* she thought defensively. She turned her attention to another restaurant, a small place on Larchmont Boulevard that offered ordinary fast food, but whose cook made some of the best pies and cookies anywhere.

Sara marched into Eric's office with a printout of her column and dropped it onto his paper-strewn desk. "Round two," she said stiffly.

"That's the spirit! Go and look for a good little lunch place and then go home—take the night off. All we have to do now is wait for the explosion when he reads Sunday's volley."

Sara was relieved to be walking away from her desk for the day. A churning conflict was building inside her and she didn't want to be alone with herself. She placed a call to her godmother from the lobby of the Chronicle Building. "Could you meet me for lunch at the Scotsman in Beverly Hills? I'm hungry and I need company."

"Of course," Aunt Elizabeth's youthful voice came back enthusiastically. "When?"

"In an hour." She rang off feeling happier. It was possible to make too much of something, and that's what she was doing with this Paul Edgerton affair.

Since she had some time to kill, Sara spent it walking along Rodeo Drive a few blocks from the restaurant. As she casually glanced at the fashionable windows, something tightened in her breast. The area was too reminiscent of Paul—everything was in the "right taste."

She stopped herself, knowing what was happening. She was being guilty of reverse snobbery. But at least she recognized it. Paul seemed so maddeningly content with his opinions.

Aunt Elizabeth was chatty and good humored. She was a woman who still turned heads—even at her age. She wore a draped dark-gray suit with a short swinging cape set off by a fresh rose on her lapel. No laced-up Oxford shoes for her—she wore some rather dashing gray and black pumps, and an expensive black lizard bag completed her outfit.

Just the sight of her lifted Sara's spirits. Aunt Liz never let things get her down. It was fun sitting cosily in a bow window at a table for two watching the parade of people go by on the sidewalk. The air conditioner was fighting a losing battle with the odors rising from the hickory grill, and the cheerful, deafening tide of human voices made a good backdrop for an intimate conversation at a small table.

"Whatever possessed you to come here, love?" Aunt Elizabeth's sharp blue eyes assessed Sara's face. "You look tired. Is something troubling you? Remember, I've known you a long time... don't hedge."

A huge need to tell someone about the last few days rose irresistibly in Sara's heart. She looked into the shrewdly loving old eyes and made a decision. Even though Aunt Liz knew everyone in town, she was scrupulously discreet.

"Well, there is something..." she began. And

the whole story unraveled itself as they had their cobb salad, cheese-grilled potato skins, and fragrant coffee.

Aunt Elizabeth listened intently. When Sara came to the date with Paul Edgerton her fine mouth formed an "Oh" of silent commentary. "Somehow I shouldn't think you two would be compatible. Yet, there is another side of him, my dear—a very well-hidden person that exists beneath that overbearing, but stunningly handsome exterior."

"Wait until he reads my column, Aunt Liz... he'll be blazing mad!" She stopped, suddenly aware of a speculative expression on the face opposite her. "You think there's a secret side to him?"

"Possibly." An amused smile answered her. "I know him tolerably well. His mother belonged to a chamber music association in Boston, and when I was traveling in concert I was often invited to their home—a beautiful old place full of nineteenth century atmosphere and fine art treasures. Paul is the younger of the two boys; there is a sister also who fled the propriety of the family home to become a model in New York. She's quite lovely and didn't take the family name professionally. You've probably seen pictures of her—Madelyn de Lucca."

Sara knew the name. In her mind she saw the classic oval face, pure and Madonna-like, with waves of dark hair shadowing enormous eyes. Now that she knew the relationship, there was a touch of Paul in the lips and chin, and especially the eyes. "I've seen her pictures, but not lately."

"That's because she got married five years ago, to the Marquis Yves de Bertil, who has an estate in the Bordeaux-Sauternes area and is a wine prince, as my dear Artur used to say. Yves produces a small vintage, but it is exceedingly select. He sells only to the finest, such as Taillevent in Paris, Le Pavillon and other such citadels of wine snobbery," she chuckled. "Artur was an old friend of Yves' father. That's how I know about it. Their vineyards, so the tale goes, date back to Roman times when the homesick procurators of the restive provinces of muleheaded, rebellious Gauls planted vines from home and attempted to improve the rather heavy local brews."

"Is Madelyn happy?"

"I believe so. Yves isn't an effete specimen of an inbred nobility. He's a down-to-earth businessman with a deep love for his land, very much in tune with nature." She paused to enjoy a bite of potato skin. "That's why Paul has such a strong interest in wines. He spends time with Madelyn and Yves and has a mind like a vacuum cleaner for information."

"He seems obsessed with wines," Sara said. "He said he longs to retire to a château and grow fine grapes...."

"Not likely," Aunt Elizabeth smiled. "He's not the type to settle down. Too restless. It's part of his problem."

Sara's curiosity was running amok. She needed to know everything about Paul Edgerton, if only for her professional files. "What about his brother?"

The older woman shrugged. "Edward is quite a different proposition. He's a banker, through and through. One gets the feeling that he was born wearing a three-piece suit. He's on the board of several gilt-edged investment trusts and several banks. Not fly-by-night modern banks, but old ones that arrived with the Pilgrims." She shook her head, smiling reminiscently. "I think he overawed poor Paul in his youth. Their father died when Paul was seven, and Edward was several years older. Edward took him over, along with his mother and the family home. He's not at all like Paul, but short and rotund, with piercing eyes and a very large thundering voice. I find it difficult to talk to Edward. He has a habitual expression that can convince you you must be wrong, no matter what you may be saying." She gave a short laugh. "Edward's wife is a prune-faced Camille—she enjoys delicate health and her security as one of the social elite. They have no progeny. Edward must solace himself discreetly among the lower classes. I saw him by chance in his car on a country road with a rather unkempt little blonde one day. He's been wary of me ever since."

She resumed eating, seeming to have turned off all further interest in Paul Edgerton. Sara seethed with a desire to know more. "That would explain some of his problems, but not everything," she prodded gently.

Aunt Elizabeth looked up with an intentional

mask of innocence. Sara realized she was being played with. "Oh, you mean Paul. Of course he has problems. Isn't that just what I was saying?" Her face dropped into lines of seriousness. "Being brought up by the redoubtable Edward can't have been easy. Paul, for all his size and aplomb, is basically a lonely man—have you noticed? No, I suppose you don't know him well enough," she amended.

Sara willed the revelations to continue.

"I suppose you're wondering why he never married."

"How many female Paul Edgertons could there be?" she said sharply. "It must be difficult finding a mate to match his exalted status."

"You may be misjudging him, Sara," was the quiet reply.

"His attitudes are Edwardian. How old is he, really—in physical years, I mean?"

"Thirty-four or -five, I should think. But he's hardly been celibate. He *is* quite attractive in his elegant way." She smiled and Sara kept her face from revealing any reaction. "When he was in college—Harvard, of course—he had a passionate attachment to the sister of a classmate. She was a Texas girl, and vastly unsuitable in the family's eyes. Poor Paul. At vacation time they invited her to the family home in Boston and delicately dissected her. Even Madelyn, usually his champion, didn't uphold him. The girl fled to Texas in tears—she never wanted to see him again. And Paul was crushed. The girl wrote him a bitter letter, telling what she thought of Paul's kind of people. The letter was quickly burned. I heard all of this from a friend of the family, Mable van Anselm, who saw it.''

"He must not have loved the girl. A real man would have done anything to keep her," Sara said.

"But things weren't as simple as that then. He was quite young and callow and he was loyal to his family. The experience changed him. He went out with suitable girls thereafter, but his heart wasn't in it. There had been so many generations of Edgertons who were trained from birth to suppress their own desires to the greater glory of the family. Paul hadn't yet entertained the thought of rebellion."

"It's hard for me to comprehend families like that."

"They exist, believe me. But, to continue, Paul's strength was about to reveal itself. First, there was a tug-of-war with Edward, who refused to accept that Paul wouldn't study business and join the family financial tradition. But Paul was drawn to literature and became pigheaded. He graduated cum laude, I believe, with a fine grounding in the humanities. The Vietnam war had begun and Paul was drafted. Before he left he used the power of the Edgerton name to get a commitment from a Boston paper to send back reports on the war.

"Because of his qualifications he was sent to officers' candidate school and attached to a general's staff. When he came home again he held the rank of captain." She stopped and looked at Sara. "Am I boring you, dear? I do go on once I'm into a subject."

"Not at all, Aunt Liz. I'm glad to know about him. Maybe I can be more charitable about him and some of his slashing criticisms of harmless restaurants."

"I was just thinking of writing his mother this morning. Poor dear, she still doesn't quite know what happened to her obedient little Paul. She expects him to come to his senses any day and return to the fold. You're very fortunate to have parents who give you freedom, Sara, remember that."

"But how in the world did he become a restaurant critic?"

Aunt Elizabeth nodded to the waiter for her coffee cup to be refilled. "I'll have to tell you the rest, then. Paul had done very well with his dispatches from Vietnam. I'm told that his writing was perceptive and compassionate."

"Where did he lose those qualities?" Sara asked with a hint of cynicism.

"Be patient, child." She sipped thoughtfully for a moment. "At home again he found Madelyn in rebellion and leaving for New York. His mother, urged by Edward, was determined to have grandchildren, which Edward's wife couldn't produce. The family line was in danger of being extinguished. Paul must marry, and soon. He escaped for several years by studying journalism at Northwestern and taking newspaper assignments in

Europe and the Middle East. He sent back a regular column about his observations. He always did love food, so among more serious subjects he discussed the culinary customs and interesting restaurants in the countries he lived in. His vivid descriptions of food fascinated people and they asked for more of this kind of material.

"Meanwhile, his mother was terrified that he would marry a foreigner—God forbid! She was busy searching for a suitable mate for Paul."

"And she found one?" Sara asked. She was beginning to feel she knew too much about Paul for comfort.

"A girl from impeccable bloodlines. Dear Paul returned home to a *fait accompli*, full of his mother's iron will and emotion. She expected him to settle down, teach writing at Harvard or somewhere appropriate, marry the girl and produce children. Rather unenlightened of her, of course. So, there was Paul, ranged against his mother and a girl he hardly knew who was now pursuing him mercilessly. He couldn't be true to himself and everyone else, too. The pressure from the girl, combined with Edward's heavy disapproval of him, his mother's tears, and the girl's hopeful family, quite put him around the bend—as my Artur used to say."

She took a dessert menu from the waiter. "Let's have something sinful. Ah, crème caramel...that will be lovely."

Sara hurried to order. She didn't want to stop the flow of information and Aunt Liz was easily distracted. "Look there, Sara," the older woman said in a low voice. "I'd swear that the man at the end of the bar is that new English television star. He *does* send out strong signals."

"I don't feel a thing," Sara said. "Come on, Aunt Liz, finish your story. You've left everything dangling!"

"Paul escaped again. He came to California and got his job at the *Tribune*. He's been here for four years. His background gives him entrée into local society, and his personality, which has become more astringent lately, makes people think that his taste is without rival. He is a rather splendid specimen, with an appeal all his own, don't you think? I see him at parties where the women are making ridiculous efforts to draw his attention."

She sighed and then laughed. "I haven't had such a gossip in years! But you did startle me with your news. The whole situation of yours concerning Paul and the newspaper columns is... titillating, to say the least, and maybe perilous—but I think you can carry it through. Just don't be unfair to the boy. He's at a disadvantage in this little charade, though you might do him a great good." She laid a gentle, warning hand over Sara's. "Think carefully how you involve yourself with him, my dear. You both have areas of vulnerability. Now—how is dear Bill? He reported to me that he finds you a good companion, even with your eccentric taste in clothes and wigs. Now I know what he was referring to. You should have told me about your Olive Gadwall business earlier and saved me the worry that you needed guidance with your wardrobe."

They talked about Bill and other mutual friends until Aunt Elizabeth finally noticed her old silver and black chauffeured Rolls cruising slowly past the restaurant for perhaps the third time. They parted with embraces and kisses, and Sara started home with a lot to think about. Paul Cabot Edgerton was so much more than a snob. He had taken on new dimensions, but unfortunately they only made him more interesting.

AMONG THE MAGAZINES and bills in the day's mail was a thin, blue air mail envelope from France. Jean-Claude hadn't written for weeks and Sara was starting to worry.

This latest letter found him restless and unhappy with his job. "Nothing will develop here, I feel it in my bones," he complained. "I need a change. My creativity is dying. I need to hear your woman's wisdom before I do something rash and quit everything here...."

She sat down and fired off a letter to him: "A genius like yours can't be held back," she said, half in jest, "but even geniuses have to learn patience. There's time enough for the world to discover you...." She sensed his dissatisfaction keenly. He was quick to think the worst of his situations, yet he had always been the very one to cheer her up when things weren't going well. She had to urge him to take time before making any big decisions with his life.

She walked to the corner mailbox with the letter. When she returned the red light on her answering machine was blinking. She pressed the playback switch and heard her caller's message:

"Sara, this is Paul Edgerton. I thought you might be free to do something amusing tonight, like drive up to Santa Barbara for a quiet dinner at El Encanto. I'll be at my apartment all evening in case you come home in time." There was a pause, then: "Please call me anyway. I need to hear your voice."

She stared at the telephone. If she called him what would that mean? She wasn't ready to take the responsibility for letting him come any closer. Some time during her lunch with Aunt Elizabeth she had made a decision not to play with Paul Edgerton's life. She couldn't let herself start to care for a man whose reputation she intended to undermine. Sara Courtney wasn't a Mata Hari, no matter how much Eric might encourage intrigue.

She played Paul's message back another time, a lump of regret forming in her tight throat as she finally erased the message from the tape.

CHAPTER SEVEN

THE TELEPHONE RANG AGAIN later that night and Sara didn't answer it. There was no message, only the disconnecting click on the recording tape as the caller hung up.

Sara buried herself in her notes for her book, recreating in her mind one special springtime with her parents when they had been master teachers at a music academy in Asolo, high in the Italian Alps.

The phone rang once more and Sara picked it up this time, tired of being a coward. It was only Aunt Elizabeth.

"Forgive me for calling so late," the lilting voice said, "and for talking your ear off at lunch today. Old women love to remember, don't they?"

"It was fun, Aunt Liz, and very good for me."

"That's my point, dear. I've been concerned that you're working too hard—never thinking about anything but your job. What about coming up to the house Saturday night—I'm having a lovely musicale in the salon and I desperately need a cohostess."

Sara had never refused an invitation from her

godmother. "Of course," she replied, "I'd love to come."

"I'll send the car around for you at seven-thirty. Saturday, then?"

Sara spent the next day away from the *Chronicle*, at Eric's request. His spy on the *Tribune* reported that Paul Edgerton was trying to find out who Olive Gadwall was, and he might have his own informant in the *Chronicle*'s city room. Until Eric could unmask the culprit Sara was to stay away.

"And that's an order!" he laughed. "You have enough assignments in your briefcase to keep you busy for a year. Just get the copy to me by courier and I'll do the rest."

Sara called Bill McCormack and coaxed him to escort Olive Gadwall to lunch at a new Basque restaurant. She smiled at his painful groan on the other end of the line.

"Come on, Bill—old Olive needs a fella."

"And I might see someone I know. A judge or another lawyer who has it in for me. My swinging image will be in shreds!"

"I promise you she'll look no older than thirty. What's the matter? Aunt Liz said you enjoyed my company," she goaded playfully.

"Okay, but only thirty!"

"I'll meet you there at twelve sharp. Look for a sultry lady."

"Dear God—"

Norma had left Sara a wig that Rita Hayworth would have envied—long red waves with a Veronica Lake drape over one eye. Sara wanted to have fun today, to laugh and let her problems fall away. A shadow of heavy emotion had hung over her for days now. She felt terrible about not returning Paul's call, but it was better that he think her rude.

The important thing was not to find herself alone for a while. If she kept moving, seeing people, she would give herself time to let go of her nagging fascination with Paul Edgerton.

Bill was a perfect lunch date. He didn't fall apart when he saw her in her red wig and slit skirt. He even enjoyed the deception when a young lawyer from his firm came to their table asking to be introduced.

That night, after dinner with Norma in a Hollywood natural food place and a depressing French film about love and revenge, Sara had no more excuses for staying away from her apartment.

The light on the answering machine was flashing again, and a pang of expectation shot through her. The first message was from Eric, who had had no success in finding Paul's spy. The second caller didn't identify himself before he spoke.

"I'm disappointed that you didn't answer my call last night," the silken, masculine voice said. "But Edgertons are persistent. I have a very special evening planned Saturday, one that I know you will enjoy. If I said or did anything to offend you the other night, I am most truly sorry. You see, Edgertons need to be given a second chance sometimes. I would be grateful if you...." The automatic timer on the machine had cut off the rest of the message, but Sara didn't need to hear it.

She wanted to call Eric and throw Olive's wigs onto his desk for someone else to wear. She *wanted* to see Paul again. She could have wept.

But she didn't pick up the telephone to call anyone—not Eric, not Paul. Instead, she took a cool shower and curled up in bed with a restaurant guide to Los Angeles. Until she had her head screwed on straight she wasn't to be trusted to make any decisions at all. She was as bad as Jean-Claude, she growled to herself.

She set the clock for three-thirty in the morning. She was planning to visit the Central Market before dawn and get the flavor of the bustling produce exchange. Eric wanted her to write a piece about exotic vegetables. With her press pass she would have access to the loading docks and try to interview several growers.

The day was crisp and cool, perfect October weather, and Sara threw herself into the experience of the Central Market with relish. A cacophony of voices speaking Spanish, Japanese, and Italian greeted her appreciative ears as she threaded her way among high stacks of produce boxes. The smell of moist earth and fresh greenery made an exquisite perfume and Sara followed her nose to the area of the lesser known European and Oriental vegetables.

After several hectic hours of jostling and trying to have multilingual interviews with the busy men and women, Sara finally retired to her car to transcribe some of her notes.

Then, following an impulse, she drove to Santa Monica, north along the Pacific Coast Highway, stopping above Malibu where there was an almost deserted stretch of sandy beach. She brought out an old car blanket, carried her shoes, and walked until she was well away from people. She was still discovering things about her new home, places where she could be alone to think when she needed to.

The sea was a cleansing force, reminding her that she was just a tiny part of a magnificent universe. What reason did she—little Sara Courtney—have for feeling cheated by life?

She would do her job as Olive Gadwall and pursue a normal social life—with people like Bill McCormack. If she still had a burning curiosity about Paul Edgerton in the future, maybe the mysterious ways of fortune would place him in her path once more. But for now...she had a career to take care of.

It was already seven o'clock when Sara returned home. On the way back from the beach she had suddenly remembered Aunt Elizabeth's musicale that evening. She barely had time to clean up and dress, let alone find something ready to eat in her refrigerator.

Another letter from France was in her mailbox, postmarked Paris. She knew at once that something was wrong.

"My dear Sara...." She read quickly as she kicked off her shoes and headed for her bedroom.

Don't be shocked, but I have quit Le Moulin de Mougins—thrown myself into the arms of Fate. Who knows where I shall land! I'm looking for a very great opportunity here, but I despair. It is California where my future awaits me, I think now. Therefore, my best of friends, I am thinking of joining you there. Can you find me a place in one of your good restaurants?

All my love, Jean-Claude

P.S. I won't take up much room.

Sara didn't know if she should spank him or rejoice. Why couldn't he have waited a few more days to quit? Her letter would have arrived by then. "You crazy Frenchman," she said, grinning at his scrawl. She would attempt another letter to him later tonight, after Aunt Liz's party. He couldn't just arrive without a great deal of thought about a new job here.

It would be good to be with a crowd tonight, even Aunt Elizabeth's crowd. These events could be a trial, involving mandatory tête-a-têtes with high-strung artistic friends of her parents who had known her when she was a baby. She usually found herself cornered by an elderly Romanian gentleman who loved telling long anecdotes about his brilliant musical career.

Still, when Elizabeth de Lacy sat down to play the harpsichord nothing else mattered. She was an artist without peer, her fingers strong and vital, sparking with energy. She made her instrument a heavenly, soaring vehicle for her genius. Then, beauty filled the salon, wiping away whatever earth-bound concerns her guests might have brought with them.

Sara just had time to shower and throw on her favorite lavender-print silk dress. The garment was low cut with its own long scarf of brilliantly colored butterfly wings that could be tied over the shoulder or bodice for any degree of modesty. She had a pair of mother-of-pearl butterfly clips to hold her heavy waves of hair just off her forehead. The musicale wasn't an event that inspired her to do an elaborate hairstyle.

She saw the dark silhouette of the ancient Rolls-Royce parked just below her window. She made a pass at her face with a light pink blusher, jammed her feet into her bone-colored sandals, and left the apartment, struggling to put on her coat as she went. The chauffeur was courteous and silent, a man who had the look of long patience on his face. Sara sat back in the deep leather seat and tried to clear her mind.

Soon they passed through the high gates of Bel Air and wound along its dark hilly roads. The air was crisp and clear, the city below her ablaze with pinpoints of light flickering brightly against the black night. There was a pungent scent of sage and mountain lilac. She could almost pull free of the heavy, gnawing knot of regret that sat at the center of her breast and made it hard for her to draw a breath without thinking of Paul. Her afternoon on the isolated beach had only been a temporary healing.

She was starting to believe that something in her genetic programming drew her magnetically to men who were wrong for her. *Shut up, Sara,* she thought and pressed her fingers hard against her temples to relieve the tension in her head.

Elizabeth de Lacy's house was a Mediterranean-style California mansion from the 1920s, with thick stucco walls, hand-made red tiles on the roof and a welcoming open courtyard. Elaborate black wrought iron gates guarded the heavy, beveled-glass front door.

The car drew slowly into the cobbled courtyard. Gregory, the butler who had been with the household forever, opened the door to her. In his Jeeves voice that always made Sara smile he said, "Madame wishes to see you right away."

Then he led her to Aunt Elizabeth's baronial bedroom, which overlooked acres of rolling lawns and tiled Spanish reflecting pools.

"Thank goodness you're here!" a theatrical voice said as the door was being opened. "We have had a terrible accident!"

Sara saw immediately what Aunt Liz was referring to. There, dressed in yards of emerald green chiffon, was her godmother, sitting uncomfortably in a wheelchair with one leg extended and a bandage around her foot and ankle. "Aunt Liz, what happened?" Sara reached to take the pale hand that was held out.

"I was taking the air this afternoon, watching the glorious sunset, when I fell." Gregory stood behind her chair, nodding somberly. "The doctor has only just left and the gardener has trapped the gopher. He will be dealt with."

"Gopher?"

"Yes, gopher!" the old woman echoed. "That's how I fell. The busy little beast had dug a hole exactly where I take my walks and I twisted my ankle rather badly. I don't blame him for it, but you see the trouble he caused us all."

"It can't be comfortable for you like that," Sara sympathized. "Why don't you cancel the musicale?"

"It's much too late to call it off. You'll just have to fill in for me. Do be a dear and take over, will you? I'll make an appearance when the painkiller has taken hold."

Sara leaned to kiss the white cheek. Aunt Elizabeth's silver hair was perfect as always, gracefully draped back from her fine-boned face and caught in a soft twist at the neck. But her blue eyes looked tired. It was the first time Sara had seen them without their sparkle. "I could never be the hostess that you are, but I'll do my best."

The older woman smiled. "Of course the kitchen staff will take care of the buffet and Gregory knows the guests. He can give you their names as they enter. The piano accompanist arrived an hour ago to prepare. I'm having the winners of the regional opera competition sing for us tonight. It should be delightful. They're all so fresh and young." She sighed and winced in pain. "Damn it—I've trudged up and down high mountains in my day, and it has to be a common garden gopher that brings me to my knees! What irony!"

Sara stepped out onto the mezzanine corridor that surrounded the open foyer, and looked down at the heavy-glass front door. The first guests were arriving and Gregory hurried discreetly down the curving staircase ahead of her.

The fragrance of Aunt Elizabeth's favorite red roses filled the grand entrance hall. Her rose garden was extensive, providing the house with a constant supply of the beautiful flowers. She even had a hothouse for her most valuable specimens. Sara's mother had hinted long ago that a young European nobleman and amateur botanist had once fallen passionately in love with Aunt Elizabeth, and that was why a claret-red rose was named Heavenly Elizabeth.

She walked slowly down the stairs. Gregory was taking the coats of a newly arrived cluster of guests, greeting them formally. Sara knew some of them.

The pianist was at the hundred-year-old Steinway in the music room playing light classical pieces as a background to the growing chatter of the guests. Sara wouldn't have to do anything herself to make the party come to life. There was a unique liveliness to the house that made people feel they were having a wonderful time.

Elizabeth de Lacy didn't care much for electricity, preferring to light her home with an extravagant number of beeswax candles. There was a soft golden glow to every room but the kitchen, which for practical reasons couldn't afford to be dimly lit. As a result, Elizabeth by candlelight had the look of eternal youth, as did all the other ladies of a "certain age" who came here.

Sara stood at her post by the great glass door, feeling almost happy. The familiar music took her back to her childhood; the guests seemed more European than American. She didn't realize that she had been staring past the foyer with a slight wistful smile on her lips until Gregory said softly into her ear, "That's Rupert von Schlegel, miss. He's the impresario who has brought the young singers."

She quickly recovered herself and extended her hand to the dour old gentleman just arriving with a group of latecomers.

"May I introduce my guests," he said without a flicker of warmth. "My associates from Vienna, Dieter Rau, fräulein Erika Ansel, her escort Paul Cabot Edgerton, and the performers for the evening's program...."

Sara froze, rooted to the spot. Her eyes searched the blur of faces for the one face that would match the name she was afraid she had heard. Paul's eyes found hers first. He was removing his fawn leather gloves, ready to take his turn to be received. The look on his face was difficult to fathom—was it amusement or disdain? She couldn't tell in the brief, awful instant of recognition.

"Fräulein..." Sara repeated woodenly, taking the graceful hand of the young Viennese woman.

"How delightful," was the reply in lightly accented English.

Paul hung back until the three singers had been introduced.

"Elizabeth de Lacy, I presume?" he said under

his breath as he held Sara's hand for a moment longer than a normal handshake.

"My godmother has had a little accident. She'll be with us later." She searched for more to say, but couldn't.

"Your godmother? This *is* a coincidence...."

"Yes," she said in a flagging voice, wishing with all her might that she could vanish into the floor.

He took the elbow of the Viennese woman and proceeded inside without a backward look.

Her knees turned to water. With one look—with one touch—Paul had managed to throw her composure into a cocked hat. Her first thought was that Aunt Elizabeth had set up the whole thing. She hadn't really fallen into a gopher hole at all, but had purposely invited Paul Edgerton to pursue a matchmaking plan of her own. Sara knew she was being dangerously paranoid. Everyone in the world was *not* trying to get her together with Paul Edgerton! There really had been a strange series of coincidences.

Still, Sara could picture her godmother sitting upstairs with a Mona Lisa smile. She must have known that Paul was invited. She made up the guest lists. If she had been trying to be helpful, it was a terrible error.

Now what was Sara supposed to do? She couldn't help noticing that Paul's date was classically beautiful, tanned and muscular—probably from lots of skiing at Chamonix or Vail. This was the night that Paul had tried to reserve with Sara on her answering machine message. At least she had the pleasure of believing that the fräulein was his second choice.

Sara kept well away from Paul and his group, busying herself with trips in and out of the kitchen and butler's pantry to check on the hors d'oeuvres, the drinks, and the buffet preparations. She stood far back in the salon when the program introductions were made by Rupert von Schlegel. Then, when the two sopranos and the tenor began their arias she breathed a long sigh of relief. There was no more for her to do except wait until Aunt Elizabeth decided to make her entrance. Then she would go home.

The music room was high ceilinged with delicate painted plaster work depicting frolicking maidens and shepherds. Near the Steinway stood Aunt Elizabeth's greatest treasure—a German harpsichord once played by Bach himself. Its fine lacquered rosewood was embellished with gold baroque motifs. Sara listened to the tenor sing the soaring notes of "Celeste Aïda" and let her eyes drift upward to the ceiling.

"Ah, for the simple life." Paul's voice breathed very close to her. She felt the small hairs rise at the back of her neck. He stood a little behind her, leaning casually against the wall with a crystal wineglass in one hand. The flicker of candlelight from the wall sconce reflected in his golden eyes as she turned her face to him. She put her finger to her lips and hoped he wouldn't say more.

"You are a mysterious lady, Sara Courtney."

"He's going to be a great tenor one day," she said against the direction of his words.

"I earnestly pray he will. But we really do have some unfinished business, you know. Would you care to slip out to the terrace for a while. I shan't bite."

Rather than continue the nonsensical conversation where it might bother the guests, Sara allowed him to take her hand and lead her from the room, along the glass-walled morning room and out to the terrace garden. With every step she felt she was going closer to a destiny she was powerless to change....

CHAPTER EIGHT

THE TERRACE WAS DESERTED. A faint scent of roses was carried on the night breezes and Verdi's rapturous song of love created a romantic mood of expectation. Sara steeled herself against it.

"If you're cold I can get your coat," Paul offered. He led her down the wide flagstone steps and into the garden.

She wanted to stop. She was already too far from the protection of the house with its safe glow of lights. "I shouldn't leave my guests for long," she said, wishing for an easy escape.

"They seem well-occupied without you," he replied dryly, and continued to lead her away from the house. The music was like a distant dream now, and they were enveloped by the night shadows made by the vine-covered arched trellis that marked the garden path. Paul still hadn't released her hand. He turned her to him so that they stood facing each other in silence. Then he raised her hand and gently kissed the tips of her cold fingers. His lips were soft and warm. His touch carried a charge of male potency affecting her fragile nervous balance.

"Didn't your godmother teach you that it's impolite to ignore a gentleman's invitation—two invitations, at that?" he scolded with controlled intensity.

Sara could see the glinting force of his eyes, even in shadow. "It was rude of me not to respond," she admitted, slipping her hand from his. She couldn't tell him why she hadn't called him back. It was childish of her to think she could solve her problem by ignoring him.

"As I said—" he took her hand a second time, turning it upward and brushing the palm with a provocative back-and-forth touch of his lips. "—Edgertons are persistent." He returned her hand with a little bow. "But we're not self-punishing, Miss Courtney. I won't ask again unless you wish it."

Her throat was tight. She looked back at the glowing lights of the music room, unable to speak past the constraining lump of emotion. He knew just what to say to make her feel wretched.

He smiled suddenly down at her. "You do wish it, don't you, Sara?"

"I..." she managed to say, feeling foolish.

"Still cautious? Are you afraid there may be something...powerful between us?"

"No—not really." She was recovering, forcing her thoughts back to logic. "As I told you, I have obligations. This isn't a good time for me to... to...."

"Start an affair? Is there ever a perfect time?"

She didn't answer his question. "I'm really sorry to have been rude. And I'm sorry I put you to the trouble of finding another date for tonight," she couldn't help adding.

"Erika? It was only a matter of a telephone call. Usually I have no trouble."

She could sense him smiling at her. "I'm sure you don't. You have a reputation to protect." She turned to walk back to the house and felt his hand on her shoulder stopping her.

"What an intriguing woman you are," he whispered, now very close to her face. "Would you mind very much sacrificing a single kiss to my curiosity? I have to know if you are real."

She stood perfectly still, not allowing the pressure of his hand to bring her back toward him. "I don't give kisses as sacrifices," she said evenly. He was behind her. She could hear his breathing and it thrilled her, even as she knew she must leave this place at once.

"Fair enough. Then you won't mind if I put my jacket around your shoulders to stop your shivering. It *is* the cold, isn't it?" Without waiting for a response he removed his coat and draped it over her, leaning close and brushing her ear and cheek with his lips.

"Don't, Paul," she said in a small voice. "I want to get back to the house."

"Do you usually affect men this way? You know, you're causing me to lose a lot of valuable sleep lately. Everyone calls me but you. There's a female right now who writes me passionate love letters. And here I am, making an ass of myself one more time with Sara Courtney. Why do you think that is?" He turned her around to face him and she didn't resist.

"Maybe you need to learn humility," she was rash enough to reply. She wanted to say something to break the rising physical attraction that was building between them in spite of their banter.

"You don't think this is a humbling experience, begging a woman who has scorned me? I've never begged a woman in my life, let alone stood in the freezing night wishing with all my heart that I was making love to her."

"You've never held back from something you wanted?"

"Never."

"Then why *are* you standing here in the cold, Mr. Edgerton?"

He laughed suddenly. "Trying to stop being afraid of you, madam. You make me feel like an adolescent—awkward and...." He smiled down at her defensive expression. "Damn you..." he groaned softly and bent his head so that his lips grazed hers, then touched them again and again until her lips parted slightly against his alarmingly gentle assault. His arms came around her and she was surprised to feel a strong trembling in his body. Her head was swimming with the delicious feeling of his warm lips on hers, the arousing, sensuous explorations of his tongue, and her own hungry acceptance. A thrill of primal urgency crept along her spine, and she could only stand there, virtually helpless, because Paul's coat was encircling her shoulders and his arms held her in a fierce embrace. The scent of him, the taste of him in the long, delicious eternity of their kiss, swept away every skeptical shred of resistance in her. She was with him in a capsule of amazing tenderness and desire. Her body was trapped against the length of him and she felt the stirring of his passion. Everything in her said *Yes*! The last thing she wanted to do was to think. This was too sweet, too much like being home at last...!

He pulled his head away a little to look at her in the dappled shadows. Her face was fiery hot and she could feel his rapid breath against it. "Humility isn't a word that appeals to me very much," he said roughly, kissing her forehead and playfully catching at the wisps of auburn hair that were whipping at her face in the light breeze.

He took her once more deeply into his embrace and they kissed as if they knew everything that would please the other, as if they had kissed for a century, a thousand years—they simply belonged in each other's arms.

A clear tenor voice was singing one of the beautiful arias from the opera *La Bohème*. Holding one of her chilled hands between his warm ones, Paul echoed the tenor's words of love. "*Che gelida manina*—what a cold little hand." From the shadows his eyes were gleaming. "It was worth the risk that you would slap my face."

Sara caught her breath. "This wasn't supposed to happen. I didn't want it to."

"I know. But do you want it to stop now?" His eyes were challenging her, as they always did.

He held her easily in his arms, her head resting against the fine cotton fabric of his shirt. His heart was beating loudly in her ear. "There are reasons why it has to," she said very seriously.

"That's terribly dramatic, my lady," he said as he nuzzled a kiss into her wisping hair. "Are you married? Pledged to another?" She shook her head slightly.

"I have it!" he teased. "You've taken your vows and are about to enter a nunnery...and I'm a cur for distracting you...."

At that she had to smile. "No—none of those."

"But it *is* a matter of conscience—something dark and brooding that you aren't able to speak of. Something out of *Wuthering Heights?*"

"It isn't very simple, Paul," she said, trying to stop the shaking in her body.

"A compromise then: would your conscience allow you to accept an occasional dinner date with an admirer? Nothing more than that—no attempt on your virtue, no pressure—just a kiss now and then to keep him from perishing?"

She felt the intensity behind his casual words. If she said no, that would be the end of things, and she would regret it the rest of her life. "I think I can make peace with myself," she capitulated.

"I knew you were a reasonable woman beneath your facade of mystery and reserve."

"I mean it, Paul," she said, trying to disregard the tremors inside her. "I'm not going to get involved." The words sounded ridiculous after what had just happened between them.

"How can we get involved if we're just friends out for a dinner now and then?" he asked, sounding innocent. "Now, let's go back inside before we both freeze to death. I don't want you to change your mind again." He put a guiding hand at the small of her back and let her walk ahead of him into the house.

As he removed his coat from her shoulders he leaned close, not to kiss her, but to whisper, "If I can arrange something to make Erika happy, will you let me drive you home? I see you don't have your car."

She flashed a curious look at him. "How did you know that?"

"Gregory. Edgertons may lack humility, but they make up for it in stealth."

"I'm not sure I like being checked up on," she said warily.

"But I intend to know all there is about you. I'm a journalist by trade, remember?" He opened the door from the terrace, standing back to let her enter. "Until later, then...." His fingers brushed lightly across her lips. Then he disappeared into the crowded room.

Sara needed time to collect her thoughts before resuming her duties as hostess. The warmth of the room wasn't enough to stop the sporadic little shivers. Paul had disappeared from sight, but her senses were filled with him. His fine cologne still clung to her, the sensation of his powerful arms around her left a lingering memory of need and comfort—and a hunger had been awakened that she thought she would never feel again.

Not since Jacques, she thought ruefully. But it wouldn't be like that this time. Jacques was totally selfish, a man who used women, a man without heart. And Paul was...what? The man at The Right Table, the snob? But much more. She wouldn't be standing here feeling shaken to the very bottom of her toes unless there was a lot more to Paul Edgerton than that. She wouldn't have put herself into this vulnerable position. Long ago she swore that there would be no affairs. If something developed with Paul it would have to be commitment, a word she doubted he knew.

Gregory stepped from the butler's pantry to tell her that her godmother wished to see her. Glad of an excuse to dismiss thoughts of Paul, she took the service stairs up to the second floor. Aunt Elizabeth was preparing to make her entrance, adjusting a crutch under one arm.

"I'm going to need a little support to get down the steps, but I think I can manage. Is everything going well?" Her voice was dramatically cheerful.

"It's a successful evening, Aunt Liz. The tenor was wonderful and the two sopranos are just now singing."

"And the guests—did Gregory do his part?"

Sara nodded and helped Aunt Elizabeth arrange her Chinese-silk embroidered stole so that it partly concealed the plain wood of the crutch. The two women made slow progress down the curving staircase, with Gregory looking on like a worried mother hen.

Aunt Elizabeth stopped to catch her breath at

the first landing. "Did Paul Edgerton come?" she asked. "You haven't mentioned him."

"I wish you'd warned me."

"Why? So you could make a getaway? Don't be annoyed, my dear, but I had an intuition that you should see him just once in some other context, not in some wretched restaurant where he is being the great gourmet. Was I right?" She cast a wise eye at Sara.

"I'm not sure. It might have been better to leave well enough alone."

"Ah, youth! Such a complicated time of life." She was ready to take the last of the steps into the foyer.

"Please, Aunt Liz, no more little surprises."

Her godmother threw her head back in horror. "On my oath. That's the last of my involvement in the affair," she smiled. "Do be careful, but give the boy a chance. Now, stand aside—I'm going to hobble to my musicale and finish the evening properly."

Sara felt Paul's eyes on her and met his gaze with a slight smile of acknowledgment. A dinner date once in a while—that was a safe arrangement. An intelligent one. When she had begun her involvement with Jacques they had seen each other constantly, from morning till midnight, and beyond. It was a roller-coaster of emotion, each day going faster than the last. Their relationship had been obsessive and headlong from the start.

With Paul she had the power to control the rate of fall. It was an odd way to describe what she was about to do, but it fit.

Sara felt a shaky hand take her elbow, and turned to meet the beaming white face of Anton Saolescu. He wanted to talk to her, had looked for her all evening, he said. She smiled and looked interested, happy to give the bent old gentleman another chance to relive his past. It must have been hard for him to outlive most of the people who had known him as a celebrated musician.

"Is your divine godmother going to play for us tonight?" he asked in a wavering voice. He always referred to Aunt Elizabeth in extravagant terms.

"She can't use the pedals until her ankle is better." Sara was aware that Paul was walking toward them, overcoat and car keys in hand. His imposing appearance effectively stopped the conversation.

"I'm afraid I must take this charming lady away from you," he said. "I have permission to drive her home." He respectfully nodded to the elderly man.

"You know who her parents are?" Saolescu wheezed. "Great musicians...great...." He turned his faded eyes elsewhere and shuffled off.

"I hope I wasn't intruding," Paul said.

"Poor old dear."

"As of a moment ago I'm a free man. Erika will be well cared for by Herr Rau and I have been given permission by the hostess to escort you home. Am I being properly humble?" He was on his best behavior and completely charming.

"Temporarily." She smiled at him and was glad that Aunt Elizabeth had invited him tonight.

They left the party while the second soprano

and the tenor were in the throes of a tragic farewell scene, sending their powerful voices out into the night air. A stray neighborhood dog paused in his evening rounds to throw back his head and howl along with the final long note of the aria.

"Another music lover," Paul laughed.

They drove slowly down the winding Bel Air roads. Paul's hand reached to cover one of hers. "Do you feel up for an Irish coffee at a little place I know?"

Her fingers curved comfortably around his. She shouldn't. "I don't think so, Paul," she replied. "I was up at three-thirty this morning and I'm out of steam."

"What were you doing at that hour? A paper route to ease the poverty of the genteel writer?" His Boston accent made him sound the perfect snob.

"I was out doing some background research." She thought fast. "Eric said he might buy some free-lance pieces for his paper if he likes my style." *Almost true,* she excused herself.

"Forgive me, Sara, but you'd do better writing for the *Tribune* instead. How Eric allows that lurid prose in his food section, I can't imagine. Nothing less than yellow journalism."

Sara flushed. "You mean that woman...?"

"What do you know about this Olive Gadwall business? Eric must have said something to you." He disengaged his hand from hers and gripped the steering wheel. His jaw was set.

"Paul isn't telling anyone," she said truthfully.

"Well, it's damn bad form. I'd appreciate it if you could get old Eric to talk about it."

"I can't promise," she evaded. "He seems to think he's doing something good for the general public."

"I don't accept that. I've spent almost five years trying to lead the public gently by the hand into the land of good taste, and I'll not stop now just because a bourgeois leveler like this Gadwall person thinks all men should eat with their fists and guzzle bad wine!" He stomped his foot on the accelerator and zoomed the Mercedes out into the traffic on Sunset Boulevard.

"Paul, watch out—" Sara said nervously.

He let the car coast to a safe speed and released the death grip on the wheel. "I haven't been myself lately. I didn't mean to upset you." He glanced over at her with an apologetic set to his elegant face. "I had no right to let myself go like that. Have dinner with me Monday night, will you? I'll behave myself. I really need to be with someone like you who has her feet on the ground...and doesn't take me too seriously." He lifted her hand to his lips for emphasis.

At the door Paul kissed her gently, expertly, and with tenderness. Sara could feel him holding himself in check.

"I won't use up all my tokens in one night," he said softly, extending a formal hand to her as a sign of good faith. "Until Monday, then. And thank you, Sara, for saying yes at last. My ego couldn't have borne it if you had refused me again."

She eased herself inside the doorway and was grateful to be alone in her sanctuary. Even at this pace things were starting to go too fast. Her heart was beating unsteadily and her emotions were frayed from the effort of being reserved with him.

Now she understood why fraternizing with the enemy was a crime punishable by death during a war. If you got close enough to discover that the enemy was warm and human, how could you point a gun at him?

She had all day Sunday to debate the wisdom of fraternizing. The Sunday Food and Entertainment section of the Chronicle glared out at her with its bold new format. Olive Gadwall in full battle cry. She could imagine Paul's reaction. She had torn him apart in print, attacked his sacred citadel and made him look like a fool for criticizing the Indian restaurant.

The telephone rang several times that morning and once again in the evening, but Sara's instincts told her not to answer. She even disconnected the message machine for the day. If it was Eric, she would see him in the morning. If it was Paul, she didn't have the heart to hear what he would say.

It was Sunday evening before she remembered that she had meant to write to Jean-Claude. In his present mood he might do anything on impulse. She had to persuade him to be prudent for once in his life. She wrote:

> Please, don't plan to come to Los Angeles right away. It will take time. I can't openly

talk to chefs about you, but I can use my contacts to see what the chances are for you. Just sit where you are until I can uncomplicate my own life first—please! I *don't* have a large apartment, and I'm in a very peculiar position professionally....

CHAPTER NINE

MONDAY MORNING SARA LEFT her car in the underground garage of the Chronicle Building and took the elevator to the newsroom. There was the usual Monday buzz of activity in the air, general meetings in the many cubicle offices, the setting of weekly assignments by the editors.

She was preoccupied with her thoughts as she threaded her way through the rows of desks and display terminals. In the far corner the staff of the food and entertainment section was holding its usual animated, loosely organized meeting. Eric was in the midst of it, laughing. His face looked just like the Cheshire cat as he saw Sara and motioned her to hurry over.

"A star is born!" he said to the group as they reached out to give her pats of approval. "But now we have to work like hell to keep Olive Gadwall's identity a secret. Nobody—that's *nobody*—outside our core group must know. You've never seen Olive Gadwall and you're just as curious as the next guy. That's *all* you say! If this makes our sales go up you'll see the results in your own pocket books. There'll be spies and prying. Woe to any loose lips!"

Eric dismissed the troops and sent them back to their desks. He made a convincing general.

"Come into my office, Sara. I'll tell you the rest."

She sat down in front of the desk on one of his two straight chairs. "This isn't going to work, Eric," she began.

"Of course it will," he said brightly. "I've got the payroll office to change their books so that your name doesn't show up as one of the employees. He can't possibly trace you. We've done it...it's war from now on. I haven't had so much fun in years!" He stopped at the expression on her face. "What's wrong?"

She shook her head. "I don't want to declare war on anyone."

"You've been out with him again, haven't you?" His shrewd eyes were on her.

"Unintentionally." She delivered an edited version of the evening at Aunt Elizabeth's. "My godmother is a friend of his—she even knows his family in Boston. He...wants me to have dinner with him tonight." She waved her hand in a gesture of helplessness. "I'm even having a hard time being irritated with him."

Eric blew out a silent *Phew*! "Do you realize that old J.B. Quarles, the Great One, upstairs in the executive office, is actually chuckling over the whole thing, pleased as punch. That's just what he said—'pleased as punch.'" Eric raked a hand through his sandy hair. "Everybody here is excited. We've got something to rivet public attention. It doesn't happen too often for a section like ours. We're prepared to stand behind you, Sara."

He searched her face for a positive reaction. "For God's sake, don't look like it's the end of the world. Nobody knows who Olive is—that's the fun. And when things settle down you can get off the hook. Edgerton will never know, I swear! You can fall in love with the man for all I care...."

"Don't be ridiculous. I'm not going to quit. But I do feel like a fraud, and nothing will change that."

"I don't know what to say, Sara, except that old J.B. wants to give you a salary that will reflect your value to the paper. He's calling this Edgerton affair the Great Broccoli War."

She grimaced. "Circulation should be jumping."

The phone jangled, interrupting the conversation, and Eric answered. "What!" he yelled back, and slammed the receiver down. "You've got to get out of here, Sara—now! The Boston Tea Party is on his way up in person, breathing fire."

He scrabbled some sheets of her rough copy together. "Take your stuff and work in the women's lounge. I'll send for you as soon as he's gone."

A rush of adrenaline brought her to her feet. She grabbed her papers and rushed for the door.

"Not the elevator...take the stairs," Eric barked after her.

Sara let Eric's excitement drain away from her as she tramped up the seldom-used concrete stairs. Maybe now was the time to confront Paul. She had a satisfying picture of Paul and Eric listening to her tell them both off, as if they were children. But it wouldn't work, she thought dismally. She was as much to blame as they were. She had agreed to the idea—she had gone out with Paul just to satisfy her damnable feminine curiosity. She had made a real person out of the man at The Right Table, and she had to take the consequences.

The lounge was deserted and she sank into the old over-stuffed couch. She grew tired of watching the big clock on the wall and went to freshen her makeup.

Returning to the couch, she tried to read a dog-eared magazine from a collection of forlorn back issues on a side table. She thought about going home. The door opened and the assistant food photographer, Fern, peered inside.

"Eric sent me up. It's safe now." She laughed. "That was one angry man! But he's a real dish—if you like them big and kind of British looking." Fern waved her hands as she talked. "Eric handled him like a lion trainer. We could hear the roars from outside the office. Edgerton was demanding to meet Olive Gadwall face to face, then he accused Eric of being Olive, and Eric had a laughing fit. Then things got quiet and we couldn't hear, until Mr. Edgerton stormed out, sputtering."

"Spare me the sordid details. I'll hear them soon enough." Sara gathered her things.

In the elevator Fern asked if Sara had ever seen her rival. "He's a friend of my godmother."

"I guess that makes it harder to keep it a secret. But don't worry about any of us talking. You'll be safe." She gave Sara a friendly pat. She was an eager new staff member, young and cheerful. Sara appreciated Fern's good intentions.

Eric was leaning back in his swivel chair with an ear-to-ear grin on his face. "Come in, Miss Gadwall," he said. "Did you know that you are a mummified anachronism? You are a plodding, bleeding heart old maid who is willing to exchange bad food and poor service for compliments and sob stories from know-nothing maître d's. You have bastardized the standards of good taste." He lowered his voice in an imitation of Paul's: "In short, madam, you are the worst thing that has happened to food since the hot dog!"

Sara sat down heavily and drew a breath to answer, but Eric gestured for silence. "He had some words for me, too, dear Olive. I am a dunderheaded nincompoop for printing you and he questioned my competence as an editor. Food is a serious business, he warned, and not a subject to be made into a ratings circus."

Eric was enjoying himself, but Sara couldn't share his feelings. Paul had a right to be angry.

"He mentioned innate good manners and I was agreeable," Eric continued. "I suggested that he could stop his loud replies to you any time he wished."

"What did he say to that?"

"Well, he called me a cretin and swore to unmask the dreadful witch. He has an awful temper, but I do admire his way with the English language, and said so."

"It just gets worse, doesn't it?" she said wearily.

"I really think this little war of ours will be good for him, in a strange way. He's been the darling of the social set too long. A man just doesn't have opinions like that without having some pretty bad insecurities...a sense of being cut off from the rest of the world."

"Oh, I see—we're doing this out of compassion."

"I didn't mean to sound patronizing. I actually like the guy. Sure, he's way out of line, but I get the feeling he's been stagnating on the food circuit, wanting to do hard-hitting reporting. There's frustration written all over him."

"He used to be a foreign correspondent—Europe and the Middle East. Really, Eric, I wish I didn't know a thing about him. I hit a very deep nerve with him, and I'm sorry I did."

"Wait a minute, girl." Eric brought his chair to an upright position. "I didn't mean to let him off the hook entirely. Are you going to sit there and let him call you a dessicated old maid? He will, you know. Where's your dignity?"

"That's a good question. Where's everybody's dignity?"

Eric leaned over to take her hand. "Go home, Sara. Take a hot bath and relax. Nobody's going to find Olive, remember that."

IT WAS EASIER said than done. Sara couldn't settle down at home. As much as she wanted to be the sophisticated, clever woman who let everything roll slickly off her back, she failed.

She dredged up her scattered notes on the Scotsman and forced herself to write something worthy of Olive Gadwall's new reputation. She was already getting behind in her well-publicized column. She looked at her notes about Mon Château and set them down again. She felt deceitful. Her heart wasn't in it. The fact that thousands of new subscribers would be panting to see the latest gourmet challenge this week only added to her misery.

An appealing vision of quiche Lorraine bubbled into her mind's eye, luring her from her desk to the kitchen, where she sublimated her frustrations by preparing a delectable feast. It felt therapeutic to have her hands in pastry flour. The balancing of herb flavors was a familiar pacifying ritual that took her back to thoughts of happier times.

While she waited for the good smells to start wafting in from the kitchen she called Aunt Elizabeth to ask about her ankle. In turn, Sara was subjected to a subtle catechism about her drive home with Paul.

She countered by describing his visit to Eric's office that morning. "Oh dear," Aunt Elizabeth said with a chuckle. "Your Mr. Hartley sounds like a reasonable man. He was wise not to get into a rage in kind."

"I wish you hadn't..." Sara started.

"Hadn't invited Paul to my musicale? Why in heaven's name not? You were obviously dying to see him again."

"Was it that obvious?"

"Like the nose on your pretty face. So...what are you going to do about this fascinating, naughty man of yours?"

Sara could feel her godmother's canny smile on the other end of the line. "I've thought about leaving the country. I don't know who Paul Edgerton is—Dr. Jekyll or Mr. Hyde."

A clucking sound of sympathy sounded on the line. "You must understand Paul's boyhood, Sara. The utter repression of his own liberty and dignity by Edward, and unfortunately, by his own mother, also. It was enough to put him in a temper for life. Your editor has put his finger on the problem: Paul can do far more than be a food critic."

Aunt Elizabeth turned her conversation to other things—the singers at her musicale, the impossibility of using a crutch for a week when she had so many things to do. And then, in her usual oblique way, she remarked, "Paul was so handsome the other night, wasn't he? He's one of those big men who can carry off evening dress like a prince."

Sara snorted. "He also told me that all he had to do was lift the telephone and women come running."

"How unsophisticated of him," she sniffed. "Something must have injured his ego...something you said, other than an unfavorable mention in Olive Gadwall's column."

"I may have fed the fires a bit," she admitted. "I didn't return his calls last week. He tried to invite me to dinner and then again to your party."

The old woman's laugh boomed into Sara's ear. "Sara, Sara! If you want to attract him you're going about it the right way. Refusal is good for his soul, the poor thing."

"But you said he was refused by the girl he loved in college because of his family's interference. That didn't damage his ego noticeably."

"Are you blind, child? That's why he made such a point of his masculine appeal to you. Of course you must believe him to be irresistible. He's never quite sure about women—can't trust them, you see. That's why he's become a smooth and devastating lover. *Control,* my dear. He has to be sure that his women are submissive. He *is* a good lover, they say."

"I'm not sure I follow your complex reasoning, Aunt Liz, but Paul Edgerton has many sides and lots of problems, and I haven't the expertise to unravel them all...."

"Then why are you going out with him again?"

"I didn't say I was—"

"But of course you are."

"If you weren't my beloved godmother I'd hang up on you!" Sara felt as if the older eyes could look right through at her.

"When...?" the relentless voice prodded.

"Tonight—you sorceress."

"It makes me wish I could drop some years. Paul is the kind of man to stir up all the female hormones. Have fun, darling." She hung up.

Sara knew she must appear ridiculous to that

woman of the world. But what did Aunt Liz really know about the conflicts that swirled around her situation with Paul? *Probably everything,* she thought, feeling like an indecisive ninny.

She took the small quiche from the oven, steaming and fragrant, and picked half-heartedly at the light, flaky crust. Her mind was on the night to come and all the possibilities it brought with it. She let her thoughts recall Paul's kisses in the garden. The reaction of her body was immediate, expectant, wishing there had been more to remember—imagining what might have happened if she hadn't been so defensive. Why had Aunt Liz bothered to tell her that he was such a good lover? It was a rotten thing to tell a girl who was still unsure of which way she wanted to jump.

Paul hadn't said where he was planning to take her, but it would most likely be to one of the finer restaurants. It was impossible to imagine him taking her to a middle-of-the-road eatery. She carried her plate into the bedroom and assessed the lineup of dresses in her little walk-in closet. Everything looked so old.

If she hurried she had time to do some quick shopping. She jumped into her car and drove to a small boutique on the edge of Beverly Hills where she knew she could find just the right kind of understatedly chic outfit she needed.

Two hours of browsing and pondering later, she was back home hanging up her purchase—a slim cocktail sheath in creamy wool jersey with a draped little jacket of the same supple material.

The simplicity was part of its charm. Even jewelry wouldn't work with it.

She dressed with care. Her hair cooperated with her efforts to sweep the shiny russet waves into a large side clip, making a loosely twisted knot behind one ear. The effect was more French than American. The new dress slid sensuously over her figure. It mattered very much that she look collected and smashing.

Searching in her dressing table she found a box containing a real rosebud that had been treated with lacquer and mounted on a gold stickpin. She held the small red-orange flower against the bodice of her dress and saw that it was the right choice. The rose, secure in the folds of the gracefully draped neckline, glowed with a warmth no shiny stone would possess. The outfit was completed with buff-toned suede evening slippers and a small matching clutch bag.

She set just enough of a blaze to seem cheery in the small fireplace. Aunt Elizabeth's chauffeur had delivered a bundle of oak firewood earlier in the month.

The buzzer sounded exactly on time. Sara took a deep breath before opening the door. Paul stood there, straight and tall and exactly as her senses remembered him from Aunt Elizabeth's garden. Her heart slipped into an uneven rhythm. The spark of light in his deepset lion's eyes, the sensitive twist of his lips demanded her full attention. Paul's tall figure was made all the more impressive by the fine tailoring of his charcoal-gray suit. Elegant was the only word for him.

There was a large bouquet of long-stemmed red roses in his arms. "Lovely women should be surrounded by flowers," he said warmly, his handsome face drawing into a smile.

"They're wonderful," she said as she received them. "But this isn't done much any more." They were expensive and how nice it was to feel the cool satin of maidenhair fern and smell the tender fragrance of the velvety rosebuds.

"I cast no aspersions on liberated women, but I'm old-fashioned. I like to follow the manners of a pleasanter time." He rolled an appreciative eye over Sara and made a courtly bow that said more than any verbal compliment.

"Then, by the rules of good manners I shouldn't let you stand there in the hallway while I put the flowers into water and get my jacket." She hoped she sounded as jauntily confident as he did.

Paul seated himself on the couch that faced her fireplace, while she found a tall vase and brought the roses to the coffee table. He was looking around the room with interest.

"You've made a very pleasant nest here." He smiled at her again. "It's a place where one wishes to stay. A peaceful quality, a sense of order and beauty."

His glance lighted on the picture that hung over the mantel. It was one of Sara's best loved possessions, a copy of a painting by the nineteenth century Dutch-English artist, Alma-Tadema. It showed a clear azure sea and a balustrade over which roses bloomed in profusion. A young woman looked out toward a delicate sunrise, her head turned so that only a glimpse of her features could be seen. Her dress was of the ancient Greek style, and on her feet were jeweled sandals. Golden-red hair, the color of Sara's own, was tinted with the pearly lights from the dawn sky. Her graceful figure leaned against a marble pedestal that held a carved head, veiled and enigmatic—like a sybil's. The girl seemed to be waiting. Why was she waiting and why did the marble head smile behind its filmy drapes? Sara had always dreamed about the scene. Even now the painting could draw her into a magic world.

"A lovely thing," Paul said. "You could have posed for it, I think, except that Alma-Tadema left this earth around the turn of the century."

Sara looked at him, wondering how he could have so nearly picked up the truth—because that was why her father had bought the painting. "My father said the same thing. It was a birthday gift when I came of age."

"A man after my own heart. I would like to meet your father."

Sara changed the subject. "Would you like a drink before we go? I don't know if I have anything you would like...."

Paul stood up. "Our reservations don't give us much time. Perhaps—if you're still offering—a nightcap later." He took a fireplace poker and subdued the crackling flames, but the old oak logs stayed alive with color.

It was raining lightly when they started out. The side windows of the Mercedes were dappled with tiny prisms of light and the windshield wipers made a rhythmic pattern as they whipped back and forth. Paul drove toward West Hollywood and then north along the famed restaurant row of La Cienega Boulevard. He had started a tape of Chopin waltzes. The small self-contained world of the car began to fill with fantasy and expectation.

Conversation didn't seem important. Their silence was a communicating one—not of strangers, but rather of a deep affinity. Sara tried to push back the thick, intoxicating mood that was growing inside her, the little flurries of excitement.

Paul turned toward her as they sat at a stoplight. She met his gaze and their eyes held for a moment. He smiled as a man would at a woman that he loved and possessed. There was no mistaking the look, yet Sara couldn't summon up any irritation at his quick assumption of such a role. His strong presence was something she found warming and irresistible.

He spoke quietly. "I'm happy when I'm with you, Sara—very happy."

Then the light changed and he moved the car expertly through the heavy traffic. Sara hugged the words to herself, turning them in her mind. They felt better than any compliment she had received for a very long time. They trickled into the deepest part of her heart and started to fill the empty place left by Jacques, the aching void a lost love leaves behind, full of unspoken questions and regrets.

She was afraid to say anything in reply. She looked at Paul's finely etched profile. She couldn't be falling in love with this opinionated, egocentric man. If he was what he appeared to be at all. For he was changing before her very eyes. He was happy when he was with her—it was so simple and wonderful!

She thought of the slashing, caustic pen that he could wield so ruthlessly, but ended up making more excuses for him. She hoped that when they reached the restaurant her common sense would reassert itself. "Where are we going?" Her voice was steady.

"L'Orangerie. I want to test their *veau avec sauce trois moutardes*. I haven't been there for a while and even the finest chefs can become dull when the acclaim of critics makes them forget they're not perfection. I plan to keep them on their mettle."

The magic moment was gone, the fragile mood destroyed by Paul's cool words. Sara sighed. "Isn't it hard to keep on being the arbiter of taste," she asked pointedly, "checking up on chefs and their egos? I think I'd hate to have your job."

He looked indulgently at her. "A good chef never minds feeding a discriminating palate."

The parking attendant took their car and Paul led her into the restaurant. Sara's first sight of L'Orangerie was a visual delight: soft muted-orange table cloths, delicate French chairs upholstered in stripes of orange, yellow and green, a tall fresh-flower arrangement emphasizing one wall. Silver sparkled, candlelight glowed at each table, and the lights were soft.

They were seated at an intimate table, and Paul smiled across at Sara. "Shall I order?"

The hovering waiters who had not called Paul by name, but obviously knew him, stood with pencils poised. Paul did consult her taste in cocktails, and when she asked for sweet vermouth with sparkling soda and lemon he raised an inquiring eyebrow.

"I like gentle things," she told him. "And drinks not too potent."

He gave the order, with a twelve-year-old scotch for himself, then returned his gaze to her. "And what about men?" he asked probingly. "Do you like them gentle or potent—or both?"

"I like them kind." She tried to keep her voice even. "So many men have to be proving something—pressing and winning...."

"Hmm. I think you don't fully approve of men, sweet Sara."

There was his pompous voice again. "I only approve of men or women if I think they deserve it," she said stiffly.

"Then you believe in equality of the sexes?"

What a strange question! "I believe in the best of male and female qualities being equally respected." She took a studied sip of vermouth, trying to deal with the uncomfortable emotions he could rouse so easily in her.

"It's nice here," she offered when he didn't respond. "The colors give a happy feeling."

Paul nodded, saying nothing, just swallowing his scotch slowly. All at once his face was shadowed. In the flickering light of the candle a look of profound sadness and loneliness showed around his sensitive mouth and moved in his haunted eyes. Sara had to look away. She wanted to touch his hand, hold his head against her breast and tell him...what?

"My godmother tells me you have a sister in France," she tried again.

His eyes lost their in-turned look. "Yes—Madelyn. She's married to a man for whom wine has been a family affair for hundreds of years. You'd like her." Some animation returned to his face. "She stands up to Yves, who's a bit stodgy concerning the rights of women. There's a fine brain in that beautiful head and there have been considerable changes in Yves since they married." He smiled, as if he was really seeing Sara for the first time since they sat down. "Yes, you would love my sister. She's quite happy now." He swirled the last of his drink in his glass, as if the word happy was something that puzzled him.

"I visit them on their estate in the summer when I can. They produce some special wines with a small vintage. Shall I order some for us?"

"And that's what you meant when you said you wanted to have a little château of your own," Sara asked. She wanted to have him tell her about himself, not hear it as gossip from other lips.

"Did I?" he smiled. "I should have my head examined. I don't believe I could stay on a tiny plot of earth, no matter how fine. Didn't Elizabeth tell you I had restless feet?"

"She didn't say it quite that way."

"Well, I'm not known for my ability to set down roots. My five years at the *Tribune*—that's the longest I've stayed anywhere."

"And where will you go after this?"

"It's a big world. I'll find someplace," he shrugged.

Sara watched the play of expression on his face. Paul Cabot Edgerton was a bedeviled man. There was something eating at his heart.

The waiters hovered again, and orders were given. He chose the medallions of veal with three-mustard sauce as he had intended. For Sara he decided on salmon poached in wine and dill. She was beginning to understand his high handedness. It was only a mask for what lay beneath. She was more certain than ever that she could reach him.

His face grew relaxed in the pleasant surroundings. He wasn't showing the caustic humor and machismo that seemed to ride on his broad shoulders ready to take over. Unconsciously, she sighed. He responded immediately.

"Something is troubling you. I've sensed it all evening," he said softly in a low, fluid voice. "You affect me very strongly, Sara. I don't know much about your life, but I suspect there has been loneliness as well as culture and music and family love."

She was surprised. He was asking her the very things that concerned her about him. "Everybody's lonely at times. I'm sure you are." She noticed a twitch of emotion move across his face.

"I'm trying to find out what I want to do with my talents. I'd like to be truly useful in this world, not just live a superficial existence."

He smiled with a strained twist to his lips. "Much of the world is superficial, m'dear. We who understand this can make a good living pandering to the organized superficialities of society." His voice was filled with wry bitterness. It hurt her to hear it. "I'll confess to you, Sara: I'm not too pleased with Paul Cabot Edgerton's byline as a food critic, even on a good paper like the *Tribune*. As you say, work should be meaningful, and God knows the world needs meaning. Yet, who am I to sort it all out?" He gave a quick burst of laughter. "Once I thought my mind might make a difference in the world. Now I have fewer illusions."

A hard knot sat in Sara's stomach, taking her appetite. How could she keep up with her deception? He was confiding in her, coming out of his guarded fortress, trusting her with his private thoughts.

From across the table he smiled at her with heart-wrenching attractiveness. There was no way she could live with her secret and keep seeing Paul. It would tear her apart. It stood like a thick, menacing wall between them. She had to let him go from her.

The food cart arrived at their table and the rituals of a fine restaurant began. Sara was rebelling at the idea of never seeing Paul again. But her allegiance had to be to her career...to the *Chron-*

icle. She had no right to go back on her contract with Eric.

This thing between Paul and her was just an episode, an interlude in her life—her career was too important to toss aside. Hadn't she almost given up everything for Jacques? She wasn't going to be such a fool again.

Paul was eating with apparent enjoyment, encouraging her to taste and sample everything. He spoke to her about his genuine love of music and was unabashedly sentimental about Chopin. She didn't want to like Paul Edgerton as a man...she couldn't!

Sara coolly watched the relieved smile on the waiter's face when Paul ate the last morsel, put down his fork, and sent his compliments to the chef.

"You actually liked the veal?" she ventured, watching him dab his lips with the napkin. Her tone held a challenge and he looked at her quizzically.

"Excellent. Did you want me to complain? I will, if it would fulfill your expectations of me. How is the salmon?"

"No complaints," Sara smiled. "You'll have a hard time being mean about this meal."

"Not you, too," he moaned. "Is there a conspiracy of females intent on destroying my peace of mind?" A long-suffering smile moved briefly on his lips. "Since you expect me to be a pedantic snob apparently, let me bore you with a description of French *nouvelle cuisine* as it compares with traditional *haute cuisine*."

"I have no choice?"

"None. And please don't speak until I'm finished." He was trying to be amusing, but his light remarks were heavily tinged with sarcasm. He demanded that she do as he wished. Rather than pursue the matter and make herself seem touchy, she listened with half an ear to his pronouncements on French cuisine. She found herself watching his lips and dragged her eyes away. She knew those lips were capable of teasing her body to high response. And he knew it, too. It was apparent every time he caught her watching him, and a change would come over his brooding amber eyes—a look that said, *You know very well what pleasures are possible between us.*

Dessert was a blessed interruption of Paul's lecture and the silent seduction by his eyes. For her he had ordered coffee and a melt-in-the-mouth lemon mousse tart, refreshing and not too sweet. She wished she had more of a stomach for fine foods tonight, but Olive Gadwall's discriminating taste was far, far away right now. Even Sara's observations of the service and decor weren't those of a sharp-eyed critic. Paul Edgerton, the man who was just finishing his toast rounds, brie and coffee, was all she could think about.

He asked for a taste of her tart. "Too sour," he decided, mulling his forkful.

"Just right," Sara smiled defiantly.

"I'm the critic." He made strong eye contact with her, communicating his dominant energy.

"So you are." She found it hard to look away

from the masculine focus of his gaze. It made her want to fight him and love him at the same time.

While he was pulling out his credit card he asked, "Shall we go to a charming little bistro not far away for a liqueur?"

She nodded, not wanting the evening to end, and not knowing what she would do with him when it did end. If this was to be her last date with Paul she wanted to have something to remember besides a game of cat and mouse.

CHAPTER TEN

IT TOOK ONLY A FEW MINUTES to get to Paul's special place. Here, the car attendant called him by name. Sara felt irritated when the young man gave her an appreciative look and winked at Paul. She wasn't just one of Paul's long line of vapid "friends," she fumed. She detested the locker-room camaraderie some men had about women.

The bar was intimate, done in the decor of the twenties. Large photomurals of dreamy Maxfield Parrish paintings covered the walls. The tables were on several levels around a small dance floor. Very tall vases of flowers stood in the corners, the carpet was rich with oriental tones, and velvet drapes echoed the deep blues and reds. Overhead, a huge crystal chandelier filled the high curve of the ceiling, tossing darts of light on everything. Crystal teardrops hung from wall sconces, casting dim light on the tables on the upper level.

Paul gave her his arm as they were shown to a good table at the edge of the dance floor. Muted classical guitar music was being piped into the room, while a quartet of musicians rested between sets.

Looking across at Paul she caught the same

deep look he had given her earlier at dinner and her heart responded unevenly. He was self-assured and maturely handsome—a man, not a boy. The look in his eyes summoned up everything feminine and receptive in her. Her pride begged her to resist this tide of animal magnetism. It wasn't a mere myth that there were great archetypal patterns of male and female emotions. She felt almost helpless to draw herself away from Paul's intent, silent messages. He was watching her with a slight smile that said he found her delightful—and he wanted her.

He ordered for them. Espresso, amaretto liqueur and a bowl of unsweetened whipped cream. "I like to make my own cappuccino."

He took a cube of sugar from a silver holder on the table and began turning it over in his hand. Sara was fascinated by the play of his strong fingers. They were finely shaped hands, the nails well-cared for. So might the hands of a renaissance man have been, she thought. Dexterous, sensitive, powerful, yet without the appearance of brute strength. The hand of a thinker, perhaps, or even an adventurer or artist.

His fingers sensuously caressed the sugar, turning it, feeling along its crystalline edges, as though he touched a warm, living thing. The fingers became suddenly still and Sara raised her bemused eyes to meet Paul's steady ones. They reflected a golden light from the chandelier. The corners of his lips tightened with amusement. She was being played with, teased without words, and worst of all, it was exciting her. Those knowing hands could draw, if they desired, deep response from her body—he knew it and so did she.

The little orchestra had picked up their instruments again and were now playing in a rippling, flowing rhythm. It wasn't today's music with its heavy gonadal beat or overexcited disco sounds. This was music a man and a woman could dance to, moving toward a far more penetrating fusion of energies. This wasn't music for children, or even for adults who still enjoyed the swift flashing movements and undisciplined explosions of the adolescent body. Rather, it spoke of passionate restraint, promises of delight, tenderness and of a woman's surrender to masculine power.

Sara collected her thoughts, annoyed that they had strayed so far. Was there still some delayed reaction to her loss of Jacques? Did she still need to prove that she was a whole woman, capable of passion?

A hand was being held out to her and Paul was coming around to help her from her chair. "Shall we dance, my Sara?" he asked as if there was no need for an answer.

He lifted the soft matching jacket of her dress from her shoulders and draped it carefully on the chair. Paul drew her close to him, moving easily into the rhythm of the old song, "Blue Tango." The haunting melody wrapped them in its warm spell and Sara felt Paul's arm strongly around her waist, sending pleasurable heat through the thin wool knit of her dress. His other hand cradled her own and brought it up against his chest. He bent his head and kissed the fingers he had captured so gently.

"It's not the cold little hand I kissed the other night," he breathed. "But I'm having trouble remembering the promise I made to you then—something about your virtue...I can't recall."

She felt his smile against her fingertips, and then the tiniest dart of his tongue, just once. A stab of pleasure careened along her spine. "You promised no pressure on me," she barely whispered, unable to remove her attention from the stirring, coiled serpent of sexuality that was rousing from its long slumber within her.

"Ah, yes," he said. "That was before I was so absolutely certain that I wanted to make love to you."

"Don't say that," she begged softly.

"I have to, my Sara." He pulled her tighter until her breasts were almost aching with the pleasure of his hard chest. Anyone looking at Paul would see a tall, energetic man dancing with a young woman, but Sara knew that an invisible force had reached out to her, wrapping her in a mindless urgency that blocked out everything but the vivid moment they were sharing. She flowed with him, desiring to be part of him. Paul's lips touched lightly against her forehead. If she raised her face ever so slightly to his, there in the dim light and the sparkling flashes from the chandelier, she knew that his lips would find hers and she would be completely swept away.

Even the gentle touch of his lips excited more fire in her than had ever been with Jacques. How could she have thought his body so desirable? The difference was so evident now, even with just Paul's touch.

The music ended and he released her, although he held her hand as they returned to their table. He bent to seat her and spoke low next to her ear. "I won't forget my first dance with Sara Courtney."

The espresso was delivered just as they sat down, and Paul concocted their drinks, sending a waiter running for a touch of nutmeg before Paul found it satisfactory. "The trick was taught to me by an old gourmet in Harry's Bar in Venice," he said. His eyes still held their intense gaze. She felt drugged by the promises in them.

Sipping at her tiny cup of creamy coffee nectar, Sara tried to make casual conversation, all the while only too aware of the pull between them. He was telling her about how the famous Harry's Bar had been started with a gentleman's agreement between two men, almost strangers. She heard just part of his story, reveling in the dark vibrancy of his voice, which caressed her regardless of what he was saying. If time was passing, she was unaware of it.

"Will you risk another dance?" he offered.

She blinked her eyes like one waking from a trance. "Paul...don't you think...I mean, what are we doing?" She let the question dangle, expecting him to know what she meant.

"I thought it was obvious, my friend," he said. "We're doing something we both enjoy very, very much."

"We're playing a dangerous game, Paul. And I can't go on with it. I'm not prepared to take the consequences."

"You think this is a game with me?" His face was suddenly severe.

"I think we should leave. I have an early appointment at UCLA to make a computer search for my father...eighteenth century music literature. He likes to adapt the older modes for their concerts...." She was suffering under Paul's scrutiny.

"As you wish, m'dear—but I regret not having one more dance. Were you afraid?" He prodded her to a strong response.

"Why do you insist on thinking I don't know my own mind?"

A slow, cynical smile grew on his face. "Do you?" he said briefly, and raised a hand to call for the check. A chill settled between them.

It was raining when they left the bistro. Paul was silent except for the necessity of dealing with the parking attendant. He drove her home and slid the car to the curb in front of her building.

"I'm sorry for speaking so sharply," Sara said lamely. "I hope I didn't spoil your evening. It really was very nice...." She put a hand on the door latch.

"Let me, Sara," he ordered and came swiftly around to open her door. The warmth of his hand as it took hers held a powerful charge of male energy.

"Don't bother to walk me up," she said. "It's late and you'll just get wet in the rain." She started to walk away, wanting to escape his sphere of emotional influence. It was hard enough to have said what she had—she couldn't stand it if he demanded explanations from her.

But his footfalls joined hers. He took her arm and gave her a peculiar smile. "A gentleman always sees a lady safely to her door—at least that was how I was taught. Indulge me, Sara. I find it difficult to let you go."

On the elevator going upstairs she rummaged in her purse for the key. Her hands weren't steady. At the door Paul took the key and turned the latch, standing back to let her enter the apartment. Then he followed, shutting the door quietly behind him.

There was still a bright orange glow and lazy licking tongues of flame in the fireplace—not enough light for Sara's peace of mind. She went quickly to switch on the lamp beside the couch, then turned to say her final good-night to Paul.

With a gasp she found him close beside her. His arms were around her before she could move.

His insistent hand urged her chin upward until his lips found hers—not demanding, but possessing her mouth as if such kisses were well understood between them. He felt a small responding movement of her body and drew her even closer.

Sara didn't want to fight him. She desired all he

desired. His lips began a teasing path, starting with the corners of her mouth and progressing by small sensual degrees, finally pulling her lower lip into his warmth and drawing her tongue to his. Paul's hand steadied her head as he went on with his deep, exploring kisses. She shivered with pleasure. If he hadn't held her with such a strong embrace her knees would have given way beneath her. And he knew it... he knew it! She didn't want to be a weak, submissive, adoring female.

His tender explorations continued with the softest of kisses on her eyelids and face. With a wordless murmur he brought one hand up to caress the swell of her breasts, cupping them upward. She knew she should push him away. Instead, her arms went slowly up until they clung to his shoulders and the sounds she heard were from her own throat, low and primitive.

The muscles of his arms and torso tightened as he picked her up; his smoky topaz eyes met her turquoise ones, his will challenging hers for a long moment. She couldn't hold out against his demanding strength. He sensed that he had won. "Yes, Sara... yes," he whispered as he lowered her onto the couch, still cradled in his arms.

Her shoes fell from her feet and Paul clicked the lamp off, leaving them in a half-light where every breath and heartbeat was magnified.

His fingers found the zipper of her dress, easily urging the fabric down from her shoulders, exposing her to his gaze. Then his lips were hot on her breasts, his tongue making electrifying patterns around her hardened nipples. One lone sensible thought penetrated her mind. "Paul—please!" Her voice was shaking. She pushed his head from its place close to her breast.

"Let me, Sara. You want to.... You want to...." His hand slid along the contour of her body and hinted at pleasures to come as he caressed her leg and eased the skirt of her dress up to her thighs. She held her breath against the sheer wonder of his touch and a raging battle burned inside her.

"Not like this," she managed to whisper. She put her hand over his to stop its path.

"I only want to please you, Sara. Let me give you something that can make us both so very happy." He was gentle again as his lips came to hers in the tenderest of kisses. "Let me, my darling..." he begged. "How sweet—how utterly lovely you are." He caressed her breasts lightly. "You'll see. It's going to be wonderful. I know how to make you purr."

She pulled back sharply. Something about that last word was too horribly familiar...too much like Jacques! She suddenly couldn't bear to be touched. Those smooth confident honeyed phrases—the expert technique! She remembered only too well when it was used on her before...and she felt sick.

She dragged the folds of her dress up to cover her bare skin. "You're very good at everything, aren't you, Paul?" she said into the shadowy face above hers. The taste of him was still in her mouth, delicious and addictive, and she had trouble speaking.

"Is this where we have a long talk, Sara?" Paul said wearily. "We should have had it before this, but I thought what you needed was love."

Tears burned into her eyes. He was still manipulating her and she wouldn't allow it! "I don't need anything, not a thing...except a man who lets me be myself. I don't want you to put me into the same mold with your other "friends." I don't work that way. You don't even know me!" Her voice was rising with her desperate frustration.

"Sara," he said as he reached to wipe a tear from her cheek. "Did it ever occur to you that you didn't let me know you?"

"How could I?" she shot back. "You were always Paul Cabot Edgerton, the expert. Wine, truffles, women—it's all the same. You as much as said so on the first night we had dinner. You look at me and see a woman who doesn't swoon at your lofty highness and you say to yourself, 'I've got to have her...I've got to show her how great I am...what a fantastic lover I am. I'll have her begging for kisses before you can say Jack Robinson!' " Sara was stunned to hear the poisonous words tumble from her lips.

Paul just sat there, watching her. "Well, m'dear," he laughed, " 'nuff said. I'll pack me truffles and be off. It's been grand." His words were ridiculous, but the sting in them was too real. He stood up awkwardly, adjusting his tie and quickly passing a hand through his dark disheveled hair. "I was going to try out some new moves I just perfected. Guaranteed to please every taste. So sorry you'll miss the debut."

"That's unfair," she said to his back.

"Funny," he said in an odd voice. "I thought we had something rather special, when all the time it was too much wine and firelight."

He walked to the door and turned back to her. "Do you think you're the only one who can be hurt?"

She stared at him mutely while he let himself out the door.

Returning to the couch she pushed the pillows back into shape so that they were plump and innocent. She wanted no reminders of him. But she was fooling herself. Her own body was a reminder that couldn't be set to rights with a few pats like a pillow. She felt nauseated and sick to death of herself. Well, that was the end of it. All she had to do was tell him he was a loathsome user of women, and she could guarantee that he'd never darken her door again. *Clever girl,* she mourned bitterly. *You have such a lovely way with words. Why be decent and tactful with a man when you can just as easily rip him apart?*

His parting words hung on the air like an agonizing reproach.

Her bed was cold. The sheets touched her with smooth impersonality. She curled up miserably in them to wait for morning.

CHAPTER ELEVEN

FAR AWAY ON THE COBALT HORIZON the sea and sky met with a shimmer of delight. Scattered on the warm stone floor of the ancient terrace were two small jewelled sandals and the finely woven garments of a man and a woman, discarded in their haste. Now, clinging tightly, their bodies moved together in a slow intoxicating rhythm upon the great gryphon-footed couch.

"I can't let you love me," the dream woman said. "There are secrets between us." Her long carnelian-colored hair had fallen from its combs and the man's fingers were entwined in the heavy curls.

The dream man raised his head from her flushed, warm breast. "Oh, my dearest darling," he whispered in a voice heavy with passion, "nothing you can do will stop me from loving you."

Their lovemaking continued as the colors on the horizon changed slowly to dawn light. They became part of the greater rhythm of nature, part of the sea and the sky, children of eternity.

The dream woman cried out to the man to stop. Agonizingly, she reached up and peeled away the suffocating mask she was wearing. The dream man pulled his body from hers, a look of shock and bewilderment in his beautiful golden eyes. Her exposed face was contorted with sorrow. "I can't let you love me...!" she cried again.

Great heavy tears were starting down her cheeks onto the couch. They became a flood and the bittersweet waters called down an answering torrent from the sky. The sea roared in with a high wall of salty waves, lashing at the protected terrace of their love.

She watched helplessly as the dream man was torn from her arms and carried away from her into the blue abyss. He was gone forever. And she had destroyed him.

SARA WOKE FROM THE DREAM shaking, the pillow soaked with her tears. It was too horribly real. The bedside clock said five-thirty. Almost daylight. The residue of the dream was like a cold ghostly hand squeezing her heart. She had to get out of bed and shake the images.

She stood for a long time staring through her bedroom window. Outside there was no sea. The sky was dark gray.

A grim smile crossed her lips. She had put into the dream everything she feared...and all that she hoped for. The lovers were herself and Paul, and she was filled with remorse. A psychiatrist would have an easy time of it with her transparent symbols. She had subconsciously stepped into her painting. She had always secretly wondered what the young Greek woman was waiting for as she leaned against the marble balustrade gazing out to sea. Sara had just finished the painting for the artist by sending a dream lover to the woman's couch.

Sara was satisfied that she had simply taken her own problems and dramatized them, using the painting as a catalyst. Even so, she averted her eyes from the picture as she walked through the living room toward the kitchen.

"A basket case," she muttered. She didn't take the time to brew her morning coffee, but put some water on to boil for a cup of instant.

Her senses were thoroughly sated with memories—whether they were memories of Paul's very real touch on her body, or the dream man's caresses, she didn't know. The thought of Jacques right now was laughable. He had been the first, but that was all. With him she hadn't experienced having every nerve in her sensitive flesh burn with the electricity of a lover's kiss. She had deceived herself into believing she had reached the heights, but only now did she know that there were greater heights yet. Heights she might never reach, she pondered thoughtfully as she sipped at the black brew in her cup. Never.

The piercing noise of her door buzzer jolted her, causing her to spill some of her coffee onto her robe. Who else would it be but Paul? Hadn't they said enough cruel words to each other?

She went wearily to the door and opened the peephole. In the yellowish light of the hallway she could see a pale face and two bloodshot eyes. "Jean-Claude!"

She rushed to open the door to him. The tall thin Frenchman with two battered suitcases in his hands staggered inside, looking more dead than alive. "I knew if I could reach you everything would be good," he said in fractured English just before he collapsed on her couch.

"Good Lord—what...?" She didn't know where to start.

"I fly all the night...standby from Orly. Five hours to wait in Canada...it was terrible, *chérie*, you cannot imagine." One arm hung limply to the floor while his feet struggled to push off his heavy wet shoes. "This is paradise," he sighed brushing his blond hair off his face with his hands. "Have you a crust of bread for a dying man?" His face quirked into a boyish little smile and Sara knew that his pathetic performance was designed to keep her from being angry with him for arriving this way at her door.

"You are very naughty, Jean-Claude," she said. *Méchant.*"

"*Oui,*" he said, not at all guiltily, "but I am here, *non*?"

"That you are," she smiled. "Here, you can finish my coffee while I find some dry bread and old cheese for you."

He rolled his eyes in appreciation of her meager alms.

"You didn't receive either of my letters?" she called back from the kitchen.

"Hmm," he replied evasively.

"This isn't the best time for you to land at my

door. You're welcome to stay on my couch for now, but I can't just introduce you to the great chefs of the city. That will take time."

"I shall bring them to their knees," he said with his eyes closed.

She stood over him with a small dish of cheese and bread, more pleased than she would admit to him. For five minutes she hadn't had a single thought of Paul.

"First, you should take a shower, my impulsive friend, then we need to have a serious talk."

Sara dressed for the day as she listened to the sounds of the shower and Jean-Claude's baritone voice singing like a choirboy. Maybe some odd intuition brought him here when she needed him. She smiled to herself. But it served him right to be stranded en route for five hours.

Jean-Claude emerged from the steaming bathroom clean and cheery, wearing Sara's blue terry-cloth robe. "Today I start my career," he announced jauntily.

"It's not even dawn yet. Why don't you sleep a few hours and then we can talk?"

"I'm coming half around the world and you want me to sleep?" He swept her up into a hug. *"Non, non, non!* First I show you my new discovery—*oeufs Jean-Claude*. You sit here and watch what I teach you."

He started into the kitchen, the robe flapping around his long skinny legs. He looked like a French stork. "You notice I am talking good English now?"

Sara sat down on one of the kitchen stools. "You should, after all the lessons I gave you."

"I have an English girlfriend three weeks ago, and she like me to make love to her in English. Can you imagine! What girl will refuse to make love to a Frenchman who talk the beautiful language of Abelard in her ear? But... she was a little bit crazy and I was not really in love. So—pfft! I am gone with the wind."

"You left France because of a girl you didn't even love?"

"Of course not. She was an interlude only. I have better reasons."

He was opening and closing her cupboards with a growing expression of Gallic disdain. "What has happened to you, Sara? This is the kitchen of a poor little working girl on the Left Bank."

"I haven't had much time to cook for myself lately," she sighed. The whole idea of food left her completely indifferent. "I eat out most of the time, remember?"

He jammed his fists against his waistline. "A good *chef de cuisine* cooks, not just sits at the tables of other chefs. I am disappointed." He stood forlornly in front of the half-empty refrigerator. "I was hungry."

"I used the eggs yesterday to make a rather good quiche. I can heat it up for you."

"Next it will be frozen dinners, eh?"

"Never-r-r!" she said, mimicking his accent.

They sat at the breakfast counter of the kitchen while Jean-Claude ravenously ate the rest of the quiche. Sara's nerves were numbed from the intensity of Paul's lovemaking and their bitter farewell. She put her throbbing head into her hands and listened while Jean-Claude chattered in French and English about himself.

"I would have stayed," he said. "Le Moulin was very good for me, but the *chef de cuisine* hated me. Jealous, like a husband with horns. I take his secret recipes, he says. I only improve them, I say to him. He wants me to go away, but the owners think I am okay. But they don't want to lose the big chef... what to do? Then one day le Comte de Monfort come into the kitchen especially to compliment me for my *terrine blanc et noir*, and that is the end of Jean-Claude at Moulin de Mougins. If I don't leave this instant, the big chef tell me, he will cut off my head. So—I am a genius of cuisine without a kitchen, and I think: Where is the best place for such a man to be recognized?" He raised his heavy blond eyebrows so that his young forehead was creased with deep horizontal lines.

"Where indeed?" Sara said ruefully.

"*Ah oui!* Exactly! Where my precious Sara is. You have escaped from the pain of misunderstanding and so do I. And so here we are, both to make a new life in a new world, just like in the movies."

"Not quite," she cautioned.

He waved his fork in agreement. "*Bien sûr*—of course! You will have to introduce me to the chefs and then let me impress them. All I need is a chance."

"You're going too fast. First I have to think about what to do. I'm Olive Gadwall, the secret restaurant critic. The chefs I know don't really know who I am, do you understand?"

He shook his head. "Nothing is impossible in America."

"Not to mention the problem of your getting a work permit. You're an alien now."

"What a terrible word. I will cross that bridge when I go to it," he said soberly.

"The proper thing would have been for me to arrange a job for you and then you get a work permit before you ever came here. But...."

He shrugged his angular shoulders. "Just find me a chef of good reputation and I will take care of everything. You worry too much, Sara."

She frowned at him, sitting there so cocksure of his ability to break down international laws and be famous. "Let me make a phone call...to a woman I know." She had cast her mind out to snag any possible help and had stopped at Aunt Elizabeth. She would be charmed with his audacity and talents. "But right now I have to finish my column for the Wednesday issue and I'm not in the mood to do it."

"You are in love again?" he said with canny eyes fixed on her pale face. "The heavy eyes, the lips arranged so...just like with Jacques."

"No—" she fired back. "Not just like Jacques. This isn't like anything in my past. And I can't talk about it yet."

"Forgive me," he said with mock humility. "I thought I see the signs of...." He stopped when he saw that Sara's eyes had filled with tears and she had turned her face from him. "Ahh..." he murmured, pulling her to him in a gentle embrace. "I am here now. I understand everything. *La, la,* mademoiselle, I am the exper-r-rt on love." He purposely made his accent worse. Sara smiled through her burning tears.

"Oh, Jean-Claude—I'm glad you're here!" She gave him a kiss on his hollow, stubbly cheek.

"I knew you would see it this way," he grinned. "Now... you must work on your writing and I will sleep shortly on your sofa, *oui*?"

"Oui," she answered. "I have to take my column to my paper and then go out to UCLA for an hour or so. I'll be home around noon. We can have lunch somewhere I can afford and then go to see a very special woman in Bel Air."

Jean-Claude's snores of deep sleep punctuated Sara's morbid thoughts. She sat dully staring at her notebook. It pained her to think that only a few hours before, she and Paul had made the couch a place of blissful discovery—almost.

She tried in vain to feel like Olive Gadwall. Her column was nearly finished, but she still had to reconstruct her evening at L'Orangerie. It was agony seeing Paul in her mind's eye across the table from her again, remembering the words he spoke.... What could she say about food when it had been secondary to everything else?

Sara forced herself to concentrate. Her hand started making a line of words on the paper. One phrase, another....

"This isn't like so many of the noisy crowded overcharging watering holes of the elite," she wrote. "There is no aura of obsequious service here, no excessive display. There appears to be only beautiful tasteful decor, unobtrusive courtesy, and excellent food. I have been to L'Orangerie once only, but that once was memorable." She chose the last word with care.

In reviewing her menu favorites Olive Gadwall made a passing remark about the delicate lemon mousse tart and gave high marks to the three-mustard sauce on the veal. She had a stubborn desire to mention Paul—to write his name—to force him to think about her, even if he only thought about Olive Gadwall.

At the next table, by happy coincidence, Paul Cabot Edgerton was eating the same fine dish with obvious relish. He also seemed to be enjoying the wines, the brie cheese, and the rest of his meal. His dinner companion—a woman, of course—had a smile on her face after tasting what appeared to be dilled salmon. If he writes a cruel column tomorrow, remember, dear readers, Olive was at the next table and watched him actually enjoying his meal!

She was purging herself of frustration. If she had just stopped for an instant and rationally thought about things...if she had been satisfied with a kiss and not been hungry for more...she wouldn't be sitting here with this ache in her breast and the longing in her body for Paul's taut strength, his gentle urging touches that could make her moan with pleasure. She was like an addict, unable to think of anything but the way their bodies fit together so perfectly, so sweetly in the foreplay of love. In an adolescent way she wanted him to desire her just as much. She imagined she could feel the pull of his desire for her.

"And so, Mr. Edgerton," she continued:

> I had the dubious pleasure of sitting near The Right Table, observing the master at work. Don't be surprised if I watch you at other places, too. But don't be nervous—I am a much gentler sort than you. You see, I won't correct your mistakes with malice. Just think of me as a kindly old maiden aunt who wants to improve your manners. The world doesn't turn to your command, dear. *Ciao!*

She put down her pen and typed a final draft as fast as her fumbling fingers allowed. She had never liked women who punished men, but this wasn't quite like that. This was the only way Paul Cabot Edgerton would listen to her now. She needed to make a dent in his tough carapace, even if it made him more angry than he already was.

She left Jean-Claude snoring on the couch and

drove through the rain-slick streets to the Chronicle Building downtown.

Sara thrust her column at Eric before he could say more than hello. "Read it first."

He read silently, put down the pages, and looked intently at Sara's pale haggard face. "The war's still on, I see. Good girl. I half expected a soft heart and backpedaling, but you came through like a trooper."

"Olive is back, Eric," she said firmly.

"So I see. You've just put Paul in a devilish position, thinking he's being watched everywhere he goes. You really know how to turn the knife. What did he do to deserve it? I'm asking as a friend." His face was concerned. He wasn't being the hard-hitting boss at the moment.

"Isn't this what you wanted?" she said defensively. "The Great Broccoli War and all that?"

"Calm down, Sara," he soothed. "I told you I didn't want you to continue if it's going to tear you up. I only want to hear from your own lips that you can handle this assignment and stay on an even keel." He leaned back in his chair and tapped the tips of his fingers together. "I don't want you hurt. Edgerton's not worth it. No story is."

"I'll be just fine."

"Hmm. Well, old Eric doesn't want one of his people on the casualty list. I won't ask about last night with Paul. It must have gotten too personal for comfort."

"It did."

"Okay." Eric brought his chair back up with a

snap. "Let's assume Olive lives up to her threat and appears incognito wherever Edgerton has dinner. By a stroke of luck my informant at the *Tribune* is getting me next-week's list of restaurants for Edgerton to review. I'll have it by Friday. It fits right into our plans. By tomorrow, when he reads Olive's comments, Paul should be irked, but by next week he'll be out of his mind. And the circulation is going up, up, up!" Eric had slipped back into character with gusto. "Hey, I thought you were going to send me your copy by courier. I still don't know if we have a spy in the newsroom."

"I felt like getting out of my apartment. And there's something I wanted to check out in the *Chronicle*'s morgue."

"You aren't looking for ammunition in Paul's past...that's getting a bit obsessive, isn't it?" Eric's eyes were trying to read hers but she quickly turned and left his office.

SARA STARED at the blank face of her video display terminal. Something like self-punishment made her press in her access code on the word processor that enabled her to retrieve all the back issues of the *Chronicle,* as far ago as 1922, when the paper was first published. PAUL CABOT EDGERTON, she typed methodically, then waited for the green lines to start running across the screen.

She watched in morbid fascination. The society column of the paper had mentioned him dozens of times in the past four years. Women's names—

lots of them. Balls, *thés dansants*, the Founders' Room of the Music Center, the opening of the horse-racing season... all the things that he had told her were superficialities of society. And he was a participant in every one of them!

But three years before he came to California there was an article on the op ed page, contributed by Paul as a young reporter on assignment from his Boston paper to cover a hot spot in the Middle East. It wasn't exactly a news story, more of a human look at the ravages of continuing revenge in a world that he believed wasn't big enough to allow revenge to continue. He wrote about how the children were taught from birth who their enemies were, and how they were instructed in the use of army rifles as soon as they could lift one....

Sara couldn't bear to read to the end. This was the Paul she loved, the one who once had dreams of making a difference. She commanded the memory bank of the computer to return to the society columns.

There he was again, the Paul Edgerton who had to change. She had to make him change. Gossip linked the Boston epicure to ballerinas, starlets, daughters of oilmen. The snooping columnist clucked that "Our Paul Edgerton can't hold off much longer. He has to make a choice. But what red-blooded American stallion would leave such a delightful stable to service just one mare?"

Sara counted three quotes from different women that "It was love." Somehow Sara wanted to believe that she hadn't hurt him last night. If she could prove to herself that he was used to a hit-and-run insincerity it might soothe the very real sense of guilt she was feeling.

She shut off her access to the newspaper's files. Her curiosity had only made her feel worse. There were the two Pauls, as clear as day. She loved the one and had almost given herself to the other. But weren't there also two Sara Courtneys? What if the false Sara—Olive—really *could* teach the false Paul something about honesty and kindness... what if one day the real people could find each other and start again? Anything was possible in this amazing universe, she mused. Why couldn't Olive make a better man of him?

Remembering the afternoon tea Aunt Elizabeth had arranged with Jean-Claude, Sara gathered her purse and raincoat and left the building, waving goodbye to Eric rather than speaking to him.

She drove out to Westwood and UCLA, where a patient librarian explained to her how to order a computer search for the information her father wanted. She was back home by eleven. A delightful aroma of fresh basil and garlic filled the corridor outside her apartment. Jean-Claude had discovered a specialty market on the corner and the twenty-dollar bill she had left for him.

He was shaved and dressed, swathed in a large white kitchen towel as a substitute for a chef's apron and happily preparing a French version of a pasta with pesto sauce. It couldn't have been more welcome to her frazzled nerves. Just the thing to wake up her taste again.

"So," he said as he served up the two plates of pasta, "we have a tea with your godmother."

"I think she'll adore you. Just don't do anything outrageous."

He shoved a large coil of green pasta into his mouth and grinned.

CHAPTER TWELVE

SARA DRAGGED JEAN-CLAUDE from her kitchen, which he was determined to reorganize. She had to make sure he had something decent to wear when he met Aunt Elizabeth for the first time.

They spent the early afternoon shopping and found a reasonably priced suit, some slacks, a jacket, and a good-looking sweater for him. The faded shirts that he had brought with him and his work-worn jeans wouldn't do. Several shirts and a pair of loafers also went onto Sara's credit card. "You can't wear your sandals and white socks," she told him tartly when he resisted the new shoes.

He had watched unhappily at her earlier inspection of his luggage. The only good things he owned were two silk ties, it seemed. They had been gifts and he had wrapped them carefully in tissue paper.

"This was from *maman* on my last birthday." He had held up a golden paisley print. "And this," a plain dark-blue, "from *oncle* Claude, for whom I was named."

"Thank heavens you have something good," she had sighed. His face had flushed under her assessing eyes. "What did you do with your salary all this time?"

"Some I send to *maman*, and the rest...there are girls, you know, they like pretty things."

"Well, you've got to reform. Forget the girls and get to work. This isn't Paris or the south of France."

He had drawn up in stiff dignity. "I do not like to take charity, *mon amie*. But I will soon get money for all of this."

"Nonsense! Of course you'll pay me back, but now is the time you need things."

He disappeared into the bathroom of the apartment with his packages and emerged looking quite handsome in his dark-brown slacks, toast-colored turtle-neck knit shirt and new gold-toned corduroy jacket with leather elbow patches. He looked more mature, and Sara was proud of him.

"You look trustworthy," she said as they drove up Aunt Liz's steep hill. He gave her an insouciant shrug and swiveled an implike eye toward her. "Jean-Claude, I'm not going to all this trouble for you to be cute." She accelerated up the winding road.

He put a calming hand on hers. "Do not worry, Sara. I know very well your American idioms—I will be a young man above reproaches, *n'est-ce pas*?" He made his face look very sober.

Aunt Elizabeth's old Gregory opened the door to them. His usually formal face wrinkled with a welcoming smile. Jean-Claude managed to look very French, very boyishly appealing and competent, all at one time.

They found Aunt Elizabeth seated by her tea

table with her satin-slippered foot on a small ottoman. She was definitely on the mend and her face showed good color. As Jean-Claude kissed her hand with a graceful gesture her eyes rolled expressively at Sara. It took only moments for her to fall under his spell.

Over tea she discussed ways to introduce him to certain of the better chefs in town. "It's such an inconvenience, Sara, that you write under a nom de plume and no one knows you except as that Gadwall person. The next choice to help Jean-Claude would, of course, be Paul Edgerton." She stopped to observe Sara's negative shake of the head. "Well, Eric will have to do—and Bettina Straus," she said to Jean-Claude's inquiring face. "She's the editor of that delightful little guide to the best restaurants in the area." She sipped at her tea while Sara and Jean-Claude waited for her next disclosure.

"Yes," she was saying, almost to herself, "that's the very thing! Bettina sponsored Sigmund Heep when he was an aspiring chef and came to establish himself here. You *have* been to La Gazelle, haven't you, Sara?"

"Not yet, but I've heard raves about it. Sigmund Heep is making quite a name for himself in the best magazines."

"Just so," her godmother agreed. "A prima donna, but he's a rising star and well connected. Also, he's a kind fellow and truly an artist with food. He should be free Monday. He owes me a favor or two."

After a few more cryptic statements about food and patronage in Los Angeles it was all arranged: Aunt Elizabeth would give a small luncheon. She would invite Sigmund Heep and Eric, Bettina Straus, Sara, and Mr. Chollie, the local amateur gourmet of the society A-lists. Jean-Claude would prepare a menu of his choice and then join the table afterward for conversation. "And applause, if you're as good as Sara says you are," she said. "Of course Paul Edgerton would be an asset...." She paused, but Sara's face said no. "Well, then, let me arrange it."

She guided Jean-Claude into a conversation about his life-style, his training, and his family and he loved the attention.

"Your *tante* Liz is of an indescribable kindness and *très charmante*," he said to Sara while their hostess smiled broadly.

"And where are you staying?"

"With Sara, whose friendship is like the warm fire of her apartment."

"You soon will have a job and can afford your own place," Aunt Liz said firmly. "You can count on that, I think."

As they said goodbye, Aunt Elizabeth stopped Sara. "Why don't you check out La Gazelle tonight? Then you'll know something about Sigmund Heep's tastes and Jean-Claude can enjoy your disguise—which I hope I never have to see."

Jean-Claude was bubbling over with plans during the drive home. "I will outdo this Sigmund Heep," he declared.

Sara laughed at his irrepressible ego. "I can see pictures of you in *International Cuisine* and *Gourmet* already."

"So—shall we attend this restaurant of the famous chef?"

"By all means. I need material for my column."

She called for reservations, giving Jean-Claude's last name, Monsieur Roland. When she checked her answering machine there were several calls with no messages left on the tape. Why should Paul risk being put down again, anyway? He was probably out tonight with one of his stablemates who could make him feel wonderful.

She barely had the cynical words form in her mind when the telephone rang. A rush of adrenaline impelled her toward the desk, but she stopped short of grabbing the receiver. She knew the recorded message would start after two rings, and she waited, then picked up the receiver to listen, while her hand covered the mouthpiece. "Please leave your name, phone number, and time you called," her own voice said to her, "and I will get back to you as soon as possible...."

Don't hang up, she thought fiercely. Then a resonant voice exploded in her ear. "Good God, Sara, I'm forced to talk to this mechanical monster! Your blasted machine is an insult to civilized relationships. I've spent a terrible time since I saw you. Won't you please call me and put me out of misery? I don't much like the way we left things between us. Dear girl, I beg you, let us at least talk. Don't leave me twisting slowly in the wind. I'm abject...." The tape cut him off with a loud beep and Sara set down the phone.

Jean-Claude was waiting on the couch with a glass of sherry for her. She joined him and tried to seem natural, but the sound of Paul's voice made a constricting lump in her throat and she sipped quickly at her small glass of warming liquid. She looked up to see Jean-Claude's concerned face. His sympathy tipped her emotions over into tears.

He set down his drink and held out his arms to her. "*Ma chérie*, you must not...." He gently stroked her hair. "I have seen your sad face when you think I do not see. Now you have a silent telephone call and now.... Please—are we not friends of the most close nature? Sister and brother? Let me carry a part of the trouble also."

Sara was tired of "the story," tired of her stupidity that got her into such a mess—but she patiently explained to Jean-Claude about Paul, the man at The Right Table who had made a strong romantic approach to her, not knowing that she was his bitter rival, Olive Gadwall. "It started out as a lark," she said. "Remember when I wrote you how much fun it was going to be...? Well, it all came back and stung me. And then last night...." She forced herself to give an impersonal description of her evening with Paul and the terrible way it had ended only hours before Jean-Claude's arrival at her door.

He let out a soundless whistle. "What kind of man is this Paul, to walk out on a lovely woman after such an interlude?"

"I drove him away," she said tonelessly. She didn't want to meet Jean-Claude's eyes.

"Then do something to bring him back, if you want him."

"I can't fight all his problems and my own, too. Some girl he wanted to marry turned him down because his family didn't approve of her...."

"And so now he has no trust of females," Jean-Claude said knowingly.

"I guess. But can you imagine what would have happened if everything had gone *right* with us last night? It would be even worse now. I'd have more on my conscience, including Olive Gadwall. There'd only be that much more for him to be disillusioned about when I got around to confessing everything to him. Everything's impossible, completely impossible!"

"Then you wish to be rid of him?"

"No, of course not. But I won't pretend he's reformed just because he says he's sorry. It has to be deeper than that. I have to know that he sees me as a person, not just a female who arouses his masculinity and is different from the other shallow dates he's been having."

"*Ma foi*, Sara, *mon amie*—you have changed very much in six months."

"I learned a lot from Jacques about valuing myself," she said defiantly.

"Women!" Jean-Claude said and threw up his hands. A rapid knock sounded at the door and Jean-Claude answered it. A delivery man stood there with a huge arrangement of several dozen roses. Sara saw them and came to look at the card, detaining the man for a moment.

She quickly ran her eyes down the words on the card: "Let these things of beauty speak for me. I have no words to tell you into what an abyss I have fallen. I dwell in darkness. For the sake of a blooming love, Sara, be kind."

She shoved the card back into its envelope. "Tell your boss that the lady refused the delivery." The man appeared truly surprised, but went away with his roses.

Jean-Claude looked astonished. "That is not a good thing, to throw the flowers of a man into his face."

"If he thinks I'm going to forget how he acted.... It probably works every time. A few flowers.... Oh, shut up, Jean-Claude!"

He closed his mouth and made a sign of surrender with his hands.

Sara looked at her watch. "It's almost six. I've got to put on my damned disguise. You'd better wear a shirt and tie, not that polo knit. This isn't Paris!" She stalked into her bathroom and slammed the little door. As she soaked in a hot bath praying that her temper and nerves would settle down she regretted being sharp with Jean-Claude.

She stared darkly into the box that had her assortment of wigs, compliments of Norma, and tied her hair back the way she had been taught. Then she pulled on the salt and pepper wig and pressed her hair up under it. The frumpy suit that she sometimes wore as Olive felt heavy on her shoulders. Sensible shoes and drab makeup finished the ensemble. She no longer looked herself. She looked at least forty years old—forty hard years at that.

The phone rang and she reached to answer the bedroom extension, ready to give Paul Edgerton a lecture on sincerity. It was the florist. "Madame," the voice said, "the gentleman requests that I deliver the flowers to you. He says they don't belong to him, but to you, and that I can't keep them since he paid for them. He...is angry. What do you wish me to do with them?"

"The flowers are mine? Good. Will you please send them to the nearest convalescent home. Ask them to distribute them to the older patients." She hung up briskly. She knew that Jean-Claude had heard, and she was ready to snap his head off if he said a word.

She kept thinking about the note. The more she thought, the more patronizing it seemed—and his effusive telephone message, too. It felt good to be mad at Paul. It eased some of the deep regret that coiled inside her.

Jean-Claude looked up when she came into the room. For a moment his eyes blinked oddly, and then he realized it was indeed Sara. He started to laugh, but Sara cut him off. "Come on—it takes ten minutes to get to La Gazelle."

He sat silently beside her in the car. She felt his suppressed amusement, but refused to join in the humor. She was driving aggressively, passing cars without her usual caution.

Jean-Claude pulled at her sleeve and said plaintively, "*S'il vous plaît*, Madame Gad-a-wall, have a kind heart not to drive as a taxi in Paris. My nerves are in small pieces." He gave her such a pained, pitiful look that she eased her foot back from the accelerator. "This is my fault, Sara. I have intruded on your life to an uncomfortable situation. I am guilty to come without asking you."

Sara felt awful. "It's not you, and I never want you to feel unwelcome. I'm just making a mess of my life, that's all, but it's...it helps to have you here. It keeps me off the roofs of tall buildings," she said with a little wry smile.

He sighed. "I will not give unwanted advice, *chérie*, except that you must not take all things as they appear to be. Do not go at the fast conclusions. I desire to see this Paul Edgerton and draw up a conclusion of my own."

"Aunt Elizabeth will oblige you, I'm sure."

"Now you are mad with her, too?"

"Let's forget Paul and have a good dinner. See that sign down the block? That's our place."

They left the car with the valet and went into the pleasant restaurant. The decor was in shades of grays and muted lavender against a spectrum of whites—from creamy bisque to bone and ivory. The murals on three walls showed shadowy dancing female figures among a variety of delicate white and violet flowers, and with them gamboled dreamlike gazelles. The low booths were upholstered in lavender and the tablecloths were a bisque-toned linen. A big bowl of white marguerites presided over a buffet table of salads.

Sara and Jean-Claude were seated at one of the wall booths. The place was nearly filled. Jean-Claude looked out of place with the plain older woman at his side. He was still trying to keep his face straight, but when he let his eyes wander to her wig and face the corners of his wavering lips struggled to stay serious.

"Relax," she said. "I'm not mad any more."

Sara opened her napkin onto her lap and let her gaze take in the big open room. She was curious about the much-lauded food of Sigmund Heep. Eric would be pleased that she was reviewing La Gazelle.

She was idly letting her thoughts move when a flash of a face was reflected in one of the antiqued mirrors, making her stiffen involuntarily and catch her breath. Paul was here! His eyes met hers in the distant mirror, but she saw no flash of recognition.

"What is it, Sara? What do you see?" Jean-Claude put his hand over hers.

"Look straight ahead and to the right-hand wall. Paul Edgerton is there."

He scanned the booths interestedly.

"Don't be so obvious."

"Do not ruffle the feathers, Madame Duck. He will not take notice. I am only one of many admirers," he smiled. "It is the big man, *oui*? Dark hair...handsome...."

She nodded, not wanting to look herself.

"Ahh," he said with irritating perception, "I can understand now, but I fear he is engaged with two ladies."

His warm hand clasped around hers, helping to get her racing heartbeat under control. "Do not regard him, Sara. Let us order our food."

"In a minute." Her eyes were back on Paul. He was turned sideways to her, his full face reflected in the mirror for Sara to see. The women with him were, as Jean-Claude had noticed, very well-turned out. One was older, perhaps in her early forties, not a natural blonde, with an aura of great attention to her looks. The second was in the bloom of her twenties, delicately pretty and using her very large eyes to best advantage. A waiter was just serving them and Paul was laughing. They seemed to be bantering flirtatiously together. The older woman tapped Paul's hand with hers to emphasize a point and he caught her fingers, holding them for a moment of eye contact.

Sara's solar plexus twisted as she watched, and she flared with silent anger. So this was the Paul so deep in an abyss of darkness...this professional bachelor in a silk suit enjoying himself with not one, but two doting females. Poor Aunt Elizabeth, Sara thought suddenly. Of course she must have known he would be here. Her romantic old heart probably thought that they would meet across a crowded room and—*voilà*.

On impulse she said to Jean-Claude, "I must know what they're eating. We'll have the same thing. I'll write about it in my Sunday column and let him know that Olive is never far away. I'd like to do some comparison tasting tonight."

"But how shall we find out what he eats? Will you stand over his plate and watch?"

"Almost." She looked around the restaurant. "The restrooms must be through that door beyond Paul to the right. You could walk past the table on your way there."

"Ah ha!" he said conspiratorially. "You will excuse me for a moment...."

Jean-Claude unfolded his tall frame and sauntered toward the far wall. As he neared Paul's area a waiter moved into his path and he was forced to stop momentarily behind Paul. Jean-Claude turned his head to scan the table and then went on his way. Minutes later he retraced the same route, paused near Paul's table on the pretext of studying his watch, and returned to the booth beside Sara.

"My eyes tell me—now I must look at the menu. *Oui,* it is here. Your Paul is enjoying—let me see...." His finger ran down the listing of fish. "*Alors*, it is turbot *braisé au champagne*. A *garçon* was removing the soup bowls. I know from the color it is sorrel soup. For the ladies, the older one has a *salade verte* and...*oui*...it must be *côte de veau à la bonne femme*." He shuddered. "I do not like to put bacon with veal...."

He searched the menu again. "For *la charmante*, it was *salade niçoise* only. She is careful of the diet. Her figure in some years will be going to *embonpoint*."

His description of the young charmer as inclined toward plumpness pleased Sara. Paul's aristocratic tastes were supposed to run to women who could never be too rich or too thin. He was slipping.

"Well then," she said. "We will have the same. What will it be—fish or veal?"

"I tell you, Sara, no matter what is said by Sigmund Heep, the veal with the bacon is a combination for plebeian taste. Give to me the fish."

While they waited for the first course they sipped their cassis with lime, which Jean-Claude had ordered. Seeing Paul in his tête-à-tête with the women was like watching a scene from one of those 1930s society movies. She felt detached and cool as soon as her anger subsided. It was a stroke of good fortune that put her here to see Paul's duplicity and gave her a scoop for her column as well.

By the time their main course arrived Paul's party was being served dessert. Jean-Claude had judged well—the younger woman took only coffee, but Paul and the older woman had made selections from the dazzling confections on the dessert cart.

"What wines did they have?" she asked.

"I am not so fast as to read labels while reading my watch. I suspect that the cellar of Monsieur Heep is not *distingué*—not like a cellar of Europe."

"We'll ask a waiter. Tell him I recognize Paul from a society picture and want to follow his choice of wine and dessert."

"I think *le grand* Paul will soon be leaving. We may relax then, *hein*?"

Poor Jean-Claude. Sara felt a wave of remorse. "I'm sorry," she said. "I've burdened you with all of this...this foolishness."

"Do not think of it," he said affectionately.

Paul Edgerton squired his ladies out past their booth without a glance. Sara's unruly heart contracted while she watched him. He was smiling slightly and the curve of his lips was one guaranteed to draw a woman's dreams. Sara saw the older woman looking at him and knew exactly how he was affecting her. The sensation of his lips on her own became vivid again and sweetly painful. She turned back to Jean-Claude and caught his eyes on her—an expression of pity which he wiped off hastily with a smile.

He tried very hard to make amusing small talk during dessert, reminiscing about an irascible old chef named Jules who had taught him everything about dessert making. "But it is good, this *carbielle royal*. Chef Sigmund Heep is clever. His thin round of chocolate is crisp, of course, but not hard to cut, and the meringue—*la, la*!—*tendre* as a kiss. Just right for a lady."

He balanced a forkful of coffee-flavored whipped cream, meringue, nuts and chocolate, holding it out to her. "Here—open." He thrust the sweet tidbit into her mouth. "*Bien*. Now, how is yours?"

Sara had a slice of cream-filled pastry ring with strawberries and pineapple. It had been Paul's choice. She pushed her plate toward Jean-Claude for him to sample. They both agreed that the chef had firm control of the dessert situation.

They drove home at a leisurely pace. Jean-Claude was satisfied that Sigmund Heep was a chef to match his own high standards. "I will need a way to come to work," he announced. "Have you no Métro?"

"A busy bus system, that's all."

"Not like the Paris Métro. I do not want to stand on streets and change from bus to bus. Los Angeles is sprawled across many miles. And then I wish to have freedom to go many places, to find good vegetables and meats."

"You'll need a car pretty soon. I can't always be with you."

"There is no need. I simply borrow your car, if you agree. For tonight I must go to find the best ingredients for my menu. This luncheon with Sigmund Heep must be *extraordinaire*!"

"I'm too tired to go with you. Sure, take the car," she said as she pulled up to the curb in front of the apartment. "Just get it back in one piece. I suppose you have a valid French driver's licence and some kind of identification...."

Jean-Claude gave her one of his most appealing smiles. "Sara, you are the angel of goodness. What would I do if you do not help me?"

"You'd get along just fine." She handed him the keys and started to open the car door. "You'd charm the ladies and be so disgustingly French that no one could refuse you anything." Sara knew very well that she was forgiving of Jean-Claude's penchant for women. On him, though, it looked boyish and amusing...on Paul Edgerton it was abominable!

CHAPTER THIRTEEN

LONG BEFORE DAWN Sara was dimly aware of the clatter of pots and pans in her kitchen. She drifted in and out of sleep, trying to lose herself in darkness, avoiding having to face the responsibilities of her waking life.

"Sara, *lève-toi*—get up!" Jean-Claude's penetrating voice jangled into her state of unconsciousness. "I need you to taste something...." His eager face peered into her room. "Quickly! There is no time...." He disappeared again.

She groaned and threw back the covers. Groggily she slid her feet into her lacy satin slippers and threw on her sea-green caftan. She could smell garlic cooking, and shallots, too. Wine, and the distinctive odor of burning butter. Starting her day at seven o'clock with a dish meant for a luncheon wasn't very appealing at the moment. She glanced in the mirror, ran her fingers hastily through her shoulder-length waves and made a face at herself.

The kitchen was smoking from the butter. The window over the sink had been thrown open, letting in a chilly breeze. Jean-Claude, wearing her too-short terry-cloth robe, was singing to himself and doing a fast dance between the stove and counter top. "Now, Sara! *Vite!* Stir the salmon slices into the sauce while I arrange the spinach about the platter. I burned the butter and I have to start again."

"I don't believe this," she said, bemused by the high level of activity in her little kitchen before she had even had a glass of orange juice. There was a candle glowing on her round dining table, and two places were set with her best china and flatware.

Jean-Claude snatched the frying pan from her hand after she had sautéed the slices for a short while. "*La!* Just enough! Now, sit down. If you say *terrible* I will prepare something other for *tante* Elizabeth and Sigmund Heep."

She took a steadying breath and dipped her fork gingerly into the thin salmon slices that sat in a nest of finely seasoned chopped spinach. It was a delicate portion and a delicate fish, flavored with sensitivity so the wine didn't compete with the garlic and shallots, and the blend of ingredients made the tongue wish for more—even at 7:00 A.M. The hint of lemon brought out the freshness of the salmon.

"Marvelous," she pronounced. "Do it this way for the luncheon and Aunt Liz won't want to lose you to a restaurant. She'll try to keep you for herself!"

"It is worth the risk," he grinned at her. "I am thinking to serve *un secret des moines* after this. What do you feel?"

Sara remembered very well the time she and Jean-Claude first concocted the rich and wonderful "monk's secret" at the Cordon Bleu. Meringue, liqueur, candied fruit, ice cream.... "Not this morning," she begged. "And maybe it's too rich for the luncheon." The thought of sampling a dessert was more than she could bear.

Jean-Claude brought in two of her crystal wine goblets and set them on the table. "I have found a very good riesling. Since I have been working for many hours in the night I wish to celebrate our new collaboration in fine cuisine."

He poured two servings of the chilled white wine and lifted his glass, about to make a toast.

The doorbell made its jarring peal twice in quick succession.

"What is that?" Jean-Claude said. "Only telegrams at this early hour, *non*?"

"Probably from my parents. Could you get it?" She picked up her glass and lifted it to her cheeks, feeling the coolness on her skin. Through the transparent liquid she watched Jean-Claude go to the door and open it. The refraction made his angular form swim in and out of focus. Then she saw a flash of red and a second form.

Jean-Claude said something, then the clipped words of the visitor reached Sara's ears: "One must learn not to be surprised by anything, mustn't one?"

Paul! He was standing ominously in her doorway, holding a large bouquet of red roses in his hand. Sara's body froze. Jean-Claude hesitated, then looked back at Sara with a question on his face as Paul started inside.

"I'll only stay a moment—less than that," Paul said.

Jean-Claude tried to block his entrance. *"Mais non, Monsieur!"* he objected, but Paul was already standing at Sara's table with a hard sardonic set to his face.

"A homey little scene, Sara. What is this—the end of a long continental evening... and not even a French wine?"

Sara set down her glass and said the first thing that came to her: "You have no business—"

"I suppose not, but I had the ridiculous notion that I might find you alone, without... guests. I didn't want my flowers refused again."

Sara was mute. What could she say to him that he would accept? There was Jean-Claude, wearing her robe and holding a wineglass. And there she was in casual attire at seven in the morning, her hair looking as if she had just come from bed.

Paul tossed the flowers onto the table and started back to the door. "No need to see me out. I know the way."

Jean-Claude raised a detaining hand to Paul. *"Non*, you do not understand very well. Sara and I are intimate for many years. It is not what you think...."

Paul's lips twisted oddly. "It is exactly what I think, and it matters not at all, *oui*?" He made the little French word seem nasty on his tongue. "Goodbye, then, whoever-you-are," he said to Jean-Claude. He gave Sara a dark look over Jean-

Claude's shoulder. "And farewell to your lady."
Then he wheeled and left.

The color had drained from Sara's face. Jean-Claude shrugged, "I try to explain to him...."

"You said we were intimate. Do you know how different that word is in French and English?"

"Sure. It means we are close friends."

"It means we are lovers. Dear God, couldn't you have said something else—anything else?"

"*Intime* is not intimate? *Mon Dieu!* But he is jealous. This mean he cares about you, *mon amie*."

"Not Paul Cabot Edgerton." Her mind searched for an apt description of him. "He's more like a wounded lion crashing around."

"Such a strange way to think about a man you love."

"I think I've hurt him, Jean-Claude—not once but twice. What does a man do whose ego has been damaged?"

"If he is like most men he will want to hurt in return."

"And if he isn't like other men...?"

"He will turn the hurt onto himself."

Sara began to shiver. "But I don't want that. I—"

"Then go to him, *chérie*. Tell him this and take him to your bed like a woman who truly loves a man." Jean-Claude was sipping thoughtfully at his wine. "Find him in his hiding place for wounded lions."

Sara started laughing uncontrollably. "Oh,

Jean-Claude, you're wonderful! Everything is settled by making love—how French of you!"

"Mais oui," he winked naughtily. "What else?"

When her laughter stopped she was miserable again. Even if she went to him and loved him she couldn't be completely honest about herself. And he would be the same Paul Cabot Edgerton with the same dark corners of bitterness and superiority, unchanged. The walls would still be there to separate them no matter how closely they held each other—no matter how exquisitely their hungry bodies made love.

"Ahh, Sara," Jean-Claude said softly. "My coming was not such a good thing, *hein*? And my English is a terrible weapon...."

She put her hand over his. "I'm almost glad you used the wrong word to Paul—and met him at the door like you lived here. I couldn't have planned it better."

"Then you are just as much crazy as your lover is. Oh, I forget—your newspaper is here. I was reading the section for restaurant jobs." He handed her the rest of the *Chronicle*. "I have read the restaurant column of *La* Gad-a-wall, and it is full of fire. I am not sure I approve of such methods to make a man love you." He made a little clucking sound with his tongue.

Speechless, she wondered what she would have done if Jean-Claude hadn't been there, if she had opened the door to Paul and he hadn't been forced to defend his honor by insulting her. What if...what if...! What if she weren't Olive Gadwall and Paul didn't have his touchy ego? A futile sigh escaped her lips.

"I want to introduce you to Eric Hartley, my boss," she said out of the blue to Jean-Claude.

"Soon?"

"Right now, this morning. As soon as you get out of my silly short robe and I put some clothes on."

She had a few "what if" questions to ask Eric, and she wanted to ask them before she lost her nerve.

ERIC GREETED SARA with a bear hug. "The switchboard hasn't stopped ringing since the morning edition hit the streets. Everyone wants to take sides. It's fantastic! I'm thinking of starting an Olive Gadwall fan club.... Uh oh, Sara, you have that look again. Out with it."

"First, I want you to meet my dear friend Jean-Claude Roland. He's a genius chef who's just arrived from France."

Eric put out his hand to take Jean-Claude's. "Welcome to the *Chronicle*. If there's anything I can do, just ask."

"There's nothing you can do for him, Eric, thanks just the same." Jean-Claude looked embarrassed at Sara's tart reply.

"Okay, Sara, let's have it. What's eating you today?" He folded his arms across his chest and leaned back a little, waiting.

"Eric, what would you have done if I hadn't

been here—if you had to find another person to be Olive?"

"Unfair question," he smiled winningly, but uncomfortably.

"Would you have started this war with another Olive?"

"It might have occurred to me," he evaded.

She suddenly ran out of steam. She had Eric on the run and Jean-Claude miserable—what did she hope to accomplish by this little power play?

"Do you want me to find a replacement?" Eric asked.

"I...I'm not liking this job any better as your dumb Broccoli War heats up, Eric. I don't know how to undo what I've done, and I still have a gut feeling I have to teach Paul a lesson."

"So...what do you want me to do?"

"Nothing—nothing at all. I just had to complain one more time."

"Will it help to know that circulation is rising, and that Paul Edgerton probably has a fat raise in his own pay envelope this month? You're doing each other a real favor, if you look at it one way." He let down his stiff posture. "Listen, Sara, I don't interfere with people's consciences. If yours is killing you—and it sounds like it is—then tell me. I can be Olive Gadwall for a while."

She almost said Fine, go ahead and do the dirty job, but she couldn't let go of the one lifeline she still had to Paul.

"I really wanted you to meet Jean-Claude," she said. "I'll be a grown-up now and bite the bullet."

"Stout heart," Eric deadpanned. "And I'm looking forward to Elizabeth de Lacy's luncheon next Monday. Very nice to meet you, Jean-Claude...."

Sara took Jean-Claude to the Farmers' Market on Third Street and introduced him to the largest oranges he had ever seen, the most delectable papayas, kiwi fruit, and other exotic things from the tropics. He gave a critical eye to the several bake shops, sampling their wares for the sake of research, he claimed.

Jean-Claude loaded up with fresh produce, especially bunches of very expensive herbs, for his further culinary experiments in Sara's kitchen. When they returned home she put on an apron and joined him in her tiny work area.

For the next few days she and Jean-Claude lived in a world of their own, cooking, laughing, and remembering all the silly things they had done when they were students together. Paul's Thursday article had been predictable—aloof and cutting. He had addressed himself directly to Olive:

> As for manners, madam, mine were formed long before I was born, in the genteel traditions of my kind. Yours, I suspect, came over on steerage by way of Ellis Island—and not too long ago. Cease and desist, I beg you, before your tatty origins are revealed in their entirety. I wish to spare you and your family further embarrassment....

Sara felt sorry for him. What must his readers be thinking? His tone had moved from the ridiculous to offensive. What might have been a forgivable and even charming Paul Edgerton was sounding like an insufferable snob, even a bigot. That couldn't be the real Paul. She must have driven him to it, and now he was flailing out at the world like a wild man.

The shadow of her concern for him hung over her activities, even though she was outwardly enjoying herself with Jean-Claude. Later in the week they went for lunch at La Gazelle, with Olive Gada-wall wearing her long red wig and Jean-Claude starting to enjoy his role as gigolo to middle-aged women. He was also trying to decide if Sigmund Heep was a worthy master to serve under. If an offer were to be made, what would he do?

There were no more messages from Paul on her answering machine, no more florist deliveries, and Sara felt empty. Her contrary emotions wanted the attention but rejected it. She had a long talk Friday night with Jean-Claude about what might be wrong with her. "I never felt unstable before," she said in frustration.

"I am telling you what I see, *chérie*. In Paris I always think that you had not a happy childhood, as much as you tell people you are happy. Yet there is a searching. You were lonely as a child, I think. For me, food is a sensual expression, an obsession of my French genetic heritage. But for you, *amie*, I see that food is something else: You find security in the structure of a fine kitchen. You find your true family among the *paternelisme* of the older chefs. You make the preparation of food become a substitute for loving—a child who has spent too many years without the nighttime kiss of a *maman* and *papa*."

Sara simply nodded her head when he finished his analysis. "Maybe you're right. I don't know," she said wearily. "That doesn't excuse my cruelty. I feel as if I've dragged Paul into a deep, frightening hole and he's fighting for his life."

"Perhaps he is. Olive Gadawall has made him seem less than he prides himself to be. She says: 'Paul Edgerton is the emperor without the new clothes.' Now if the emperor has no clothes, how will the emperor win respect of his people?"

She smiled at him, amazed at his simple wisdom. "Then I'm the little boy in the fairy tale who dared to tell the truth? I don't remember what happened to him in the end. He was probably flogged and exiled."

"I don't know, but I do know that the emperor sent away the tailors who created his invisible royal robes."

"I'd love to believe that that's what I'm doing. But right now the emperor is on parade in his birthday suit and the people are laughing at him. I hope he can survive it."

"If he is the man you believe him to be, he will be happy for what you are doing. Believe me, *mon amie*."

"Then why do I feel so terrible?"

"Because you love him. I wish I understand this

kind of love, myself." He sighed. "Now, are you writing your article on La Gazelle for Sunday, or not?"

"I'm writing it. I didn't want to stir Paul's devils again, but I think I have to. And thanks for playing Sigmund Freud. I had to think about some things."

When Paul read her La Gazelle piece he would have to find another way to attack her than impugning her ancestry.

"Dear Paul," Olive Gadwall wrote, "I'm so very sad. To think you had to search in the cellar of your prejudices to attack me! Would it help you to know that I proudly wear my Mayflower Descendants pin? Tsk, tsk, dear boy—straighten up! Pay attention to your food, and please—try to remove your well-shod foot from your mouth.

By the way, did you enjoy the veal at La Gazelle? Didn't you think it was just the tiniest bit overdone and overrated for the price? And do you really think a Château Dupuis '79 is the proper choice for the turbot *braisé au champagne*? Even my middle-class escort noticed that the sorrel soup was slightly off color. Since you are a good friend of Chef Sigmund Heep, could you prevail upon him to have his waiters tend to the rest of us as genially as they do to you?

Until next time, my dear, remember that your Olive is just a glance away. *Ciao!*"

Sara was going to have to be more clever with her disguises now. She and Norma spent all day Saturday experimenting with rubber glue and soft plastic facial features. They almost caused Jean-Claude to drop a soufflé when Sara surprised him near the stove looking like the Wicked Witch of the West, warty nose and all.

"Mon Dieu!" he whispered sharply. "You will have everybody in the restaurants to stare at you—with eyes standing out from heads!"

"Not subtle enough, I guess, Norma," she called back to the bedroom. "We'll have to come up with something else."

Norma was proud of her art. She was thirty-one, had never married and probably never would. She didn't care about what other people felt were necessities. Although she lived her life around dazzling costumes and make-believe she had a stubborn insistence on looking plain and nondescript. If there could have been a real-life Olive, it was dear Norma Johnson. Generous to a fault and happy to live vicariously through the movie-studio people she worked with, Norma was becoming indispensable to Sara's alter ego.

"How about if I make you look like an Agatha Christie character—Miss Marple, say?" she chirped, peeling the wobbly long nose from Sara's face.

Sara winced. "I want to look like a thousand other ladies you'd walk past in a shopping mall. Show me how to change the shape of my nose a little, and get some wrinkles in the right places."

Norma searched through her makeup case and came up with a small piece of rubberized skin that fit onto the end of Sara's nose, just altering the shape enough to give her a new look. She applied a crinkly film to her throat and under her eyes and finished with a blue-tinted short, curly, gray wig. "We'll downplay your big blue eyes and lashes a bit," she said, as her deft fingers worked with a gray pencil to drab out her lashes and brows.

"You don't think this is how I'll look in thirty years...?" Sara asked, screwing up her face and making a mass of tiny wrinkles pull across her pale cheeks. "Now—I want to try this myself." She peeled off the layers of her disguise and started from scratch while Norma watched impatiently. "Sit on your hands if I make you too nervous," Sara offered.

Jean-Claude bowed deeply and swept his arm in a broad arc, grazing the floor with his hand. "May I have the pleasure of serving *le soufflé au homard* in the principal dining room, mesdames? It is a recipe which I personally copied from Chef Jean Plet of Hôtel Plaza Athénée."

"And what wine does the chef recommend to go with his lobster soufflé?" Sara sniffed.

"Ah, Madame Gad-a-wall, I would serve a Clément Blanc, but we must be satisfied with a California chablis."

Sara turned her half-finished face to him with a growl in her throat. "Arrgh! Another wine snob. I don't think I can stand it!"

CHAPTER FOURTEEN

THE WEEKEND HAD PASSED without a call from Paul. Sara was intensely aware of the absence of contact with him. The fun of trying out new disguises and going out with her friends only spread a thin layer of pleasure over her distress.

When she read her Sunday column about La Gazelle she hadn't felt comfortable. How could a woman who thought she was in love with a man do what she was doing? She was fooling herself to call it love. But what was this feeling—as if she had a connecting cord to Paul Edgerton, and she couldn't possibly cut it and drift free from him, no matter how painful the cord was?

Jean-Claude nudged her into activity. "You think too much about your suffering. You are more French than I am," he laughed. "Let us go. My salmon is already growing old, and I can wait no more time."

They were busily assembling the luncheon ingredients which they should have done earlier, but Jean-Claude had spent all of Monday morning in search of absolutely fresh salmon. He had changed his menu a dozen times, now settling on a more simple treatment of the fish. "The flavors must sing," Jean-Claude insisted.

"You know, Sigmund Heep is a pretty good chef," he said with a straight face as they started to drive to Aunt Elizabeth's. "I can teach him a few tricks of my trade to make him better-r-r." His French drawling accent was exaggerated for Sara's benefit, she knew.

"If you don't behave yourself today you'll never-r-r have a second chance in this town."

AUNT ELIZABETH'S DINING ROOM overlooking the western rose garden was breathtakingly decorated with huge bouquets of her special hothouse roses in a riot of colors. The cheery tablecloth on the oval table was antique linen from old China, embroidered with more bright flowers. It was from the palace of the last empress, Aunt Elizabeth explained to Jean-Claude, who had complimented it effusively.

He made the sign of the cross over his chest. "May I be worthy of such delightful ambiance," he said earnestly and Aunt Liz was charmed. She was doing well with her injured ankle and was using a silver-tipped ebony cane now. It was an elegant accessory to her long black brocaded Tibetan dress.

Sara worked with him in the huge kitchen and enlisted the regular cook, a sweet older woman named Marie, to chop the scallions for the cold cream of avocado soup. He quickly assumed a paternal air, efficiently getting his two assistants to do exactly as he commanded. Sara smiled to herself as she followed his orders. He was going to be one of the great chefs, no doubt about it. He had the instinct for balancing flavors and coaxing even the most prosaic dish into excellence.

Aunt Elizabeth left them alone while she served light aperitifs to her guests in the adjoining garden room. Jean-Claude had insisted that no stronger drinks be served.

Sara gave him a kiss for luck and joined the party as it was moving back to the dining room. Two graceful cloisonné candelabra were lighted just for their decorative effect. To one side of Sara sat Bettina Straus, a garrulous comfortable woman of Aunt Elizabeth's vintage, who was obviously of good breeding and long acquaintance with the best things of life.

Bettina was a woman who remembered when more entertaining was done in private homes than at restaurants. She was a mine of information about Los Angeles in the last fifty years and an amusing table partner. To Sara's other side was an old crony of the ladies, the man known as Mr. Chollie. He was a sort of perennial presence at lavish parties. Aunt Elizabeth had chosen her luncheon guests carefully. These were the people who still carried weight with the old guard, whose patronage could make or break an aspiring chef.

Sigmund Heep arrived last. He was an imposing figure of a man, about forty, tall and lean. Vitality crackled around him as he was presented to his fellow guests in turn. He paused at Sara's place with an appreciative glint of the eye before accepting his position next to the hostess.

Sara observed him carefully. The renowned and

feared Sigmund Heep was almost an exact mirror image of Jean-Claude, only twenty years older; his light-brown hair and thin face, the gesturing hands, the obvious self-satisfaction. She prayed that everything would go well.

Aunt Elizabeth set the tone for the meal. She tapped lightly on one of her crystal wineglasses. "I shan't introduce you to the man in my kitchen right now because he is very busy. We will see him later. I want no false praise, no compliments just because you are in my house. You are all here to judge impartially whether this young chef deserves a recommendation by you. Now, Gregory—please serve the first wine...and to all of you—*bon appétit*...."

After that rather formidable beginning it took a few minutes for conversation to become normal. The wine was tasted dutifully and the velvet-smooth *crème d'avocat glacée*, Jean-Claude's soup, eaten thoughtfully. There were two kinds of rolls, subtly enhanced with the flavors of rosemary and poppy seeds. They made a delicate balance with the cool smoothness of the avocado soup.

Sigmund Heep said very little. Sara watched his lips and eyes, but couldn't fathom his emotions. He greeted the presentation of the main course with a sternly assessing face, fanning one hand over the plate to draw the flavors to his flared nostrils—sensitive ones, Sara was sure.

"This is simply marvelous," Bettina raved. Aunt Elizabeth was withholding comment, but she gave Sara a large, delighted wink. The mouth-watering aroma of the sautéed salmon in vermouth sauce and lime sent Mr. Chollie into an eye-rolling ecstasy.

"Heavenly. I haven't had better. Who is this young man, Elizabeth? I demand to know right now!"

"In due time." She smiled serenely and motioned for Gregory to open the second bottle of wine. Sara noticed the label—Jean-Claude had found his Clément Blanc among Aunt Liz's collection of fine wines. And his salmon was truly a work of art, arranged in almost Japanese simplicity with a tomato purée and truffle to one side.

Eric arrived late, apologizing profusely because of a crisis in the *Chronicle* office. He took his place at Aunt Elizabeth's left. Sara caught his eye and asked silently: "What's the matter?"

He shrugged his shoulders. "Tell you later," he mimed back at her. She knew his concern had something to do with Paul.

Jean-Claude's salmon dish livened the party considerably. Everyone was talking about the terrible or wonderful state of foods in Los Angeles—depending on which conversation one joined. Bettina was an enthusiast, and Mr. Chollie was proud of spreading gloom about the future of fine cuisine and good manners.

"The only one who upholds the old ways now is that Paul Edgerton," he said in a sententious voice. "Sorry to see him making a fool of himself with that other critic. He shouldn't have to apologize for his opinions. Really a matter of class, I think—"

Aunt Elizabeth cleared her throat loudly and changed the subject back to food. "Sigmund, what do you sense about our cook's background and future?"

He raised his eyebrows dramatically. "His background is obvious—either French or Viennese. I understand very well his reasoning in marrying the flavors and textures. One is born with such feeling or not. I cannot say more until I see what he offers for dessert and how he is in person when I shake his hand." Heep's mannerisms were amazingly like Jean-Claude's, Sara noticed again. What if they were too much alike and couldn't stand each other?

Gregory brought out a bottle of Aunt Elizabeth's champagne and started to pour it into the fine tall tulip goblets. Behind him Marie appeared carrying a silver tray. Jean-Claude's dessert was about to be served in Aunt Elizabeth's cut crystal sherbet glasses—apricot compote with *sabayon*.

The six glistening concoctions emitted the most wonderful smell of kirsch and almond as Marie moved around the table. For the first time Sara saw Sigmund Heep break into a wide smile. "He has the touch," he breathed to himself.

Jean-Claude bounded from the kitchen close on the heels of Sigmund's statement. He was wiping his face with a kitchen towel. A flurry of applause greeted him. "Bravo," Aunt Liz said. "Everyone—may I introduce our chef, Jean-Claude Roland."

Sigmund Heep stood to take his hand in a hearty shake. "So—you wish to work?"

Jean-Claude nodded his head. "Not just to work, but to create a fine kitchen."

"Of course." He dismissed the statement as self-evident. "What do you think of starting in La Gazelle tomorrow? I will work you hard for two weeks. I will find out what you do well and what you ruin.... Is this okay with you?"

Jean-Claude hesitated and Sara was about to jump up and tell Sigmund Heep that he would take the job. "And after these weeks, what...?" he pressed. Sara felt the color leaving her face. She could see the opportunity about to fly right out the windows of the room.

Sigmund's eyes flared quickly and Sara gritted her teeth, waiting for him to tell Jean-Claude to forget it. Instead, he slapped the young chef on the shoulder, laughed with a loud bellow, and said, "Maybe I will let you open my new little restaurant for me. It's up to you to prove how good you are."

Bettina interrupted. "But what happened to that chef you hired from Paris?"

"Family trouble—a sick wife. My L'Intime opens at the end of this month. I cannot be at two restaurants at once like a magician. Then Elizabeth de Lacy presents me with a gift from heaven—a chef who knows what to do with food. What do you say... let me train you in my way of doing things, and I see if we have a new chef at L'Intime!"

"You will be satisfied with me, monsieur, I promise."

"I do not like to be proved wrong when I make a judgment. Cook for me tomorrow." He raised a warning finger. "If you do well by me I will treat you like a prince. If not, I will make sure you do not even wash dishes in a good kitchen again. Do we have a deal?"

They shook hands heartily and everyone at the table clapped. "I'm adding your new little place to the next edition of my book," Bettina promised. "I suspect it will outdo La Gazelle. Your decorator let me have a peek inside."

"L'Intime is not to be compared," he said firmly. "It will be unique—a meeting place for lovers, a place for the soul to renew itself with the finest cuisine."

"You sound very romantic, Sigmund—not at all like your public image," Aunt Elizabeth teased.

He growled good naturedly. "And you, young man...." He looked imperiously at Jean-Claude. "I do not tolerate lateness. Be there at nine."

Jean-Claude made an instinctive little bow to the master and Sara smiled to herself. Sigmund Heep was completely in charge.

Sigmund departed and the party started to break up. It couldn't have gone more smoothly. Mr. Chollie and Bettina clucked approvingly at the whole transaction and left soon after, thanking Aunt Elizabeth for the chance to see the birth of a great new career. Bettina threw her arms around Jean-Claude's neck and gave him a smacking kiss. "Dear boy, you were magnificent!" she gushed. "Come along, Chollie, we've still got Marian Hosmer's tea...."

Sara was itching to ask Eric about the trouble at the office, but Jean-Claude was wound up in his victory and Sara had to be a part of the celebration. "I've never heard Sigmund like that," Aunt Elizabeth said. "You had him hypnotized. It was the dessert. What potion did you wave over the *sabayon*?"

Jean-Claude smiled like an angel. "He recognized my understatements. He is a genius himself. We will work well together. And, *tante* Elizabeth, you have given me new life. I will be grateful for all my years." He raised her hand to his lips for a heartfelt kiss. "If ever I can be of service...."

She patted him on the cheek. "Just be sure that I get a good table when I come to L'Intime and that the lights aren't so bright that every woman there looks ten years older than her escort."

"For you, candles," he said.

ERIC HELPED THEM to the car with the things Jean-Claude had brought from Sara's kitchen. "The poor devil," Eric said in mid-thought.

"Jean-Claude?" Sara asked, surprised at the word.

"No—Paul Edgerton. The managing editor got word today that Paul wants to sue us for harassment or invasion of privacy, maybe both. The legal department's getting nervous."

"Oh, no...."

"He can't do it, Sara. We've got the First Amendment behind us. I'm thinking of letting the gossip column handle it. 'What handsome restaurant critic wants the law to fight his Broccoli War...?' Something like that."

"Nothing doing! Eric Hartley, I've let this thing go along pretty much the way you wanted it, but I don't want us to play dirty. Let Olive handle it. Anything between me and Paul has got to stay between us—period. Promise me that."

"Sure, honey, sure. Just tell me the rules of this crazy war as you make them up, will you? I don't like playing in the dark." He shrugged on his overcoat and stalked off to his car. "Oh, by the way, Western Union's trying to get hold of you. They'll probably call your apartment," he said as he backed abreast of her car. "And here's the list of places Paul's dining this week." He handed her a white envelope.

Jean-Claude was almost unmanageable on the way back home. "I don't want to go to the apartment," he said. "I want to drive up a high mountain or go to swim in the ocean. I will put on my tennis shoes and run for many miles! Didn't I tell you, my Sara, that this is my land of opportunities?"

She reached to give his wildly gesturing hand a squeeze. "I'm really happy for you."

"And not so happy for yourself, I think?" He stopped his ramblings and looked seriously at her tense face.

"I wish I could separate Olive from Sara and be coolly professional."

"At least accept that you cannot, and do not hold the fires to your breast like Sainte-Jeanne d'Arc. How will you have appetite for my cooking, hein?"

"I'm acting like a martyr?"

"Do you love Paul Edgerton or not? It is simple. If you do, then find a way to let him know you as I know you."

"He thinks you know me *too* well," she laughed as she turned her car into the underground garage of her building. Jean-Claude was having his usual calming effect on her.

While he cleaned up the mess in her kitchen, Sara listened to the message on her telephone machine. Western Union had called. A voice read the telegram:

"Sara, dear. Change in schedule. Papa and I arriving on eighteenth. Benefit at Music Center. Then time for us. Tell Elizabeth not to fuss. Love. Mother."

"It's just like them," Sara said to Jean-Claude. "They're probably filling in for someone who couldn't make it at the last minute. They always were softhearted about rearranging their vacations to help out a friend. Not like other concert artists, who wouldn't change a date if a bomb fell on them."

She glanced at the wall calendar. "That's next week. I'll have to call Aunt Liz. When mother says 'no fuss' she means give us just a small parade and hold the elephants. She'd be crushed if there wasn't a reception or something."

"And what are we doing tonight, *chérie*? Do we stay inside and eat the leftovers, or is Madame Gad-a-wall in need of a restaurant for her column?" He popped a piece of rosemary roll into his mouth and looked expectant.

"You're restless. Okay, where do you want to go? We have the whole city to choose from."

"What is in the little envelope of Eric Hartley? A list, I think?"

She glanced back at her purse on the desk. "If we go to one of those places, Paul might recognize you."

"Not if the gentleman with you is wearing a moustache." He held up a strip of salmon under his nose to show the effect.

"Norma didn't leave me a moustache. She didn't think I'd be needing one."

Jean-Claude disappeared into her bathroom and returned with a good approximation of a red moustache made from a curl in Olive's long red wig. He looked very strange.

"We shall not kiss, of course," he said. "Now, what is in your envelope?"

Sara didn't really want to go out, especially to see Paul again. And now with a threatened lawsuit he would be watching like a hawk for his nemesis, Olive Gadwall.

She pulled out the folded paper, a photocopy with the *Tribune*'s letterhead. *Monday dinner at George's Acropolis—8:30.*

Jean-Claude was reading over her shoulder. "And what is that?"

"A Greek place in the Valley. I don't know if I'm up to raw lamb and goat cheese," she said sourly.

"...but grape leaves and baklava, *chérie*! Why not? It will clean my palate of my own cooking. I grow tired of *nouvelle cuisine*."

"Never say that to Sigmund Heep." She looked skeptically at him. "Give the Acropolis a call and invent a name for the reservation. You'll be impossible until I give in."

GEORGE'S ACROPOLIS WAS DARK, crowded, noisy, and smelled of a riot of pungent flavors, not the least of which was the permeating aroma of oregano and broiling lamb. It was known as a fun place to dine when one felt in the mood for Greek music, costumed waiters, and an ebullient owner-maître d'.

Jean-Claude was ready to fall under the restaurant's Mediterranean spell. He steered Sara by the elbow through the closely arranged tables, trying not to lose sight of the young woman who led them through the jam of activity. "Are Monday nights always this busy?" Sara managed to shout.

"Every night's like this. George has a lot of friends." The hostess disappeared, leaving two large menus on the table.

"Order anything you like," Sara said with a wave of her hand. "I'm too tired to care. Places like this dull my senses anyway." What she didn't say was that she had lost all pleasure in tracking down Paul Edgerton.

Jean-Claude grinned. "Let me take a little stroll to find Monsieur Edgerton's table first. It will aid with the menu selections, *non*?"

"Whatever you want to do," she sighed.

"Do you wish to leave?" His brow furrowed in concern. "I'm sorry to make jokes if you do not feel well."

"I'm all right. Go ahead. I'll soak up some atmosphere until you get back," she smiled weakly. She didn't want to spoil his victory evening.

Jean-Claude returned after a long absence. He was carrying a large carafe of dark red wine. "A most friendly place," he said over the din of voices and music. "Somebody put this into my hand and said something in Greek."

He poured the wine and picked up his menu. "Paul Edgerton has not come in. I asked George himself, but there is not even a reservation made in his name. I will have a *moussaka* and Greek salad, I think."

Sara pondered over her wineglass while Jean-Claude made light conversation. Why hadn't Paul come? It was after nine already.

"Sara," Jean-Claude said after another stretch of time. "I think we have been to a red herring."

She smiled dimly at the fractured idiom.

"What if Paul Edgerton—in his anger—made a false list of restaurants, knowing that you will use it...?"

"That would be clever." She took Eric's stolen

list from her purse and started to read the rest of it. Chez Frenzy on Tuesday...Mary's Bar and Grill on Wednesday.... "A rock music supper club and a sandwich place on Santa Monica Boulevard," she said. Her eyes ran down the list. Le Faux Pas and a place called Duck Soup rounded out the week.

When the poisonous flare of her first reaction eased, she started to laugh. "I would have done the same thing. At least we know he has a sense of humor. But he may not expect old Olive to have one, too. She's going to have some fun with Paul's red herring while Eric tracks down the genuine list. Olive is going to give a certain noisy Greek taverna a send-off it doesn't expect." She looked around at the happy crowd. "Give me the menu, garçon!"

After Eric hung up she suddenly felt very much alone in her apartment. The two pages of her column lay before her, carrying her strange lovelorn message for Paul. She wondered, not for the first time, if what she was doing was at all rational. "O what a tangled web we weave, when first we practise to deceive." Until recently that saying had seemed tired and old, but now she saw how frighteningly true it was.

Sara grabbed her coat and left the apartment building. She hadn't taken a long walk since she left Paris, but Los Angeles hadn't been a place that invited leisurely strolls—not like the banks of the Seine, or Montmartre, with the constantly changing array of art displays and the sense of long history underlying everything. In Los Angeles people didn't seem to stroll, they walked briskly, holding onto their purses and packages—or else they ran, dressed in velour exercise suits with designer labels.

But today she needed to walk. Something about the Greek restaurant had awakened her own need to be part of a larger family of human activity. She was becoming stuffy, just as she had accused Paul of being.

She thrust her hands into her pockets and walked from her apartment up toward Sunset Boulevard, then west, aiming her steps into the little breeze that was blowing from the ocean several miles ahead. But mostly she watched the faces of the people who passed her—faces from every part of the world, in every shape and color. She felt as if the phrase *melting pot* was taking on a reality for the first time in her mind. These were the people she wanted to write for. They were the ones that Paul Edgerton wouldn't acknowledge as occupying equal space in his little world. But this *was* the world.

Why couldn't he see that? And how could she ever truly love a man who separated himself from most of the inhabitants of the earth? Did that first Paul Edgerton—the one who roamed the globe and wrote perceptive articles about the very human dilemmas we all face—still exist somewhere?

When she turned the latch of her apartment door again Sara was more distressed than before she'd left. In all the books she had read on romantic love, she had never known a case like hers. There was absolutely no way of living happily ever after with a man whose values were so estranged from hers.

She wasted the rest of the morning staring out the window wondering about that first Paul Edgerton and if they would have fallen easily in love. Once upon a time, they might have, but not now.

ERIC DIDN'T COME AT LUNCHTIME. Sara thought of phoning him and noticed that her red message light was on. She punched the playback button, half expecting to hear Paul's voice—hoping, really, that he had called. Instead, Eric spoke to her in his business voice: "I'm running late for a lunch meeting. I'll send a messenger around before three to get the column. Later—"

A second message followed—a comforting voice she hadn't heard for many months and had almost forgotten the sound of: "Sara, sweetheart, it's papa. Sorry to miss you. We're in Paris, planning to fly in Friday noon on TWA flight 215. Elizabeth's sending her car to meet us. It'll be wonderful to see you. Mother sends her love. Tell Elizabeth not to go to any—"

"Trouble," Sara finished the sentence. The machine had cut off his final word. Dear papa. He was the quiet, easy-going one of the remarkable partnership of Elena Talbot and Jonathon Courtney. He was gentle, tall, and patient to a fault. The stabilizer of his wife's whirring propellers, he always liked to say with a wry smile. Hearing his soft, even voice made Sara wish he were here already, with his arms outstretched to her for a big hug. In the old days she had always looked forward to the time she would spend with them when they returned from a concert tour. Laughter and affection would mark their visits during the few weeks of rest and practice before the next tour.

Oh, papa, she thought urgently, *don't let mother say too much to some newspaper reporter at the airport!* Her mother knew the secret of Olive Gadwall. What if, by some terrible chance, she gave an interview at the airport and in her usual effusive manner blurted out that her dear sweet daughter was writing the Olive Gadwall food column: "...how delightful. We always knew she was creative.... I hear she's in rivalry with some snobbish critic in town...."

Sara could see it all now. Eric would kill her, but only after Paul had consigned her to the lowest regions of hell and the *Chronicle*'s readership had plummeted upon learning that the great war was over and the formidable Olive was only some pianist's daughter.

She picked up her partially read morning paper and saw that Talbot and Courtney were scheduled to perform Saturday night at the Music Center, replacing the much-heralded Russian string quartet, one of whose members had defected in San Francisco a week ago. The quartet's remaining three members were flown home immediately while the defecting cellist was taken to an unnamed place of seclusion. The Los Angeles concerts, whose purpose was to raise money for world hunger, would have been canceled if the piano duo hadn't agreed to perform.

The scheduling decisions were usually papa's, Sara knew. It was like him to help a charity in need. Maybe he had arranged this fill-in concert so that the whole family could be together. She suspected Aunt Elizabeth of writing too freely to them about little Sara's personal situation.

At three o'clock exactly Eric's messenger came to the door to collect her column and handed her a manila envelope. For Your Eyes Only, Eric had written across the face of it. Another bit of spy business.

Inside was a single sheet of paper with the

names of several restaurants and a series of numbers beside each. How very secretive, she smiled to herself. Eric had added a note of his own at the bottom:

> Paul's personal code. It took me all of five minutes to figure it out. He'll be having dinner tonight at the Tinderbox on Las Palmas. Phone in your comments before ten and I'll have them rushed for tomorrow's column. Gung ho!

SARA WENT THROUGH THE MOTIONS of assuming her Olive Gadwall persona. Norma hadn't any other plans for the evening and was delighted to join her. Reservations were made for eight-thirty under the name of Grundy, and Sara tried to forget that there was any problem in her life greater than deciding which entrée to order at the Tinderbox.

She was shivering a little beneath her warm coat as she waited for Norma to bring the car around to the front of the apartment building. The expectation of seeing Paul had made her nerves slip from under her control. Her shivering didn't stop even in the warmth of the car, and she hoped that Norma couldn't feel the vibration on the other side of the bench seat.

"The Tinderbox just reopened," Norma said by way of making conversation. Sara had been silent for the drive into the center of Hollywood. "A couple of the gals at the studio sing here at night.

They don't waitress or anything. They just do a couple of numbers from light opera and such." Norma's pale face lit up with expectation. Sara found herself wishing she could do a few simple makeup tricks on her friend and bring out the pretty woman who had retreated behind Norma's plain facade.

"It's tough for a theater person to get a start in this city," Sara offered. "They all seem to be marking time as waiters and waitresses."

"You'd be amazed how many guys think I can help get them an audition with some bigwig at the studio, just because I work there," Norma said in her pleasant high voice. "It's pathetic. I never know if a guy's asking me out because I'm so nice or he just wants to get in the door."

In the yellowish glow of the streetlights Norma's face had the look of long practice at being disappointed in men.

"Well, we know why the men will be singing at our table tonight," Sara said in an effort to lighten the mood. "They'll be there because we're paying them to sing. Simple as that."

"Damn right," Norma laughed.

SARA WAS WEARING the same disguise and outfit she had worn for her meal at the Greek restaurant, and Norma had made sure that the whole effect came together naturally.

"Miss Grundy," Sara said to the brightly costumed girl at the desk. "Party of two."

Sara's eyes scanned the shadowy stair-stepped

levels of the restaurant. It had once been a theater-in-the-round. A tiny stage was set up at the open end of the horseshoe-shaped room. On the broad curve of the risers were dinner tables, each having a small shaded lamp in the middle. The second show of the evening was about to start.

As the hostess led Sara and Norma down into the theater area Sara strained to locate Paul's table. She didn't dare ask if Mr. Edgerton's party had come in. But she didn't need to.

The hostess stopped at an empty table to seat them and then said in a confiding voice: "See that gentleman over there? That's a famous restaurant critic. The owner's in a stew because the soprano got sick tonight and sent a replacement he doesn't know. We're all on our best behavior. I apologize in advance if you don't get the best service. It's all going to Mr. Edgerton's table."

"You don't think you could find us a table a little closer to Mr. Edgerton's, do you? My friend here is a great admirer of his." Sara put on her best appealing expression. She was debating whether to risk insulting the hostess by pressing a ten dollar bill into her hand.

"No problem, ma'am," the woman replied cheerfully. "Tuesday nights are a little slow, so there's room to choose. Follow me. He's got a table right in the center of things."

"The right table," Sara said, and the hostess laughed at the little joke.

"My boss sure hopes it's the right table. Is this close enough? It's the best I can do."

Norma nodded and they were seated. Sara kept her face away from the light. After she propped up the large menu in front of her she slowly moved herself into a vantage point to observe Paul's table.

Her first surprise was that he seemed to be alone. The second was that the waiter was removing an empty martini glass and replacing it with a full one, leaving a small carafe full for another serving. But Paul wasn't the type to gulp down several drinks before dinner—double martinis at that. The strongest thing Sara had seen him drink was a gin and tonic or a single shot of unblended scotch.

"Well, there he is, in the flesh," Norma said in a whisper from behind her own menu. "Do you think he'll be suspicious?"

Sara watched Paul for a long moment before answering. A sharp contraction in her solar plexus sent a flare of heat up her spine and she felt short of breath. Was he drinking because he was beaten at his own game by a rival food critic? Or was he staring into his glass because he couldn't forget Sara Courtney—couldn't get the thought of her out of his mind?

What if he knew the effect he had on her, how his very touch electrified every nerve in her body. Would he even care, now that she had refused him in so many ways? She watched him and wished with her whole heart that she had accepted his flowers, tried to explain Jean-Claude—anything to make it possible for them to be in each other's arms again. But here they were, not ten feet away from each other, and a million miles apart.

"Sara, I was asking you—do you think he'll guess who you are?"

"Oh, sorry. No. No, I don't think he'll know. He doesn't look well."

Norma screwed her face in disbelief. "What do you mean? He looks terrific. God, Sara, he's the dark, brooding type. They all have those shadowy deep-set eyes and that sexy serious mouth. It has nothing to do with his health. Now, what are we supposed to be eating tonight?"

Sara's table was placed slightly behind Paul's. He would have to turn around to see her, but she could see him very well. She chose from the selection of pasta dishes, not giving her order much thought.

Paul still hadn't had even an appetizer yet and Sara picked at her salad course, wondering what was wrong with him. If some woman had stood him up he was taking it very hard. Or was it the lawsuit?

"Well...?" Norma asked after she had devoured half of Sara's salad as well as her own. "You're staring holes through the poor guy."

"Shh," Sara said. "The show's starting."

The lights in the room dimmed and the stage lights came up, revealing a young man and woman dressed in frontier costumes. The master of ceremonies announced a selection of old Broadway favorites and a small orchestra started the familiar introduction to "Surrey with the Fringe on Top" from *Oklahoma!* It was bright and happy. Sara tried to observe Paul's reaction, but it was too dark.

The singers were excellent and the audience showed its appreciation with enthusiastic applause. The comic song from *Annie Get Your Gun*, "Anything You Can Do, I Can Do Better," got laughs. Sara felt uncomfortable hearing the silly confrontation between the man and woman, each challenging the other. It sounded ridiculous, this battle of the sexes.

Everyone stood to clap at the end of the group of songs. The lights came up again and Sara looked over at Paul's table, but he was gone, an empty glass the only sign that he had been there at all.

"He's just gone to the little boys' room," Norma explained.

"I don't think so. The waiter's clearing the table and setting it again. Paul's gone," Sara said flatly.

"Busy fella. Probably had another date. Don't spin your wheels. Isn't Olive supposed to be rating this place?"

"I'm not very hungry, Norma."

Sara ate only part of her *spaghetti alla marinara*. It was perfectly good food, but she couldn't taste a thing. She begged off having dessert. "I'm sorry, Norma. I'm not good company for you. We'll do it again when I'm feeling more together, okay?"

Norma signaled for the check. "I'm not complaining about a meal I don't have to pay for. It's fine, whatever you want to do. You really look kinda puny. What is it? A flu bug?" Her face drew into wrinkles of concern.

"Maybe," Sara said dully.

As they passed the desk on the way out, a new singing ensemble was beginning a scene from *Kiss Me Kate*. Norma went to retrieve their coats and Sara couldn't resist stealing a fast look at the reservations book. There was Paul's name—reservations for 8:00 for one person. So—his mood had nothing to do with being stood up by a companion. There never had been one in the first place. She felt a mixture of elation and sadness.

Back in her apartment, alone again, Sara picked up her phone to call the night copy editor at the *Chronicle*. "Add this to the column, Jerry," she said, taking a deep breath that was more like a sigh.

The Tinderbox was a delightful place, the singers fresh and talented, and the Italian food honest and enjoyable. The audience was truly entertained—all except one man. Dear Paul, what's wrong? I haven't much heart for the stalking game when the prey looks so sad. Where is the old self-satisfied tilt to the head, that superior curl to the lip? Has romance come into your life, perhaps, and departed again? Every man needs the love of a good woman. I pray you give the sweet lady a chance, whoever she may be. Forgive old Olive for intruding, but I've always told you that I care. *Ciao*.

"That's laying it on a bit thick, isn't it?" Jerry asked.

"Just print it. Eric knows what it's all about."

"Sure, Sara. But it sounds more like the lonely hearts column."

"Pish tush!" she scolded in her Olive Gadwall voice.

A key rattled in the door lock and Jean-Claude burst in, breathless. He swept Sara up into his arms and swung her around in a circle. "*C'est incroyable! Incroyable!* Sigmund Heep is a giant! La Gazelle is good, but L'Intime will be better. I am so happy, Sara!"

Sara looked steadily into his sparkling eyes. "You had a good day, then?" she teased with understatement.

"I had the best day in my life! He likes my way of work and he is teaching me certain refinement of style, but I will allow this because he is a genius like myself! And when L'Intime opens in two weeks I will be in charge under the benevolent supervision of Sigmund Heep. To think—I am here only a few days and I have the opportunity of lifetimes!" He tried to pick Sara up again, but she stopped him.

"There's something else, isn't there?" She was suspicious of a certain glint in his eyes, one that she had seen before.

"How do you tell? Okay—there is a girl. She comes to the kitchen with her *école de cuisine*, and our eyes meet... and—"

"Jean-Claude Roland, listen to me." She put

her hands on her hips. "First things first. No love affairs with little girls in cooking classes for at least two weeks. Please, please, give your full attention to your job. I know how you are."

Jean-Claude looked horrified. "What do you think—I am some kind of idiot?"

"Your heart lights on the nearest tree, just like Lord Byron."

"It is different, this girl. Her name is Dulcie McNatt and she is a serious student of the arts at the university. She is not a silly girl. And she is waiting for me outside. First I have to tell you I need your car a little more longer."

Sara just looked at him. Another impossible male in her life. "Go ahead. Just bring back the car undamaged. And the girl, for that matter. Her father may be large and mean."

The sooner she could arrange something for Jean-Claude in the way of living quarters and car, the better. If he was going to embark on an affair it wasn't going to be in her living room!

CHAPTER SIXTEEN

EARLY THE NEXT MORNING Sara padded to the front door on slippered feet, trying not to wake the sleeping Frenchman on her couch, but she needn't have troubled. She snorted in frustration. Wherever Jean-Claude was, her car was also. How long could this go on?

She retrieved the morning paper from outside her door and pulled out the food and entertainment section. While she poured her first cup of coffee and stirred the cream and sugar into mocha-colored swirls her eyes were rapidly assessing the Consuming Passions column. She wasn't sorry she wrote it.

Sara popped a piece of whole-grain toast into her mouth, chewing as she mulled over the current status of the seige. Paul was probably reading her column right now and planning his nasty retort. She hadn't the least idea what the day would bring.

She waited until she knew Eric would be in his office before she called the *Chronicle*. She had prepared her defense in case he objected to today's column.

"Hey...what's all this lovelorn business?" he

chided offhandedly. He always started genially, then got tougher.

"Just a hunch," she evaded.

"Did you know that the copy editor called me late last night to make sure you hadn't flipped your lid?"

"I'm not surprised. But let me develop this, Eric. I think Paul wasn't expecting Olive to change her tactics. It could be interesting." She was pleased that her voice sounded so professional—so totally opposite to the uncertainty she was feeling.

"Anything you say. You've had the right touch so far. Go with it for a while and see what he does."

"Thanks. Now where's Paul going to be for the rest of the week? I'm no expert on codes."

Eric's easy laugh sounded in her ear. "That's a left brain function—man's realm. Or is it right brain? Anyway, Olive needs to be at the Green Terrace tonight. Thursday's the big one—Cliffside is having its grand opening tomorrow night. Invitation only. Edgerton's going, but not Olive, it seems. I smell a plot. But Bettina Straus is a good sport and she's happy to add Mademoiselle Corinne Thierry to the guest list—that's you—and an escort. I told her you were a free-lance gourmet food writer for a small Paris magazine. We have a chance to scoop Paul on Sunday."

"Did you have an escort in mind?" she asked in an obedient tone.

"That's your domain. He should be able to keep his mouth shut and just smile."

She put down the phone and lifted it again, her fingers quickly tapping the push-button pattern to ring Bill McCormack's law office.

He listened politely while she described her predicament. "I'm writing all this down in my memoirs. Be warned," he joked. "I want my descendants to know what I went through to give a certain journalist a start."

"All heart, Bill," she laughed. "See you tomorrow."

Sara called Aunt Elizabeth next. She had to make sure there wasn't a mixup at the airport Friday and the reporters didn't get her mother talking. It would be awful....

"I was just about to call you, Sara. Isn't it wonderful about the concert?" the old voice raved. "Your father phoned me yesterday. Now tell me, how is Jean-Claude? Did things go well on his first day at La Gazelle?"

"I think they went too well, Aunt Liz—that's the problem. Sigmund Heep thinks he's terrific, the plans are still on for Jean-Claude to be the *chef de cuisine* of the new restaurant. But...."

"What's wrong, dear?"

"Jean-Claude's a hopeless romantic. Worst luck, he met a girl whose cooking class was taking a tour of the kitchen. He stayed out all night with her, and in *my* car. He needs a spanking."

There was silence on the line for a moment. "You can't have a normal life of your own with that young stallion dashing in and out of your apartment at all hours. You need your privacy and he needs his."

"I can't throw him out. He doesn't have enough money for rent, let alone a car, and I haven't saved very much to lend him."

"Of course. He must stay here on the grounds. I have that little gardener's cottage just standing empty at the end of the lane. If he's willing to share his life with a few stray cats he can perch there for a while. I'll see if I can find a ramshackle car somewhere."

"It sounds heavenly."

"I'm a firm believer that a lady needs peace and dignity in order to develop her own personal relationships properly."

Sara hesitated to say more. Aunt Elizabeth had done too much for her already.

"Well..." the dramatic voice prodded. "There's more, isn't there?"

"Is there any way I can stop the press from doing an airport interview with my parents? If mother accidentally says anything about me—about Olive—I'll be in the worst mess! I wish I could pick them up myself, but I'm not sure of my scheduling for Friday yet and Jean-Claude has gone God-knows-where with my car."

"I'll simply go myself with my driver. Don't think any more about it. The secret will be preserved. By the way, how is Paul?" Sara could feel Aunt Elizabeth's canny gaze almost piercing through the receiver.

"Did you see my column this morning?"

"Hmm," she affirmed. "*And* I read between the lines. Don't you think you're treading on rather thin ice, taunting the poor man like that?"

"I didn't think I was taunting him. I... well, I wanted to show his readers that he could be human."

"Is that all it was? What a relief! I was thinking you still carried a torch for the poor dear and were doing some complicated kind of public confession of feeling for him. Young people nowadays do the oddest things in the name of love."

"I don't know if I'd call it love," she said as heat rose to her face.

"Well, it's the damnedest ritual I've ever seen—and I've seen a lot. I've even taken a subscription to Paul's paper, just to follow your peculiar odyssey of discovery. Where will it end, I ask myself?"

"Probably nowhere," Sara said, tensing under the pressure of Aunt Liz's scrutiny. "I don't know...."

"I rather thought you didn't, my dear. Now do be sure to come to supper on Friday. I'll take care that there won't be interviews at the airport. And tell our young French Lothario that I'm arranging living quarters for him as soon as possible. Be of good heart," she said cheerily and rang off.

As soon as she set down the telephone it rang again, startling her. It was Jean-Claude, sounding sheepish.

"I am desolate about your car, Sara," he said. She could visualize his mobile features trying to look desolate. "But the night proceeded longer, and I was with Dulcie in her apartment. And now I am at work at La Gazelle...." His voice lifted on a note of helplessness.

"I'll take a cab to the restaurant," Sara said, trying not to sound forgiving. He needed a lesson before she would tell him that he was being given a free cottage and car.

"I am desolate," he repeated. "I will repay your kindness."

"No need. Just keep your mind on your work."

"I want you to meet Dulcie. She is an angel of heaven. *Never* is there a woman like this!"

"I'll be there for my car within an hour," she said briskly, "and I'll pick you up at the restaurant after work tonight. I'm taking Norma to dinner at the Green Terrace first."

It was only two miles to La Gazelle and Sara decided to walk. The restlessness in her body demanded a release. She bundled up against the cool winds that foretold rain. Her soft light-blue wool coat had been a gift from her parents a year ago, and she loved pulling the sash tightly around her waist and feeling herself wrapped in its protective warmth.

She had gone half a block when she sensed that a car was keeping pace with her, just a little distance back. She turned nervously, calculating what she should do. She wished there were other people on the street at the moment, but there weren't, and the nearest apartment building had a security gate in front. She quickened her steps.

Out of the corner of her eye she saw a metallic flash from the grille. She didn't want to seem afraid. She was sure she could reach the little row of shops at the corner in thirty seconds. She didn't look back a second time, only held tighter to her purse and tried to look purposeful and confident.

She felt the car advancing on her pace, finally pulling into a driveway just in front of her, blocking her path. The passenger window slid down and she looked up to see Paul's face and his white Mercedes. "Hope I didn't frighten you," he called out.

"That was an awful thing to do!" she shouted harshly. "I was about to yell for help." She was shivering uncontrollably.

"Forgive me, Sara. But I had to talk with you and you don't make it easy for me. Won't you get in? I can take you anywhere you're going." His face looked drawn and tired, his eyes almost believably sincere.

She stood watching him, still shivering, her arms crossed rebelliously in front of her. He was being a gentleman after he'd just scared her out of her wits, and she could hardly collect her thoughts for a simple yes or no.

"Sara, listen to me," he said. "I really am sorry. I didn't think—" He leaned over and opened the passenger door for her.

She walked like an automaton toward the car and got in, sitting with her purse planted on her lap, exactly as Olive might do. She couldn't think what to say to him now that he was so close and after everything that had happened between them.

He reached across her to close the door again and the nearness of his body was paralyzing to her. She felt the way people do in nightmares, where everything you could ever want could be yours if you would just reach out and take it... but you can't.

She could only sit and wait for him to speak, while the soft caress of his cologne revived memories. Paul draped an arm over the back of her seat and looked at her for a long moment. "I'm here to tell you, you were right," he said in measured tones. "I've had a lot of time to think about what happened to us the other night."

"Paul," Sara said shakily. "This isn't the best time for me to talk." She was unprepared to answer whatever he had to say. It was difficult enough just to be suddenly with him.

"Then don't say anything, Sara, let me talk." He ran a finger along the line of her throat and touched her lips. "I know I looked like a jealous fool standing at your door with my posies in hand that morning. I have trouble controlling my reactions to things. I don't think I've been jealous before or so thoroughly rejected by a woman in a very long time."

Sara didn't know if she could believe his words. They always came so easily, tuned to the occasion and designed to take him to his goal. She felt his hand on her shoulder, resting as if it was so natural to him.

"Jealousy is an insidious thing. Then everything became clear to me. I had bungled into the reason you had been holding me at arm's length. I was so blind when you kept telling me you had complications in your life, that I didn't for a moment think you might have a current lover."

"I don't—" she started to say, but her voice constricted in her throat.

"You needn't explain," he said. "I won't put you in that position. It was none of my business. But maybe someday there will be a time when you need me. I just wanted to let you know I'll be there for you. And don't worry—there won't be a panting suitor bothering you again until you are free." He straightened up and put the car into reverse. "Now, where do you want me to take you?"

"I don't have a lover," she managed to say. He must have known how condescending and insulting he sounded. Patting her on the head and telling her he forgave her—how generous of him!

He let the engine idle at the curb and turned to smile a doubting smile at her. "Sara, I said it didn't matter any more. I hoped you would see that I understood."

"I don't think you do." If she had to have a confrontation with him she wouldn't be responsible for the outcome. "Did you think I sent you away because of some scruples I had about sleeping with two men at once? Or maybe because I was afraid my lover would find us in flagrante?"

"The thought had occurred, yes." His face was studiedly controlled. "You say you haven't a lover, but I ask you this: If I should come to your door at an early hour will there be a French gentleman preparing your breakfast?" The words had a strained playfulness.

"He isn't my lover."

"Only a very casually dressed cook, then?" His face was looking straight ahead as he drove slowly up the street.

"He's an old and dear friend. I told you; I haven't got a lover."

"And what were we, pray tell?" The old acid was back.

"I don't know.... We were just something that happened," she said, confused.

"Just something between the cognac and a good night's sleep?"

"Please, Paul...I don't understand it yet."

"It was really quite simple, Sara," he said without looking at her. "We found each other attractive and we did what grownups do."

"No, that's not fair!" Her eyes were hot from the angry tears that pressed against them trying to come out. "I don't make casual love to men."

"Oh?" She saw his eyebrows rise slightly. "You were a virgin, Miss Courtney? Was I going to be the first?"

"What we had could have been something special, but it ended up badly."

"And whose fault was that?" he bit back.

"Nobody's. All I know is that it wasn't right.... It wasn't the way it should be."

"That's a funny way to descibe it, m'dear. It was your idea to make it end when it did. Or is that a complaint about my technique? I've been told I'm rather good."

Sara's temper rioted out of control. "You're revolting! It has nothing to do with technique.... It has everything to do with honest caring."

"Since when are you giving lectures on honesty and virtue?" he returned nastily.

"Paul—stop the car! I'd rather walk. And this time, please don't think you have more things to say to me. I haven't the strength!"

He braked hard and she had the door open before the car had come to a full stop. She had to get away from him before she started crying, because once the tears started she didn't know if she could ever stop them. "One more thing," Sara said with whispered intensity as she left the car, "if you ever again want a woman who has a mind of her own and doesn't rush into your magnificent shadow, do her the courtesy of respecting her. Give yourself the rare experience of viewing a female as an equal."

She turned back to her apartment and didn't look to see if the white Mercedes was following. She knew it wasn't.

She could barely see the telephone book to find a cab company's number. "Damn you, Paul Edgerton! Why do you ruin things for yourself?"

She ordered a cab, then spent the next twenty minutes mentally rewriting the script that they had both acted out so stupidly in Paul's car. Maybe he was always so volatile, so quick to attack when he felt threatened. Until he changed there was no way on earth they could ever have anything more than purely sexual encounters—and that she would never allow.

She knew of couples who were compatible in bed but fought like demons the rest of the time. She had tried to explain her fears to Paul. But he hadn't understood.

Sara collected her car from Jean-Claude, who looked as if he hadn't slept for a long time. She didn't want to hear his apologies again and told him she'd come for him at ten. He was dying to tell her all about the heavenly Dulcie, but the subject of lovers made her queasy.

She aimed the car in the direction of the foothills above Pasadena, northeast of the central Los Angeles area. Driving along the Angeles Crest Highway, maneuvering the curves and sharp switchbacks, she allowed her eyes to wander toward a horizon studded with pine trees and tall native California holly. Everywhere she looked was green, freshly washed from recent rains. The pungent smell of pine sap hung in the misty droplets.

After an hour of driving she was high enough to see patches of old snow here and there in the sunless crevices of the canyons. The air was cold and penetrating—exactly what Sara was seeking in her flight from the murky mess she had made of a simple affair with a man.

But maybe there was no such thing as a "simple affair." What if fiction and fairy tales had made it only seem so? She parked near the summit of Mt. Wilson and looked out over the cloud layer that covered the cities below.

It was starting to grow dark down in the Los

Angeles basin. She watched as the sun began its long descent into the western sea. Sara's appetite was nonexistent and the very thought of putting on a disguise and going to the Green Terrace for dinner was repugnant to her. She had never defied Eric, but this time she had to. The gourmet game had soured in her mind, at least for now.

She wanted to be finished with Olive's campaign to reform the man from The Right Table—a desire she knew was like a surgeon wanting to stop removing an infected appendix halfway through the operation. She and Paul had a lot to resolve before they were fit company for each other.

The drive back to reality was slow, giving Sara time to fill her lungs with the healing fragrances of the wild spring herbs that grew along the road.

The first thing she saw when she returned to her dark apartment was the red glow of her telephone machine. She was considering disconnecting it for good. It would be just as well for her to miss some calls. She played back her messages with a resigned clench of her jaw.

"Sara," the low voice said. "It's Paul. I don't want you to return the call, just know that I had no intention of upsetting you today. Edgertons have never been cads, believe it or not. Maybe we can meet for a civilized drink and start fresh."

Sara looked for a long time at the little silent machine, wondering if a civilized drink with Paul would solve anything. That was so much like his pattern of thought. To her mind a good cup of strong, black coffee might lead to more sensible discussion. But neither choice was an option. She had already told him what he could do to make himself decent company for women.

Jean-Claude was floating on a romantic cloud when she picked him up outside La Gazelle. "Don't tell me—you're in love for the first time," she chided him and his silly facial expression.

"*Absolument!* And she loves me. This time it is not like other women. I am to marry Dulcie McNatt!"

"After one night," she said skeptically.

"It was eternity! We stay awake all the night trying to think how to be together and not separated. Her father gives small money for her sharing an apartment with three girls, and I am imposing my presence on your living room sofa." He shrugged his shoulders dramatically. "One does not commence a love affair in circumstances of this sort."

"And now you feel doomed to celibacy...."

"I will work harder than ever in my life to make money for a place for us. She will finish her studies in two months and her father wants her to return to Wyoming—a place of desolation for a beautiful girl. She cannot be an artistic spirit in the wilderness of wild West." He was genuinely unhappy and Sara couldn't hold back her good news any longer.

"What if I told you that Aunt Elizabeth has offered you her gardener's cottage until you can afford a place of your own? It has a separate entrance from the lane at the rear of the property. You seem to have a ready-made lovers' nest."

"I would think to be in paradise! It is truly? *Tante* Elizabeth has made such an offer?"

Sara nodded, happy that her dear, emotional friend was ecstatically in love. "You'll have to do a little cleaning out. There are some cats who live there, too...."

"I will be Hercule, who cleaned the stables of Augeias!" He threw his arms around Sara, hindering her view of the road.

"Stop," she gasped. "Aunt Liz is also trying to find you an old car. But I want to know what's going on at the restaurant. What does Sigmund Heep think of his bleary-eyed new chef? It's a wonder you didn't cut your fingers off with a sharp knife, in your condition."

"Ahh, but I know to separate my genius from my romantic heart. Sigmund is a strange man—a tyrant, but he only wants the best food for his kitchen."

"And L'Intime?" Sara wanted to keep his attention focused.

"There is just one little problem, but I make it clear with Sigmund."

"And...?"

"I will tell you when we are comfortable in your living room," he hedged, and Sara didn't press him.

When Jean-Claude had poured himself a glass of sweet vermouth and found a comfortable position on the couch he looked up at Sara's inquiring face and finished his news.

"Two weeks after we open L'Intime we will have a grand opening."

"That's customary," she said.

"Sure. But he is inviting Paul Edgerton to criticize my cooking. What do you think, Sara—I will cook exquisite food for this man who wish me dead, and he will then ask to meet the great new chef... and my reputation will be a ruin before I am starting. He will cut me in small pieces in his newspaper."

"*That's* your little problem?" Sara marveled at the understatement.

"*Oui*, but it is okay now." His eyes twinkled with mischief. "I just tell Sigmund that Paul Edgerton once found me in the apartment of a beautiful lady of his, with very little clothing on my person, and if Paul Edgerton recognizes me it will be the end of everything."

"I suppose Sigmund thought that was funny." She cringed at the thought of sounding like an easy woman playing two men off against each other. "You didn't mention my name, I hope."

"Madame," he said, placing his hand over his heart. "I do not play with the honor of a lady. Sigmund tells me to grow a moustache very fast and keep my chef hat on my head. He has had experience of this delicate sort of affair himself. And now, my dearest friend, I must ask one more time for your car and I promise to bring it to you before morning."

"Dulcie is waiting?"

"We will be married before two months. Remember I have said this!" He caught the keys as Sara threw them, and he disappeared out the door.

CHAPTER SEVENTEEN

JEAN-CLAUDE WAS true to his word. When Sara woke early and dressed to buy a copy of the *Tribune* at the corner market, loud rolling snores were vibrating from beneath the bedclothes on the sofa. Sara caught a fleeting drift of perfume as she walked through the living room. Cinnabar, she decided, and felt she was beginning to know something about the amazing Dulcie McNatt.

She couldn't wait until she got back to the apartment to start reading Paul's Thursday column. She stood next to the newspaper vending machine and pulled apart the paper as fast as her chilled hands could go. Her eyes read quickly past the other lead articles and stopped, fascinated, at The Right Table.

Open letter to hapless old maids who have nothing better to do than offer gratuitous advice to men of the world: The condition of my heart seems to concern you, but that may be because the shriveled organ that passes for your own has had so little to stir it. I find that sad, my dear Miss Gadwall. Whatever you may think of Paul Edgerton, pray do not worry about his love life. Perhaps it is yours that needs tending. Stop by my table some night when you are studying my plate and allow a true gentleman to set your heart a- flutter. Then return to your chilly garret and write that I have no knowledge of real life. In my prayers I beg the Creator to give you some small joy before you go to that great common table in the sky, old thing.

He said nothing about the Tinderbox. The rest of his column was a list of the best California wines of the year.

> There is no restaurant review today, but next week I will have a full assessment of a marvelous new establishment in town—Cliffside. Cheers.

Prickly as ever, Sara thought. Unrepentant. She had hit a nerve, she was sure of it. To devote his entire column to a rebuttal of Olive's plea for more humanity was a victory for her. She was flushing him out into the open, forcing him to show to the world that he could be flustered—even forcing him to forgo a restaurant critique. Paul Edgerton was on the run.

She prodded Jean-Claude's inert body when she returned to the apartment. "It's already eight-thirty."

"I will soon die of love and no sleep," he murmured from beneath the pile of blankets.

"Would you rather have Sigmund Heep finish you off with a cleaver?" she threatened.

While he stood under the hard spray of the shower, Sara reviewed her disguises for the day's masquerade. Cliffside was a place that would test her fear of heights. She had seen it once or twice during construction. Its name was apt, since it sat on high stilts, jutting out of an almost vertical hill along Coldwater Canyon. The view over the San Fernando Valley and beyond would be spectacular.

It would be the kind of place where a lady could wear a veil and look terribly *soignée*, according to the preview hints that had been leaked to Los Angeles Magazine. Paul wouldn't think to find Olive there in a black silk suit and gloves. Norma's black page boy wig—one that Sara thought made her look like Theda Bara—would be perfect with her cloche hat. And just a little extra rubber tilt to the nose. Very twenties and chic. She wished Eric could be there to see her. He loved intrigue—the mysterious mademoiselle, and all that.

Jean-Claude pulled himself together with the speed of light and pocketed her keys. Sara said *adieu* to her little car once more, hoping that Jean-Claude wouldn't be arrested before he could get a proper license. She wasn't sure her insurance covered visiting aliens without work permits who hadn't taken the time to see to the little legalities of life in the United States.

She looked up absentmindedly at her Alma-Tadema painting over the mantel. The Greek woman still gazed out over the deep-blue sea, waiting.

And the veiled statue of the sybil still held its secret. The glance threw Sara's pulse out of rhythm for a moment with the memory of that strange, vivid dream. She could still feel the dream man's touch on her body.

She drew a long full breath to come back to normal. Real life wasn't like that, she reminded herself. It should be, but it wasn't.

And real life included housecleaning, something that she had neglected for too long. Her mother never noticed things like that, but Sara had a vestige of pride anyway. She spent the day at a leisurely pace cleaning, dusting, and rearranging her apartment. She had turned over part of her closet to Jean-Claude reluctantly, aware that that gesture made him seem more permanent here than she desired. But she had to get his things out of sight and not draped over chairs as they had been since he arrived.

She started her transformation into Corinne Thierry early, becoming by degrees a stranger to her mirror. By 7:30 she was a symphony in black—the silk suit, hat and veil, gloves, evening sandals and sheer stockings, not to mention the wig. Her lips were vibrant red, her eyes exaggerated with kohl.

When Bill stood in her doorway he just stared. "Well, I'll be damned!" he said.

"Monsieur McCormack? Aimez-vous votre demoiselle de compagnie?"

"Whatever you said, I'll follow you anywhere," he grinned.

"I asked if you approved of your female companion tonight?"

"If I didn't think your disguise would come off in my hands I'd like to touch the goods."

"Typical chauvinist pig," she laughed. "Anyway, most of it's real. Norma just taught me some tricks."

Bill was agreeable to being the silent date. In fact, he was enjoying the idea of watching Sara play the role of Parisienne at the exclusive gathering. "I'm trying not to be hurt that Bettina didn't include me on her guest list."

"Don't feel alone, Bill. Olive didn't make it, either. And I think I know why."

"Edgerton?"

She nodded and adjusted her veil so that she could move her lips without brushing against it. "He's losing his grip, Bill. He's actually afraid Olive will dog his steps and make him look silly. At least he'll be feeling safe at Cliffside."

"Corinne Thierry, was it?" Bill reminded himself.

CLIFFSIDE CAME INTO VIEW as they rounded a hairpin turn on Coldwater Canyon. Its high plateglass walls and cantilevered decking were strung with tiny white lights that made the restaurant appear to be floating on air. Sara shuddered. Her vertigo wasn't a joke. If she enjoyed liquor more, this place would tempt her to have a steadying drink of something strong.

The cars were being whisked away by attendants

to unseen side roads and Sara and Bill entered Cliffside, to be discreetly questioned and approved of before being allowed to penetrate the interior. Mademoiselle Thierry and escort were expected.

Cocktail waiters appeared immediately to take orders and Sara ordered a lime and tonic, speaking slowly in French to be sure he understood her. With her highball glass securely in hand she felt prepared to explore the restaurant. Bill tagged along mutely beside her as she chattered to him in French about the decor and the crowd.

Cliffside was dimly lit, which made the view out the huge windows all the more stunning. Millions of lights flickered in the blowing night air below.

She left Bill at the bar so he could have some fun and walked slowly through the crowded room. Men gave her second looks, which she returned with a boldness new to her. She soon realized that there was no danger of Bettina or anyone else exposing her identity, since this "exclusive" opening night was packed with people and the darkness of the room prevented visibility for more than a few feet.

It was inevitable that she would bump into Paul, nonetheless. It seemed fated to happen, even in this crowd. Sara felt she could cope with it tonight. He would be on his best behavior in this setting. She wondered how many of the sleek females here had been flattered by his attention and thought they were being made love to by a prince of a man who thought they were extraordinary.

She stopped the bitter train of her thoughts and

tried to think like a restaurant critic. She jotted some notes in French on her small memo book, trying to do a fair assessment of the decor without her own jaundiced state of mind intruding. In the press of the cocktail crowd she had a hard time holding her pen steady. A slight jostling against her elbow stopped her writing completely. She put her note pad away again and when she looked up she was face to face with Paul.

"Well, hello," he smiled. She started to move away with only a brief, polite acknowledgment, but he kept his eyes on hers. "I don't think we've met. I'm Paul Edgerton." He quickly shifted his glass to his left hand and reached out to take hers.

She gave him a gloved hand. "Corinne Thierry," she said briskly. *"Je ne parle pas—"*

"And I'm terrible at French. I'm sorry." He stood looking down at her with a helpless but charmingly masculine expression. Oddly, she didn't have her usual physical response to him. Instead, she was annoyed by the way he held her captured hand and spoke very carefully. "I... *je suis un journaliste. Le... le Tribune."*

"Un journaliste?" She smiled mysteriously from behind her protective black veil. A plan was percolating in her busy brain. It was too tempting... *"Ahh! Vous êtes un correspondant international? Un journaliste sérieux? J'adore les journalistes sérieux!"*

He hesitated a little. "A serious journalist? Well, in a way, yes. *Oui. Les restaurants, la cuisine, les vins...."*

She frowned in disappointment. *"Quelle dommage,"* she said sadly, then removed her hand neatly from his and walked away.

Paul may not have been able to translate "quelle dommage" into "what a pity," but he could read the look on her face. Her entire body language had just told him that she found him unworthy of serious conversation. It was a new experience for him. Sara started back toward the bar where Bill was being congenial. She sampled the hors d'oeuvres on his little plate, still feeling the exhilaration from her meeting with Paul—a secret satisfaction. *"Délicieux,"* she said.

"I thought they were pretty good, myself. Also, I've seen a couple of my old buddies from the Bachelors who're ready to pay me handsomely for your phone number. I told them you were hopping the first plane to Paris in the morning. Just nod your head if you're getting a kick out of knocking 'em dead in your gorgeous getup."

She nodded, smiling, then leaned close to his ear to whisper. "If sexy veils and languid eyes are what all men react to, then the nice girls of the world are going to a lot of trouble for nothing."

"It's the nice ones they bring home to mama."

"And keep a little on the side." She thought of Paul's proper brother Edward, as Aunt Elizabeth had described him, with his acceptable wife and the mistresses for his pleasure. "Just another Edgerton family tradition," she thought aloud.

"You talked to Edgerton already? Did he give

you a hard time?" Bill put a protective arm around her waist.

"I think I gave him something more to think about," she said, her eyes straining to find the tall man above the crowd.

Instead of a formal restaurant dinner the head chef and his associates had arranged two lavish buffet tables along both sides of the room. The tables were covered with elaborately decorated trays of representative dishes from the regular menu. There were fourteen entrées, five soups, a variety of salads and vegetable marinades. The wines and desserts would be served individually at the tables.

Sara and Bill took small portions of a number of dishes and retired to a table for two just back from the high windows and the unnerving sheer drop to the canyon floor. Sara knew that many eyes had followed her and she was certain that Paul was aware of her.

She ate heartily, tasting Bill's assortment of entrées and drinking more wine than was usual for her.

"Something really loosened you up, kid," Bill said under his breath as she held out her empty glass to try the next type of wine. "I think I was more comfortable with the old Sara. I didn't feel like I was defending a camp against invasion from every direction. Frankly, I feel tense." He was smiling, but Sara knew what he meant.

"I'll behave," she whispered. "And, Bill— you're a very good sport."

"Yeah," he said, casting a defensive eye around him at the various men who were watching Sara.

She didn't look around for Paul as they left. It was part of her new attitude. She had come here to do a job and she had done it. Along the way she had confirmed what she had suspected but not let herself believe: Paul's male ego was so hungry for attention that it would be practically impossible for him to make a commitment to one woman.

She asked Bill in for coffee, but found her apartment in confusion. Jean-Claude was packing his clothes. Her own closet was being emptied of his things by a strange female, and Bill said he thought he'd better say good-night.

Jean-Claude gave her a kiss and put up his hands in horror. "This *is* my Sara, is it not?"

"Just what is going on?" she managed to say as the front door closed behind Bill's departing back.

"*Tante* Elizabeth says she has worked all the day to make my new home prepared. I have only to come with my possessions."

"And this must be Dulcie," she said. The young woman with the short brown hair and large brown eyes stopped at the doorway to the bedroom, her arms loaded with Jean-Claude's clothing. She put out a struggling hand and took Sara's.

"I hope you don't mind..." she said, realizing how it must have looked to Sara.

"Do you need a ride to Bel Air?" She was tired but willing.

"The Rolls-Royce is coming soon for us from *tante* Elizabeth."

"Isn't that wonderful?" Dulcie enthused. "My stuff is in your car and we just have to move it to the Rolls."

"We are pledged to one another," Jean-Claude said proudly, putting a loving arm around Dulcie's shoulder.

"You're *both* going to move in?"

Dulcie's young pretty face and delicately formed body managed to seem dignified as she looked lovingly at Jean-Claude. "We don't need more time to be certain of our commitment. We're sure this is it."

Sara leaned to give them both a kiss as they sailed out of her apartment in answer to the sound of a horn outside. "Wish us luck!" Dulcie called back.

Suddenly, the apartment was very quiet. The only evidence that Jean-Claude had ever been there was the stock of good food in her refrigerator, including two bottles of French wine. The thought of wine wasn't appealing at all right now. Her only real acquaintance with it was as an adjunct to cooking, and tonight's little splurge had left her feeling a bit odd in the stomach.

She could hardly wait to rid herself of the French disguise and wash the heavy black eye makeup from her face. No doubt Jean-Claude was explaining to his Dulcie that the woman she met tonight wasn't exactly Sara Courtney.

Propped up comfortably in bed with her down pillows and a comforter, Sara thought about her article on Cliffside. Should she reveal to her esteemed rival that he shook her hand and even had a passing conversation with the dreaded bourgeois writer? She decided not to. Instead, she would ignore her opponent completely and do a straight review of the new restaurant. Paul could wonder how she managed to penetrate the exclusive affair. He might even recall his strange encounter with the exotic Frenchwoman. But he would certainly put a closer guard on his secret restaurant lists from now on.

FRIDAY MORNING Sara's phone rang early. She awoke with a groan. Paul's presence was still with her from the disjointed dreams that had haunted her night. The phone rang for a second time and she reached over to answer it.

Eric's brisk voice said, "Hi—you can't be asleep, you owe me two stories. Up, up, up!"

"People have been killed for less than that," she grumbled.

His voice changed. "What's the matter? Did you see the grand Edgerton at last night's bash?"

"Yes, all dashing six feet of him. I even talked with him."

"Good God! He didn't catch on, did he?"

"I was very French and very disdainful. He was too busy trying to salvage his pride to wonder who was watching him from under the black veil."

"I suppose you rubbed his patrician nose in it for your column," he said hopefully.

"I decided not to, Eric. I'd rather he thought some about the brief encounter with the Frenchwoman who didn't approve of his kind of journalism. I'm writing this one differently—serious and dignified. If he wants to play the fool, let him. Olive won't even bother to notice that he was there."

"Well, okay." Then, after a pause he said, "what about the Green Terrace Wednesday night?"

"I didn't go, Eric. I'm truly sorry, but I felt... ill all afternoon and I just couldn't force myself to see Paul again so soon."

"So soon?" Eric was barely containing his curiosity.

"We had a nasty confrontation Wednesday morning. It was personal—"

"Look, Sara, old Eric wasn't born yesterday, and I've got a lot invested in this whole Olive Gadwall business...."

She sighed heavily. "I'm handling it, Eric, that's all I can say."

"I'm not experienced enough to give advice at this late stage, but I wish you'd gone to the Green Terrace. My source tells me that Edgerton was unimpressed with it and is going to tell his readers it's just the kind of deadly dull place Olive Gadwall would enjoy."

Sara's eyes opened fully for the first time and she sat up in bed. "At least he's using me as a comparison."

"Judging by our mail, Olive has inspired a lot of timid people to venture out into the world of restaurant sampling. Edgerton may have the four hundred on his side, but, by damn, you've got the four million!"

Sara was feeling better. "I don't know when I'll be able to get to the Green Terrace. My parents are coming in a few hours, and I'll be tied up through the weekend."

"Sorry, kid, we've got to get you to the Green Terrace before Sunday. I'll have my secretary make reservations for lunch today. Paul won't be there, so we can be ourselves, right?"

"But Eric, I wanted to go with Aunt Elizabeth at noon to pick up my parents at the airport."

"Don't disappoint me, Sara. Elizabeth can do the honors."

"One more thing though...."

"What's that?"

"After Paul reads my story on Cliffside we'll have to find some new way to discover his eating plans."

"Right. I'm hoping for some kind of public surrender soon. I think the guy's about to break."

"He's got a long line of very blue blood behind him, Eric. Don't count on Boston surrendering too soon."

CHAPTER EIGHTEEN

AFTER ERIC'S PHONE CALL Sara stayed in bed just long enough to do a mental inventory of her wardrobe and the long day ahead of her. Lunch with Eric would fade into the press conference at the hotel, which gave little time before Aunt Liz's dinner and reception.

One of her old standbys was her plum-colored Chanel-style knit suit. It would take her through the day and into the evening if she wore it with her soft-pink ruffled chiffon blouse and single string of pearls. She always felt confidently well dressed when she completed the outfit with matching plum bag and high-heeled pumps and kid gloves. Conservative, but feminine. She had worn this ensemble for her first interview with Eric.

She washed her hair and did her nails, feeling acutely that there was unfinished business in her life. She could get dressed up and go to functions and have men compliment her, but she would always feel that it was an empty exercise. There was something so basic in her need for Paul, and just avoiding him wasn't going to cure it. Someday, somewhere, they *had* to meet again...they *had* to look into each other's eyes and say exactly what was in their hearts.

Until that moment she would have this painful stirring of desire, this need to feel his body pressed close to hers. But now was a time to stay clearheaded. There was a full day ahead of her, which would need all her energy and focus. She looked forward to being with her father and mother again after so many months.

Her hair was brushed into a soft French fold at the back of her head and small curls escaped over her ears. Stress had made her eyes seem larger than usual, almost dreamy, and she admitted to herself that she looked very attractive, as well as intelligent. She recalled how Paul's face had looked the first time they met, at the Indian restaurant—the appreciative glance, the masculine response... and her own involuntary physical sensations when he took her hand.

A shudder of remembered pleasure went through her as she looked in the mirror. Paul had looked at her last night, too, and given an appreciative glance—his programmed reaction to a goodlooking woman. Or was there something in her eyes that drew it from him, even when she was masquerading as someone else?

"Intellectualizing and hoping again," she said to the mirrored face. She snapped her purse shut and left to meet Eric.

Eric was waiting for her at an excellent table, drinking a glass of mineral water. The Green Terrace was a stunning version of the popular plant-laden restaurants that were in every big city. Small paths wound around tables set on flagstone. Flower borders and great tubs of trees and shrubs made a friendly forest out of the high-ceilinged, skylighted room. The garden ambiance allowed one to forget the busy boulevard and traffic jams just outside the walls.

Eric greeted Sara with a silent wolf whistle and handed her a menu. "I like the place already," he said cheerily.

Sara looked around and saw quite a few tables of well-dressed women, and many groups of men in business suits having their executive lunches of large salads and omelettes. The Green Terrace, Eric reminded her, was close to the financial area of Century City.

Sara ordered a salad of marinated cooked vegetables surrounding an avocado half, which was stuffed with a mixture of cooked rice and shrimp. Eric had an appetite for something more filling, settling on a casserole of salmon and scallops in wine sauce with shallots. They were given a separate bread menu and chose a loaf of rosemary bread, an Italian regional specialty.

The bread came first, hot and crusty in a napkin-lined basket, exuding an aroma that activated Sara's indifferent appetite. Eric wanted a glass of white wine, and Sara ordered tea.

She was pleased with her salad. The creamy garlic dressing carried a flavor that took her back to happy times in France when she and Jean-Claude had nothing better to do than try to outdo one another in their experimental cooking.

Eric was enjoying his casserole with hungry concentration, and the plump round loaf of bread disappeared quickly. "Whew!" he said, picking up a last stray crumb from the bread basket. "Paul was right about this place, Sara. Olive just can't help liking it, don't you think?"

"Of course she'll like it. When I'm done with the mouth-watering descriptions people will be standing in line just to catch a whiff of the fresh-baked breads."

"Paul is going to look pretty pale with his tired old prose. If he's smart he'll read Olive's Sunday column and rewrite his own for Thursday. Either way, you'll win," he chuckled.

"Winning isn't everything," she said quickly, and then regretted it because she saw Eric's keen inquisitive eyes perk up.

"Listen, young lady...there's nothing wrong with what you're doing as Olive Gadwall—not a thing. It's seat-of-the-pants journalism and everyone enjoys it. The world's too sober as it is."

"Just don't nominate me for a Pulitzer Prize," she smiled.

He looked over at the dessert cart, which the waiter was wheeling up to the table. "What about some of this chocolate cake and maybe a blueberry cream tart?" He signaled his choices. Sara sipped her tea and tried the blueberries.

Eric put a friendly hand on hers. "I can see that Paul's loaded with brooding charm. But he's not exactly a happy man. Guys like that can drag a girl down with them."

Sara looked down at her hands. "He really

should be doing hard news, foreign affairs... human interest stories."

"It's hard to think of him doing human interest. You're sure you've got the same man?"

"Just look in the old *Chronicle* files, Eric. He used to be so different—years ago."

"Ahh," he said. "Woman, the healer of male souls. That's a losing fight, Sara. You can't bring him back to himself if he won't cooperate. Is that what this is all about?"

She just stared at her hands. "I know he's a better person than the one who writes those columns...."

"Hello there, Eric!" A portly, middle-aged man with a grandfatherly face and wide-awake eyes was holding out his hand to Eric.

"George—good to see you!" Eric rose quickly to shake hands. "Sara, may I introduce you to the editor-in-chief of the Los Angeles *Tribune*, George Strickland. This, sir, is Sara Courtney. She's the goddaughter of Elizabeth de Lacy. Her father is Jonathon Courtney."

"Delighted," he said. "Elizabeth is an old friend and I've had the pleasure of hearing your parents in concert many times. I hear they're arriving today."

"Yes, I'm joining them in an hour." She smiled up at the perceptive eyes of Paul's boss. "I've enjoyed reading your paper in the few months since I've moved here from Paris."

"That's the spirit. Don't bother with that rag Eric works for." He gave a rich laugh and clapped Eric on the shoulder.

"I have to keep up with the food fight your restaurant critics are having. It's really amusing," she said.

"For the time being, Miss Courtney. My restaurant columnist is about to blow the food fight wide open. Watch for it."

"George likes to tease me," Eric winked at Sara.

"No, really. Paul's got something up his sleeve that he wants to spring on Olive Gadwall. He isn't an easy man to know lately, I must admit, but we can enjoy our strange journalistic feud for a little longer I think, before it burns out."

Someone called out to him and George Strickland left, sending greetings to Elizabeth and shaking Eric's hand again. On that note Eric paid the bill, gave Sara a peck of a kiss and sent her on her way. "Don't let George spook you. He's just trying to make me nervous. Crafty as a fox."

DRIVING OUT to the posh Beverly Wilshire Hotel, Sara began to write her column mentally. She wasn't going to be put on the defensive. Paul could plot his strategies, it wouldn't change what she had to say to him in print.

What could possibly account for the long line-ups for a table at the Green Terrace? she planned to ask Paul. *Don't take my word for it, but ask the many well-dressed men and women what drew them to this lovely establishment. I'd wager it was the food first and foremost—the too-tempting breads, the too-good desserts. It doesn't require a snob to detect the fine preparation and imagination that is lovingly blended into the dishes here. In fact, a snob might miss half the fun by searching too hard for the elegant and overlooking the simply delicious. Ta ta!*

It was three o'clock when she reached the hotel, and found that her parents hadn't checked in yet. Thinking that the plane must have been delayed, Sara inquired at the desk if she could find a typewriter and a quiet place for a few minutes. She hurriedly sketched out her review before she forgot the words. By that time she caught a glimpse of activity in the lobby and rushed to be folded into her parents' arms.

Tanned from two weeks in the Rome sun before their final performances in Paris, they were as energetic and magnetic as ever. Sara almost wept with delight as she looked into her father's reassuring face, grinning at her while her mother's very blue eyes brimmed over with happy tears. Aunt Elizabeth orchestrated the luggage and got everyone up to the beautifully decorated suite of rooms.

"Don't forget. Press conference downstairs at four-thirty, then my house for dinner at six. I want to get both of you home and asleep early tonight. Elena, why don't you lie down while you talk to Sara?" Elizabeth suggested, before letting herself out of the suite quietly.

"Elizabeth tells us Jean-Claude is here and is about to launch a career," her father called back from the large dressing room where he was unpacking. He stood a full foot taller than her mother, with a handsome head of light-auburn waves, his genetic gift to Sara.

Her mother bounced tentatively on the bed to test its softness, then drew a comforter up over herself and laughed a tinkling laugh. "You and Jean-Claude had to come halfway around the world to find your careers. I find that poetic somehow." She reached her hand out for Sara's. "Sit beside me, darling, and tell me why you're so terribly nervous about our saying something personal to the press. Elizabeth thinks you're falling in love with somebody, is that true?"

"She mustn't have explained my problem very well, mother."

"Yes she did," her father chuckled. "Mother just wants to hear it all over again. It feeds her romantic sensibilities."

"Your poor man must be beside himself with irritation," Elena Talbot said.

"It'll be nothing compared to what he'll be thinking if he discovers who Olive Gadwall really is. Aunt Elizabeth is a dear, but she's living back at the turn of the century in male-female matters."

"She says the gentleman is very attractive. What a delicious little stew you must be in."

"It's just a publicity campaign, and it won't go on long."

"And Jacques? Do you ever hear from him? You didn't write us about him, so we assumed it was over." Her mother's clear-blue eyes looked eager to absorb every bit of information about Sara.

"Jacques has gone on to his next excitement."

"Elena," her father called good-naturedly. "We'll have time for all that later."

"Thanks, papa," Sara mimed silently. He understood.

Sara slipped out to let her parents unwind. The hotel had arranged a meeting room for the press conference and Sara browsed in the little art and fine-clothing shops until the reporters and camera crews arrived. When they did, Sara tried to blend into the crowd.

Jonathon Courtney was a master at handling the press. He projected a friendliness that kept journalists from asking too-sharp questions. With him in control it was more like a get-together of old cronies who loved music. It was so comfortable, in fact, that Sara thought the press conference would never end. She signaled her mother that it was growing late, and her mother in turn smiled winningly at the ladies and gentlemen of the media, announcing they had another engagement and were leaving.

They just had time to get to Bel Air by six o'clock and be welcomed by Aunt Elizabeth into her garden room for a candlelit family supper.

The house was decorated with roses from the garden and the special greenhouse. Gregory was doing his duties as butler and bartender and Marie hovered welcomingly over a buffet table spread with a large assortment of delicacies.

Sara's parents were being embraced by a steady stream of old friends. Sara left the receiving line to find Eric, who had come in earlier and was circulating already. She hoped to avoid a long-winded chat with old family friend Anton Saolescu tonight and depart early. Aunt Elizabeth's chauffeur would drive her parents back to the hotel.

Elizabeth de Lacy floated by, in a long mauve-silk at-home gown, enhanced by her usual red rose. She gave Sara a light tap in passing. "I forgot to tell you, dear, I've invited Paul. He did so wish to meet them...."

For a moment Sara stood alone, aware of a sinking spot in her stomach. She might be able to handle having Paul here—she'd come a long way since her earlier indecisiveness—but Paul and her mother talking to each other.... It could be terrible! Her mother was famous for her unscheduled remarks anyway, and with all the tittering from Aunt Elizbeth, Elena Talbot might just think it was sweet to bring Sara and Paul together. A cold sweat began in her hands. She had to get close to her parents and stay there.

Moving through the crowd was a wearisome process. People spoke to her and she had to answer. She found Eric. "Aunt Liz invited Paul," she said under her breath. "Be a friend and head him off. I've got to stay by my parents."

"Too late," he said, turning to take Paul's extended hand.

"I expected to run into Sara," Paul said

smoothly, "but you're a surprise, Eric." He gestured with his cocktail glass at both of them.

"Why is that, old boy?" Eric struck an urbane pose to match Paul's. "Don't *Chronicle* editors belong on the social circuit?"

"I was hoping to find Sara alone, frankly, and not in a tête-à-tête with her literary mentor."

"I'm not sure I like your tone," Eric bristled and moved a protective arm around Sara's waist. "Back off, Edgerton."

Sara watched the tension escalate quickly between the two men. She looked defiantly at Paul. "Please, Paul. I told you we didn't have anything more to say to each other, and certainly not tonight." Just being close to him made tremors start in her body. "I've got to be with my parents now, so please excuse me."

As she walked away she heard Paul's voice say acidly to Eric, "I've come to expect this from the lady...." Eric's reply was lost to her. Sara was seething with irritation. Paul acted as if she should apologize to him for having a normal life apart from him. She wouldn't stand for it. She wouldn't be bullied.

She hurried to find her mother and father and shake off the emotions Paul had stirred in her again. *Would it always be this way between them?* She didn't know if she could live with this unresolved and frustrated pain inside her. Perversely, she hoped that Eric was giving Paul a dose of his own medicine—two men who could spar equally well with each other.

Sara stood unobtrusively on the edge of her parents' animated circle. The receiving line had dissolved into informality and moved away from the door.

An old friend of the family, Carlo Segenti, turned and saw Sara. He was the distinguished maestro who would conduct at her parents' concert. "Ah, *piccola*!" he beamed. "How beautiful you have become. Can this be the shy *piccione* who sat on my knee at six years old and would only whisper replies to the things I said to her?" He drew her into a bear hug against his fine ruffled shirtfront and gave her a resounding Italian kiss. He was still the very image of the dramatic maestro. His hair had more gray than she remembered, and the lines in his strong, sensitive face were a little deeper. As he let her go Sara saw over his shoulder the expressionless face of Paul Edgerton with Aunt Elizabeth beside him.

Segenti moved to allow them into the circle, but he kept a loving arm around Sara's waist. Paul's strange eyes followed that arm to its resting place where the maestro had a firm, friendly grip on her hand as well.

Elizabeth made introductions and Paul's face changed to charming, his mellow voice saying just the right things to interest Sara's father and make her mother glow with pleasure. Then he turned politely toward Sara, as if they had met once or twice before, but no more: "Good evening, Sara—maestro. This appears to be a homecoming of sorts for everyone."

Sara knew what he meant beneath his words and she bristled at his tone. The maestro laughed. "Sara is one of my best friends for a long time. We have met all over Europe, have we not, *piccola*?" Sara nodded slightly and smiled, and he went on: "And each time we met after an absence, there was something we always did. Do you remember, *cara mia*?"

"How could I forget?" Sara had always loved this tall lone man who lived with music like a mistress. She could sense Paul's judgmental thoughts. They grated on her. He had no right.

"Then why do you not see if I have forgotten? I came straight from Roma."

By this time Sara's parents were smiling indulgently and Paul's eyes were intent. For Sara, memories were streaming back—happy ones. She felt like a child again. So many times the little Sara had reached into Segenti's right breast pocket to find the small gift that he always had for her. It was their own small ritual, and by his smile tonight she knew that a gift again waited for her.

She slipped her hand into the warmth of his pocket and encountered something small and soft. Slowly she drew out a tiny satin jeweler's bag.

Segenti's face was delighted. "Do you know how long it is since I see you? More than four years. So I have never given the coming-of-age gift. I only hear from others how Sara is a grown-up woman." He took the bag and opened it into her hand. A sparkling antique ring of clustered dark Italian garnets and gold shone on her palm.

The maestro pressed it onto a ringless finger. "Be a happy woman, *cara*, as happy as you are lovely." He kissed her hand gently and she reached up to kiss his aristocratic cheek, murmuring her thanks. Her mother drew her close to examine the ring.

"It's beautiful, Carlo—and her birthstone, too."

Paul was seemingly forgotten in the little celebration. Sara noticed a strange expression on his face before he turned away. Carlo was still holding her hand so she couldn't follow Paul if she wanted to—and worse, Aunt Elizabeth was watching with eyes that saw too much.

For a while Sara was enveloped in the wave of friends who moved about her parents. Her mother leaned toward her. "He is a handsome man, your friend Paul. And full of passion—I can tell. He was bothered by Carlo's gift to you. That tells me that you have a jealous lover on your hands." She smiled affectionately. "Why don't we invite him to stay after the reception, just family, and get to know each other better?"

Sara fixed her mother with a warning look. "That's impossible, mother. Don't even suggest it. I just hope we can get through the reception without a scene. Paul Edgerton doesn't understand my situation at all. Please, mother...!"

"I like men with that impetuous spark in their eyes—it was one of the first things I noticed about your father." She laughed. Jonathon Courtney heard and gave her a mock-impetuous glance.

Sara wanted to find Paul and tell him that what he was thinking about her had nothing to do with reality. She knew he didn't believe her denials of a relationship with Jean-Claude, and he would be more than willing to believe that she hopped all over Europe with men like Carlo Segenti.

It was important to her to set him straight, even if nothing else was straight between them. She edged away to find him, feeling combative herself, stubbornly wanting to have it out with him. But she was forestalled by Aunt Elizabeth's voice, which was raised above the general buzz of conversation.

"Some of you have asked to see my rose garden. I would be delighted to show off my greenhouse to anyone who will walk into the garden a little way with me. Come on, Sara, you must help me." She fastened one strong arm into Sara's. Escape was not a possibility. She looked around to find Paul, but he wasn't in her line of vision. But he was here somewhere—she could feel him. She was still tied to his emotions in spite of herself.

Sara walked through the garden, along the softly lighted paths, beneath the shadowy trellis where she and Paul had once kissed, and into the Victorian-style greenhouse. Gregory went ahead inside, turning on lights.

Aunt Liz's special roses blossomed in huge tubs. Tuberous begonias in hanging baskets thrived beside a remarkable collection of sub-tropical plants. Each type of growth was in its own section and regulated by the most precise humidity and temperature controls. Exotic bromeliads and hanging ferns made an emerald background for the roses—miniatures, floribundas, teas and moss roses. The whole building held the lovely moist breath of growing plants and a sweet, heady rose perfume.

After people had wandered about enjoying the sheer beauty of the place, Aunt Elizabeth made special introductions of her favorite plants. She was just finishing when Gregory came to say she was wanted on the telephone—long distance from London. "Will you turn out the lights and close up for me, Sara dear?" she asked.

A few rose lovers lingered for a while as Sara waited restlessly for them to leave. Her nerves felt on edge. At last she was alone.

She went to the main switch box by the greenhouse door and began to turn off the series of lights. The graceful Victorian glass building was in darkness except for filtered light from the waning moon in its westward path. Sara stood just inside the door, savoring the feeling of this miniature paradise. It was something to be shared, she thought and sighed heavily.

There was a sound just behind her and she turned with a start.

"That was a very big sigh for such a popular young woman," Paul said evenly.

Sara's gaze went to his face, which was shadowed. "You startled me...."

His lips twisted into irony. "Forgive me. I'm blundering as usual."

Sara said nothing.

"I was hoping we might take this opportunity to have that civilized drink together. I don't like my affairs left unresolved." He stepped toward her.

The force of his emotion was far stronger than his words. Sara wasn't going to be goaded into having any exchange with him on his terms. She had some things of her own to say.

"My silent lady of mystery, still? A mystery to me, but well-known to other men, I gather." His cynicism was overpowering.

Sara looked directly into his shadowed eyes. "You seem to want to believe that I have a long and checkered past, Paul. Does it make you feel better about yourself? Would that make it easier for you to approach me, thinking I wasn't worthy of you?" She decided to slice through the angry wall between them.

He looked at her for a long moment, as if trying to read her mind. "You're hardly a virgin, Miss Courtney," he smiled slowly. "Haven't we established that already?"

"The Vestals went out a long time ago," she bit back. "I'm a twenty-five-year-old woman, and my past is a lot more innocent than yours, I'm sure. The double standard doesn't work today. I won't be made into a fallen woman while you merrily graze among your herd of female admirers!"

"Spare me, m'dear. I thought we had something very special when first we met. Here's a woman of quality, I thought—a woman I can communicate with, who is understanding and keenly perceptive. But I neglected to see that this woman had some strange need of her own to reduce my self-esteem to shreds and make a parade of her other men for my benefit." He turned away from her.

Sara stepped in front of him, blistering to tell him how stupidly mistaken he was, but controlling her tongue. "You've made your own little world, Paul, where everything revolves around you. From that vantage point anything that challenges your ego is an enemy. You don't know me very well at all."

He looked down at her with an indulgent half smile. "Frenchmen for breakfast...newspaper editors for dinner...Italian conductors to train you in the ways of men...that was a touching scene with the ring. It surprised me that your parents have condoned such open fondling of their daughter even when she was a young girl. Was it with your consent, Sara? I ask because I worry about you." He watched her face solicitously.

Sara couldn't believe his delusions. The moonlight haloed around his head, striking a glitter from his amber eyes. She could still find him a figure of romance—tall, beautiful and...terrible. Why did she care at all?

"Well?" his voice rasped. "Did Segenti love you like an Italian male and a father figure all in one? Did he teach you to prolong a man's agony and expectation?"

That was enough. All her pent-up misery flared

into fiery anger. More than anything, she wanted to hit that handsome face with its awful power to disturb her—to stop those lips from hurting her more.

Almost as if in a dream she felt her hand come up and slap his cheek. Yet, even as her hand struck his skin and felt the roughness of his beard under the surface a thrill spiraled up her arm and pleasure flooded her. Slowly, in the distorted time of intense emotion, she saw her arm fall away and a flash of naked anger gleam in Paul's eyes. Then the strange time warp exploded....

Paul caught her hand and dragged her close against his body. She tried to push away, but his strength was superior. Swiftly he thrust her hands behind her and imprisoned them in his heavy grip. With his other hand he took hold of her hair and gave her head a backward pull before he bent his lips to hers.

She gasped, as he forced her lips apart, and she felt the intrusion of his hot tongue searching hers. The taste of him was what she had longed for—but not with this fury! Then slowly his half-open mouth moved with heat and lust to her throat. He groaned and released her hands, drawing her thighs hard against him. She refused to find pleasure in it—she resisted it and let her arms go limp at her sides while his hands moved in the darkness of the moonlit shadows, enticing her to join his angry passion.

Impatiently he pulled her soft blouse up from her skirt and then his groping hand discovered that she wore no brassiere. Sara stayed perfectly still, waiting for him to realize that he was alone in his mad explosion. She was trembling from the effort not to respond to the scorching heat of his mouth on her breasts.

She wouldn't cry out this time—wouldn't tell him to stop. He would only scorn her imaginary scruples. This time she would let him do as he wished, then he would have to live with the consequences of his punishing domination of her.

His urgency increased and he moved his hand along the curve of her body, pressing up under her skirt to blaze a tantalizing path to her most sensitive places. His knowing fingers caressed and stroked, daring her not to respond. She knew now that she wouldn't—that he could force no passion from her this way.

"It's no use, Paul," she whispered as his provocative touches failed to arouse her. "I won't join you in this—"

"I don't believe you, Sara..." he said thickly. He grasped her body tightly to him and brought them both down until they were lying on a bale of planting moss and he was tugging at his belt buckle. "You want this as much as I do...." Sara could make no rational contact with his eyes. She felt sick....

"Paul Edgerton, I'm ashamed of you!" Aunt Elizabeth's sharp tones cut the air like a knife. Paul stood up in hasty disarray, leaving Sara gasping with relief.

"I came to see what had kept you, Sara," the

older woman said evenly. "You were somewhat engrossed, to say the least, but there was an element of one-sidedness to this nasty scene that caused me to remain and observe, where otherwise I might not have—and your words, Paul, confirmed my opinion."

Paul stood back and drew breath to speak, but Aunt Elizabeth refused him the courtesy of a reply. "Very little shocks me. But to use a woman's emotions and body like this—with not a word of love, not a gesture of gentleness—to assert your control only, is to me an act of the most outrageous cruelty."

Paul tried again to speak, and she waved him to silence. "I have regarded you as a gentleman. I'm so very sorry to have been mistaken. Come, Sara." She moved to take Sara's shivering arm in hers. "Paul, it would be best if you left without returning to the reception. When you feel that we can speak honestly, I would like to talk to you."

Sara watched Paul cross the threshold and hesitate. He turned toward her. "If I tell you I am profoundly sorry, it wouldn't convey the real depth of my failure, Sara. It was unforgivable. You have every right to despise me...." He looked at Aunt Elizabeth who stood, a queenly figure, in the semidarkness. "I don't know what is happening to me. Believe me, I wouldn't cause either of you pain...." He turned and walked with long strides toward the parking lot.

"We'll go in the back way and you can repair your appearance," she said to Sara. "Of course you know the man is madly in love with you, desperate to capture you."

Sara could barely hear her godmother's words, lost as she was in the awful, swirling tides of regret and misery.

"He's a compulsive type," Elizabeth continued, "I've known men like Paul, my dear."

Sara managed a wry smile. "I realize that, Aunt Liz."

"But once you can get a man like that on the right track you've got a devoted lover for life, believe me. I can see the good in him, even after this. His past casts a terrible shadow over him still."

"I don't care any more." Sara walked faster, intending to get her purse and coat and leave as soon as she could. The older woman put a hand out to stop her at the door to the kitchen.

"Sara, do you recall my little tale about Paul's love for the Texas girl, so long ago? Well, she didn't just leave his life simply, she made a point of telling everyone he knew that she had made a fool of him—that she had slept with other men while they were engaged. It was spite, of course. The poor girl wanted to hurt him. But think about it when you are more calm—"

"No more stories, Aunt Liz. It's finished. The end."

"I suppose you're going home to brood. I don't advise it."

"I've got a review to drop by the *Chronicle*."

Aunt Elizabeth cocked her head and looked at her. "Are you as tough as you're sounding?"

"I'm taking care of myself," she said back. "Tell mother and papa I'll call them in the morning."

"And not a word about this...?"

"Not a word. And thanks." Sara squeezed her godmother's hand warmly.

CHAPTER NINETEEN

THE FIRST THING SARA DID when she returned home was disconnect her answering machine and take the phone off the hook. The next thing was to take a hard, cold shower and wash the remembrance of Paul's touch from her body. It was like a ceremony of completion, the end of a very long ordeal.

This was the end of the silly Olive Gadwall-Paul Edgerton feud, as well. Monday she would tell Eric that she planned to quit. She might even go with her parents on tour for a few months until she found another job. Or, if Eric was still a friend after Monday, he might find her an assignment in another city where the *Chronicle*'s parent company had a newspaper. Whatever developed, it wouldn't be in Los Angeles!

She dressed for bed and went to slide the deadbolt across her door. She glanced up at her painting and gave a soft grunt deep in her throat. Maybe the Greek woman was simply gazing out at the beauty of the sea and sky—not at all waiting for a dream lover to sweep her into passionate embraces. And the veiled statue was just that: a statue with a veil. Her damned imagination had managed to make everything into more than it was every step of the way.

She spent Saturday with her parents, driving them to the Music Center to rehearse with Carlo Segenti and the L.A. Philharmonic, then back again to the hotel to rest and have a light supper before the performance. Sara indicated that she didn't want to talk about Paul Edgerton or Olive Gadwall, but would much rather hear what her parents had been doing since she'd heard from them last.

She stayed backstage in the wings during the concert while her mother and father delighted their audience with their virtuosity. Jonathon Courtney's arrangements of Ravel, Stravinsky, and Liszt brought standing applause and shouts for encores. Sara was so proud of those two creative darlings who happened to be her parents.

A benefit ball was scheduled afterward on the huge stage, which was quickly cleared and a Viennese backdrop lowered in place, chandeliers and all. Sara hadn't the heart to stay for it. She kissed her mother good-night, gave her father a hug, and excused herself. Maestro Segenti would return them to the hotel.

At her doorstep someone had left a florist box. She picked it up and brought it inside, but didn't open it. She didn't want any more apologies from him. Apologies were cheap and easy to make.

As if to defy the very concept of fine cuisine or superior taste Sara picked up the phone and ordered a pizza delivered to her door. Then she turned on her television set and waited for the delivery. The late news was giving a few minutes to the benefit at the Music Center. There were her parents, Aunt Liz and Maestro Segenti, dancing under the Viennese chandeliers. It seemed peculiar to be watching them from this little electronic box, but she was still glad she was home curled up in her robe and alone.

WHEN SHE WOKE THE NEXT MORNING she was on the couch. The television was on and the apartment smelled of pizza, some of which still lay cold and unappetizing in its oily box on the floor.

She retrieved her *Chronicle* and set it on the kitchen counter next to the florist box, not caring about either of them. The phone rang and it was Jean-Claude.

"How are your mother and father? How was *tante* Elizabeth's party? I got home from work too late to see you there...."

"Everyone's fine," Sara said. "What about your love nest?"

"Ah, my Sara! My life is one foot in heaven right now! Dulcie loves me like *une ange*. You must visit us today. Come to lunch for *oeufs Jean-Claude* and something from Wyoming that Dulcie taught me, ranch-fried potatoes." He pronounced it gingerly.

"My family will be visiting friends, so I'm free. What time?"

"Twelve. But you say nothing about my little present to you. Did you not notice?"

Sara thought quickly. "The flowers?"

"Ah *oui*. From Dulcie and me."

She glanced over at the box, imagining the wilted flowers inside. "They were beautiful, Jean-Claude," she lied. "How sweet of you both."

"I take care not to send the same color of roses as Paul Edgerton—did you notice?"

"Hmm. Well, it was dear of you to think of me. I'll be there at twelve."

After she hung up she opened the florist box and saw the dozen pink and white blooms, long stemmed and now very, very sad. She set them in ice water in the refrigerator, hoping that she hadn't killed them.

At eleven-thirty she was dressed casually in jeans and a cashmere sweater, ready to leave for Jean-Claude's cottage. The *Chronicle* still lay rolled up with a string around it. Even the thought of Olive Gadwall was repugnant. There were other things to do with her life now. She tied a silk paisley scarf in her bouncing ponytail and enjoyed being comfortable.

There was a gravel lane at the side of her aunt's property that led to the gardener's cottage. Sara stopped her car beside a very old Japanese compact car with a crumpled front fender.

She walked the little path to the adobe cottage and knocked on the low oak door. Dulcie answered, but her eyes showed no welcoming light. "Yes?" she asked.

"Dulcie, it's me—Sara."

"I don't believe it." She put a hand to her mouth in surprise.

"The last time you saw me I was the lady in black. We never did get properly introduced, did we?"

Dulcie took her hand, laughing, and drew her inside, where a crackling fire was roaring in the high, open fireplace. Jean-Claude was standing next to the stove in the midst of preparing biscuits. "Am I not a domestic man?" he grinned at her.

"Your home is very cozy," Sara said as she looked about the single large room that was theirs. An old daybed served two purposes, she assumed. A few fat dormitory-type pillows were on the stone floor, and posters adorned the walls.

Over lunch Jean-Claude watched Sara and didn't ask questions about Paul. He did confess, however, that he and Dulcie had ulterior motives for asking her over.

"My father doesn't understand about Jean-Claude," Dulcie said while she cleared the plates and brought apples and cheese to the table. "I shouldn't have told him anything."

Jean-Claude explained: "The father of Dulcie imagines that a man who cooks food for a living is not worth his beloved daughter."

"Daddy's a rancher and a businessman," Dulcie said. "He got mad when I said we were thinking of getting married."

"It is difficult for me to understand—a man of great money who does not know French cuisine as an art. He thinks I cook hamburgers and make milk shakes," he said disdainfully.

"He's going to make a terrible scene, Sara. He and mama think I'm under the influence of a

Svengali or something. They're talking about coming here and bringing me back home!" Her large brown eyes were brimming with tears, and Sara found herself empathizing with Dulcie.

"We know you have good ideas to help," Jean-Claude said in an expectant voice. "How to convince monsieur McNatt I am no wolf, and no clumsy cook in a hamburger place?"

Sara looked at both of them. "Don't you know what you should do? It's perfectly clear to me."

"If I go to her father he will see I am not a large Wyoming cowboy and he will refuse to consider me. What does he know about Frenchmen?"

Sara had to suppress a smile. Jean-Claude was so very French. If Dulcie's father was as she described, there was a basic cultural problem. "I have a perfectly good suggestion: Show him what kind of cook you are. Let him come to Los Angeles and judge for himself what kind of prospect you are for his daughter."

Jean-Claude looked pained. "How will he even know what is good food? He eats steaks every day of his life."

"I'll bet he listens to experts, though. Why can't he bring along a food expert or two to help him decide?"

Jean-Claude's expressive French face went through several degrees of agony before Dulcie threw her arms around his neck and cried, "He'll do it! I know Daddy, and he'll give a man a fair chance. He just has to go by the book. You're right, Sara. He'll take the opinion of an expert.

Jean-Claude, honey, that's what we'll do!" She ran over to Sara and nearly knocked her from her chair. "I love you!"

On the drive back to her apartment Sara thought how simple it was for her to come up with answers to other people's problems. It made her happy that she could help her favorite Frenchman and his beloved Dulcie. Maybe it was a sign that she would have clearer insight into her own situation from now on. She could hardly wait for Monday and the meeting she planned to have with Eric at the *Chronicle*.

For the rest of the day she worked hard at her desk arranging the chapters for her book. Her last act before going to bed was to drop the morning's *Chronicle* into the trash basket—Cliffside, Green Terrace, Olive, and all.

SARA WAS AT THE OFFICE before Eric arrived. One of the staff greeted her cheerfully and laid the morning's *Tribune* on her desk. He pointed to the first page and went about his work, dropping copies of the newspaper on several other desks.

Sara looked at a box and its headline in bold type:

A CHALLENGE

Paul Cabot Edgerton, the *Tribune*'s man at The Right Table, challenges Miss Olive Gadwall of the *Chronicle* to a public contest of taste. Mr. Edgerton requests an early response from Miss Gadwall. His representative will meet with hers to establish the protocol for the contest—the date, location, and judges to be announced by both newspapers.

Sara turned the paper face down on her desk. "Sorry, Mr. Edgerton, but Miss Gadwall declines." No more Broccoli War, no broadsides in print. She wanted only to disconnect herself from him entirely.

Eric arrived carrying his own copy of the *Tribune,* passed by her desk, barked an order for her to follow him and went to his cubicle office. Sara was right behind him.

"Eric," she started, "I have to talk...."

"Did you see it?" he almost shouted, ignoring her words. "That was what Paul had up his sleeve—a challenge! It's brilliant! What a media event!"

"Don't count on me." She had to raise her voice over his.

He stopped and gave her the floor.

"Eric, I've thought about this whole thing until I'm blue in the face and there's only one conclusion that's right for me: I have to let Olive go."

"Is this the final verdict, or is it just temporary?" He sat down and swiveled his oak desk chair to face her.

"It's final. I'm sorry to do this to you, I truly am, but I can't go on in a battle when I've lost the stomach for it...and that's not a pun," she smiled grimly.

"And your contract—what about that?"

"Can't I break it?"

"Only if I twist some arms in the legal department."

She looked into his clever blue eyes and knew that he was still in charge. "What if I quit—just walk out...."

"You wouldn't do that. You're an honorable lady, and you will want a good referral to your next job—unless you're quitting to get married and have some guy pay all your bills." His easy-going voice wasn't unfriendly, just telling her the facts of life, and she realized it.

She took a deep breath. "You told me you'd let me out of this if it got too difficult, Eric."

"I did," he nodded. "And I will. But not before Olive Gadwall faces Paul Edgerton in the gourmet contest. Today changes everything." Sara looked helplessly at her boss's determined face. "I've already had a call from George Strickland and we're drawing up the ground rules. Paul wanted to have it be a wine tasting party... covered labels and silver spittoons. I told him we wouldn't go along unless half the contest involved food tasting, as well."

"I can't believe you went ahead without asking me."

"My dear Sara, as of Friday noon when we lunched together at the Green Terrace you were still on Edgerton's trail. How could I know you had undergone a metamorphosis over the weekend?"

"All right, Eric. What if I go through with this

ridiculous challenge? *Then* will you help me get out of my contract?"

"I'll do everything in my power to get you a job you'll love, Sara. That's a promise."

"Will you give me a little time to think about it?"

"Don't ask me to leave the great debate up in the air for long. George is pressing me for a date already. He envisions Olive and Paul doing network talk shows...."

"Has he asked Paul if he wants to do it?" She had to know if they were both being railroaded.

"It was his idea in the first place, according to George. Edgerton wants to get the debate out in the open. If I were in his shoes, and as good a journalist as I think he is, I'd do the same thing."

"Just...not this week, okay? I want to spend some time with my parents and not have any more pressure for a while."

"What pressure? You're the one who's whipping yourself, as far as I can see. I don't want to be the heavy in this drama."

"Do me one more favor, Eric. Be Olive for a couple of weeks. You said you would if I asked, and I'm asking. Let me take a break."

He looked at her for a long moment, saw that she was serious and said, "Sure, honey. I guess I can fill in for you. But what will I tell George about a date?"

She looked at the large wall calendar behind the desk. "Tell him the world won't end if Paul has to wait until the seventh."

"Wednesday the seventh," he said. "That'll be final, then. Wish me luck when I start writing like Olive Gadwall, though. It won't be easy to reproduce your special tone."

"Eric...you're really very nice," she smiled, close to tears.

Walking out of the Chronicle Building and into the underground parking garage was like leaving behind an enormous burden. Sara now had almost two weeks to clear her brain of its stupid obsession. If she had the strength to tell Jacques to leave her life, then she surely could forget Paul. And once she let him go she could honestly wish him well. He was a good journalist. He did have sensitivity in certain ways. He just didn't know the first thing about the mysterious and delicate ways of love.

She went straight to the Los Angeles Central Library and checked out an armload of books about wine. It would be bedtime reading when she felt like it. She owed that much to Eric and the *Chronicle*. And there was a wine-tasting seminar being offered at UCLA this weekend. She wouldn't want to embarrass Eric by letting Paul win that part of the contest without a struggle.

L'Intime was due to open Friday night. Jean-Claude would be in a wild flurry of preparations with Sigmund Heep, so Sara wouldn't ask him for wine advice yet. Maybe Aunt Elizabeth would enjoy teaching her some of the subtleties. And Armand, the husband of her godmother's cook, was once the owner of a good little restaurant. Perhaps he would help. There was hope.

But for the next few days Sara planned to forget everything related to her work. She and her parents were flying up to San Francisco in the morning to visit old friends and arrange a recital at the beautiful old Opera House. April in the city by the bay would be crisp and clear, and Sara hadn't seen it since she was a child.

They became tourists, riding on noisy, jerking cable cars and eating sourdough French bread at Fisherman's Wharf. Sara realized how isolated from the world she had allowed herself to become, even in the midst of the chic restaurant crowds. She had been so intent on debunking Paul Edgerton that she herself was in danger of turning sour.

In the long nights in her Nob Hill hotel room, high above the city, she thought about Paul the young man, with the idealistic soul who had once cared so deeply about the problems of his world. In her own foolish, impractical way, she would always have love in her heart for that other Paul Edgerton. It didn't matter any more if he knew it or if he resented her digging into his past. She could even forgive him his punishing behavior in the greenhouse. Maybe it was possible for a man to be driven by something beyond his control. She made no excuses for her own treatment of him.

They returned to Los Angeles Friday morning, in time for Sara to call Jean-Claude at his cottage and wish him luck with his opening dinner that night.

"I am without my sanity!" he proclaimed. "But all will be perfection! Dulcie is sitting on the pins and needles today. Will you and your kind parents bring her with you tonight?"

Sara agreed. Dulcie had a large stake in Jean-Claude's success and would be a nervous wreck if she weren't surrounded by calmer people, and supportive Aunt Elizabeth was away for the week.

The opening night of L'Intime was understated and quiet, a far cry from Cliffside's social extravaganza the week before. Sigmund Heep was a cautious, intelligent man, wise in the ways of restaurants. He intended his newest place to be a hideaway with its own atmosphere of delightful intimacy. The unimposing facade would attract only those who wanted a departure from the see-and-be-seen interiors of the popular restaurants.

They were among the early patrons to arrive. It was a matter of word-of-mouth, rather than invitations, that provided the patronage for the evening. Bettina Straus and her friends were coming in later, and a theater crowd was expected around eleven o'clock for late supper. Dulcie was very subdued as they were shown to their table—the right table. Sara smiled. Jean-Claude had reserved a place in a secluded section of the room, partially hidden from general view by two kentia palm trees in pots. The chairs were deep and soft, upholstered in moss-green cut velvet; the linen was shell-pink. The lighting was neither dim nor harsh, but indirect and flattering.

Sara examined the menu and knew at once that both Jean-Claude's and Sigmund Heep's tastes were represented. The staff was well rehearsed but nervous.

Sara's party ordered from the menu, and Dulcie leaned close to Sara to speak. "I don't know if I can stand knowing how worried Jean-Claude is back there!"

"Rest assured," Sara soothed. "He thrives on tension."

Dulcie shook her head. "But too much tension can break a person. This morning I called daddy in Wyoming and asked him to come down here some day soon and judge Jean-Claude. I thought he'd agree and bring one or two experts. But he's going to do more than that...!"

Sara couldn't imagine what could be so terrible. "What is he planning to do?"

"He got on the phone and found out who was the biggest and the best in the gourmet world. You know who's coming to see Jean-Claude? Austin Gilbert, the chef who has the famous television show in San Francisco...and a friend of daddy's who's president of the Gourmets de Los Angeles...and he even asked Julia Child! Can you believe it? She's agreed to have Daddy fly one of her friends here who works with her program. And another chef from a famous place in New York. I'm scared to death!"

Sara understood her concern. "What does Jean-Claude say about it?"

"He's delighted. He hasn't a doubt in his fine French head. But, Sara...!" Her pretty round face was flushed. "I wanted daddy to invite you—

Olive Gadwall—to be sure we got a good review, but his friend from the Gourmets said it should be Paul Edgerton, instead."

Sara's heart sank. It could be a disaster if Paul recognized Jean-Claude from his one encounter at her apartment. Even with his new moustache he was still unmistakably Jean-Claude. Dulcie didn't seem to know about that little complication and Sara wasn't going to tell her. "I'm just as confident as Jean-Claude that everything will go beautifully," she said. "Your father will be proud of both of you." Dulcie smiled a dubious smile and tried bravely to be cheerful for the rest of the dinner.

L'Intime's decor wouldn't attract raves, but that was one of its charms. The arrangement of the tables and potted palms and low decorative partitions gave the restaurant the ambiance of a private dining room. There were no distracting velvet wallpapers or art collections on the walls, only simple oak paneling and thick burgundy-colored carpeting. One wasn't aware of the conversations at the next table. The decorator had made L'Intime intimate.

The invitational formal opening would be in two weeks—long enough for the restaurant to have worked out its unevenness. Sigmund Heep had no need for concern, however; the first night was close to perfection.

When Sara's party had finished they wanted to go to the kitchen to congratulate Jean-Claude, but the waiter said the kitchen was a madhouse and visitors would only make it worse. Everyone understood. Sara returned her parents to the hotel and drove Dulcie to her little cottage.

Dulcie didn't want to be left alone. "I can't wait until he comes home! Won't you stay with me until he's back?" she pleaded.

"I've got to be up early for my seminar at UCLA. Give Jean-Claude a kiss for me and tell him I knew he was a genius from the first day I met him. He was wonderful!"

BACK AT HER APARTMENT BUILDING, Sara collected her week's mail and papers from Norma, who had held it for her during her absence. Curiosity made Sara read the Wednesday *Chronicle* first—Eric's first try as Olive. He had played it safe and written a glib reply about the contest and padded the rest from notes she had fed into her word processor about the Basque place and Stella's Place, the English Tearoom in Pasadena. There was no mention of Paul until the end.

> I wait with bated breath for our encounter on the seventh, dear Paul. I much prefer you to be sharp of taste than sharp of tongue. May the better half win!

Sara cringed. She wouldn't have said it that way. Eric was being too cute.

Among her newspapers was the Thursday copy of the *Tribune*—probably Norma's. Paul's column was featured on the front of the food section, not on page three where it usually was.

"The thrill of the chase will soon be over for both of us," he had written.

I look forward to the opportunity to dignify our relationship with an unguarded handshake. It can't have been entirely satisfactory for you, dear Olive, to spend these weeks taking shots at me from behind protective covering. And I must confess, I've had much to ponder during our well-attended little war. Leave your weapons at home when you come, and I shall do the same. I believe the rules of the Geneva Convention should apply, don't you?

Sara put the paper down and stared at it as she sat at her dining table. Some of the sting was missing, the defensiveness. He almost seemed to address Olive as an equal. Or was she reading too much into his words?

Her fingers moved to open one of the dozen envelopes that waited for her and her bemused mind didn't notice that that particular piece of mail had the logo of *Epicure International* on it. As she was pulling out the letter she started to focus her attention again. The letter was from her former editor, asking if she would be interested in doing a regular feature on American foods, trends, and fads. Mention was made of her old column which she had written as Niece of a Hundred Chefs. It was a modest offer, but an interesting one. How much more might they pay her if they knew she was Olive Gadwall as well?

She set the letter aside. It only added to her conviction that there were other avenues for her to investigate in the future. Right now she had to get some sleep and be ready to explore the almost mystical domain of wine tasting at the seminar in Westwood.

Something bothered her very much, though, as she lay in bed waiting for sleep to stop her busy mind. Something about the tone of Paul's column didn't feel right. He was no longer the adversary. What was he up to? Was he really becoming a more decent person? Had Olive actually done some good?

Her heart was beating faster than it should, alert and expectant—as if it had a counterpart out there somewhere, beating in the same dynamic rhythm. *Pish, tush,* Olive's words whispered, *the very idea. Pish, tush!*

CHAPTER TWENTY

APPEARANCE (color, depth, clarity):
NOSE:
TASTE:
EVALUATION:

Sara's notebook was quickly filled with key words and phrases, names of too many grape varieties, and insiders' comments from the three wine experts who led the seminar. For $150 she had purchased a total immersion in the lore and appreciation of wines. Thirty other people had done the same.

The morning hours were devoted to the abstract subject of wines and their history. The afternoon was a hands-on tasting experience. By four o'clock Sara had learned the subtle differences in color between an immature red Bordeaux and a fine mature red Bordeaux, an eight-year-old sauterne and a very old classic sauterne. She tasted every type of wine and analyzed it.

In all her years of knowing wine as a part of good cooking she had never actually studied the grape like this, mostly because she wasn't much of a drinker, and alcohol always left her feeling less than alert. The challenge was a week and a half away. She was now glib enough to bluff her way through a wine tasting, she thought.

She called Jean-Claude late that night to give him her educated opinion of his first night as *chef de cuisine*.

"Will Olive write about me soon?" he asked. "I wish to show the praise to the father of Dulcie. Is it to appear in tomorrow's newspapers?"

Sara would have to call Eric at home and ask permission to phone in a quick review of L'Intime for the late edition of the *Chronicle*. It might be too late now for the morning edition. "Don't worry," she said after some thought, "you'll have something to show Dulcie's father. When is he coming for the great judging?"

"In six days. I will be magnificent!"

SUNDAY'S CONSUMING PASSIONS COLUMN included a brief but enthusiastic critique of L'Intime, complete with superlatives and Olive's belief that this new chef was a star on the horizon of fine cuisine. Mr. McNatt would have to be impressed. The main part of the column was another heavy-handed attempt by Eric to impersonate Olive. For Sara it was like watching a favorite recipe fussed with by well-meaning friends until it had lost its original flavor. It was painful to watch.

Without conferring first with Eric, Sara wrote a short piece for Olive Gadwall's Wednesday column:

Do I sense an awakening of a finer spirit in my associate from the *Tribune*? A fairness newly emerging? I pray that when we finally meet on Wednesday next, we will come—to paraphrase Shakespeare—not to bury each other, but to praise our noble craft. May the victors in our bloodless contest be our dear readers, and may they live to tell their grandchildren of a time when a better way was found to settle passionate differences. *Ciao!*

She could hear Eric's low chuckle as she read him her short column. "I was that awful?" he queried.

"You were fine, Eric, you just weren't exactly Olive. I had to respond to the challenge in my way."

"I was hoping you would. We'll run it Wednesday. Does this mean you're back?"

"Not completely. There's one more column I have to do—a kind of parting shot. I want it to appear the morning of our contest, and that will be the end of it."

"Anything you say," he agreed. "Old Eric isn't Olive, I know, but bear with me on Sunday's column. I'm thinking of retiring Olive after you leave and finding a regular food critic with a real name." There was a pause, then he added, "You *are* still planning to leave, aren't you?"

"As soon as the big show is over. Have you decided where it's to be?"

"Paul wants the judging to be at Mon Château's private dining room. I told him it was all right with us."

"Who are the judges?"

"Two senior accountants, actually. From one of the big companies in town. They'll keep the tally of hits and misses. Simple as that. Either you know what kind of wine it is, or you don't. Same with the ingredients of the mystery dishes."

"Paul agreed to this?" she asked, surprised.

"George insisted, and I go along. The public likes to see numbers and charts on their television screens. Edgerton wasn't thrilled. It keeps him from using his large vocabulary after every sip of wine. But the contest is being set up by *Les Amis du Tastevin* and three of Bettina Straus's favorite chefs, including Sigmund Heep. No objections, I trust?"

"Any chance Paul will be given help by his pals at the wine-tasting society? Advance information?"

"He's probably asking the same thing about you and the chefs. Don't worry. It's the event that counts. The media want a colorful contest, that's all."

"Then Paul and I are just props for a show?"

"That's a crude way of putting it, Sara, but you know how fickle the public is. They like to be entertained."

"That's not the kind of journalistic career I had in mind," she said testily. "Doesn't it bother you that nobody's concerned with the reasons Paul or

I would select a certain thing during the contest? Wouldn't you rather have us show a true appreciation for the wine and food we're being tested on?"

"I was only saying that it doesn't matter who wins what, just so it's fun for everyone who watches."

"Yes, sir," she bit off. "The editor's always right."

"Give me a break," Eric said, sounding exasperated.

IF SARA HAD had the courage she would have picked up the phone after that and called Paul at his home to commiserate, critic to critic. Oddly, she felt closer to him in the last few days than ever. But it was best to let Olive die a natural death and send Sara Courtney back into the world of journalism with her own by-line for the world to read.

During the week she saw her parents and Aunt Elizabeth for lunch and a scattering of dinners, and kept an ear tuned to Jean-Claude's preparations for his big test. It was important to her to start writing some sample columns for her own portfolio. She wanted to show more about her real abilities—the history and lore of foods, the sheer fun of dabbling in a kitchen. She had been so sidetracked with Olive's campaign to reform Paul that she'd neglected the very reason she was a food writer in the first place.

Thursday evening her parents invited her to Mon Château for dinner. Her mother wanted to visit "the scene of the crime," the place where the gourmet challenge would be decided.

Being there in that charming rural-French room with its great warming fireplace and the familiar smell of burning oak logs brought up a confusing array of memories. Sara wanted to excuse herself and leave—there seemed to be ghosts in Mon Château's dining room.

Sara and her parents were graciously greeted by the maître d' and shown to the same table by the fire that Sara had shared with Paul. The coincidence was unsettling.

Sara's nerves were on the alert, her chest felt tight as if emotions had been stored up inside and needed release. She tried to concentrate on making conversation with her mother and father and enjoying her first course salad, but she felt Paul's presence intensely.

The arrangement of the tables and high-backed upholstered chairs made it difficult to see everyone in the room and Sara was growing more anxious every second as the dinner proceeded. As if a spell had been cast on her, she felt shivery and cold.

The dinner was a quiet one. There were no interruptions by fans who recognized Sara's parents. Mon Château was a place where privacy was respected as much as good food.

"What's the matter, dear," her mother asked. "Are you catching something? You're so pale tonight." She put a hand over Sara's cold one and warmed it with hers.

Then it happened—just as Sara sensed it would. Paul appeared on the other side of the room walking toward their table with a stunning woman on his arm. Sara closed her eyes and tried to use her will to keep him walking out the door, but he arrived at her table anyway.

She arranged her face into pleasant indifference and watched as he greeted her parents. "Sir, madam, it's a pleasure to see you again. And Sara, of course." He inclined his fine head toward her as if they were slight acquaintances, no more. Sara looked into his eyes and couldn't read them. He *had* to recall their last meeting! Her pulse quickened at the flicker of intensity she detected in his amber eyes. He turned to his companion, a raven-haired beauty, who was very pregnant and seemed to be intimate with Paul. She clung tightly to his arm as he made his greetings. "May I introduce Madelyn de Bertil."

The face was familiar and the name was somewhere in Sara's memory, but the two didn't connect at first. Instead, a wild series of conclusions moved through Sara's mind: This was Paul's mistress... he was showing Sara that he had other interests and obligations in his life... he wasn't changed at all; that had been Sara's own delusion....

"Madelyn is my sister," Paul continued, jolting Sara out of her morbid thoughts. "She's on her way to San Francisco to join her husband on wine business." Sara felt like an idiot. Of course she knew that face! Paul directed his words at Sara's parents, while Sara struggled for equilibrium. There he stood, self-possessed and beautiful in her eyes, his voice still carrying that special quality she once thought she loved.

Jonathon Courtney addressed Madelyn: "And will you be back here to watch your brother face Olive Gadwall? It should be interesting."

Madelyn looked at him with her large dark eyes and smiled. "My husband Yves wants to return to France quickly, which leaves me little time for my dear brother. But I'll hear all about it from him. Poor dear! To think a woman has finally brought him down from his lofty perch...." She glanced impishly up at Paul.

"What a traitorous thing to say," he laughed easily.

"But it's true, darling," she chided, and looked directly at Sara. "I've never seen him so wonderfully challenged on his delicate points of pride." She reached up and gave him a light kiss on his cheek.

Paul became formal and stopped the banter. "We won't keep you from your dinner, but I wanted to tell you how very much I admire you both for your contribution to music. From the bottom of my heart." He extended his hand to Jonathon, made a courteous little bow to Elena, and looked briefly at Sara. "Good night, then."

"I hope we'll meet again," Madelyn said genuinely.

When they were gone Sara's mother was smiling. "He really is a charming man, Sara. And his sister, too. Don't you feel anything for him at all?"

"We started off wrong, mother." Sara's whole body was trembling from the sudden, jarring revelation that she still loved him, that she couldn't stop loving him, no matter what outrageous things he did or said.

"Things can start again, can't they?" her mother asked innocently.

"I'm about to do that, mother. I'm quitting the *Chronicle* after my contest with Paul. I'm already looking for another job, preferably not in California."

Dinner ended on an awkward note, with Sara's father trying to keep pleasant small talk alive while easing his wife off the subject of Paul Edgerton. Sara was grateful to him for that. It gave her mental space to think about Paul. Why couldn't she just admit that she had done a bad job of rebounding from Jacques—that she still had a lot to learn about men?

SARA SPENT THE WHOLE OF FRIDAY in the Central Library thinking about Paul and trying to be interested in rare cookbooks from the last century. If she wanted to call him she would have to walk a long distance to a pay phone and people would be listening nearby. There was little chance that she would weaken and call Paul in that setting.

It was four-thirty when she arrived home. The phone was ringing as she put her key into the lock, and her pulse quickened.

Jean-Claude's voice groaned into her ear: "Sara. *Mon Dieu,* I thought you would never get home!" After a strangled gulp he went on, "*Je suis très malade*—seriously I am sick. I have no person to assist me but you. This place is desolate."

"Jean-Claude, stop," Sara commanded. "Where are you?"

"At L'Intime. Only two of my kitchen workers are here...the others are also *malade*. Like flies they drop away to fly home. What am I to do?" His voice rose to a trembling squeak. "I cannot beg Sigmund to cook...his chefs are busy...I cannot change the day of my judging by the father of Dulcie...everyone is here to see me—chefs from far distance. Sara," he pleaded, with more gulping sounds, "you are my only hope!"

"Hold on, Jean-Claude, I'll be right there."

Whisking off her dress and climbing into jeans and a sweatshirt took only a moment. She grabbed a sweater coat and rushed to get her car. Jean-Claude wasn't just being dramatic—he was in big trouble and he sounded awful.

It took exactly fifteen minutes to drive to L'Intime. Its newly painted white and gold sign swung in the late afternoon breeze. Flowers bloomed cheerfully in the large pots by the recessed door with its huge lion's-head knocker.

Sara drew a breath and turned into the parking lot. When she entered the kitchen, the door was standing ajar. Sara found Jean-Claude sitting propped in a corner on one of the high working stools. His face was nearly as white as his chef's coat. He moaned when he saw her.

Bit by painful bit she heard his story while his two helpers watched with expectant faces. Yesterday, it seemed, the *sous*-chef used some leftover chicken and vegetables to experiment with a new dish, some small meat pies. He wanted to try a new flavor combination. "We tasted the pies for lunch today and they are good...but..." he whispered, "all who partook of them are now as I am. Those—" he pointed toward the helpers "—are the only ones not sick."

"Go home, Jean-Claude. I'll work out something," Sara said firmly.

"*Non! Non!* I must stay...but you must cook. I will die at my place for the future of Dulcie and myself." He straightened up, hiccuping drearily. "You will excuse...." He tottered toward the door leading to the rest rooms.

Sara found out from the two helpers that the other three chefs had left for home an hour ago. She thought fast. It was almost five o'clock. If something didn't get started right now, this minute, there wouldn't be any command performance for Dulcie and her father's experts.

She used the wall phone to call Aunt Elizabeth, who had just arrived home from a trip to New York. Sara thanked God for the good timing. Aunt Elizabeth grasped the situation at once.

"You're going to need my Marie and her husband, Armand. He was a fine chef in his day, you know. They're quite capable of taking orders and cooking to Jean-Claude's style. Keep your wits about you and call me if you need anything more.

I'm sending Marie and Armand to you right now. Godspeed!"

Sara whirled around from the telephone and told the assistants to show her the plan for the evening. Not only was Dulcie's father coming with his tableful of people, but L'Intime was serving a complete dinner menu to the other patrons as well. If ever Sara needed all her bragged-about organizational sense, it was now.

The assistants were experienced and talked only enough to give her a feel for the kitchen and the food on hand. Some of it, fortunately, had already been prepared and set aside by the chefs, before the dread chicken pie was eaten. Work was begun for the salads, vegetables, and ingredients for the soups.

Jean-Claude wove weakly back to his stool, moaning and perspiring. Sara told him about Marie and Armand, and a ghost of a smile moved over his wan face. "That is fine for the general menu, Sara...but what about my special dinner?"

"You're going to cook it, my friend, only you'll use my hands to do it!"

He drew up a sigh from his toes, hunched over on his stool, and put his head on his drawn-up knees.

"Are you okay? Are you in bad pain? Jean-Claude!" Sara laid a hand on his tousled hair. He seized it with fervor for a kiss and his weeping eyes looked up at her.

She withdrew her hand from his clammy grip.

"Tell me what you have planned and I'll get started."

"Duck," he said in a rough whisper and pointed to a refrigerator door. Sara found to her relief that he had already done the first preparations of the main dish. The breasts were boned, and the dark meat puréed with cream and forced into drumstick shapes. The breasts would be baked later with their sauce.

"Okay," she said. "Now what's the first course?"

"Shrimp... with lemon-herb sauce and thin slices of avocado around it, and also the thinnest of pieces of artichoke heart."

"Good. What vegetables with the duck?"

He swallowed hard. "A coarse purée of carrots, with topping of cooked chopped bulbs of *aneth doux*."

Fennel, she translated to herself. "What else?"

He leaned back and closed his eyes. "I have mango peeled and ready for the ice-cream machine for *un sorbet* with the duck. Please, I must not think of food for a little...."

As much as Sara sympathized with him she had to smile at his extravagant way of suffering. He looked very young and vulnerable on his tall stool, slumped against the wall. His English was wobbling in and out of clarity. The bush of his new moustache covered his lip and he had cut his sideburns very high, making his nose look very large and Gallic.

Giving him time to recover, Sara scouted on her

own. She found the carrots, set them to cook, and got the fennel ready to simmer. She gave the carrot preparation over to one of the helpers. Sounds of life were coming from Jean-Claude again. "What about dessert?" she asked.

"I was planning when the sickness took it from my mind...." He rubbed his head distractedly with a long thin hand. "I was going to make *galette des rois* to go with *café*... but I need more time to do *un autre* dessert... to finish what my miserable pastry chef cannot do. *Hélàs!* I wanted a special *crème* and it is too late."

Sara's heart sank. Here was their first large problem—how could she make the delicate lemon butter cake and another dessert, too? She didn't know his kitchen or his stock on hand yet.

Marie and Armand arrived, competent, quiet, and efficient. They went to work immediately on the regular menu, setting the kitchen into the orderly rhythm that a good restaurant should have.

Jean-Claude had sunk back into a bleary doze, refusing to go home or to rest in the tiny executive office. He had a kind of pathetic nobility, his slack angular figure leaning in the corner between a table and the wall. Marie clucked her tongue toward him and made despairing gestures at Sara.

"Let him be," Armand said in a strong husky voice. "It is Jean-Claude's kitchen," he said to Sara. "Better that he tries to be here." He was a tall man with a shock of grizzled hair, his older-style chef's clothes straining over a girth larger than it once was. The helpers were jumping to his commands but looked pleased.

Armand pulled a bottle from his small bag of special cutting knives—keepsakes from his days of cooking glory. "Medicine from Madame de Lacy. He is to have one tablespoon in a little water each hour. It is a remedy against nausea and food poisoning."

Sara took the bottle of clear liquid. It had a sharp but not unpleasant smell. Armand watched her. "Madame first found it in Egypt, when she suffered from the distress of tourists."

Sara chuckled. "Come on, Marie, help me to get this down him." They stood over Jean-Claude with the remedy now fizzling in its water.

"*Mon Dieu*..." he groaned, "have I not torture enough?"

He ruefully swallowed the medicine and Sara placed a chair cushion from the restaurant in front of him so he could lean his head against it. He sighed.

"Before you go back to dozing—" Sara held his hot face in her hands "—have you any oranges?"

"*Oui*—in a box in the little storeroom behind where you will see brooms and soaps." She let his head fall back against the cushion. An idea was forming in her mind. If there were enough oranges....

She had to stop for a conference with Armand. He pointed to the paper in his hand. "I find notes here for a soup of potato and lettuce."

"Let's do it," Sara decided. It would be a good

touch before the shrimp and avocado dish. "We can make enough to use part of it for the soup of the day on the regular menu."

Armand put an assistant to work on the potatoes and lettuce. In the big refrigerator Sara found a large pile of cucumbers. They would go well with the duck course and give a fresh touch of taste and color with the carrots and fennel, sliced, cooked, and lightly sauced with a hint of dill.

In the storeroom she found the oranges—a full box of them with the perfect kind of thin, supple skins she wanted. Armand looked up from his own work with an eyebrow raised at her busy occupation with the oranges. She explained: "I remember a wonderful dessert I had once in Verona at the Tre Corone restaurant. Very finely shredded orange peel, candied in orange juice with a dash of sweet vermouth."

Armand's face was interested as she described it further. "The orange peel is arranged in a nest and that is filled with balls of frozen almond ice. It is flamed at serving and the light syrup ladled over the top."

"I remember such a dessert in Italy," Armand said. "It should not take long to make. With the ice-cream machine the almond ice is not a problem. Surely it will be spectacular and not too heavy."

She demonstrated to one of the assistants how she wanted the shredding done and started boiling the syrup.

Sara supervised the purée of potatoes and lettuce, then seasoned the smooth delicate green soup mixture with salt, dill, and thyme.

Sara felt like five people, each obeying the commands of a central brain. The bubbling syrup was thickening for the dessert preparation and she hurried to put the orange rind shreds into a collander and blanche them with very hot water to take off the bitter oils. She had to hurry. The clock seemed to be moving at double speed and sounds of waiters arriving through the back door broke her concentration slightly. The maître d', a dignified older Frenchman, came into the work area. He took the alarming circumstances in stride and Sara told him exactly what to expect from the situation. "Jean-Claude is telling me what to do, and we are doing it," she said emphatically, so that there wouldn't be anyone on the staff telling the patrons that a strange woman and her friends were really the cooks for the night. "Can you show me the special table for the McNatt party now?"

Sara looked out for the first time at the arrangement for the reserved table. The waiters had set up a long table from four small ones and given the area a feeling of privacy by a careful placement of potted palms and a decorative screen. Bouquets weren't on the tables yet. Sara had intended to arrange flowers when she first saw them sitting in a bucket of water by the back doorway. *Do the flowers after the galette,* she reminded her frantic brain.

It was time for another dose of Jean-Claude's medicine—taken without protest now. "I am cold," he muttered. His temperature had dropped. Marie brought a blanket from her car and wrapped Jean-Claude snugly in it. A shadow of color was in his face now. Warmed, he made a gallant effort to see what was happening. Sara described the various stages of cooking and he seemed satisfied.

"I smell orange. What is this?"

"I'm making an orange peel in vermouth syrup."

A faint smile curled his lips. "I have no energy to ask more. It will be good and beautiful." His emotional eyes spoke volumes of gratitude.

The syrup was ready, thick and shining. She poured the mound of orange shreds into it and stirred until all was coated with the sugary mix. The rind had kept its brilliant color and looked splendid. With a sigh of relief she set it aside, trying to remember to keep it warm for serving.

Did she dare to make the *galette* now, or should she fix the table first? No, the *galette* first—it must have time to bake and cool. Thank heaven this Breton recipe was an easy one. Sara smiled to think that Jean-Claude had chosen this traditional Epiphany cake. He must have been drawn back to his Breton roots, when the little cake was a special treat of his childhood.

It felt good to put her hands into a fine cake batter after so long away from her cooking pleasures. She divided the light mix of sugar, flour, egg yolks, butter and salt into two equal parts, then pressed them into buttered round cake pans. She glazed the tops with a froth of egg yolk and water and drew the tines of a fork over the tops, forming crisscross diamond patterns.

She was going to depart from custom and fill the cake with a cream cheese mixture enhanced with buttermilk, and salty to the taste. The cake—if all went well—should be tender and flaky, and not very sweet. It was to be served last, in place of a cheese plate, to accompany the coffees and liqueurs.

While the cake was baking she directed her mind to the flowers for the tables. With the waiters nearby folding napkins into fans, shining glasses, and setting out service utensils, Sara concentrated on creating her arrangement of flowers and greenery.

The maître d' had brought a long container that stretched the length of the table. Sara anchored baby's breath over a layer of fern, then inserted yellow and white rosebuds deeply into the ferny background. The end result looked almost professional, she thought.

She stood with the maître d' and briefed him one last time. "Just make sure this table is happy—a lot depends on it. Mr. McNatt, the host, will probably introduce you to the two chefs with him as well as Paul Edgerton, the food critic."

"Ah, yes," he said earnestly. "The man at The Right Table who argues with the lady. Jean-Claude told me. Do not distress yourself. All will be as perfect as in a dream." He gave a confident laugh that Sara wished she could share.

CHAPTER TWENTY-ONE

THE EVENING SKY was still touched with the glow of sunset. Out of the kitchen window Sara saw street lights go on and the restaurant sign by the parking lot entrance light up. Her heart was beating hard. The restaurant was about to open, and Dulcie's party was scheduled for seven-thirty, an hour from now. Jean-Claude was sleeping again. Sara suspected that Aunt Elizabeth's potion contained a good dose of tranquilizer.

A fresh flow of apprehension rippled through her. She was worried about Paul's reaction to the dinner, almost more than anything else. How would he judge her *galette,* for instance? She could hear his smooth, rich voice saying, "A fine combination of flavors wedded into a beautiful finish for a superior dinner. This young chef is innovative, Mr. McNatt...." Then, just as clearly, he was saying, "This travesty of cheese and cake, salt and sweet, should be swiftly put into the disposal to meet its proper fate. The chef has no feel for subtleties...."

A horrible thought struck her—who was she cooking for? Was it Paul she wanted to impress, or was she doing this for Jean-Claude? Did she have such a huge ego that she was imposing her own ideas on the meal even though her work tonight was supposed to be Jean-Claude's?

You want Paul's praise, she admitted silently. She wanted to see his fine lips taste the things that she had created, that her hands had touched—almost as if something of herself could enter into him.

She removed the cake from the oven. The layers looked shiny, brown and appetizing. She would have to taste it first, just in case it *was* a bad idea to improvise her own recipe. She didn't want Jean-Claude blamed for her mistake. Carefully she cut a horizontal sliver from the surface of a layer destined to be on the bottom. She spread some of her filling mix on it and popped it into her mouth. It was good.

The kitchen was a blur of activity. Fast, expert fingers were making radish roses, carrot curls, white turnip camellias—making ready trays of garnishes. Marie was finishing the sauces for the regular menu and Sara was completing the sauces for the duck and the cucumber dishes.

The restaurant sounds were increasing. The first customers had arrived. Sara looked about her with a sudden fear that nothing was ready, no matter how hard everyone had tried. Armand saw her and put a strong arm around her shoulder. *"Mise en place, mademoiselle,"* he said with a determined tone and adjusted his immaculate neck cloth. "Everything is in place."

"It really is," she said unbelievingly. She gave a

quick kiss to each of the tired assistants, and to Marie and Armand. Armand established a rhythm carving the roasts and supervising the dishes as they were readied for the dining room.

Sara's impatient eyes had spotted a small sliding door that opened into the executive cubicle. Curious, she entered the tiny office, noticing that there was an opening next to the desk for a view of the restaurant. A palm tree had been placed against it, making it an ideal spy hole close to the McNatt table. Sara intended to use it.

Her solar plexus was shivering from a delayed reaction. It wasn't going to be easy watching the long table from her hiding place in the executive office. Quietly she offered up a prayer for Jean-Claude and Dulcie to be happy. Something good had to come from all of this.

The restaurant was filling up and waiters swarmed around the pick-up area in the kitchen. Between helping wherever she was needed, Sara spied through her private window. Suddenly, it was seven-thirty and the McNatt party arrived. Dulcie was tense looking and dressed in an overly elaborate blue chiffon dress. She was followed by Paul, who cast an analytic eye around the room. The other ladies and gentlemen of the group were conservatively dressed and sleek. Sara knew which one was Dulcie's father—the big rugged man who wore a string tie with his well-tailored dark suit. The president of the Gourmets de Los Angeles had to be the one with the deep-blue velvet jacket that set off his thick snowy-white hair so well. Of the three other men, two were the judging chefs, and the two women were Dulcie's mother and the wife of the gentleman in the velvet jacket.

It was starting, Sara thought with a jolt. These people, most of whom had been abstractions until now, were here to judge everything that had been prepared in the last frantic two hours. She tried to read their faces, but knew it was a waste of precious time. She was needed in the kitchen.

Sara had to do something about Jean-Claude's appearance. He could be called out at any time by his guests at the long table. She brought a clean white chef's suit out from the pantry closet and helped Jean-Claude down from his high stool.

"We're going to resurrect you," she said encouragingly. She accompanied him as far as the rest room door. "Change into these." He gave her a grin that was almost normal and shut the door. Sara planned to touch up his face with cosmetics from her purse.

Jean-Claude took a long time and Sara was about to go into the rest room to see if he was sick again, but he came out, looking like a new man in his clean white suit.

"Sit here," she ordered. "I'm going to bring some blood back into your face." His body was still limp and unresponsive, and his hands were cold. His brown moustache stood out against his sickly skin.

Sara used her makeup base, rubbing it over his big nose and cheeks, erasing the dark circles under his eyes. She added a glowing blusher for a healthy look, then she held up her purse mirror to him. He pursed his lips. *"Mon Dieu,* you have given me my original handsomeness." He was able to grin at his joke.

"Sit still," she said. Deftly she slid his tall chef's hat onto his head and put it at a dignified angle. He reached up to set it into his usual jaunty tilt and she set it straight again.

She stood back to analyze her work. In the low lights of the restaurant Paul just might not recognize him. She gave him his triangular white cotton neck scarf and he knotted it around the collar of his coat. Jean-Claude stood up to wrap his shaky arms around her and pull her against him.

"How can I repay you?" he whispered huskily.

"Just be happy." She felt close to tears.

"I promise to make your Paul see what a misjudgment he has done to you," he said dramatically.

"If you do, you'll be a dead Frenchman, Jean-Claude, I swear! Don't you dare do *anything*...."

He grinned.

The waiters were ready to pick up the soup cups, now beautifully garnished by Marie and set onto handsome plates edged with red and gold. Scrolled between the bands of color was *L'Intime*. Sigmund Heep had only the best.

Sara urged Jean-Claude to save his strength and stay in one place. She hurried into the cubicle and looked through the peephole. The table was within easy earshot, just in front of her, and the conversation seemed comfortable among the guests. The soup was rapidly disappearing.

Sara caught a comment from the Gourmet president: "The last time I had this was at the Four Seasons. This is excellent." One of the chefs nodded in agreement. Paul was eating silently, but he was eating. Dulcie seemed so frozen with anxiety that she could hardly swallow anything.

Back in the kitchen Armand was sending out the wine for the next course. The dinner progressed in its ordered pattern and Sara's furtive peeks told her the food was being relished. The two chefs, especially, were tasting carefully and conferring. One of them dipped his finger into the dressing for the shrimp and avocado dish for a private moment of evaluation.

There were agreeable smiles when the duck was served, decorated with small rounds of puff pastry stamped with a fleur de lys pattern. The carrot purée gave color, and the green crescents of cooked cucumber gleamed in their delicate sauce. The mango sherbet in its tiny silver cups was savored slowly by the guests.

So far so good. Sara couldn't have eaten anything if her life depended on it. She was still waiting for Paul to do something or say something about the food. Sara heard an appreciative remark about the cucumbers from one of the ladies: "I've often wondered why we don't see cucumbers cooked more often...."

Paul turned his attention to her. "To be sure," he agreed. "This is a good complement to the duck."

Sara could have cried with relief. He was in a mellow mood. But how mellow? He still had to come face to face with Jean-Claude.

There was a pause while the table was cleared and the various wineglasses were replaced with fresh ones. Sara held her breath. Her dessert was ready on a large silver platter. The milky, frozen balls of almond ice lay in their nests of candied orange rind. She had put several white rose buds and maidenhair fern on the edge of the platter.

The maître d' and two waiters worked over the tray just before serving it, pouring the cognac and quickly flaming it. Exclamations from the table followed the flickering blue flames and the chefs nodded to each other. Sara wondered if she had done something too ostentatious but the faces at the table looked happy.

The waiters served the glistening nests onto crystal plates, ladling the warm sauce over the top. Dulcie watched every face around her nervously. She leaned to whisper something to her father, who boomed, "Of course it's great! Stop fussing, honey...."

"The boy's really done it," the president of the gourmet society said to his host. "I say he's first class."

Neither the chefs nor Paul said anything to that, and Sara felt angry. Why should a love story, and a career, hang in the balance of judgments by these few self-satisfied people?

After the dessert plates were removed the waiters took orders for coffee and liqueurs.

Sara's *galette* came next, sliced into thin wedges. The cheese filling stood out white against the golden crust of the cake. A murmur of interest rippled around the group as the waiters served out the small pieces. This was finger food in the same way that cheese would be for the final course.

Paul's fine hand toyed with his wedge of cake. He lifted it to his nose and smelled it, as a wine connoisseur would a cork. Then he chewed a bite with an analyzing look before popping the rest into his mouth. One of the chefs was watching. "Well?" he inquired. Paul slowly drew toward himself the plate with the remaining cake on it and selected a second piece.

"Does this answer your question?" He smiled.

For the first time, Sara had a true sense of optimism. She watched as the rest of the cake disappeared around the table, washed down by coffee or sips of liqueur.

She felt an uneven breath over her shoulder. Jean-Claude was smiling hopefully and watching the end of the dinner. "They have not tossed their plates to the floor," he said. "Maybe I am saved, *non*?"

"They're deciding right now," she whispered. "Let's not watch."

They walked together back to the work area of the kitchen. "I am a fraud," Jean-Claude said mournfully. "If they like it, it is you they are applauding."

Just then, Dulcie burst through the serving doors and Jean-Claude pulled himself erect like a man about to be sentenced. She threw her arms around him. "They want me to bring you out!" She looked around the kitchen, at first not recognizing Sara. She stopped in her tracks. "What are you doing back here, Sara?"

"For moral support, Dulcie. I just came in the back way to see how things were going. I couldn't help myself!"

"Then come on and meet my parents," she bubbled. "Everyone wants to congratulate Jean-Claude!"

Sara shook her head. "I'm in old clothes—I'd rather not. And, *please*, Dulcie, don't say I'm here. You and Jean-Claude should enjoy your success together. I'd rather not be part of it."

Dulcie tugged at Jean-Claude's hand and pulled him toward the dining room. He gave Sara a bemused look and went with her.

"It is done," Armand crowed. "Go to your little window and report to us."

Dulcie's father was standing at his place with his large hand extended to take Jean-Claude's. "The votes are in, John," he said pleasantly, ignoring the French name. "Chef Austin Gilbert will speak for us all."

Jean-Claude was trying not to slump, Sara perceived. His back was straight and even dignified. The middle-aged chef rose from his chair and formally addressed him: "We are unanimous that you are on your way to becoming a master chef. You are innovative without being too radical, and you should find an eager clientele anywhere." He moved to shake Jean-Claude's hand. "I invite you to San Francisco to be a guest on my program."

The entire table of diners stood, then, to give their appreciation. Jean-Claude gallantly went to Dulcie's mother and kissed her hand with a flourish while Dulcie glowed with delight.

He then shook Paul's hand and was detained from proceeding around the table. Sara's heart lurched. *Please!* she begged silently to any power that might be listening.

Paul's penetrating voice carried across the happy noises while Sara held her breath. "I believe we have met before—at the home of a mutual friend." He smiled at Jean-Claude. Sara watched Jean-Claude's jaw drop. "I recall saying to our friend Sara that your style was provocative. You made an impression on me then, and again tonight. You are obviously a lover of...the finer things. I intend to mention in my column that the chef at L'Intime is one to be watched and appreciated. Tell our mutual friend that I applaud her taste."

An unusual expression flitted over Jean-Claude's face as he shook Paul's hand again. "You are most kind, Monsieur Edgerton. I owe much of my present situation to the goodness of Sara and to her friendship to Dulcie and myself. I take pride in that friendship." He gave Dulcie a melting look that was unmistakably love, and then turned back to Paul. "I will give your message to Sara, sir. It may not be too late."

Sara couldn't believe Jean-Claude's choice of

words. Jean-Claude had moved on and Paul was standing quietly by himself. He was facing away from Sara's view, and she wanted to see his face. When he turned around again his face was a mask of Edgerton suaveness. He was conversing with Dulcie's family, confident, at ease in his world.

Sara couldn't watch any more. She said goodbye to Armand and Marie and left the restaurant. Her body ached with fatigue, and she drove slowly in the evening traffic. It pleased her deeply that she had been part of a happily-ever-after ending. Beyond that, she was just simply tired of everything.

Back in the living room of her apartment the phone light was flickering. When she listened to the message she heard Paul's voice and tried not to react to it. "Sara," he said from the tape, "I've just had the pleasure of a fine dinner cooked by a friend of yours, Jean-Claude Roland—a French gentleman I have encountered once before in other circumstances." The voice paused a moment. "Not that it makes much difference to your opinion of me now...but *mea culpa*, most sincerely. My judgment has been grievously bad and I...." The tape clicked off and the next message started close on its heels.

"Your mechanical secretary is a cold censor. I won't press you for another chance, yet I earnestly pray for one. You sent me away with good reason. Just try to recall the good moments we had together.... I won't forget them...ever."

The doorbell rang and Dulcie and Jean-Claude

pushed their way into the room with a bottle of champagne and wild whoops of victory. The next few hours were filled with noisy, joyous plans for the future, until Sara's eyes could hardly stay open.

Jean-Claude had had a miraculous healing sometime during the congratulations, and he made his famous omelette for them all at midnight. Sara tried to be a good sport, even though she felt removed from their strong emotions. It wasn't envy she was feeling, but numbness.

After they had gone and she was lying awake in her bed, Paul's voice kept on saying, "Try to recall the good moments.... I won't forget them...."

"Oh, damn," she whispered, and let the sobs begin at last.

CHAPTER TWENTY-TWO

SATURDAY MORNING, after she took her parents to the airport for their flight to San Francisco, Sara drove to Bel Air. In the back seat of her Mustang was enough clothing for the week, her portable typewriter and books about wines.

She didn't want to be available to anyone until the contest on Wednesday. The mere sound of a telephone and the flash of a message light was more than she wanted to live with, and Aunt Elizabeth was kind enough to offer Sara the guest wing of her house. The Mediterranean-style estate was becoming a refuge for all of Elizabeth's friends suffering from a certain kind of heart trouble lately.

Sara's new quarters were decorated in clear tones of yellow and beige, with accents of sky blue. The dormer window had a long, cushioned window seat beneath it where she discovered a calming view of the spring garden stretching out below.

Aunt Elizabeth had offered friendship and silence when Sara had called earlier that morning. "No one shall know, dear. There are times when a woman needs a place of peace."

"It's not just peace I want, Aunt Liz, it's...."

"I know. You haven't been able to fit the pieces of your personal puzzle together yet, and you have to try one more time. Am I right?" The old voice had sounded sure.

"I have to know if I've been the one who made all the mistakes, or if Paul did—and how I could have let it get so crazy when it should have been wonderful."

"I would advise you not to agonize too much. It never solves things. There is a certain old maxim that helps me: *To understand all is to forgive all.*"

"Thanks. I'll try. Do you think Paul has ever heard your little maxim?"

"No more of that now, Sara," she had scolded. "Say goodbye to your dear parents and come here as soon as you can. I plan to leave you completely to yourself. Marie will cook you anything you ask for."

At her aunt's house Sara entered into a timeless existence, with no telephone, no television, no newspapers—just as she had requested. She knew that this was the most important thinking she would ever do in her life. She couldn't let Paul just walk away from her, but she didn't know what to do to untangle their punishing web of reactions to each other.

He had his difficult past to contend with—his angers and defenses. And she had things deep inside her that still hurt. She was determined to drag them out into the light for examination—Jacques, her disappointments, her uncertainty about what she expected of herself, even her silly prejudice about people who didn't live up to their talents.

Somewhere in her ponderings, looking out of the high windows at the way nature persisted in creating beauty, Sara began to realize her own blindness, her reactiveness.

She wasn't ready to forgive Paul, any more than she could forgive herself—but she was starting to understand. According to Aunt Liz's old saying, that was a good beginning.

Sara had told Eric there was one more Olive Gadwall article she had to write. Now she knew what it would say. Propped up in the corner of the window seat with her typewriter, she began.

My dear Paul, answer me a riddle this Wednesday morning before our contest of tastes.... What is the difference between a Bedouin nomad presiding over his campfire meal, using the seasonings of his long tradition, and a Cordon Bleu chef who coaxes a subtle flavor from his stainless steel and copper pot?

If you tell me, "There is all the difference in the world! One is a man of unrefined tastes and the other is a master," you will have missed the point of the riddle. I have missed it sometimes, myself. The correct answer is, I believe, that there is no difference between the two men, for both of them give great respect to their art. And where there is respect there is dignity. Beyond that, the sophisticated quibbling we both have done is not really important. Let us tell our readers not to be afraid of their own taste, and to be willing to try that of others. Enjoy food, enjoy its preparation, enjoy its presentation. Regard the comments of critics with a grain of salt, because we are definitely not gods!

Now your Olive must go to prepare herself to meet the man from The Right Table. *Ciao!*

That would be the last time Olive chided Paul Cabot Edgerton in print. It was a good feeling to be done.

SARA TOOK LONG WALKS on the sunlit paths of Aunt Elizabeth's gardens, pausing to pick a late blooming double pink camellia for her crystal vase, leaning to inhale the healing fragrance of an old-fashioned moss rose, dropping in to have a cup of herb tea with Dulcie and talk about Jean-Claude.

The books on wines got careful reading, and for several hours late Tuesday night Jean-Claude coached Sara for the contest.

"I still don't find it pleasant to spit out each sip of wine," she complained of the time-honored ritual.

"If you swallow it all," he laughed, "you will be a little drunk at the end of the tasting. Then what will your public think?"

Jean-Claude, Dulcie, Aunt Elizabeth and Sara had sampled and evaluated more than twenty towel-shrouded bottles from the de Lacy collection of wines. Only Aunt Liz knew them all in the blind testing. "In my day a lady of refinement made a point of educating herself in the fine points of the gentleman's world—wines, cigars, cognac. I don't regret my early indulgence of male egos, but I wouldn't teach a daughter of mine to do it. Let the man make an effort to understand the things that are important to a woman, I say now!" Her clear blue eyes sparkled with determination and the accidental swallowing of some of her own good wines.

"Why, Aunt Liz!" Sara said. "You sound positively liberated!"

"I always was," she grinned. "I just didn't let all the men know it. In my time we had to play lots of games to survive. Thank God it's changing." She looked meaningfully at Sara.

Wednesday Sara moved back into her apartment, feeling that she knew herself better now. She had come to accept that she loved Paul with all her heart, and that her love was so strong and unshakable that it couldn't be altered by anything Paul said or did. This love had moved far beyond egos and old hurts. Hadn't it been tested in so many ways already?

What Paul felt was, strangely, not so important. She knew that someday—if there really was justice and order in the universe—their love would find a way to come together. If she had learned anything in her days in the quiet, sunlit guest room in Bel Air, it was to accept life and be patient.

SARA PAID CAREFUL ATTENTION to her disguise, starting early in the afternoon. Norma worried over her like a frantic hen, bringing out every wig and old movie costume she could find.

Sara had to calm her down. "I want to be Olive Gadwall. When the public sees me on the television screens I want them to feel satisfied...that was just the way they pictured the old gal. I want Olive's first and last appearance to leave them happy."

The contest was scheduled for 7:00 P.M., timed so that most of the Los Angeles viewers were likely to be having their own evening meal. Sara arrived at Mon Château in a taxi. She wouldn't drive her own car, and she certainly couldn't have Aunt Elizabeth's chauffeur bring her.

The woman who stepped from the cab at six-thirty was fifty-ish, with pleasantly styled graying brown curls and a navy-blue tailored suit. Her shoes were dark blue and sensibly low heeled. Around her neck a pair of tortoise shell reading glasses hung from a gold-toned chain. People who looked interestedly at her face saw a friendly, middle-aged lady with brisk step and a very average, very comfortable appearance.

Sara took a deep breath and plunged ahead up the steps to Mon Château's familiar front door. She was aware of lights and television cameras, and a sprinkling of applause as she went quickly to the private dining room at the side. Eric met her there with an encouraging smile and a thumbs-up sign.

"Paul's over there," he said, "in the center of that circle of reporters and cameras."

Sara looked for him and saw the top of his head over the crowd. She moved with dignity to meet the judges and speak briefly to George Strickland, Paul's editor. She nodded as she heard the rules: there would be twelve wines tasted and twelve foods. The wines must be identified by variety first, with extra points added for naming the year and the vineyard. The foods must be identified, and extra points given for naming the ingredients in each dish. Sara saw that the scores would be flashed onto a mechanical scoreboard at the end of the room. The television lights made the room very hot, and as the time grew nearer for the contest to begin the noise level increased.

Sara sighed, feeling like part of an old Roman spectacle. George Strickland spoke up: "Before you sit down, the TV people want to get a shot of the moment you first meet." He brought Sara to a place beneath the scoreboard and Eric accompanied Paul.

The two rivals looked at each other while the cameras whirred. Olive put out her hand first to take Paul's. A slight smile was on his refined lips, not exactly condescending, but more of real amusement. "At long last," he said as he took her hand. "I'm not disappointed, Miss Gadwall. You are exactly as you led me to picture you."

"A dessicated old maid, as you once threatened to call me?" she said in the motherly sounding voice she had rehearsed with Norma.

Paul deftly raised her hand and kissed it. "A gentleman may be forgiven his barbarities if they spring from ignorance, I hope." His eyes were full of golden lion's confidence.

It was Sara's turn to smile. "Perhaps... perhaps."

"Then, dear lady, pray let us get on with our little matter of taste, shall we?"

"To be sure," she said, mimicking his elaborate manners for the cameras and winking at Eric.

There were two tables in the center of the room, each draped in fine white linen and set with silver and several empty wineglasses. Nearby, a long serving table bore a line of twelve covered dishes and the anonymous wine bottles. The *sommelier* of Mon Château and the maître d' stood by as the official servers.

Sara allowed Paul to seat her. For an awful moment she realized that this would be the last time he would ever hold her chair and lean his body close to hers as he had just done. It was the last time they would share words or touch hands. Her heart suddenly constricted tightly, leaving her breathless. Noble sentiments and high resolves to the contrary, Sara Courtney was already feeling lost without Paul Edgerton in her life.

She forced herself back to attention, setting down her navy-blue handbag beside her chair and opening the white linen napkin onto her lap. She turned her head slightly to acknowledge the man at the next table who had just taken his place. He looked back at her with a formal nod of his head.

Olive Gadwall folded her hands primly in front of her, waiting for the judges to explain to the watching public how the contest would be run. Sara felt the comforting shape of Maestro Segenti's little Italian garnet ring and turned it around on her finger, just as she realized with horror that Paul had kissed that same hand a minute ago. She slipped the ring off quickly and dropped it into the pocket of her suit jacket, praying that he hadn't noticed it.

A coin toss between the two editors determined that the first half of the contest would be the food tasting. Sara felt good about that—it was home territory.

The maître d' brought out the first covered plate. "I will present both the lady and the gentleman with a bite of the first prepared dish. They will have one minute to taste, then write their description on a pad of paper provided for them. I will ask them please to close their eyes as I am serving."

He approached Olive's table and she obediently closed her eyes, waiting to be fed the first portion. She felt like a fledgling bird in a nest waiting for its mother.

"Open, please," the serious voice said.

The tangy, complicated flavors of a good fondue spread pleasantly through her mouth and she smiled as she swallowed her morsel. She looked quickly over at Paul, who was thoughtfully rolling his bite for a thorough evaluation.

Olive wrote *fondue*.

The maître d' read both answers. "Correct. Now, please, name the cheese in the fondue."

Olive knew the distinctive flavors of Gruyère and Romano and Parmesan. She wrote that, plus the fact that the butter in the mixture was unsalted.

"For naming the dish, one point each," he instructed the scorekeepers. "For naming ingredients...two points for Monsieur Edgerton... four points for Madame Gadwall."

Olive Gadwall watched as a large 3 appeared next to Paul's name and a 5 next to hers. A few people clapped at the score, and Olive wished they hadn't.

The next dish was a cold paté served on a light cracker. They both identified it and knew that it was made from calf's liver and chicken liver, with butter, sherry and brandy. Six points went to each.

As the contest proceeded the room grew more silent. By the final dish the score was Paul Edgerton, 24—he had missed the conch stew and white veal stock entirely—and Olive Gadwall, 37. Olive glanced at Paul as the last of the twelve tastings began. He was looking straight ahead, like a soldier on parade, showing not the slightest emotion. Did it gall him so terribly to have lost the first round of the contest? She didn't feel completely comfortable as the victor. They were still fighting each other, even in this ridiculous contest.

And why wasn't he sweltering under the heat of these lights? His dark gray wool gabardine suit was every bit as hot as hers. But she had a heavy layer of rubberized makeup to contend with. She slipped off her jacket for relief and felt ready for the final dish. Each dish in the contest had been progressively more difficult or obscure. Paul had been tripped up on the tenth and eleventh. She had, mercifully, once made a conch stew in Mexico when her parents had taken a long vacation in Guadeloupe and she had come to know the hotel chef.

Olive closed her eyes for the last time, being told that the twelfth was a soup. It was a familiar flavor—celery root, onion, leek, cream...celeriac soup, very smooth and quite subtle. She wrote her opinion of the dish and the maître d' nodded his head silently, while waiting for Paul to make up his mind. The maître d' read Paul's answer and made his final announcement:

"Ladies and gentlemen—for the celeriac soup...Madame Gadwall five points. Monsieur Edgerton did not correctly identify it."

The scoreboard flashed the new numbers: Paul Edgerton, 24—Olive Gadwall, 42. A scattering of applause went around the little room, the covered dishes taken away by waiters, and an intermission announced. Sara was surprised by the score. Paul knew much more about foods than the numbers showed. What had happened to him tonight?

Paul stood up and graciously came to Olive's table, offering her his hand in congratulations.

"I bow to your knowledge of fine cuisine."

Sara adjusted her voice to a soft, low register. "And I admire your humility."

"I believe you're the first person to say that, Madam, and I look forward to not having to be humble after the wine tasting." He smiled maddeningly at her, and her carefully guarded emotions started to slip from her tight control.

"But isn't humility a good quality, whether or not one wins?" she chided.

"Your middle years have made you wise, dear nemesis, and I defer to your wisdom once more." He nodded his head and retired to his table, where a plate of dry biscuits and small cubes of mild cheddar cheese had been placed. It was time to clear the palate of the variety of food flavors and prepare for the wines. Olive's table received a plate of biscuits and cheese, also.

The windows were opened briefly to air the room, and no smoking was permitted for the remainder of the contest. Olive nibbled on a biscuit, wondering what Paul was thinking. What made him say the things he had said to her? Was he putting on a show of gallantry for the cameras only?

The *sommelier* stepped forth with his first bottle of wine. It was swathed in a cone of white paper to conceal its label. Sara knew the reason for the white tablecloth—from her wine-tasting seminar she knew it was the perfect background for assessing the color of the wine in the glass.

Six tulip-shaped, stemmed glasses stood at each table. The first wine was poured and Olive Gadwall picked her glass up by the foot, very carefully examining the color against the white background before bringing it to her nose and then to her lips.

She stole a glance sideways at Paul, who was masterfully going through the proper motions that Olive had awkwardly done. *Dry before sweet, young before old, modest before fine*—that was the order of wines for a classic tasting. On that basis, Olive wrote her evaluation. This was a dry white wine, bone dry. Jean-Claude had given her a muscadet last night that was identical. She wrote the name and an approximate vintage.

The *sommelier* regarded her answer and Paul's, then announced that both were correct as to name and year. Paul had correctly named the château and got an extra point.

The next series of white wines were easily identified by Paul. Olive struggled to name a Chenin Blanc and a German Riesling from Mosel. She was lucky enough to make two accurate educated guesses. The others she failed to name at all.

This was Paul Edgerton's territory. The scoreboard numbers edged higher next to his name, until, after the white wines, Paul had an over-all total of 38 points and Olive had gained but a few to 47. At that rate she was going to lose the contest. Eric's face looked tense.

The glasses were replaced with fresh ones for the rest of the tasting. Paul took small bites of his biscuits and cheese between wines and Olive did the same. She knew she should care more about winning.

A rush of pleasure went through her when she recognized the Zinfandel from the 1981 California crop. Jean-Claude had made a point to show her the deep blackberry hue near the top of the glass, darkening at the bottom until it was almost opaque. "It looks like a vintage port," he had said as a hint. It tasted strong and slightly sweet. She guessed at Napa Valley for its origins, and was right.

Four more reds crossed her lips. Paul knew them all. She used every spare shred of knowledge she had gathered and made guesses on every one...an Anjou Rosé, an Italian Chianti, a Cabernet-Sauvignon. Sometimes she was right, but not often enough to keep the worried look from Eric's face. Before the last wine the score was Edgerton 56...Gadwall 56.

The *sommelier* appeared nervous as he poured the final glasses of wine. "I wish you both good luck," he said as they lifted their goblets of palish, pink-red liquid. It wasn't the heavy, sweet dessert wine that Olive expected, according to the customary sequence, but there was no rule that a wine tasting *had* to proceed from dry to sweet.

She passed the fragrant, fresh-smelling wine beneath her nose and tasted it. She knew at once she had tasted this recently. In fact, she had drunk it here, at Mon Château...with Paul! *Beaujolais nouveau*, she wrote quickly. This was the new wine that everyone was racing to taste first in New York and Los Angeles. She had a strange, quivery feeling in her body as she looked over at Eric and gave him his own thumbs-up signal. Her hopeless frustration with Paul was breaking out of control. The modest little Beaujolais had been the last straw to her composure.

Sara was feeling light-headed in the roomful of cheering people and whirring cameras and lights. A blur of numbers flashed on the board... 58...58. The *sommelier* was announcing that there was a tie. "The last selection was a Beaujolais nouveau, ladies and gentlemen, correctly identified by Miss Gadwall and Mr. Edgerton."

Her chair was being eased away from the table and she found Paul next to her, helping her to stand and meet her audience behind the television cameras. "Are you all right, old dear?" he whispered into her ear. "Shall we do the final lap for our public?" He was smiling charmingly.

She let him take her arm and lead her to a place beneath the scoreboard where microphones were being held out toward them. A voice called out, "What do you think about the tie?"

Paul chuckled agreeably. "The better critic won."

"Does that mean you're happy with the score, Mr. Edgerton?"

"Miss Gadwall is a formidable adversary in print and out. I found her a delightful opponent and a true lady. I have no complaints." He lifted Olive's hand for a public kiss to show his sportsmanship. His lips brushed close to her hand, but then, swiftly and unnoticed by others, there was the searing warmth of his lips in a firm pressure before he drew away.

She looked up sharply, as if he had struck her. His eyes were glinting with amber flecks, his lips lifted into the slightest of amused smiles.

"Miss Gadwall—Olive—" a woman shouted for attention, "—will you and Mr. Edgerton be doing this again soon? Will you ask for a rematch, since you tied tonight?"

Olive shook her head and Paul answered for her. "My point was made. I brought the lady out of hiding, and I shall be satisfied with the results. And now, ladies...gentlemen...I have an appointment tonight and I beg your leave to attend to it." He looked at Olive and smiled again. *"Ciao."*

CHAPTER TWENTY-THREE

THE MORNING AFTER THE CONTEST Sara wanted more than anything to stay in bed wrapped in a cozy cocoon. She didn't want to know what was happening in the world outside or what the newspapers had written about the great challenge. She needed her own comforting walls around her while she sorted out the conflicting emotions that sleep had mercifully dulled for the long hours of the night.

Mostly she was irritated with herself for having been weak enough to let Eric talk her into going through with it. She hadn't been the aggressively crusading Aunt Olive that her readers had expected to see. Waves of embarrassment rippled through her when she thought how easily Paul had taken command just by being suave and pleasant in front of the media. He had treated Olive as he might have treated one of his mother's friends, solicitously and courteously. And she had just stood there in front of the microphones, stilted and light-headed, while Paul answered for her.

The ringing phone jarred her out of her thoughts. She hesitated, letting it ring long enough for the answering machine to take over. Then she played it back, not knowing what she would do if it were Paul.

"Hi," Eric's voice crackled in her ear. "Call me back, Sara—at the office. I know you're there, damn it! I've got news."

She sighed and dialed the number. "Ah ha!" he said. "Who are you avoiding—Edgerton?"

"I'm tired, Eric."

"I've got news that will perk you up!" She was silent and he barked, "Are you there, Sara?"

"Yes, go on—what's your news?"

"You sound like the end of the world. I've been getting calls... last night and this morning. Everybody's jostling for an interview with Aunt Olive, alone or with Edgerton. You've captured the media. Sara?"

She groaned.

"Is that any way to greet tidings of sudden success? Listen to this—a woman's magazine, one of the biggies, wants to do a cover story on you and your 'enchantingly clever ruse of disguise.' You represent the feminine drive for parity in the bastions of male supremacy. Wait until they see the real you! They hinted at a contract for a monthly column. Now you can take off the fright wigs and be yourself. Talk show offers are rolling in, local and network."

"I can't think about it now." She heard the tiny quaver in her own voice. "I'm tired. Haven't you forgotten that I'm retiring from Olive Gadwall?"

"Retire!" he exploded. "While you're right on the brink of syndication? Is this the Sara who wanted to be a real journalist—be really tops in her profession? Are you listening?"

"Mmm, yes, Eric." His voice sounded like ocean waves crashing futilely against a far shore, and she was only half aware of what he was trying to say to her.

"Just think, you can be a feature writer about more than just food. You'll be able to pick and choose things you want to talk about—and there's money in it, Sara. You can be comfortably independent. You can afford to tell off all the food and wine snobs in the country!"

"I don't want to take on the whole food industry. Lots of my best friends are chefs and serious cooks...even if some of them pander to food fads and social chic." She sighed again. "Just take people's names, and tell them Aunt Olive is on a vacation. All of this has been too much for her middle-aged nerves."

Eric breathed an improper word. "This is serious—an opportunity that most journalists would grab for."

"I *am* serious. I just can't cope with anything now."

His voice changed. "I'm sorry, honey. It's Edgerton, isn't it? But life goes on. He's not the last smooth bastard you'll ever meet...likeable as he is."

"What bothers me...well, I think he let me... that he saw to it that the score was tied."

"That just doesn't make sense. A man like Edgerton.... Hold on," he interrupted, "there's something I have to read...."

She felt like hanging up, but that would be unkind. Eric was trying to help. From his point of view she must seem wildly impractical—a fool. She held the phone a little away from her ear, hearing indistinct conversation on the other end of the line and a lot of rustling of paper. Then Eric's voice shouted onto the line. "My God! There's something you haven't seen yet!" His tone was a mix of hilarity and excitement. "Sara, are you still there?"

"What's going on?"

He gave a strangled chortle. "You'll have to see for yourself. I can't just tell you. It wouldn't be fair. Get the morning *Tribune* and read Paul's column, pronto! Call me back!" He hung up.

A rush of fear surged through her. What had Paul done now? And where could she find a *Tribune* without going out? It occurred to her that Norma was visiting friends overnight. Her paper would still be on her doorstep.

She threw on her terry-cloth robe and ran down the hall to Norma's door and grabbed up the paper, then back to her living room while her fingers fumbled with the rubber band. She flipped open the paper to the food section, letting the rest of it drop to the floor.

There was a write-up of yesterday's contest, with a headline, THE TIE. Her eyes rolled past it to Paul's column.

Hail and farewell, my friends of the Right Table! By the time you read this Paul Edgerton will be far away, flying toward Rome.

A desolate, empty feeling gripped her heart. Her eyes sped on.

> I look forward to springtime in Italy. I have gone back to my first love, international reporting, and I will now be the European correspondent for Tribune Enterprises and their network of fine newspapers across the United States.

Sara drew a heavy breath—Paul was gone! Somehow, she had still hoped...in a small corner of herself....

> Do not worry. The Right Table will continue in the capable hands of Bettina Straus. Already many of you know her Guide to Restaurants in Los Angeles. Who better could I find? This is not to say that I will forget food entirely, and no doubt I will sometimes lapse into a bit of gourmet whimsy as I move about the capitals and byways and report to you what I see there.

Sara was about to drop the paper to the floor with the rest of the *Tribune*, but something else caught her eye.

"Now to an even more urgent matter," he had written.

> You have all been drawn into my controversy with Olive Gadwall of the *Chronicle*. It

hasn't always been fun for me, even if it did provide amusement for our public. The redoubtable Olive—may she be blessed for her courage—is responsible for the fact that I'm going to do what I should have been doing in this difficult world: trying to see what makes sense and reporting it to you as honestly as I can.

And that brings me circuitously to my point: I have a proposal for Olive Gadwall (née Sara) behind her clever disguises. My dear, will you marry me?

Sara gulped and read on, stunned.

You've done your best to bring me to my senses. Despite my boorish attitudes and unforgivable behavior, I have longed to tell you how much I love you. Ponder with all of your heart and decide if you want to travel this world with me and use your own fine writing skills as well. What joys could be ours!

Two weeks from today I will be at a sidewalk table for two at the Ristorante Tre Corone in Verona, Italy—the city of Romeo and Juliet, my dearest. All arrangements for your journey have been made. At 8:00 P.M. the candles will be lit, the wine cooling and the roses will bloom against the fine white linen of our table. Strollers will be walking past and many lovers will be hand in hand. My heart will be beating with excitement, lovely Olive. I will be tense with hope, for this will be the most important day of my life. In my pocket will be a wedding license and after dinner a city official, a friend of mine, promises to marry us in the Renaissance rooms above the Piazza dei Signori, where Dante's statue broods among the flights of pigeons.

I pray you, *bella signorina*, be kind! Am I the Right Man at the Right Table? I await your choice.

My readers, my friends—thank you for your patience. You are not witnessing the end of Paul Edgerton. God bless!

The last words were blurred by the tears in Sara's eyes. The whole thing was outrageous and yet she loved it! So he *did* know who Olive Gadwall was! But when? And how?

It was crazy!

Her memory showed her the wide curved sidewalk of the Piazza Brà in Verona, where more than once she had sat at one of the tables of the Tre Corone. It was so simple to picture Paul sitting there, handsome and aloof, waiting... for her!

A flash of pure joy careened through her. She hadn't lost him! No matter if he was high-handed and overbearing at times, she loved him. She loved him! She had no illusions about him now, or about his true quality beneath the surface. And there was no question about what she was going to do.

The doorbell and the phone rang simultaneously. She picked up the phone. It was Eric. "Hold on," she said and went to the door.

A man stood there with a florist box. She tipped him and opened her box. Several dozen roses spilled out—and two large envelopes addressed "to Sara" in Paul's handwriting. She longed to read it, but Eric was on the phone, waiting. Reluctantly, she picked up the receiver.

"Well..." he said. "I admire the man. When he does things, he does them right. I'm truly happy for you, Sara, even though this leaves me in a hell of a mess!"

"I'm sorry, too, Eric. You know I have to go...."

Eric's voice softened. "I know, honey. But put up your storm windows. Someone has leaked the truth about who Olive is, and the press will be all over you any time. They haven't had such a romantic happening for years."

"Oh, no, can't you head them off?"

"Too late."

"Lord! What should I do?"

"Hole up—go to your godmother's and wait for it to die down. Better yet, give your exclusive interview to the *Chronicle*. We'll treat it any way you like."

"I've got to get off the phone. Flowers just came and there's a letter from Paul that I can't wait to read! Let's have lunch and talk then."

"Pick you up at twelve-thirty. But, just to add a serendipitous note, old J.B. Quarles is ready to offer you a special correspondent's job like Paul's, for the big *Chronicle* chain."

"Eric! Hang up!" She set the phone back into its cradle. For a moment she held the letter to her cheek. It was typical of Paul, fine and impetuous, his writing a headlong, powerful scrawl against the conservative paper. She began to read:

> Beloved Sara. I hope by now you have gotten over being angry at me for so publicly declaring myself. But, my darling, I felt I had no other course. My recent inexcusable behavior closed all other doors to you. Believe me, Sara, I have never acted in such a way before—I plead the desperation of a man who is so deeply in love that he sees through jealous eyes, because of his uncertainty about the cool little lady he adores. On sober thought I realized that you had every right to doubt my intentions from the very first, but you were driving me mad with mixed signals, too.
>
> I owe my final awakening from stupidity to our friend, Jean-Claude, the estimable young genius who had the courage to invite me to lunch at his restaurant yesterday and talk to me like a *grand-père*.

Sara made a sound between a snort and a laugh and read on, her hand shaking.

> Don't be angry with him, I beg you. I suppose you know he had a very bad conscience about his illness on the momentous McNatt Judgment Day. He made a clean breast of it to me and I absolved him. He said he could only repay you by helping us to get together

because he knew you loved me. I could have kissed him! He didn't leave much out, my dear—the painful truth of Olive's identity, your unusual childhood, your expertise as a Cordon Bleu cook, and yes, I know about Jacques, too. No wonder you resented my pseudocontinental approach and all my talk about mature human beings doing what comes naturally, without a word about something that I did not fully understand—what love can do.

I also know—with great embarrassment—that the wise Elizabeth has told you my own tale of disastrous relationships with women, starting with my poor dear mother and the jilting girl of my puppy love period... and my days as a prowling, miserable, utterly absurd man of the world. Well, most beloved Sara—I have grown up now. I can only say that my life will never be truly complete without you. I will not overwhelm you, Sara—you are an independent being and I want your friendship as much as your love. I do want to cherish you, dearest heart, and walk with your hand in mine beyond forever! Come to me, Sara—

Paul

Holding the letter close to her breast, Sara felt tensions and fears unknot in her solar plexus. Happiness moved in her like a warm flood. She smiled, thinking of the dreary Sara who had begun the day an hour earlier. The world was wonderful again. Paul might be far away, but she felt a potent link with him.

Theirs wouldn't be a union where the woman's work was absorbed completely into the man's. It would be a partnership. She would accept some of the offers that Eric had rambled on about so enthusiastically.

She closed her eyes and saw Paul in Verona with that smile on his lips that never failed to make her heart melt. Almost, she could feel his hand holding hers across a candlelit table and breathe the fine scent of his cologne.

The telephone intruded on her waking dream. "Sara, dear." Aunt Elizabeth's voice was soft. "I have forgiven that darling man. What a romantic he is—so like my Artur. Of course you are accepting him," she said as a kind of afterthought.

"Of course!"

A delightful, soft laugh answered her. "You can't know what a relief this is for me. I'd begun to blame myself for bringing you two together—questioning whether I'd lost my touch."

'Oh, Aunt Liz—" Sara felt the quaver in her own voice "—how awful if you hadn't!"

"Then you won't punish him any more on account of Jacques?"

"Who told you about Jacques? Jean-Claude?"

"I told him not to meddle, but it was like asking a fire not to burn. It was all done from love, my dear. Don't be hard on him."

"I know. It worked out, so I won't be mad at him."

"And you must call your parents in San Francisco. We've all been so worried about your sad little face when you thought yourself unobserved."

"Was I so transparent?"

"Yes.... When are you going to let Paul know you accept?"

"I have no address."

"But surely you could get it," Aunt Elizabeth urged.

"I'm going to play it his way. He'll just have to suffer, too."

A rich chuckle came from the other end of the line. "If he calls me, what shall I say? He might, you know."

"Tell him it's a secret."

"You are an evil child. But it's almost irresistible. I understand. Tomorrow we will shop for a trousseau, my gift." She hung up before Sara could answer.

Immediately the phone rang again. This time Jean-Claude's voice spoke, hesitantly. "*Chérie*, you have read the writing of Paul Edgerton this morning, *oui*?"

"Yes. And he told me in a letter what you had done. Jean-Claude, you're not to be trusted...but I love you anyway."

He gave a slightly embarrassed laugh. "*Zut*... you and that Paul would never get straight unless somebody does something. I owe you so much, Sara. I feel not right in my heart about the deception of my cooking and so I tell him the truth. He is a good man, not unreasonable—and he loves you, *sans doute*. You will go to him, *oui?*"

"*Oui*. But you can't tell Paul if he asks. Chef Roland, my compliments—you saved the whole casserole by adding the right ingredients at the last minute."

"*A bientôt!*" he laughed.

The rest of the day flew past. Eric rose to the occasion, deftly handling reporters who wanted a look at Olive Gadwall in real life. Some photographers snapped her picture as she hurried out of her door with Eric on their way to lunch. All afternoon her phone rang with requests for interviews, but she declined comment. One evening paper carried a picture captioned, *Chronicle Editor Protects Aunt Olive... will she jilt the critic at The Right Table?*

Even the TV news gave a jocular mention of the local romance, saying, "All's fair in love and broccoli wars." Sara felt uneasy. She was glad that Paul was far away in Rome. The voracious media attention was hard to take. It made their love seem trivial. But for all the temptation to fly right now to Rome and throw herself into Paul's arms, she wouldn't. She wouldn't change the romantic script he had written. They would both wait until Verona.

Her parents returned from their successful concerts in San Francisco, Seattle and Vancouver. They decided to stay in California until their next tour to Washington and New York. They would use Sara's apartment after she had gone.

The busy days became a mad blur for Sara. Only the nights were memorable, when her thoughts of Paul grew so strong that she felt she was with him. So many times she reached to pick up the phone and track him down, just to hear his beloved voice. But something told her not to. It was as if both of them needed to play out the delightful drama. Her feminine nature was being satisfied by making him wait in suspense, and his dominant male nature was probably reveling in her sweet malaise. She reread his letter a hundred times.

The speculation went on in the press. Eric had coerced various chefs into writing for the Consuming Passions column while he looked for a permanent critic. Olive Gadwall would be no more. The *Tribune*'s gossip columnist clucked about the romance, asking titillating "will she or won't she" questions, with pictures of Sara and Paul.

"Anything for circulation," she said tartly to Eric, who was having fun with it all.

"All you have to do is Telex Paul and make the announcement," he remarked.

"And take all the romance out of it? Never, Eric. I want to look as beautiful as possible and appear like a vision of love at his table. Don't deny me that!"

At night Sara slept with dreams of Verona. She walked with Paul in its medieval streets, stopping for the sweetest of kisses, and woke again, longing for his touch—the gentle touch that she knew he was capable of.

What was he doing now? He had been silent, no letters, no calls to anyone. There were terrible moments when she wondered if he was playing with her. Could this be his ironic last word for deceiving him? Would she arrive at Tre Corone and find no one waiting?

Time was speeding and yet crawling at a snail's pace. One day her father appeared at her door with a gift of beautiful matched luggage. She cooked a quick lunch for him and he reached across the table to take her hand. "What's wrong, darling? Are you having eleventh hour jitters?"

She nodded and whispered, "Suppose he's not there." Then she burst into uncontrollable tears, all her fears welling up at last.

Jonathon Courtney came around and held her against his comforting chest. "He'll be there, baby. Don't worry. This is romance, it should be wonderful and fun. Don't let him down. Enjoy what he's doing, creating beautiful memories for you both."

She looked into his handsome, loving face. "Would you...might you have done the same thing?"

A glint of amusement came into his eyes. "Quite possibly, my darling." He would say no more.

SHE SIGNED AGREEMENTS with the woman's magazine and the *Chronicle*. J.B. Quarles, the man who sat in the highest office at the *Chronicle*, called her in for a fatherly interview, and wasn't the ogre that everyone had portrayed him to be. Big, in his eighties at least, and looking every year of it, he handed her an envelope with a bonus check. "Tell me," he boomed, "are you going to meet Edgerton in Verona? I'll never tell your secret."

When she said yes, he laughed heartily and kissed her cheek as if he shared a common male delight in Paul's victory. "We're expecting big things from you, Sara," he said as they parted. "Good luck."

Sara had one last thing she wanted Eric to print under Olive Gadwall's by-line after she was in Verona. In it she told her readers that she had gone to meet the man at The Right Table—*The Very Right Man*, she wrote.

THEN THE DEPARTURE DAY CAME. Her lovely new wardrobe was packed, her hair was shining and styled by one of Beverly Hills's best salons. Aunt Liz and her parents kissed her with a few loving tears at the departure gate of the airport. Two reporters with cameras loomed out of the crowd to snap pictures.

Exhausted from a sleepless night and the very early flight time, Sara slept most of the way to Milano. It was a delight to walk out into the soft spring air at Malpensa Airport. The special enfolding ambiance of Italy gave her its eternal gift of happiness. The flow of fluid Italian speech and the appreciative male glances lifted her spirits high.

Of course Paul would be waiting in Verona!

This was reality, not a dream anymore. When she was collecting her baggage she heard a mellow Italian voice calling for Signorina Courtney, and a rotund young man wearing a chauffeur's cap at a rakish angle smiled broadly when she answered.

"Signorina Courtney, I am to drive you to Verona. My name is Luigi. *Benvenuto a Italia!*"

They were soon driving from the airport in a Fiat sedan, old but well polished. With Italian courtesy Luigi found out that Sara was meeting her fiancé. He kissed his fingers in a dramatic gesture. "Do not worry, I get you to Verona in plenty time."

Now that she was moving swiftly toward her rendezvous she began to shiver inside with a strange mixture of joy and fear. They were moving through the streets of Verona now and familiar sights made her feel comforted and welcomed. Lights were being turned on in the piazzas, and the old buildings glowed in the mellow light of early evening. The small, ancient city was as she remembered, filled with modern vitality and medieval charm. Passing through a gate in part of the old Roman wall, she glimpsed the first-century Arena a block away and her heart started to lurch alarmingly. Paul was somewhere close by.

The car drew up at the entrance to the Hotel Due Torri. Luigi refused a tip. "I am already given that," he smiled. *"Felicità, Signorina."*

At the desk she couldn't resist asking if Signor Edgerton was registered. The concierge smiled. "*Si*—he has gone out an hour ago and has said he will be late in returning. Do you wish to leave a message?"

Sara shook her head. Her pulse was racing wildly. He *was* here! She had to smile. But he hadn't met her. He was playing out the scenario to the letter.

In her quietly elegant room she ordered tea and unpacked, hanging up her very special wedding suit. Aunt Liz had insisted on buying the terribly expensive creamy raw silk skirt with its matching feather-light cashmere knit jacket, trimmed with binding and buttons of silk. The blouse was a froth of fine ruffles at the throat, a delicate amber shade echoing the color of Sara's hair. The pumps and handbag were a soft toast color.

After a scented bath Sara tried to rest. Her travel clock said seven. No need to hurry now, she told her thumping heart. The restaurant wasn't far from here. But rest was only a word and her body rejected it. She started to dress.

The suit looked as if it were made just for her, and a pendant of dark carved amber set in gold—a gift from her mother—added just the right touch. Her hair fell easily into place, its soft waves pulled away from her face and fastened with two small gold antique combs.

Her fingertips were cold and trembling as she began her makeup. Her face looked back at her from the antique mirror, her eyes dark with large pupils. She experimented with color and shading until she felt comfortable with her look. If she had ever been beautiful, she was now. She examined that expectant face with the flush of love on it, and saw, too, the changes that had come to that face and those eyes. Now there was a newfound strength. Dimensions of awareness and understanding were there. The thought of Jacques did nothing to mar her composure. She could not be hurt by anything in her past.

She thought of herself and Paul now. It was a difficult, intense, brilliant man who waited at the Tre Corone for her. She shuddered involuntarily, realizing her own power to give him happiness or pain. To walk with him in life as a companion—growing with his kindness, laughing with him at the twists of life, and learning together—that was what she wanted.

Her wristwatch read seven forty-five. A sudden jolt of adrenaline moved her toward her door. Downstairs the concierge's eyes gave silent, eloquent approval to her appearance. Her heart lifted, although she was having trouble just putting one finely shod foot ahead of the next. The concierge called a cab for her, and Sara rode the few blocks to the Piazza Brà, a large circular park with a great fountain in the middle, walkways and trees. The wide street went all the way around the park, past old and imposing buildings that made a semicircle along the outer edges. Streets converged at angles and the Roman Arena's floodlit, austere lines shone against a still-dusky sky.

A row of restaurants curved along the far end of the piazza with lighted awnings and potted plants defining their areas on the very wide marble sidewalk. The many outdoor tables were already doing a brisk business and waiters scurried about.

When the taxi stopped in front of the arena, Sara's heart was beating faster. Across the wide curve of the square she saw the lit sign of Tre Corone and walked toward the restaurant. Now her hands were icy and her breath uneven. Forcing herself to walk slowly, she approached the tables of the Tre Corone. By her watch she was one minute late. A sense of déjà vu and timelessness overcame her, and her mind was numb. All about her well-dressed people were sitting at their candle-lit tables enjoying their evening. Wine buckets reflected the lights in their silvery sheen. The air was slightly cool, but balmy. Sara looked at the faces. Where was Paul? A frantic paralysis rooted her feet to the pavement.

Then a voice spoke gently beside her and she looked up to see a stranger smiling at her. "Signorina, are you to meet a distinguished gentleman at a table for two?" It was the maître d'.

The fear relented suddenly, leaving her lightheaded. "Yes. Signor Edgerton...."

"Behold, Signorina, just there by the boxed hedge." She followed the nod of his head and saw Paul at a table a little apart. His head was turned away gazing toward the street, and he was a lonely and striking sight behind the large bouquet of white roses that was lying across part of the table. She stared for a long moment at the sheer wonder of him. His fine profile stood out against the darkness behind him. Dressed in a charcoal-gray suit with a rose in his buttonhole, he was the complete gentleman. Every instinct told Sara to run to him, but instead she smiled her thanks to the maître d' and, holding her head high, began to walk toward his table...their table.

As though a vibration had moved between them Paul turned and their eyes met. Slowly he came to his feet, his expression so intense with love that Sara could hardly bear the light of it. His hand came out with an eloquent gesture of welcome and she put her own into it. He bowed. She felt his warm lips on her cold trembling fingers. As he straightened and stood gazing at her, tears glittered on his lashes and moved unchecked down his cheeks.

"Sara, my Sara." His beautiful voice shook with emotion. "Am I the right man at the right table?" His hand tightened painfully on hers.

Through her own blinding veil of tears she answered. "The right man—forever."

"Thank God. I've been dying by inches, and I can't tell you how much I want to kiss you, but the maître d' and other onlookers are convulsed with romantic curiosity. Oh...to hell with them all.... You're here, my darling, you're here!" He pulled her into his arms and kissed her thoroughly. Sara heard, beyond the singing of her heart, sounds of gentle laughter and a *bravo* or two from male voices.

Paul let her go. The hovering maître d' pulled out her chair for her, smiling from ear to ear. Paul took her hand again. They sat for an eternity without speaking, in complete contentment, just absorbing the mad and wonderful thing that they were doing. Then he reached into his pocket and extracted a small box marked Damiani. With formal gestures he opened it and drew out a ring that gathered light into itself—a band of gold with a center diamond that took sparkling color from an emerald on one side and a sapphire on the other. Looking directly into her bemused eyes, Paul slipped the ring on to the proper finger.

"How beautiful," Sara whispered, and then looked to see two other rings in a second jeweler's box, simple gold bands.

"I hope it isn't too elaborate for Aunt Olive's humble taste," he said, smiling at her.

"She'll make an exception in this case. Olive has broadened her appreciation of things since you first knew her."

"And are there any more skeletons in her closet that will rise up and haunt us someday, my dear?" he asked with perfect Paul Edgerton haughtiness. She thought back and searched her mind.

"Perhaps one...a certain lady in black named Corinne...."

A slow, humorous grin started on his beautiful lips. "She upset a certain pompous gentleman very much and gave him something to think about on that painful road to reform. I can even forgive Olive that." He lifted her hand for another long, tender kiss, then covered it tightly with both of his own.

"The rings are for Olive and Corinne and Sara,

when I marry them...if later this evening is not too soon, that is."

"Not too soon at all. I have it on authority from the ladies themselves."

They broke into delighted laughter. It was only later that Sara remembered with any clarity what they ate. The waiters gave good service, the courses appeared, plates came and were whisked away. Sara and Paul were ravenous, as if the release of tension had sparked their appetites.

Sara's body had its usual uncontrolled response to Paul's closeness beside her. His eyes told her that this night would be unforgettable. Paul laughed as the waiter brought the dessert—the shredded orange desert that she had prepared for Jean-Claude's great dinner for Dulcie's father. She laughed too and he leaned to kiss her sugar syrup lips. "I know everything," he whispered.

They ate and laughed and talked—but mostly they just looked into each other's eager eyes. They had all the time in the world to discover everything about each other. But Sara needed to ask one more thing.

"When did you first know?"

"When did I know I loved you, or when did I know about Olive? Shall I answer both?" His eyes teased her. "I think I loved you that night at the Indian restaurant when I had an irritating feeling that you should be with me and not Eric. It seemed right to be with you—even your delicate challenges to my taste gave me an intimate feeling that first night. How intriguing to have this ethereal, beautiful woman look me straight in the eye and give an intelligent opinion without seeming to care what I would think of her. As to Aunt Olive—I was too angry with her to suspect a connection. I should have noticed all the little clues, though—you knew Eric, you were a writer, Elizabeth was evasive when I asked her about you. It was Jean-Claude who finally opened my eyes to my grand folly. After he finished with his lecture on your great virtues it didn't matter that you were Olive or the Queen of Sheba. I just loved you, and I feared that I had lost you."

He reached for Sara's hand. "Life is worth more than the trivialities of taste. I had retreated so far from the best of myself...it took Olive to force my ego to the wall and reveal my stupidity. She was a great joke on me. Oh, Sara, it hurt damnably to realize what I had done with my life before this, but it made me love you more. That night in the greenhouse—" his voice was shaking slightly "—that night when you didn't respond, taught me more about love and commitment than you can imagine."

Tears blurred her eyes again. "We've both learned a lot." She wouldn't let him continue with apologies. The past was dead and done with. Instead, she told him about her new status at the *Chronicle*, and the other offers.

He put his head back and laughed. "The Fates are giving us gifts beyond our hopes, my darling—what a life we will have!"

THEY WALKED TOGETHER the few short blocks through the Piazza delle Erbe and then into the beautiful small square where Dante's statue stood. Sara held her roses tightly to her. In the brocaded antique rooms of one of the very old buildings Paul's friend waited with a smiling couple. Madelyn, Paul's sister, drew Sara into a delighted embrace.

"I'm so glad he's happy, Sara. And I know we'll be friends." Her husband kissed Sara's hand and looked into her eyes with kindness.

"You must spend time with us in France as soon as you wish," he said. "Our child will be coming and we will be staying close to home."

The short wedding ceremony was quickly over. Sara and Paul signed the papers. Paul's Italian friend invited them to his home for dinner the next night, and Madelyn and Yves went back to the hotel with them, since they were staying there also.

In the lobby Yves chuckled, holding Madelyn close to him, her pregnancy preventing a tight embrace. "It would be traditional to have a champagne toast, at least, but what are traditions in the face of love?" He looked deeply into Madelyn's large dark eyes. "I want to make love with my wife and so, I presume, do you, Paul."

"You are the best of brothers-in-law," Paul told him.

In their suite Sara found her clothes had been moved from her original room to Paul's, and she discovered more roses, great bouquets of them. Then Paul took her into his arms and nothing existed but his strong wonderful body and the magic of his resonant voice repeating again and again, "I love you, Sara...I love you."

Aunt Elizabeth was right—Paul was a wonderful lover. He gave the most exquisite pleasure, gently, knowingly, caringly. Many times that night they woke to kiss and murmur about the amazing joy that was theirs. There was no point of sensation that was untouched by them, each desiring only to make this night a paradise for the other. Each time they made love Paul's lips and tongue caressed her body until it ached with desire...each time his passionate touch moved down across her smooth belly a fire was rekindled in her—deep and primal, yet with the heat of a divine ecstasy. There was no name, no word possible to describe the stunning rightness of their bodies' communication.

They lay quiet at last, and he explored her lips with gentle kisses. "I never knew before, my beloved, that love could bring such feelings." They kissed deeply again. "No wonder men and women keep seeking for union, knowing bliss is in it, but finding only a painful fire that burns and exhausts, instead of this...this wonder! I love you," he whispered, and moved to join more deeply with her until they rushed together into the pure fire of love.

SARA WOKE TO SEE SUNLIGHT beaming through the shutters warming the colors of their room. What had wakened her? Then she knew. Paul lay beside her and he was laughing to himself. He turned toward her, propping his handsome torso up on one elbow, his eyes dancing.

"What's so funny?" she asked to his impudent gaze.

He leaned down to kiss her with a tenderness that melted her very soul, then drew away to look into her face. "I have been lying here for an hour blissfully enjoying my new life, and then a thought struck me that there was one thing about which I hadn't been honest with you." His face took on a mock serious expression. "Sara, it's something that will make work for you, my darling. I'm almost afraid to say it."

"Paul Edgerton, tell me this instant!"

"Very well. It's such irony—after all of our involvement with food, and all the talk about my discriminating palate. Do you realize, my love with all I know about food, that I can't even cook!" He laughed deeply until the bed vibrated with his sound.

"Not even a little?"

He shook his head. Sara burst into her own laughter. How good it felt to be part of his joy! He captured her sleep-warm body in his eager warms and their laughter dissolved into kisses.

February's other absorbing
HARLEQUIN *SuperRomance* novel

THE HELLION by LaVyrle Spencer

Rachel Hollis had only just become a widow, and who should be pounding down her door but Tommy Lee Gentry.

Tommy Lee. Crazy boy. The hell raiser of Russellville, Alabama, had three marriages behind him and a string of fast women and cars. He'd never change, the townsfolk said.

Rachel knew differently. She had been in love with him at seventeen. Now, twenty-four years later, he could still excite her more than any other man. Then again, was it Tommy Lee she really longed for, or just a wistful memory from the past?

A contemporary love story for the woman of today

These two absorbing titles
will be published in March
by
HARLEQUIN
SuperRomance

TASTE OF A DREAM by Casey Douglas

As rioting beset the Malaysian capital, two strangers sheltered in a basement—and fell in love. The madness of the world was purged with the night. With the dawn they were separated....

Until four years later in Washington, when cultural adviser Danielle Davis and logger Ryan Kilpatrick locked horns at an embassy party. The minute their eyes met, they became the intimate strangers of long ago.

Mutual need made them forget that high-handed diplomats and headstrong loners don't mix. For they wouldn't be content with just a taste of life....

A MOMENT OF MAGIC by Christina Crockett

For Susie Costain, designing Mardi Gras costumes set her free. To be creative was as necessary to her as the air she breathed.

Sy Avery understood Susie's dedication to her work. Being a gifted photographer, he, too, made certain sacrifices. But when the sacrifices included giving up precious time together—day and *night*—something had to be done.

Sy would never ask Susie to give up her work. He knew the price she had paid for her freedom—but neither knew it could cost her her life!

These books are
already available
from
HARLEQUIN
SuperRomance

SANDCASTLE DREAMS Robyn Anzelon
AFTER THE LIGHTNING Georgia Bockoven
WAKE THE MOON Shannon Clare
EDGE OF ILLUSION Casey Douglas
REACH THE SPLENDOUR Judith Duncan
SHADOWS IN THE SUN Jocelyn Haley
DANGEROUS DELIGHT Christine Hella Cott
NOW, IN SEPTEMBER Meg Hudson
A QUESTING HEART Deborah Joyce
HEART'S PARADISE Lucy Lee
THE RIGHT WOMAN Jenny Loring
FORBIDDEN DESTINY Emily Mesta
SENTINEL AT DAWN Louella Nelson
TRUSTING Virginia Nielsen
AMETHYST FIRE Donna Saucier
A RED BIRD IN WINTER Lucy Snow

If you experience any difficulty in obtaining any of these titles, write to:

Harlequin SuperRomance, P.O. Box 236, Croydon, Surrey CR9 3RU

HARLEQUIN *Love Affair*

Look out this month for

MIRRORS AND MISTAKES *Kathleen Gilles Seidel*

They were very proper Bostonians who worked hard, dress[ed] conservatively, and ate and drank in moderation. Suzan[ne] Lawrence, secretary to the vice-president of Southard-Colt, a[nd] Patrick Britten, the firm's most brilliant consultant, hid behi[nd] polite, cool facades—and led lives of exquisite loneliness. Ide[n]tical in taste, temperament and habit, they drew together in t[he] belief that they would always remain friends. Neither anticipat[ed] the powerful instinct that would overwhelm Patrick . . .

LOVE IS A FAIRY TALE *Zelma Orr*

Ami Whitelake had surrendered her dreams long ago and to[ok] satisfaction in hard work, pleasure in the wonder of nature a[nd] love where she found it—rescuing an injured mongrel d[og,] taking in a homeless boy. For Ami, Wagner's Ranch became h[er] sole source of joy. It was a chance to practise her veterinary sk[ills] in a land of spectacular beauty. She never expected to find lo[ve] there, until she met Jeff Wagner. But Jeff barely noticed h[er.] Surely he would never return her love . . .

MUSEUM PIECE *Anne Stuart*

James Elliott thwarted her at every turn, scooping up [the] treasures before she could acquire them for San Francisc[o's] Museum of American Art. It was unethical and Mary Lind[a] McDonough decided she'd better do something about it. S[he] would send him a cool letter of protest. But not before she h[ad] written an extremely nasty poison pen letter—the letter [she] would have sent if she didn't have her reputation to consi[der.] Unfortunately, she slipped the wrong letter into the envelope[.]

HARLEQUIN *SuperRomance*

Your chance to write back!

We'll send you details of an exciting free offer from *Harlequin SuperRomance*, if you can help us by answering the few simple questions below.

Just fill in this questionnaire, tear it out and put it in an envelope and post today to: Harlequin Reader Survey, FREEPOST, P.O. Box 236, Croydon, Surrey CR9 9EL. You don't even need a stamp.

What is the title of the *Harlequin SuperRomance* you have just read? _____

How much did you enjoy it?

Very much ☐   Quite a lot ☐   Not very much ☐

Would you buy another *Harlequin SuperRomance* book?

Yes ☐   Possibly ☐   No ☐

How did you discover *Harlequin SuperRomance* books?

Advertising ☐   A friend ☐   Seeing them on sale ☐

Elsewhere (please state) _____

How often do you read romantic fiction?

Frequently ☐   Occasionally ☐   Rarely ☐

Name (Mrs/Miss) _____

Address _____

_____

_____ Postcode _____

Age group: Under 24 ☐   25-34 ☐   35-44 ☐

45-55 ☐   Over 55 ☐

Harlequin SuperRomance, P.O. Box 236, Croydon, Surrey CR9 9EL.

SR1